# HIGH PRAISE FOR ANDREW PETERSON!

"Andrew Peterson has created the most brutally effective thriller hero to appear in years. He handles a plotline like his hero might a well-oiled sniper rifle."

—Ridley Pearson, Author of *Killer Weekend*

"A high-powered thriller from a magnum-force writer."

—David Dun, Author of *The Black Silent*

"Andrew Peterson scores a bull's-eye in his debut thriller novel—fortunately for readers, this is just the opening salvo in a planned series of books destined to rank among the classics of the thriller genre."

—Laura Taylor, Author of *Honorbound*

# IN THE LINE OF FIRE

"I see him," Nathan said as he ejected the spent shell and closed the bolt on another. Brave bastard, he thought as he placed the crosshairs on the running man's hip. Then something twitched on his spine and sent a shiver through his body. It was the kind of premonition he couldn't ignore. He'd felt it before and had never been wrong. He swung his rifle back toward the lodge. A man was standing in the open doorway, using the jamb to steady his stance. He found himself looking directly into the business end of a sniper rifle.

*"Harv! Get down!"*

The air cracked.

Behind him, the rock wall exploded in a barrage of hot copper, molten lead, and pulverized granite. Something stung his face. A second later, the thump of the discharge reached his position. Nathan pointed his rifle at the ground and fired. A burst of earth blew upward, giving himself and Harvey a few seconds of cover.

*"Harvey!"*

"I'm okay."

They scrambled backward as another deafening crack tore the air. *Son of a bitch!* That shot hadn't missed by more than six inches. Three more shots smashed the stone above their heads. Nathan protected his face with his forearms, but the rest of his body didn't fare as well....

# FIRST TO KILL

# ANDREW PETERSON

LEISURE BOOKS  NEW YORK CITY

A LEISURE BOOK®

September 2008

Published by

Dorchester Publishing Co., Inc.
200 Madison Avenue
New York, NY 10016

ISBN 10: 0-8439-6144-9
ISBN 13: 978-0-8439-6144-7

Printed in the United States of America.

10 9 8 7 6 5 4 3 2

Visit us on the web at www.dorchesterpub.com.

# ACKNOWLEDGEMENTS

First and foremost to my wife, Carla. Simply stated, she's been the most supportive and influential person in my life. Writing a book is a solitary endeavor, and I couldn't have accomplished it without her patience and kindness. She's an extraordinary woman and I'm fortunate to be her husband.

And to my parents, Paul and Cindy, for being so supportive over the years. To my brothers as well, Daniel, Matthew, and James. You guys are the best.

Next, to my freelance editors. Ed Stackler and Laura Taylor. You're more than just my editors, you're my friends. Both Ed and Laura have stood with me through thick and thin. They picked me up when I fell down, and kicked my butt when I slacked off. There's a lot of Ed and Laura in *First to Kill* and they have my heartfelt thanks.

To Don D'Auria, Executive Editor at Dorchester Publishing, for taking a chance with me. Thank you for being patient with this first-time author.

To my agent, Jake Elwell, of Harold Ober Associates. Thank you for representing me with class and excellence.

Thank you to Ridley Pearson and David Dun for the outstanding cover blurbs.

Special thanks to Douglas Reavie, MD, F.A.C.S. for his generous help with the post-bombing triage scene.

And, of course, to Bill Thompson, who first believed in me as an author. Hey, Bill, are we there yet?

# FIRST TO KILL

# Prologue

The warm glow from the cabin's window told a lie. The scream from within told the truth. Bound to a chair with baling wire, the federal agent had been thoroughly battered: eyes swollen shut, fractured cheekbones, chipped teeth, and worse. Kicked aside, six severed fingers lay scattered on the plank floor. The air reeked of cigar smoke and charred flesh from dozens of burns that marched up the man's arms and across his chest like tiny cattle brands. Where he'd struggled against the wire, his wrists and ankles were torn and bleeding.

"He's out again." Ernie Bridgestone grabbed the naked man's hair and yanked his head back. Bridgestone, a former marine drill instructor, was tall and lean, with a thin mustache, cropped hair, and acne-cratered cheeks.

"Leave him be. He's had enough." Leonard Bridgestone towered over his younger brother and outweighed him by sixty pounds. Aside from their clothing—blood-spattered T-shirts, woodland fatigues, and combat boots—they looked nothing alike, except for their pale blue eyes, a gift from their mother's side. They never talked about their father's gifts.

Ernie released him. "I'll give the dumb son of a bitch credit: He lasted longer than I would have."

"Let's hope you never have to find out." Leonard was also ex-military—Army Ranger—but unlike Ernie, he'd been decorated from the first Gulf War with a Silver Star, two Purple Hearts, and a Navy Cross for rescuing a downed Hornet driver. He began sloshing gasoline out of a five-gallon can around the cabin's stark interior—a pine table and chairs, a brass lamp, two bunk beds. He saved the last two gallons for human flesh, tipping the can just above the agent's head, letting gravity do the rest. The man shivered and moaned under the stinging fluid.

As the smell of gasoline fouled the air, the rain intensified. The windows flashed white. Once. Twice. Half a second later, thunder rattled the glass.

"Damn shame to torch this place," Ernie said.

Leonard parted the curtain and glanced out the window where morning twilight crept across the Sierra Nevada mountains. "I figure we've got three days, max. He said his last check-in was five days ago, and they expect to hear from him at least once a week."

"But Les saw him in town yesterday. He could've reported in already."

"Naw, he would've told us. It only took two fingers to verify he was FBI. Nobody can take what we did to him—not for five hours. No way."

Ernie spit in the man's face. "I still can't believe this asshole set us up."

Leonard nodded. "Kinda evens the score a little, doesn't it?"

Ernie grunted and grabbed the bloody pliers, wire cutters, and ice pick from the table.

"Leave those."

"They're perfectly good tools."

"Leave 'em. Don't let the anger cloud your thinking. This isn't about revenge."

"The hell it isn't."

"Let it go, Ernie."

"Easy for *you* to say." He hurled the pliers across the room.

Leonard knew his brother's anger well. In Ernie's third year in the United States Disciplinary Barracks at Fort Leavenworth, several inmates had beaten him to the brink of death for stealing a pack of cigarettes. He'd spent fourteen weeks in the infirmary—the first two in a coma.

The fed stirred in his chair and moaned. Leonard approached and crouched down like a catcher. "You got something more to say?"

"Kill nee . . . kill nee firss."

Leonard looked at his brother.

"Fuck him. Let him feel it."

"He's been through enough." Leonard stepped back, pulled his forty-five, and took aim. But before he could finish the man off, Ernie shoved him aside, an entire book of matches lit in his hand.

"Then I'll do it."

*"Ern, stop!"*

But his brother tossed the matchbook, casually as dice at a craps table. The whoosh of ignition was chilling.

The burning man leaned his head back and howled.

"Dear Lord." Leonard raised his pistol again, but before he could pull the trigger, Ernie grabbed him and yanked him toward the door.

It was too late anyway. They retreated from the gathering inferno, down the porch steps, and out to the Bronco. Leonard got behind the wheel, but Ernie stood in the rain, watching the fire until the heat forced him into the cab.

Leonard started to speak, but Ernie cut him off. "You're wrong," he said, his eyes glittering with flame. "It's always about revenge."

# ⊕ Chapter One

Stretched out on the bed of the Islander Hotel in San Diego, Nathan Daniel McBride stared at the ceiling. With a sigh he touched his face, tracing three deep scars. Marks from another time. Another world. The longest scar started at his left ear, ran down the side of his face, and ended at the tip of his chin. The next followed a diagonal path from the top of his forehead, across the bridge of his nose, and etched his left cheek. Visibly the worst, the third drew a deep arched line from temple to jaw. Nice touch, that one. At six-foot-five, two hundred and forty pounds, he'd kept himself lean and hard in defiance of his forty-four years.

He rolled toward the woman beside him. She smiled, enjoying his attention. In contrast, Mara had flawless skin. Her kind brown eyes and black hair perfectly complemented an athletic physique. In her mid-twenties, she was nothing short of stunning. But perhaps what he appreciated the most about her: She rarely broke their silent moments.

"Have I ever really thanked you?"

She slid a leg over his hips. "Thanked me? I should thank you. You're not like the others."

*The others.* It felt like a slap in the face. Denial. It was so self-serving. Mara was a prostitute. He was a john. *One* of her johns, he reminded himself. Sure, they'd been seeing each other twice a week for the last eight months, but what kind of relationship was that? Empty. Going nowhere. She was so beautiful, and he was . . . what? Did the scars make him ugly? Or something else? Like what he used to do for a living? He wondered how different his life would be if he hadn't joined the Marine Corps. Would he have a wife? Children? A home? Not just a roof over his head, but a real home, a sense of purpose, a sense of belonging, a sense of family. But he *had* joined the service, and he *had* become a sniper. And he *had* been captured and tortured in a remote Nicaraguan jungle more than a decade ago. His captors had carved him like a Thanksgiving turkey. An inch apart, dozens of crisscrossing scars covered his chest and back, making him look like a human wicker basket. By all rights he should be dead from the crucifixion the mercenaries had created. Suspended from a tree, the vertical cage had forced him to stand. After two days and nights on his feet with no food or water, the pain in his legs had been literally blinding. He'd been delirious with infection and fever. In and out of consciousness—

"Where are you?"

"Huh?"

"You were gone again."

"Sorry."

She traced one of the grooves on his chest with a forefinger.

"Are you happy, Mara?"

"You've never asked me that before." She smiled, but it didn't reach her eyes. "I can't meet you Friday."

He sat up. "What? Why not?"

"Shhhh . . . It's okay. I have another meeting. Some drug company bigwig. Karen set it up."

"Mara, if it's money—"

She touched his lips. "You're so generous to me. It's not the money."

"You could work at my security company. I can get you an apartment. You don't have to do this. It's . . . dangerous."

"I'm glad you care. Will I see you next week?"

His cell phone interrupted them. He reached over to the nightstand and flipped it open. "Hello?"

"Nathan? It's Karen. It's that big guy. He's here again." Karen's voice sounded on the edge of panic. "He's got Cindy."

"I'll be there in seven minutes. Can you make it out to the patio?"

"I . . . I think so."

"Do it. Turn off as many lights as you can."

Two minutes later he was striding through the hotel's lobby with Mara in tow. Once outside the automatic glass doors, he sprinted over to his Mustang, Mara's heels clicking on the concrete as she ran to keep up with him.

He climbed in, fired up the engine, and flipped on the headlights. Turning west onto Hotel Circle North, he accelerated to fifty. "Seat belt," he said. Mara fastened herself in as he swerved into the oncoming lane of traffic to pass a minivan.

"I thought it was over with that guy."

"Apparently he didn't understand my warning."

"What are you going to do?"

"Give him a stronger warning."

He ran the red light and smoked the tires as he made the turn onto Interstate 8. Within ten seconds he was doing eighty miles an hour as he screamed under the Morena Boulevard overpass, then down the I-5 north on-ramp. The engine roared as he punched the Mustang up to one hundred ten miles an hour.

Four minutes had passed since Karen's call. A lot could happen in four minutes. He forced the thought aside and concentrated on driving.

Nathan's phone rang. Seeing his business partner's name on the blue LCD screen, he flipped it open. A call this late at night raised immediate concern. "Are you okay?"

"Me?" said Harvey. "Yeah."

"I can't talk right now."

"Are *you* all right?"

"I'll call you back in half an hour."

"Copy that. Half an hour."

Nathan glanced at his watch as he exited the freeway.

Five minutes.

Something washed through Nathan's mind. Karen had called *him*, not the police. She could've dialed nine-one-one. He'd always suspected the police knew about her "escort service," but her girls were high-class and low-key, part of a small operation, with no more than five girls working at any given time. Karen's women weren't hookers trolling for their next twenty-dollar trick to feed a meth or heroin habit. They were escorts. Sophisticated corporate types.

Karen had called Nathan because he was a no-nonsense, kick-ass type of man who knew how to take care of business the old-fashioned way. He and his oldest friend Harvey owned a private security firm. They were also both ex-marines, and Nathan figured he still looked the part. The combination of his size, short rusty hair, icy blue eyes, and the scars on his face made him look tough and hard. His thoughts returned to Karen.

Six minutes. Too damned long.

After slowing for a stop sign, he accelerated to sixty miles an hour.

"Nathan!"

He saw it.

An orange cat darted out from the left. It skidded to a stop in the middle of the street and froze, its eyes shimmering bluish green in the headlights. Nathan executed a smooth adjustment of the wheel to the right, hugging the curb.

"Did we hit it?"

Mara whipped her head around. "No. It's still there."

Nathan eased away from the curb and braked hard for the next turn. Thirty seconds later he pulled to the curb a few houses east of Karen's place and left the engine idling—it needed a cooldown after being run so hard.

"Stay here. Turn the engine off after a couple of minutes." He reached across Mara, popped the glove box, and grabbed his SIG Sauer P226 nine-millimeter. Climbing out, he jacked a hollow-point round into the chamber and lowered the hammer, using the pistol's de-cocking lever. He tucked the weapon into his blue jeans at the small of his back and sprinted up the sidewalk. Several houses distant, a dog barked three times, then went silent. Beneath orange cones of streetlight, chest-high recycling bins were stationed in the street's gutter like silent sentries.

An off-road pickup was parked in Karen's driveway. It had been lifted and decked out with monster tires and half a dozen floodlights mounted on the roll bar above the cab. Nathan shook his head. Everything oversized and out of control, just like its damned owner. Nathan paused in Karen's front yard and listened. All quiet. He placed an ear against a dark window. No music. No sounds of a struggle. Nothing.

At the side yard, he reached over the top of the gate and unlatched the locking mechanism from its cradle. It swung silently. At the rear corner of the house he peered around a planter full of barrel cactus. Tall and slender, Karen looked cold, hugging herself in the damp air. He issued a low warbling whistle and she turned. He waved her over, and she hugged him tightly—he could feel her trembling.

"What's the situation?"

"He's inside with Cindy."

"Where?"

"I don't know."

"Has he hurt her?"

"I don't know!"

"My Mustang's down the block."

"I can't leave Cindy."

"I'll handle this."

"Nathan, I—"

"Karen, please. Get going."

She paused as if to argue, then nodded and hurried through the gate.

Nathan felt feral anger begin to radiate as he pictured Cindy being brutalized by the guy. It tightened his body with adrenaline, threatened to overwhelm him. *Not now, damn it.* He closed his eyes, slowed his breathing, and relaxed his hands. When he'd calmed his mind, he removed his shirt and dropped it to the deck. He didn't want to give his opponent anything to grab.

Pulling his nine-millimeter, he traversed the rear wall of the house, his movements precise and silent. At each dark window he paused and listened. All quiet. No sound at all. Nothing. Working his way through the maze of potted plants and patio furniture, he approached the sliding glass door. Detecting no movement, he lowered into a crouch and slipped inside.

He heard it right away: a man's voice from down the hall.

Gun leading the way, he crept down the dark hallway, toward the only closed door. Another surge of adrenaline swept through him, this time under his command. A smile touched his lips. Nathan McBride—in his environment, ready, willing, and able to kick ass.

The next sound banished the smile—the unmistakable sound of a hand slapping flesh. Nathan kicked the door so violently it tore away from its hinges and crashed into the room in a horizontal hail of wood splinters and drywall dust. Fully clothed, Cindy cowered on the floor in a corner, her legs tucked against her chest. The left side of her face showed a fresh impact.

The man leaning over her whirled around and squinted. "You."

"Yes, me." Just as Nathan recalled, this guy was solid muscle and huge, taller than Nathan by an inch or two. With his shaved head and hourglass torso, he looked like a bouncer. To anyone else he might have looked intimidating. To Nathan, he was three hundred pounds of hamburger with an amphibian's brain attached.

Nathan stepped forward and slapped him with his free hand—a wet, meaty impact on the man's cheek. He moved back and waited for the reaction he knew was coming.

The man looked Nathan in the eyes, looked at the gun, and then looked him in the eyes again.

"What, this?" Nathan said. He tossed the SIG Sauer onto the carpet at the man's feet. *Go on, reach for it. Give me an excuse. Do it!*

His expression confused, the bouncer glanced down at the gun and unconsciously wiped his nostrils with his thumb and forefinger. *Cocaine.*

If this guy had any sense of reality, he would've surrendered right then and there, because he was now face-to-face with a shirtless opponent covered in menacing scars who looked like he belonged in a bare-knuckle cage-fighting match on an alien war planet. An opponent who'd just tossed his gun over, giving away a decisive advantage. And he should've also realized that anyone who did that against a gorilla like himself had to be trouble. But this man *wasn't* thinking straight. No doubt he was accustomed to winning fights. Probably had never lost one. Well, that was about to change.

Ignoring the gun at his feet, the bouncer lowered his head and charged.

Nathan was ready.

He sidestepped and shoved the man into the wall. The guy's head penetrated the half-inch drywall and left a cereal-bowl impression in its surface. Nathan kicked him in the ass, making the cereal bowl deeper. The man grunted, cursed, and yanked himself free.

Nathan stepped back as the man snorted, clearing dust from his nose. "It's a little cramped in here," Nathan said. "Let's finish this in the living room."

"No problem."

Nathan gestured toward the door and moved aside, allowing him to exit the bedroom first. He pointed at Cindy. "Stay here." Following at a safe distance in the near darkness, he sensed his opponent disappear around the living room corner more than he saw it. Then he heard a metallic scraping sound and knew exactly what it was.

The fireplace iron.

Nathan took loud, deliberate steps down the hall and stopped four feet short of the corner. The poker's black form whooshed and penetrated the wall where he would've been had he kept going. More drywall dust flew. He kicked the bouncer's arm, pinning it to the wall, and had the satisfaction of feeling the mid ulna and radius bones snap. The hand released the iron and fell away.

"Oh, man, that's gotta hurt," Nathan said. "Had enough?"

The bouncer charged again—surprisingly fast, but not fast enough.

Nathan ducked low before thrusting upward with all his strength.

The man literally flew over Nathan's back and landed with a grunt. He rolled onto his belly, tried to use his arms to get up, and seemed surprised when one of them didn't work. His expression somewhat irritated, he fell to his side and looked at his arm.

"Broken," Nathan said.

"You're a dead man."

Nathan spread his arms and looked down at himself.

The bouncer struggled to his feet and lunged forward with a left jab zeroed at Nathan's jaw. Anticipating the punch, Nathan jerked his head to the right and snapped up with his left elbow, smashing the man's nose. *That's a bingo!* For 99.9 percent of Earth's population, that level of blunt-force trauma did the trick. Party over. Lights out. Send the babysitter home. But this man simply wiped his nose and squinted at the fresh blood on his fingers.

"It was cocked about thirteen degrees to the right," Nathan said. "It's straight now. No charge."

The bouncer grabbed a toppled chair with his good hand and hurled it. Nathan ducked. Behind him, the glass door spiderwebbed before exploding out onto the deck.

Roaring like a maniac, the bouncer charged a third time.

He never made it.

His foot caught on the corner of the coffee table, and he went down. Hard. Had the fall not landed him squarely on an overturned chair, it would've been comical. Unfortunately, his left eye socket made solid contact with the bottom of the chair's leg. Three hundred pounds of momentum. Nathan ran the calculation in his head. It wasn't pretty. If he was lucky, the eye could be saved, provided it wasn't dangling out of the socket by a gooey blue-gray tendril.

The man rolled into a fetal position and cupped his eye with his good hand.

Nathan felt it, a tangible presence evaporating from the room.

This fight was over.

An absurd memory flashed through his mind, something his mother used to say: *It's all fun and games until someone loses an eye.* The thing was, losing an eye was a damned serious injury. Eyes didn't heal like broken bones; once the optic nerve was destroyed, that was it. End of story—no more vision. That fact hit close to home with Nathan. On more than one occasion his tormenters in Nicaragua had threatened to blind him with a knife. When they'd carved his face, he'd forced himself to hold perfectly still through the searing agony so the blade wouldn't slip and take out his eyes. He shivered at the memory. As much as he resented this big man on the floor, he didn't want to see him blind in one eye. Spending the next fifty years with a glass eye and no depth perception wouldn't be a fair trade for terrorizing Cindy. A broken arm and a pulverized nose should be punishment enough.

"Come on," Nathan said. "Let's have a look. It's over, okay?"

The big guy staggered to his knees, still holding his left hand over his eye.

"I'm gonna look at that eye. If you try anything, we'll start over."

No response.

Nathan flipped a switch on the wall and squinted at the sudden brightness. He approached the bouncer from the broken-arm side, just in case there was still some fight left in the guy, which he seriously doubted. The bouncer looked pitiful, clutching his eye—beaten and bloody, like a bully who'd finally met his match.

"Let me see it. Easy, now . . . What's your name?"

He slowly removed his hand. "Toby."

Blood was streaming out of Toby's nose and running down his lips and chin. Nathan examined the eye from a safe distance. Fortunately the impact hadn't been directly on the orb itself. It had missed by half an inch, but the skin was laid open on the upper brow.

"Well, Toby, I've got good news. You aren't going to lose your eye, but you'll have one hell of a shiner." Nathan stepped back. "You had a close call here." He paused to make sure he had Toby's full attention. "You can blow this experience off, or you can use it to turn your life around, to walk a different path." Nathan watched him ponder the comment for a few seconds. Toby was a big man—huge, really—and people often associated his kind of size with stupidity. Nathan was also a big man, not as big as this guy, but he often felt people treated him as though he were all muscle and no brains.

"I lose my temper," Toby said.

"I noticed. Did *you* notice that the things I said were designed to *make* you lose your temper?"

"I can't help it."

"Yes, you can. I know from personal experience. Trust me on this."

Toby said nothing.

Nathan crouched down. "Here's what I do. When I feel

anger coming on, and I really want to hurt someone, I stop it by using a mental image. You can call it anything you want. For me, it's a safety catch. You with me so far?"

Toby nodded.

"Okay. I picture autumn leaves falling from trees and gently settling on the ground all around me. Give it a try. Start by closing your eyes and imagining it."

To Nathan's surprise, Toby closed his eyes.

"You're standing under the trees with your head tilted up, your arms out to the sides, palms up. The leaves are filtering past you, brushing against your skin. Breathe in deep; let it out slowly. See the leaves as they flutter past you." Nathan watched Toby's face change.

He looked pretty calm for a moment, then winced. "Oh, man . . . My arm hurts."

"You're just now noticing that?"

Toby nodded again.

"How high are you?"

"A couple lines."

"Do yourself a favor, Toby, and lay off the blow. You'll save a ton of money, and you'll enjoy life a whole lot more. There's lots of detail out there, stuff to notice, to use in your life. You may need some help to quit, but as soon as you realize you don't need drugs to have fun, you'll have the problem licked."

"I'll try. You fight well."

"Like I said, it's all about the details. I knew you were on some sort of high because your pupils were too wide for the ambient light in the room. I knew you were right-handed because you used it to wipe your nose. You're right-footed because you took your first step toward the door with your right foot. I wanted that info in case you were a kickboxer. I knew when you were going to charge because your eyes gave you away. Stuff like that. It can save your life. It's all about the details."

"Those scars all over your body?"

"What do they tell you?"

"Somebody did that to you on purpose."

"Why did they cut my stomach and back?"

Toby thought about it a few seconds. "No arteries."

"That's right."

"You were a soldier and got captured; they tortured you. . . ."

"Sit tight, okay? You're going to need some stitches, and that arm needs to be set. When you get to the emergency room don't lie to them. Tell them you were in a fight. Observe the doctors and nurses closely. Learn from them. Ask them questions. Ask them what they're looking for when they examine your eyes and take your blood pressure. Ask them how broken bones heal."

Toby said nothing, just looked around the room as if he were already seeing things from a new perspective.

"Make sure the vision in your left eye doesn't become blurred or doubled over time. If it does, see a specialist right away, okay? Your retina got jarred. Hopefully not too much. I want you to wait here while I bring the girls back in. They're human beings, Toby, not just objects of entertainment. They have feelings, like you. Like me."

"I should leave."

"Not yet. You need a few butterfly bandages to control the bleeding." Nathan retrieved a clean towel from the kitchen and folded it into a quarter of its original size. "Hold this over the cut with pressure. Is your truck an automatic or a stick?"

"Automatic."

"Think you can drive?"

"Yeah, probably."

Nathan patted his shoulder. "Details. Start noticing them." He retrieved his nine-millimeter from the bedroom and told Cindy to follow him. Together they left the house through the front door. They found Mara and Karen sitting in his Mustang.

"Party's over," Nathan said.

Karen climbed out and hugged Cindy. "Are you okay?" She looked at Nathan. "Is he gone?"

"No, but he will be soon. I think you'll find he's sorry for what he did. I think he's gonna tell you so."

She stared at him for several seconds. "We'll see about that."

He led the women down the sidewalk and back into the house through the front door. Karen glanced at Toby, who hadn't moved. Cindy disappeared down the hall and returned a minute later dressed in jeans and a T-shirt. Along with Mara, they started straightening the room. As Nathan had hoped, Toby apologized, even offered to pay for all the damage he'd caused. Karen said she'd call it even if he agreed never to come back, and they struck a deal. When Nathan was sure things had cooled down and Toby was no longer a threat, he motioned for Mara to follow him out to the front yard. Once outside, he removed his wallet and handed her a wad of hundred-dollar bills. "To cover the damage in the house."

She was reluctant to take the money, but accepted it with thanks and a long hug.

"You could've hurt that guy a lot worse than you did."

Nathan didn't respond.

"Did you want to?"

"At first." He answered her unspoken question: "But I saw something in him."

Mara stared for several seconds, hugging herself in the cool air. "Something in yourself?"

Nathan nodded.

"If you ever want to talk, I mean, you know, just talk . . ."

He turned to leave.

"Nathan?"

"I'll call you soon; thanks, Mara."

He retrieved his shirt from the rear deck and pulled it on. On his way back to his Mustang, he diverted over to Toby's truck, pulled a business card from his wallet, and set it against the Plexiglas cover of the speedometer, where it wouldn't be overlooked. It was a dual message he was sure Toby would understand. He slid into his car and waited. Sitting there, he ran the whole encounter back through his mind, analyzing it. Mara was right. He could've hurt Toby, hurt him badly. He knew the consuming rage Toby felt. Knew it well. But over the years since his captivity, he'd learned to control it, to use it like a tool, to make it work for him, not against him. Maybe Toby could too.

His cell rang. He flipped it open. "Harvey. Sorry about that."

"No worries. Everything okay?"

"Yeah. I'll call you back on the Clairemont hard line within fifteen minutes, if that's all right."

"You got it."

Toby walked out the front door a few minutes later, his right arm hanging uselessly. Using a pair of field glasses he kept in the glove box, Nathan watched Toby grab the business card from the dashboard. The big man stared at it for several seconds before backing out of the driveway. Keeping his headlights off, Nathan followed Toby's truck until it was clear of the neighborhood. Several minutes later he was home, drinking a bottled water on the sofa and dialing Harvey back.

His partner answered after the first ring. "All right, tell me what happened."

"One of Karen's girls got slapped around by that big guy I told you about last week."

"And . . . ?"

"I put a reprimand in his personnel file."

A pause. "Did you kill him?"

"Now, would I do something like that?"

"Yes."

"I'm deeply hurt by that comment." Silence on the other end. "I didn't kill him," Nathan said. "The circumstances didn't warrant it."

"I would've helped."

"There wasn't time. I broke a few traffic laws getting there, and a few bones after I arrived."

"How many's a few?"

"Bones or laws?"

"Is there a difference?"

"Radius, ulna, and a nose. Nothing serious."

"I'm proud of you."

"Thank you. Now, is everything okay with you?"

"I'm fine. But Frank Ortega's not. He's worried as all hell about his grandson."

Nathan sat up. "Frank Ortega? The former FBI director?"

"The same."

"Who's his grandson?"

"FBI. A deep-cover operative inside some kind of arms-smuggling racket."

"What kind of arms?"

"I don't know yet."

"Where?"

"Up north. Lassen County. Nate, he's missing. Ortega wants our help. I didn't promise anything, but I said we'd meet with him. Face-to-face."

"Tonight?"

Nathan heard his partner sigh. "Yeah, tonight. Hold tight. I'm already on my way."

## ⊕ Chapter Two

Nathan's Clairemont house was similar to every other on the block: meticulously landscaped, with a pastel stucco exterior and a tile roof. What set Nathan's apart was its state-of-the-art security system. He had installed a system of laser beams criss-crossing the yard, which, if broken, sent spotlights popping up from the lawn's corners and triggered an audible alarm inside the house. The home's interior had both motion sensors and thermal-image detectors. Some would call it overkill; Nathan called it an indulgence. He and Harvey owned a company that installed such systems. Why shouldn't he own the best?

Harvey Fontana pulled into Nathan's driveway in his Mercedes, its metallic blue paint turned into a lifeless gray by the streetlights. The same age as Nathan, Harvey stood six inches shorter, and his light hazel eyes were an extreme contrast to his tanned Latino complexion. The combination gave him an almost exotic look. Gray hair was winning the battle over the rich black of his youth.

*Join the club*, thought Nathan.

"You know I'm here," Harvey's rich baritone muttered from the driveway. "The least you could do is meet me outside."

"I am outside," Nathan said.

Harvey whipped around. "Damn it, Nate. I hate it when you do that."

He gave an innocent shrug. "Do what?" Then he hugged his business partner. "Why do you drive this big thing?"

"I'm a big man; I need a big ride. What's it to you?"

"You're an average-sized man. . . . Everywhere."

"It's good to see you too, Nate."

"How's the family?"

"Great. If you'd visit once in a while, you wouldn't have to ask."

"You know how it is. . . ."

"Yeah, I know."

Nathan's tone changed. "From one to ten, what's the urgency of tonight's meeting with Ortega?"

Harvey answered without hesitation: "Ten."

As they drove south on I-5, they enjoyed a comfortable silence, each in his own thoughts. After a few miles they turned east on I-8.

"You get a chance to look at the financials I sent?"

Nathan grunted.

"Our net worth went up another eight hundred grand this quarter."

"Just paper."

"I know money bores you, but honestly . . . You own a helicopter, for cryin' out loud, and your home in La Jolla is to kill for." Harvey shook his head. "If you ever get truly bored with your share of our company, you can always sell it to me."

"Don't worry; it's yours when I kick the bucket."

"That could be arranged."

"So . . ." Nathan's tone signaled a change of subject. "You and Ortega go pretty far back."

"I know his son, Greg, better. He was doing Middle East satellite intel for the CIA at the same time we were in Nicaragua. He transferred to counterterrorism work in the FBI eight years ago."

Nathan said nothing. He already knew all of this—knew Harvey was setting a stage.

"He's a good guy, okay?" said Harvey.

No response, just the quiet humming of the big German engine. Nathan, too, was setting a stage; he fully planned on helping Frank Ortega, but he had some conditions that were nonnegotiable.

"I couldn't have rescued you without Greg's help," Harvey said. "I know you know that. But he knows it too. Greg and I spent long nights studying satellite imagery together. He volunteered his time freely, without question. I owe him, Nate. Big-time. *We* owe him."

They rode in silence for the rest of the trip. Everything Harvey said was true, and Nathan didn't resent his bringing it up. Harvey *had* rescued him. He wouldn't have lasted another day in that godforsaken cage. In fact, he had no memory of being carried three miles through the jungle. Mercifully, he'd been in and out of consciousness, mostly out.

Nathan also knew their gratitude and loyalty remained mutual. He'd sacrificed himself to ensure Harvey's escape during their botched mission. They'd been surrounded by guerrilla soldiers hell-bent on capturing them alive, and decided to separate to give themselves the best chance of making it out. But Nathan had doubled back to cover Harvey's exit, had given his position away by firing shots to draw the pursuers, leading to his own capture and subsequent three weeks of interrogation and torture. The bottom line: Nathan and Harvey were closer than family; either of them would give his life for the other, no questions asked. If helping the Ortegas was that important to Harvey, Nathan would be there for him.

They pulled into Frank Ortega's driveway at eleven fifty p.m. It was a steep climb, snaking up to a Mediterranean Spanish–style home with a terra-cotta roof. Lit with spots, mature palms lined both sides of the driveway, creating an impressive colonnade. A dark Ford Taurus was parked in front of a detached three-car garage. Nathan figured it for an FBI vehicle, Greg Ortega's ride. The white stucco house was big, but not overly so, and the classic symmetry of its design was pleasing to the eye. A wheelchair ramp had been constructed to one side of the entrance, bypassing the steps up to the front door. As their Mercedes rolled to a stop, a Rottweiler bounded out from the side yard and loudly challenged their intrusion.

Nathan opened his door.

Harvey put a hand on his shoulder. "Maybe you should wait until Frank comes out."

Nathan slid out and took a step forward, addressing the dog in a near whisper. "Easy. Easy, now. You're not in charge here. I am."

"Come on, Nate; get back in here. That dog's going to tear you to pieces."

He took another step forward. "I'm not afraid of you. Settle down. Now." The dog backed up a step, unsure of its standing with this new pack member. Hearing something Nathan couldn't, it raised its ears and turned toward the house. Nathan looked up just as two men appeared at the front door, the older of the two in a wheelchair—former FBI director Frank Ortega.

"Scout. Come," Frank said. Its docked tail wagging, the dog trotted up the driveway, turned up the wheelchair ramp, and sat by its owner's side. The man patted the dog's back. "Good boy."

Nathan had met Frank Ortega once before. He tried to remember where, but couldn't place it. Maybe a political convention. They walked over as the two men came down the ramp, one rolling, one walking. Harvey approached first. "Hello, Frank." They shook hands. "This is Nathan McBride."

"It's an honor to meet you again," Nathan said.

"The honor is mine. You're an unsung hero, Major McBride."

"I appreciate that, sir, but I'm a civilian now."

"You've earned the title, and please call me Frank."

The man issued a firm handshake—overly so. Nathan figured it was a gesture saying, *I may be in a wheelchair, but I'm still a force to be reckoned with.* Frank Ortega had kind brown eyes behind a pronounced brow line. Thin, but not slack, he didn't have the slightest hint of a belly under his white button-down shirt. He wore tan slacks with penny loafer shoes that looked brand-new. Although he did his best to hide it, his face looked taut with tension.

Frank's son, Greg, strongly resembled his father: same piercing brown eyes, same brow line, just twenty-five years younger. Nathan guessed his age at fifty, plus or minus. Greg wore a dark jogging outfit and running shoes.

Harvey gave Greg a hug. "Greg, this is Nathan McBride."

"Pleasure," Greg said, shaking hands without a smile.

"The same," Nathan answered. Greg's handshake was not as firm as his father's, and he spent a fraction too long looking at Nathan's scars—something Nathan didn't resent; he'd gotten used to it over the years. Just a natural reaction to seeing all the damage.

"Tell me something, McBride," said Frank. "How did you know about Scout? Most people are intimidated by Rottweilers."

Nathan didn't mind being called McBride. As a military man he'd gotten used to it. Like Nathan, Frank Ortega would be in the habit of speaking that way. He'd been the FBI's top man, in charge of thirty thousand employees for two United States presidents.

"It was his body language," Nathan said. "When a dog is going to attack, it lowers its head, crouches down, curls its lips back, and shows its teeth. Scout was barking, but he wasn't singularly focused on me. He was turning his head slightly, kind of a sideways barking. He knew you'd be coming out of the front door, so he was dividing his attention between me and the door. By approaching him, I established dominance."

Frank nodded a silent compliment.

"I like dogs a lot. They're amazing animals. They give affection and loyalty freely."

Frank Ortega glanced at Harvey, but said nothing.

Nathan sensed the tension thicken. He hadn't intended the comment to be suggestive of their current situation—true or not—but he wasn't going to backpedal from it.

"Let's go inside," Frank said.

Nathan watched as Frank easily maneuvered up the ramp and through the front door. He was also acutely aware of being studied by Frank's son, Greg. The surveillance was subtle but steady, and Nathan felt resentment aimed his way. Understandable. From what he knew about Greg, the man rode a desk, as most FBI agents did most of the time. Nathan hated offices and avoided his own as much as possible. First Security Incorporated was Harvey's deal, and Nathan gave his partner free rein to run it as he wished. He had neither the desire nor the temperament to run a complex business.

Inside Frank's home on the left, Nathan saw a small library. On the right was a sitting room with a beige leather sofa and matching love seat. Straight ahead was the kitchen. But what impressed Nathan the most was the stone floor. Staring in amazement, he stopped short of a fifteen-foot reproduction of the official FBI seal, every aspect of the insignia intricately re-created in a mosaic of colored stone. Inscribed within the seal were the words *Fidelity, Bravery, Integrity*. FBI.

A small elderly woman approached from the kitchen. "Frank spent a fortune on it." Mrs. Ortega had shoulder-length silvery gray hair and a gentle, matronly face. She was thin, but not frail. With those oval glasses, she could've come directly from baking cookies or reading the *Wall Street Journal*.

Nathan inwardly winced as she strode across the symbol.

"We walk on it all the time," she said, reading his expression. "It's the floor, after all. I'm Diane; it's nice to meet you, Mr. McBride."

She offered her hand. It felt like warm bones in a velvet glove. "Please call me Nathan. This should be in a museum." From the corner of his eye, he caught Greg shifting his weight. The man was strung tight and could be a problem. Probably *would* be a problem.

"Harvey," Diane said.

Harvey bent and kissed her cheek. "It's good to see you, Diane."

"Would anyone like tea or coffee?"

"Yes, please, black coffee," Nathan said.

Harvey asked for the same.

"Greg?"

He shook his head no.

"Let's talk in the library," Frank said. He wheeled himself in that direction. His ride had no bells or whistles—simply a seat on wheels, as basic as they came. Nathan reevaluated his earlier assessment of Frank's grip during their handshake. The man had a powerful grip out of necessity, and the firm handshake hadn't been phony or intended to show off at all. The man simply had strong hands.

Despite Diane's comment, Nathan avoided stepping on the FBI seal as he followed; somehow it didn't feel right trampling on it. Frank maneuvered himself behind his desk while Nathan, Harvey, and Greg sat in tan leather chairs arranged in a semicircle. Nathan studied the photos behind Frank's desk, showing the former FBI director shaking hands with five different presidents: Carter, Reagan, Bush, Clinton, and George W. Bush. Frank stood on his own two feet in the Carter, Reagan, and first Bush photographs, and sat in a wheelchair for the other two. Portrait-type pictures of his two adult children were hung on the wall to his right: Greg and a daughter. Nathan waited through an uneasy silence while Frank reached into a side drawer and pulled out a thick file. Nathan glanced at the folder, then back to Frank.

"I know your father well. We go back a long way."

Nathan said nothing.

"He's a good man," Frank said quietly.

Nathan locked eyes. "We aren't here to talk about him."

Out of Frank's line of sight, Nathan felt Harvey nudge his foot. If Greg had noticed the gesture, he didn't react.

"No, that's true. We're here to talk about my grandson. Greg's son. He's MIA. Has been for several days now. He was undercover inside some sort of arms-smuggling operation up in Lassen County. An outfit called Freedom's Echo." Frank paused for a moment. "How much do you know about Semtex?"

"It's Czech-made plastic explosive."

"That's right. Extremely potent stuff. And we know for a fact that this group up there got their hands on some of it—a lot of it, actually. Around a ton. It was the last thing my grandson reported before he disappeared. It's likely he blew his cover relaying the information."

"That's a bad situation."

"And not just for him. Seizing the Semtex is critical. In the wrong hands it could mean several more World Trade

Center–type incidents. A few well-placed car bombs in the underground parking structures of high-rise buildings could bring them down. Unlike the World Trade Center, there wouldn't be time for an evacuation. The building falls down with everyone inside."

Nathan had seen footage of buildings being demolished with explosives. Implosion, he believed they called it. But if you changed the pattern and timing of the charges, the building could fall more like a tree, taking out other buildings like dominoes. If the World Trade Center towers had fallen sideways, it would've been worse, a lot worse.

"What exactly do you want us to do?"

Frank leaned back in his wheelchair and stared out the window like a man looking back on his life and wondering about all the things he could've done differently. "The FBI is about to send SWAT teams under the command of the Sacramento Joint Terrorism Task Force to raid the compound. They have two objectives. The first is to recover the Semtex, if it's still there. The second is to determine the fate of my grandson. Bring him home, if he's alive. But the overarching plan is to put Freedom's Echo out of business before that Semtex moves." Frank leaned forward and locked eyes with Nathan. "You two were the best covert ops team this country's ever had. I'm not patronizing you. I mean it: You guys were the best. What I need is for you to be my eyes and ears up there. I have a personal stake in this; it's my grandson, my own flesh and blood. And I no longer have the access I used to. Oh, I could make a call and get boiler-plate information, but it wouldn't be firsthand visual intelligence coming from a source I trust."

"Okay . . ."

"Essentially, I want you to back up the FBI raid. Things could go badly; there could be a firefight. You guys were the best damned sniper team in the world. The FBI could use—"

"With all due respect," Nathan cut in, "we don't do that

anymore. We aren't hired guns. We run a security business. The FBI has its own sniper teams."

Harvey moved uncomfortably in his chair, but remained silent.

"I'm not asking you to be hired guns. I'm asking you to serve as a safety net for the SWAT teams in case things go badly. These arms sellers are hardcore guys. Elite ex-military. Now they've got Semtex. You could save lives." Ortega took a deep breath and sat back in his chair. "I cashed in a major favor with Director Lansing today—to involve you in this operation. He gave me the okay, but he's considering it a 'don't ask, don't tell' situation. He doesn't want to know anything about it—only that his SWAT teams succeed. I personally vouched for your integrity. I'm putting my reputation on the line here. If you're willing to do this, then the trust will have to work both ways. You need to trust me, and I need to trust you."

"Then you must know the potential ramifications of what you're asking us to do."

Frank looked at Harvey with a troubled, almost annoyed expression, and Greg was gripping the armrests of his chair way too tightly.

"I understand the ramifications, McBride. Do you?"

Nathan said nothing.

"For God's sake, there's more at stake than just my grandson. That amount of loose Semtex on American soil makes this a national security issue as dangerous as any Al-Qaeda threat. More dangerous. These guys are Americans; they look, act, and talk like us. They blend in. They're invisible."

Over the ticking of the regulator clock, Nathan took a deep breath and let it out slowly. No one spoke for several seconds. "We have some conditions."

"Conditions?"

"That's right. Conditions. We'll find your grandson and back up the SWAT teams, but we don't want to be left standing when the music stops. Understood?"

"Clearly."

"And we'll need complete background and intelligence information on the targets and their compound."

"Of course. I wouldn't have it any other way."

"One more thing. No armchair quarterbacking. Once you turn us loose, that's it. No second-guessing our moves. We do this our way, without interference, or we don't do it at all."

"Like I said, it's an issue of trust in both directions."

Frank pushed the file across the desk.

Nathan didn't touch it. He knew what it was, what it represented.

"This is everything we have on Freedom's Echo. Everything," Frank said. "It's an exact duplicate."

Frank kept saying *we*. Understandable—the man *had* spent forty-one years with the bureau.

"I'm coming with you," Greg said.

"Out of the question."

"But he's *my* son."

*"Out of the question."*

Greg stood and squared off with Nathan. "Listen, you son of a bitch, I don't care who or what you used to be. *He's my son.*"

Nathan got up and pivoted toward the door.

"Damn it, Greg," Frank growled. "McBride, wait! Please."

Nathan stopped but didn't turn around.

"We're all under a lot of stress. Please sit back down."

Nathan didn't move.

"Please," Frank said again.

"I need some air," he said, and left the room.

Harvey stood and lowered his voice. "Damn it, Greg. What the hell was that all about?"

"Your partner's a smug asshole, that's what."

"Hey, I've known the man through life *and* death. He has a lot of faults, but being smug isn't one of them."

"Sounded like it to me."

"Well, you heard it wrong. He's *not* smug. He's confident. You can't see it because of your son's situation. You're asking us to risk our lives, and, if the situation warrants it, you're asking us to kill again. And we've said yes. But we can't have the father of the missing agent involved, much less someone who's never worked in the field. You've never killed anyone, Greg. Trust me, there's nothing glamorous or exciting about it. This isn't some half-baked Hollywood B movie. We're talking real bullets and real death. There's no place for you in this mission."

Greg looked down but didn't respond.

"Now, when he comes back," Harvey continued, "don't apologize. It won't be necessary. Nathan doesn't hold grudges, and he knows you're wound up tight. We all are. When he offers to shake your hand, you take it, understood?"

No response.

"Am I getting through to you?"

"Yes."

Nathan found Diane Ortega in the kitchen, emptying the dishwasher. "May I trouble you for a glass of water, please?"

"It's no trouble at all." She retrieved a glass from the cabinet and pressed it into a small alcove in the refrigerator. She had a face that reminded him of his own mother. "I heard that last exchange; it was hard to miss."

"It's all right."

"Will you sit with me a minute?"

Nathan nodded and pulled a bar stool out from the island for her.

"Thank you." As they sat facing each other, Diane placed her hands in her lap. "It's been difficult for Greg, his father being the former director of the FBI and all."

"I can imagine."

"Frank wasn't around much during Greg's childhood. Oh, he's tried to make up for it, but how can he really?"

Nathan knew what she was talking about. All too well.

"You've seen the pictures in Frank's office?"

"They're impressive."

"The bureau was Frank's life—still is, I'm afraid. He's always known it took a heavy toll on his family. I think if Frank had it to do over again, he would've gone to more of Greg's Little League games and birthday parties, gone fishing and camping with him. When we lived in Washington I spent countless nights at Greg's bedside while he cried, trying to explain things, but what does a eight-year-old boy really know? All he knew was that his father wasn't home." Diane's face clouded for an instant. She looked as if she were about to cry, but made a recovery. "Greg is our oldest, so he took it the hardest. I think he understands the sacrifice now, but some wounds never really heal." She reached out and held his hand. "Your father's a lot like Frank, and you're a lot like Greg."

"I'm, ah . . . not sure what to say."

"Our time on earth is limited. I'm finally beginning to understand that now. We can't change the past."

"I've killed fifty-seven people, Mrs. Ortega. It's taken a long time, but I've come to terms with it. Finding your grandson might increase that number. Are you okay with that?"

She held his hand tighter. "I don't see the world through rose-colored glasses; being an FBI director's wife has taught me that much. There are genuinely evil people out there. I'm sure you're not indiscriminate; I trust your judgment in such matters."

"Thank you for saying so; it means a lot."

"Frank and Greg know it too, but they're men, and men have a harder time expressing their feelings. It's a genetic flaw of the gender."

"Amen to that."

She released his hand. Nathan leaned forward and kissed her on the cheek. It hit him like a sledgehammer: He needed to call his own mother. Tomorrow. First thing in the morning. Nathan took a sip and left the glass of water on the counter. He entered the library, approached Greg, and extended his hand. "Can we start over?"

Greg nodded, and they shook hands.

Nathan sat back down. "Your mother's a remarkable woman."

"Yes, she is."

"May I explain my reasoning to you?"

Greg held up a hand. "There's no need. I understand why I can't be involved. We have the same policy in the bureau, and for good reason."

"We'll keep you informed every step of the way."

"I appreciate it."

"We'll find your son."

"All right then," Frank said. "There's one more vital piece of information you need." He lowered his voice. "I can't guarantee the FBI SWAT teams will know you're there. As you can imagine, it's a delicate situation with outsiders being involved in bureau business. Rest assured I'll do everything within my power to make contact up there, but you should assume they *won't* know you're there."

Nathan just stared at the man.

"That means anyone not wearing SWAT BDUs will be fair game."

Nathan nodded. "When is the raid?"

"Tomorrow at fourteen thirty hours."

"A daylight raid . . . One more question. Does my father know of our involvement?"

Frank answered without hesitation. "Yes."

# ⊕ Chapter Three

It was a windy evening in Washington, D.C., the horizon's last remnant of violet fading to black. Four miles high, lit from the amber glow of the city, thin clouds drifted toward the east. The fall colors had come early, with red and orange cherry tree leaves already tumbling down the sidewalks and gutters of the nation's capital.

The office of the Committee on Domestic Terrorism, or CDT, was located in the Russell Senate Office Building, on the north side of Constitution Avenue, across from the Capitol. Its members met in a lavish conference room in high-backed leather chairs around an oval mahogany table inlaid with red oak and cherry. The walls were adorned with oil portraits of every U.S. president. A corner table hosted a pitcher of ice water and crystal glasses. In the opposite corner, a matching table supported an elegant flower arrangement that perfumed the air with the scent of stargazer lilies. It was an impressive space, appropriate for the purpose it served: protecting the nation's security from homegrown threats.

The moment CDT chairman Stone McBride strode into the room, all conversation ended. At six-four, the senator had a commanding presence and used it to his advantage by getting close to people who were shorter—in essence standing over them—forcing them to look up. When facing the few men who were taller, he kept a comfortable distance so *he* didn't have to look up. Like the ex-marine he was, Stone kept his gray hair cut short, formal. Deep blue eyes complemented a square jawline. The man looked like a career politician because he *was* a career politician. He showed a friendly smile when he wanted something and an unfriendly smile when he didn't get it.

Now sixty-eight, the senior senator from New Mexico had earned the nickname "Stonewall" during the Korean War. It happened in March of 1951 during the advance to Line Boston on the south bank of the Han River south of Seoul. His I Corps platoon had been pinned down by machine gun and mortar fire for half an hour. In an act of rage more than anything else, he'd climbed to the edge of his muddy foxhole, stood up, leveled his M14 at the hip, and emptied five magazines at the enemy position. Bullets had thumped the ground in front of him, not one of them finding its mark. Inspired, the platoon to his left added their bullets, giving the platoon on his right the chance to advance and overrun the enemy's mortar position. Stone had been decorated for that reckless bit of bravery, receiving his nickname in the process.

"Thank you all for coming on such short notice," Stone said. "I apologize for the late hour, but the subject matter demands it." He made eye contact with everyone seated around the table. "Special Agent Watson asked for this meeting because of a critical new development. I've already been briefed, but everyone here needs to know about the new threat."

The CDT consisted of a hardworking group of five men and four women, all handpicked by the senator and representing nearly every federal law enforcement agency. It was the first group of its kind. A prototype. In theory, having a representative of each agency encouraged mutual cooperation and sharing of information. *In theory.* In reality, tension often filled the room. But despite their many differences, they all shared one thing in common: loyalty—to themselves, and to the United States of America. Without exception, everyone seated around the table shared an equally strong resolve to defend the security of the nation.

Stone turned his radar toward his right-hand man—the FBI's representative—Special Agent Leaf Watson. Watson was a career fed who'd entered the FBI academy after spending seven years in the air force as a Herky Bird driver. He was a no-nonsense guy who didn't mince words. In his mid-forties, he walked with a slight limp from a helicopter accident dating back to his time in the air force.

Watson shuffled some papers and cleared his throat. "The FBI has had an undercover agent on the inside of an arms-dealing group called Freedom's Echo for several months now. Until now, Freedom's Echo has dealt in small arms. Many of the guns aren't even illegal until they're modified to fire on full auto, which this group does. The group's located in Lassen County in northern California and operated by two brothers, Leonard and Ernie Bridgestone. You can read about this pair in your briefing packet, if you haven't already. To summarize, they're both in their mid-forties, and the older brother, Leonard, is ex–Army Ranger. Ernie Bridgestone was a marine and got himself court-martialed for killing a pedestrian while driving drunk. He spent five years in Fort Leavenworth. Both brothers had plenty of disciplinary citations in their files, and both left the military without looking back. Neither they nor their younger brother, Sammy, who works for them, got much attention from law enforcement until they came into possession of a large quantity of Semtex."

Some murmuring came from around the table. Stone McBride nodded for Watson to continue.

"Semtex is a pliable and potent plastic explosive that was manufactured originally in communist Czechoslovakia. As some of you might recall, when that regime toppled, the new government gave the world some very bad news: The old communist government had exported at least nine hundred tons of Semtex to Qaddafi's Libya, and similar amounts to rogue states such as Syria, North Korea, Iran, and Iraq. Worldwide, there could be as many as forty thousand tons of Semtex out there."

While Watson let that sink in, Stone got up, walked over to the corner table, and poured himself a glass of water. Even though he'd been briefed on all of this earlier, the number still seemed outrageous. Forty thousand tons translated into eighty million pounds. *Eighty million pounds.* How could that be? Who on God's green earth, besides the military or mining companies, needed even ten tons of the stuff, let alone a thousand tons? But forty thousand tons? Where *was* all of it? How much had terrorists already stockpiled?

Watson resumed. "We think Leonard Bridgestone made a connection with a Syrian official when he was stationed on the northern border of Iraq. He and his brother appear to have obtained around one ton. The bad news, obviously, is that the stuff's so damned potent. In 1988, less than a single pound was molded into a Toshiba cassette recorder and used to bring down Pan Am flight 103 over Lockerbie, Scotland, and an undetermined amount was used to bomb the USS *Cole* when she was moored in Yemen. Semtex was also used to bomb our embassy in Nairobi."

"Now," Stone McBride said, "we come to the point of this meeting. Our missing man is Special Agent James Ortega. All of you recognize his last name because his grandfather is former FBI director Frank Ortega, who served in that capacity under two of the portraits on these walls. Among other things, Frank Ortega is a lifelong friend of mine. We were in the same unit in Korea. James Ortega is the third generation to serve with the bureau."

"He, uh, volunteered for the job," Watson added. "When he failed to make a scheduled check-in and officially became MIA, the FBI had to assume the worst. In his last report, two days ago, he told us he saw several pallets of Semtex being unloaded from a rental truck and stacked inside the compound's main building. We've had the compound under constant surveillance since his report. As far as we know, the Semtex is still there."

The chairman leaned on the table with both hands. "I called this meeting to give everyone a heads-up on what's about to happen. The FBI will be raiding the compound tomorrow at fourteen thirty hours, local time. The FBI's Joint Terrorism

Task Force will conduct the raid, and local law enforcement will be informed of the raid only *after* it takes place. This means we can count on a certain degree of media fallout. Something of this magnitude can't be kept from the press for long. Cross your fingers, people, for all kinds of reasons. We're hitting that compound at full force tomorrow. I'll brief you afterward on the status of James Ortega, the Semtex, and the teams that conduct the raid. Until then, thank you all again for coming on such short notice."

The staff stood, gathered their notes, memos, and files, and tucked them into their briefcases. They silently filed out of the room.

As Watson started to leave, Stone stopped him. "Not you, Leaf."

Watson faced the senator.

Nathan McBride's father gestured toward a chair. "Have a seat. I've been in touch with the president. We have a few things to discuss."

Nathan's and Harvey's flight helmets crackled to life with the approach controller's voice.

"Helicopter Five-November-Charlie, contact Sacramento executive tower on one-one-nine point five. Frequency change approved. Good night."

From the left seat, Harvey pressed a preset button containing the tower's frequency and pulled the transmit trigger. "Sacramento Exec, Helicopter Five-November-Charlie is with you with information Sierra."

The tower's response came back immediately. "Helicopter Five-November-Charlie, radar contact confirmed. Maintain heading and speed for landing on taxiway Hotel. Advise upon two-mile final."

As Nathan made a slight course correction and eased the collective down a hair, Harvey acknowledged the tower's instructions. Although they could speak to each other anytime they liked through the intercom system, Nathan hadn't felt much like talking. He knew Harvey was aware of his mood; there was little he could hide from his friend. He appreciated the distance given at times like this, but sooner or later Harvey would mention it—saying something like, *You've been a little quiet lately,* or, *Is something bugging you?* Nathan fully planned on telling his friend what was bothering him; he just didn't feel like doing it now.

As if on cue, Harvey spoke. "You've been awfully quiet since we left San Diego. Want to talk about it?"

Well, there it was, out in the open where it belonged. *No avoiding it now.* "I don't know. I can't stop thinking about Ortega's grandson, how much time's passed since he last checked in."

"You figure he's been compromised and interrogated."

"Yeah, I do. Otherwise he would've made contact by now. And it pisses me off thinking about it. The older Bridgestone is ex–Army Ranger; those guys are trained in field interrogations. They probably tortured the shit out of the poor kid. Maybe still are."

"That's not the only thing bugging you."

Nathan didn't respond; he didn't have to.

"It's how far Greg and Frank are willing to go to save James. You're wondering why your father didn't go to the same lengths to find you."

Harvey had hit pay dirt. That was exactly what he'd been wondering—for many, many years. During his four-day crucifixion in the rain forest, he'd had lots of time to think about it. Hour after hour, then day after day, he kept waiting for the cavalry to arrive, hoping for the cavalry to arrive, *praying* for it to arrive. Toward the end his prayers changed; death had been welcome.

"You okay?"

Nathan nodded. "I just don't like my father knowing of our involvement. It makes this whole thing . . . I don't know, seem dirty."

"Come on, that's not fair. The CDT is a vital part of the

nation's security. It's an important job being the chairman. Of course he's involved."

Nathan said nothing.

"Despite how you feel about him, Ortega was right. He *is* a good man."

"He's a friggin' politician. It's all about money. The size of his damned war chest. Kissing babies and giving candy to kids is total horseshit. It's all about campaign contributions. Television and radio time. Mass mailings. What's the biggest issue facing a career politician? The economy? Crime? Unemployment? Illegal immigration? It's none of those things. It's getting reelected to another term. Can you believe he has the balls to send me campaign contribution letters?"

"Come on; that's not fair either. They care about all those issues; they just don't agree on how to solve them."

"I suppose you're right. Sorry, I'm just venting."

"Your father, he really does that?"

"Does what?"

"The fund-raising thing? The letters?"

"Yeah, he does."

"I'd call it reaching out."

"I call it reaching for my wallet."

"Do you send him money?"

He knew he couldn't lie to Harvey and get away with it. "Yeah, I do. The maximum amount allowed for an individual. Every year."

"No wonder he keeps sending them."

Nathan grunted.

"It's no different from any other profession," Harvey continued. "People want to keep their jobs. It's hard work being a politician, especially on the federal level. They make a lot of personal sacrifices."

Nathan knew all too well about the great Stonewall McBride's personal sacrifices, because *he* was one of them. He had an absentee dad during his childhood. Deep down he'd come to terms with it, but there was still a sliver of resentment left over, like the smell of a blown-out candle. He didn't hate his father; he just didn't feel any kind of familial bond with him. How could he? He hardly knew the man. Diane Ortega's comment was still fresh in his mind: *Your father's a lot like Frank, and you're a lot like Greg.*

"You should cut him some slack," Harvey said, "maybe try to patch things up."

"You know, you're the only person in the world I'd let say that to me, besides my mother."

"Why do you think I said it? You need to hear it. He's getting old."

Nathan said nothing.

"For your mother's sake."

They flew in silence for several minutes.

"Harvey?"

"Yeah?"

"Thanks." He turned on the Bell's landing light a little early as a courtesy to the tower. They were now a bright spot in the sky, easy to see. "You did a great job on the radio through LA's bravo airspace. You want to make the landing?"

"I do, but stay close to the controls, okay?"

"Will do." Nathan spotted the airport's beacon and made a tiny course change to put them on a straight-in final. Even as experienced and seasoned as he was, spotting the green-and-white flashing beacon of their destination airport at night was always a welcome sight. "Okay, she's yours. You've got the controls."

"I've got the controls," Harvey echoed.

"I'm on the radio," Nathan said.

In the distance, Sacramento looked like a million multicolored jewels laid out on black velvet. Visibility was good at fifty miles plus, a positive aftermath of rain. At two miles, Nathan keyed the transmit trigger. "Helicopter Five-November-Charlie's on a two-mile final."

The tower gave them clearance to land on taxiway Hotel.

Harvey made a near-flawless approach, handling the two-and-a-half-ton Bell 407 with precision and confidence. His only hitch was slowing the helicopter down a little early. It wasn't dangerous, but on a busy day with multiple aircraft in the pattern, the tower would probably ask for an expedited landing, meaning, *Get your butt in gear and land*. Harvey set the ship down near the large white H painted on the tarmac just west of taxiway Hotel, as instructed. Two other helicopters were parked in the transient area, one of them a California Highway Patrol bird, the other a Department of Forestry firefighter. Nathan went through the shutdown procedure, cooling the engine and flipping avionic switches. The four seventeen-foot rotors slowly wound down.

"Nice job," Nathan said, taking off his helmet.

"Thanks."

While Nathan went through the shutdown procedure, Harvey lifted the blanket concealing all their gear secured in the rear seats. Underneath the blanket was everything they'd need for tomorrow's operation. Nathan's Remington 700 sniper rifle was in an aluminum case at the bottom of the pile. Duffel bags contained their ammunition, spotter's scope, transmitter detector, woodland BDUs, two backpacks, bottled water, and perhaps the two most important items—their ghillie suits. A sniper's ghillie suit was an amazing piece of gear. Once donned, it broke up the sharp-edged outline of a human body by employing thousands of shaggy, stringlike, tattered pieces of fabric that hung in random disarray from every square inch of its surface. The wearer ended up looking like the Swamp Thing from the classic comic-book series. When Harvey was sure nothing had shifted during the flight, he grabbed their overnight bags.

"Did you know Frank Ortega had a daughter?" Nathan asked. "I'd always thought Greg was an only child."

"What brings that up?"

"I saw a picture in Frank's office."

"It's a sore subject. She was killed fifteen or twenty years ago. She'd just passed the bar exam when it happened—the very same day, as I recall. Some kind of traffic accident."

"That's a bad deal. Sorry to hear it."

"It *was* really bad for a while. Greg never talked about it with me. It was too painful. I think he was pretty close to his sister. He took her death really badly. We didn't talk for over a year. I didn't push, and he didn't need any pressure from me."

"I can imagine."

When the main rotor stopped, Nathan made a final shutdown check of all the systems and switches before climbing out into a cool evening with a light wind. In an unbroken tradition, he gave the Bell an affectionate pat on the fuselage after locking her up. They walked in silence toward the terminal.

It took the taxi twenty minutes to arrive, and twenty minutes after that they were checked into the Hyatt Regency in downtown Sacramento for the night.

The following morning Nathan met Harvey in the lobby of the hotel just after sunrise. Over breakfast they talked briefly about their expectations regarding the raid, in particular about what Frank Ortega had said about not being able to guarantee that their presence at the raid would be known. Nathan wasn't concerned; in fact, he preferred it that way. He and Harvey were used to working on their own.

After breakfast they returned to Nathan's hotel room, where they took a closer look at the file Frank had provided, reviewing every little detail, from topographic maps and aerial photos to the military personnel files on the Bridgestones. Internal FBI memos, along with James Ortega's transcribed reports, were also included. It was a lot to absorb, but when Nathan finished he had a pretty good picture in his mind. They retired to their rooms to catch some last-minute shut-eye before this afternoon's raid.

Unfortunately, sleep didn't come for Nathan. Staring at the

ceiling, he couldn't get his mind off James Ortega and what the poor kid could be going through at that very moment. In agony. Alone. Frightened. Hopeless. It really burned him to picture the Bridgestones doing anything they wanted. Was James tied to a chair, wired with electrodes? Screaming until his throat bled? Nathan closed his eyes and tried to clear his thoughts. There was nothing he could do for James right now. They had to find him first. Deep down, he hoped the kid was dead, not still being tortured. He made a promise to himself: If the Bridgestones had tortured James Ortega, they were both dead men.

Later that morning Harvey drove the rented Tahoe over to the airport, where they retrieved their gear from the helicopter. Within ten minutes they left Sacramento behind. Once they'd cleared the city, it was an easy cruise north on Highway 70 through Marysville and Oroville until it turned northeast into the Sierra Nevada mountains and became a designated scenic highway. The road gradually climbed into one of California's greatest natural treasures. Oaks and grassland gave way to hundreds of thousands of acres of pine forest. An hour later, Harvey found their turn onto the logging road they'd identified in the aerial photos. Using his handheld GPS device to find the exact spot they wanted, Harvey followed the gravel track for eight miles before he pulled the Tahoe off the road and parked it deep within the trees, where it wouldn't be seen by a passing vehicle.

They quickly changed from civilian clothes into woodland battle dress uniforms, BDUs, which would merge them into the native colors of the forest. They exchanged their shoes for black, dull-finished combat boots. Nathan had cut one of the cleats away from his right boot, while Harvey's left boot had the same missing cleat. Their footprints would be distinct and recognizable in the event they had to separate for any reason.

Harvey secured his Kiowa spotting scope along with twenty-five stripper clips—each clip contained five rounds of hand-loaded .308 ammo—into his backpack, while Nathan inspected his cloth-wrapped Remington 700 sniper rifle from end to end. Each of them made one final check of all their gear, making sure nothing was left behind. Harvey opened a camera-type case and removed two SIG Sauer P226 pistols. He handed one to Nathan. They both secured them into olive green holsters on their hips and grabbed five spare magazines of ammo. They slid them into slots on the left sides of their holster belts. Next they tied their ghillie suits onto their back-packs. The last thing they did was apply green, brown, and black body paint to their faces and the backs of their hands.

Nathan didn't talk during this part of the operation—it wasn't necessary—but still he noticed the occasional glances Harvey was giving him. They were both thinking the same thing. It didn't need to be vocalized; they'd come to terms with it over a decade ago. Harvey patted his shoulder. It felt good. Reassuring. If anything ever happened to Harv, he'd probably commit suicide. He couldn't imagine his life with-out Harv. He nodded a silent thank-you to his partner.

Harvey locked the Tahoe and put the keys on top of the right front tire. They didn't want an untimely jingling in a pocket. Even if the sound was quiet enough to be inaudible to humans, it wasn't to dogs, and dogs were always a concern. Shooting an attacking dog was a surefire way to give away your presence. Besides, Nathan really liked dogs—more than he did most people. All set to go, Nathan nodded, and they started up the slope, keeping fifty feet of lateral separation between them. Although getting footholds was easier due to the damp earth from last night's storm, it was still a difficult climb over decomposed granite, sand, and loose rock. After several hundred yards they took a breather. Nathan motioned Harvey over to his position.

"Time," he whispered.

Harvey slid his sleeve up and looked at his watch, where he'd smeared soap over the dial to prevent a glint of light from the sun. "Thirty-seven minutes."

"Let's do an RF check." Nathan pulled the DAR-3

radio-frequency detector from Harvey's pack and handed it to him. With a price tag of over four thousand dollars, it was a state-of-the-art device, very reliable. About the size of a shoe box, it employed half a dozen dials, various jacks for input and output, and a small six-inch antenna. The DAR-3 could pick up signals from fifty kilohertz all the way up to twelve gigahertz. Harvey turned it on and worked the dials, concentrating on the small needle. After a minute or so, he said, "We're good," and turned it off.

Nathan secured the detector back into Harvey's pack, and they resumed their hike up the canyon's wall. High overhead, a red-tailed hawk rode a thermal. The lonely whisper of wind through the pines was the only sound present. They diverted two hundred feet to the east to avoid a granite face they couldn't negotiate without climbing gear. Near the summit, Nathan slowed their pace. He turned toward Harvey, pointed to his own eyes with two fingers, then pointed to the left. Harvey nodded and set off in that direction while Nathan swept around to the right. He wanted to be certain there weren't any sentries overlooking the compound. There were countless places to hide up here; the summit's ridgeline was dense with sugar and ponderosa pines, some reaching over one hundred feet high.

After making sure the ridgeline was clear, they began scanning for a shooting position that would give them a clear view of the compound below. Although he was more than capable of hitting targets at longer distances, he didn't want to be any farther than six hundred yards. Six hundred yards was good distance, because the bullet arrived before the report of the rifle. From their current location, they needed to advance another seven hundred yards closer. Using field glasses, they took a few minutes to study the layout of the compound. Just as the aerial photos had shown, Freedom's Echo was situated in a grass valley interspersed with mature pines. Twenty or so small cabins surrounded a larger central lodge along with several other metal outbuildings, presumably used for storage.

The cabins were constructed in the classic log-cabin style, with steep metal roofs. Several camouflage-painted pickup trucks were parked next to the largest outbuilding.

Harvey secured their field glasses into his backpack before they started down. Nathan kept his head up, always scanning the area. Wind—about ten miles an hour from the west. Temperature—about sixty degrees. Humidity—mild, probably fifty to sixty percent. The scent of pines hung heavily in the air. It reminded him of his own summer camp experience. He made a low, barely audible warble-type whistle. Harvey stopped and turned. He pointed to a small outcropping of rocks flanked by mature pines several hundred yards closer to the compound. Harvey nodded his understanding. The approach to that location was going to be a little risky; the trees were sparse near the rock outcropping, so they'd be out in the open for the traverse. They'd crawl the last fifteen yards on their bellies, camouflaged by their ghillie suits. Anyone looking in their direction wouldn't see a human outline, and if they crawled slowly, an observer wouldn't see any discernible movement. Movement was what usually caught the eye.

The valley below sloped gently to the west, where the forest was much thicker. Most of the pine trees surrounding the compound had been cleared, creating a firebreak nearly two hundred feet wide, but more important, it forced any approach to be out in the open. Nathan gestured for his field glasses, and Harvey pulled them from his pack. He scanned the compound again. All quiet. No movement at all. He handed them back to Harvey.

"What do you think?" Nathan asked. "Those rock spires over there."

"Slow crawl."

They untied each other's ghillie suits, put them on, and dropped to their bellies. With Nathan in the lead, they started their crawl across the sandy surface covered with pine straw fallout. The thirty-degree slope made the trek awkward. To keep from rolling down the hillside, they had to align their bodies forty-five degrees to their actual path. Crawling on one's belly over sloped terrain wasn't very pleasant, even at a snail's pace, but the damp earth made it a little easier. Nathan hated being out in the open, even for brief periods. If an enemy sniper spotted them they'd be dead. It took five minutes to crawl the fifty-foot distance—one foot every six seconds. They made it to the outcropping without incident. So far, so good. It turned out to be an ideal shooting position. Shaped like a European cathedral, two large spires of granite each reaching twenty feet over their heads were leaning slightly to the east. The larger of the two gave them shade from the sun and put them securely in the depth of shadow. Between the spires was a flat area of sandy soil that offered a full view of the compound below and the dirt road leading into it. Staying below the compound's line of sight, they quickly unpacked their gear.

Harvey handed Nathan a stripper clip containing five rounds of .308 NATO ammunition. Harvey had used a black felt marker on the stripper clips—inside and out—to prevent an untimely glint of sunlight. Each hand-loaded round produced a muzzle velocity of twenty-three hundred fifty feet per second. Bullet time to the target at six hundred yards—just less than one second. He placed one end of the stripper clip into the breach, drove the bullets home with his thumb, and closed the bolt. He handed the empty clip back to Harvey.

"Time?" Nathan asked.

"Eleven minutes."

A gust of wind dropped a few pine needles past their position from right to left.

Harvey spoke without being prompted. "Maybe ten miles an hour. Four clicks right."

He made the adjustment to the external windage knob on his Nikon scope, while Harvey set up his ten-to-fifty-power spotter scope. Once in final position they would be lying side by side with three feet of separation between them. He shouldered his weapon and began a slow visual sweep of the compound below through the rifle's optic. "We'll call the main building zero and vector from there."

"Copy."

"Elevation?" Nathan asked.

"Nine clicks."

"Copy, nine clicks to zero. Plus three to the far side of the compound, minus two to the near side. Concur?" Nathan asked.

"Concur."

Nathan dialed them into the elevation knob of the scope. Because his rifle was zeroed for a three-hundred-yard shot, he knew an elevation adjustment for a six-hundred-yard shot was twelve additional clicks, but since they were shooting downhill, a negative adjustment of three clicks was needed.

"Here we go," Nathan said. Moving in classic leapfrog progression from tree to tree, six men in woodland SWAT gear were approaching the compound from the south, their movements crisp and rehearsed. "Six o'clock low," he whispered.

Harvey adjusted his scope. "Got 'em. I count six, with two more in flanking positions. I've got eight more moving in from the west."

Nathan tracked the second team. Six were advancing, with two more flanking for support. Both teams were advancing at right angles, staying out of each other's line of fire. Tactically sound. As the two teams approached the compound, he admired their precision and stealth. As they moved through the sunlight filtering through the trees, not a glint of reflection bounced off anything they wore. Their helmets were matte green; even their boots had a dull finish. These guys were damned good.

"Something's wrong," Nathan whispered.

"Talk to me."

"It's too quiet down there. We haven't seen a damned thing. Nothing. No movement at all."

"Okay . . ."

"Start searching the trees. I'll take the west end."

Harvey adjusted his scope and began a slow pivot around the east end of the compound. Halfway through his sweep he stopped. "Shit."

"What've you got?"

"Spotter's nest at one-five-zero east, elevation three-zero feet."

Nathan swung his rifle one hundred fifty yards east of the center of the compound and began looking in the trees thirty feet high. He saw it instantly: a sentry posted in a tree platform, the type deer hunters used. He was speaking into a radio and looking through a pair of field glasses in the direction of the advancing FBI SWAT team to the south. "They've been made."

Harvey, glued to his eyepiece, cranked it to maximum zoom. "Nate, he put the radio down. He's got something else. . . . He's pulling an antenna on a remote."

Nathan swung his rifle back to the south and began sweeping the ground out in front of the SWAT team. Through an opening in the trees he saw a mound of pine needles at the base of a large sugar pine. The pile of needles was on the side of the tree facing away from the compound. Nathan searched for other piles. There. Two more piles, also facing away from the compound.

"Son of a bitch. I think they've got M18s on the perimeter. Those piles of pine straw."

"Claymores," Harvey whispered.

"They're walking into a shredder."

"How close are they?" Harvey asked.

"Thirty yards."

"Shit, they're in range. We have to warn them. Put one in the dirt out in front of the lead man. Elevation minus two. Clear to shoot!"

## Chapter Four

Sammy Bridgestone's voice sounded metallic through the small radio speaker. "We've got company."

Ernie stood up and looked at his older brother.

"What's happening out there?" Leonard asked.

"SWAT team moving in from the south. At least a half dozen, probably more!"

"Calm down, Sammy. Are they at the perimeter minefield?"

"Not yet. Almost."

"Blow the southern perimeter when they reach twenty yards. Wait a few seconds; then blow the rest. Hustle back here. Don't wait. Understood?"

The radio clicked once in reply.

Ernie grabbed an M16 and ran to the rear door. "He shouldn't be out there alone. I'll go get him."

"Wait!" Leonard yelled, but his brother was already outside.

Nathan took two clicks off the elevation knob, aimed for a spot twenty feet in front of the lead SWAT man, and squeezed the trigger.

His rifle jumped.

The ground erupted in front of the lead SWAT member. Both teams instantly dropped to the ground. Four seconds later at least eight claymore antipersonnel mines detonated simultaneously.

From high above the effect was horrifying to watch. As if coming alive, the forest shuddered as though a giant shiver had raked across its body. "Son of a bitch," Nathan whispered. The concussive thump of the blasts reached their position a full second later. An area the size of a football field had been turned into a maelstrom of flying dirt, rocks, and splintered tree branches. An angry cloud of dust began drifting down the valley toward the west. Nathan swung his rifle in the same direction of the wind and saw the other SWAT team on the ground. If there were more claymores, they hadn't been detonated yet. The answer came five seconds later. Another giant concussion shook the forest to the west, followed by a third to the east and a fourth to the north. The compound now looked like a huge doughnut, untouched in the middle, total mayhem on the outside.

Nathan tapped his memory for what he knew about the devices—a curved block of C-4 explosive blew hundreds of small steel cubes outward in a sixty-degree pattern. Like its Scottish broadsword namesake, the claymore could literally cut a swath through the ranks. If those guys had been on their feet . . .

"I want that shitbird in the tree," Nathan said. "He just tried to frag a dozen federal agents."

"We can't see him until the dust clears."

"Break out your RF detector; let's see if the good guys are talking."

Harvey reached to his right and grabbed the detector out of his pack. He turned it on and adjusted the dials. "I'd say so; we've got a needle in the fifteen-megahertz range; signal's close by. It wasn't there before."

"Can we listen?" But Nathan already knew the answer.

"No way, encrypted for sure."

"There might be a second ring of claymores down there."

"Probably is. At least the feds are aware of them now. We saved a bunch of lives with that warning shot."

Nathan grunted. He wanted that spotter in the tree. Wanted him badly.

A few sporadic bursts of automatic gunfire began to hammer the afternoon air. At their distance it sounded like fire-crackers. "Here we go," Nathan said. "Windage."

Harvey had already given him four clicks right. From the speed of the dust cloud moving toward the west, Harvey gave him one more click right.

"Corrections to the tree stand," Nathan said.

"Give me the two clicks back on elevation, plus one more, and give me a final click right. A few more seconds . . . I can almost see him. . . . Got him. Nate, he's got a sniper rifle. He's lining up on the SWAT teams!"

Nathan swung his weapon back to the tree and saw the man bench-resting his rifle on the rail of the tree platform, taking careful aim. He was dressed in cheap catalog camo with shiny black boots. His camo cap masked his facial features, but Nathan had the impression he was young, maybe mid-twenties. He moved the crosshairs onto the man's chest, then took a deep breath and blew half of it out.

Ernie had made it halfway to Sammy's tree stand when the first salvo of claymores detonated to his right. For a split second the air seemed to shimmer as if suspended in time. Then the concussive shock wave vibrated his body like a bowstring. "Son of a bitch," he whispered. Knowing more blasts were coming, Ernie crouched down and covered his ears. The ground shuddered and shook with each progressive detonation surrounding him. The perimeter of the Freedom's Echo camp disappeared into a choking cloud of dust and flying debris.

Ernie called, "Get down, Sammy. Come on."

"I can nail some of those bastards when the dust clears."

"Goddammit, Sammy, get your ass down. Now. We're buggin' out."

"Clear to shoot," Harvey whispered.

Nathan began a controlled squeeze of the trigger.

His rifle bucked against his shoulder.

"That's a bingo," Harvey said. "Solid impact. Center mass."

Ernie Bridgestone recognized the sound. The bullet's supersonic arrival sounded like a giant bullwhip cracking.

Sammy never knew what hit him, only that something had. His mind simply wasn't fast enough to register the event. Traveling at fifteen hundred twenty-five feet per second, one hundred and eighty grains of copper and lead slammed into the side of his chest. The bullet actually missed by a quarter of an inch, but the concussive shock wave of its mushrooming form compressed his heart like a wet sponge, causing permanent failure. From thirty feet high, Sammy Bridgestone fell like a rag doll into a pile of crumpled arms and legs.

*"Sammy!"* Ernie sprinted to the base of the tree and slung his brother's limp form over his shoulder.

"I see him," Nathan said as he ejected the spent shell and closed the bolt on another. *Brave bastard*, he thought as he placed the crosshairs on the running man's hip. Then something twitched on his spine and sent a shiver through his body. It was the kind of premonition he couldn't ignore. He'd felt it before and had never been wrong. He swung his rifle back toward the lodge. *Oh, shit!* A man was standing in the open doorway, using the jamb to steady his stance. Nathan found himself looking directly into the business end of a sniper rifle.

*"Harv! Get down!"*

The air cracked.

Behind Nathan the rock wall exploded in a barrage of hot copper, molten lead, and pulverized granite. Something stung his face. A second later the thump of the discharge reached his position. Nathan pointed his rifle at the ground and fired. A burst of earth blew upward, giving himself and Harvey a few seconds of cover.

*"Harvey!"*

"I'm okay."

They scrambled backward as another deafening crack tore the air. *Son of a bitch!* That shot hadn't missed by more than six inches. Three more shots smashed the stone above their heads. Nathan protected his face with his forearms, but the rest of his body didn't fare as well. Blood began oozing from a dozen minor wounds on his back and legs.

Ernie burst through the door and laid Sammy on the floor. If the bullet hadn't killed him, the fall would have. His blue eyes stared blankly into space.

"Those fuckers," Ernie said. "Those lousy *motherfuckers*."

Leonard grabbed his brother's shirt and yanked him closer. "I nearly lost both of you out there. There's a sniper team on Eagle Rock. I just saved your fuckin' life. You were two seconds from getting nailed."

"I don't give a shit. I'm gonna kill every one of those fucks."

"Damn it, Ernie, I'm pissed too. But there's nothing we can do for him now. He's dead. If we go out there, we'll die too. I promise we'll get some payback, but *not now*."

"I can't believe this."

"Ernie, we have to go."

"Those motherfuckers."

"Ernie, *now*!"

Harvey was crouched down, looking at his partner. "How'd you know?"

"Can't explain it; I just did."

"That guy's a good shot. He nearly lit us up."

"Probably the older Bridgestone brother, Leonard. I doubt he's still there, but we need to relocate. Can you sneak a look without getting your head blown off?"

"I think so." Harvey inched his way forward, crawling on his elbows until he could just barely see over the sand. He peered through his spotter scope.

"He was standing in the doorway of the main building."

Nathan saw that Harvey was also bleeding from half a dozen spots on his back and legs.

"Nobody's there now."

"Okay, let's bug out. We'll make a balls-to-the-wind sprint over to the tree cover. Ready?"

"Yep."

The two men grabbed their packs and took off, dashing across the sloped open ground. Within seconds they were deep within the safety of mature sugar pines. They looked at each other in unspoken relief.

"I know we're not here officially, but I think we should head down there," Nathan said. "I'm betting there are more claymores, and we need to let them know about the sniper in the main building. I doubt they saw him through all the dust."

"We need to let the SWAT teams know we're coming," Harvey said. "Any ideas?"

"Yeah, we can yell."

"Any *other* ideas?"

"Sorry, fresh out. As far as they're concerned, we just took a shot at them."

"Why do I get the feeling I'm going to regret this?"

"Relax, Harv; I've got things under control."

His partner snorted. "I was afraid you'd say that. Hell, I guess it's a good day to die. Let's go."

They took off their bulky ghillie suits and started down the mountain. Two minutes later they reached the bottom of the incline. Not wanting to appear threatening, in case they were spotted, Nathan had slung his rifle over his shoulder. There wasn't much he could do about his SIG Sauer secured in his waist holster, because he wasn't willing to approach an FBI SWAT team that had just been trashed by several dozen antipersonnel mines without being armed. Their ears would be buzzing like dial tones, and without a doubt they would be thoroughly pissed off.

Harvey took out his scope and scanned the area ahead.

"I've got a spotter at one o'clock, two hundred yards. Are you sure about this? Those guys are damned high-strung. They'll shoot first and ask questions later."

"Wait here." Nathan handed Harvey the rifle and shucked off his backpack. "I'll make the approach. Just don't let anyone shoot me."

"I've got your six."

Like a silent wraith, Nathan worked his way through the trees, covering the two hundred yards in just under a minute. Twenty-five yards from the SWAT spotter, he ducked behind the thick trunk of a ponderosa and looked back toward Harvey. He had to lean several feet to his left to get a clear view of his partner. Harvey gave him the okay sign; he hadn't been seen. Now came the really tricky part; he was pretty sure how he'd handle it. The SWAT spotter had positioned himself behind a fallen tree branch, which gave him solid chest-high cover from the front and broken cover to his right. This was a small man; he could see that right away. An old adage flashed through his head. How did it go? *God made men different sizes, but Sam Colt made them all equal*—something like that. Well, this guy was a little more equal. Nathan's pistol was no match for a fully automatic MP5 in the right hands, and he figured this guy knew how to handle one. Hell, the guy was a damned expert with the thing; of course he knew how to handle it.

The downed branch where the spotter was crouched was thick, nearly two feet in diameter. Its structure fanned out to the spotter's left, while the meaty part of its splintered end faced Nathan. He judged the distance between them again—twenty-five yards, give or take. The spotter was down on one knee, sweeping the area in a back-and-forth motion with his upper body, gun at the ready. Every fourth or fifth sweep he'd keep the arc of his motion going and look behind him. Nathan studied him for about thirty seconds and formulated his plan. Precious seconds were ticking by, and he didn't have the luxury of conducting a long surveillance. He sure as hell didn't want to get sprayed with MP5 fire, so it was all about timing. He needed to make his presence known at the exact moment the man was lined up on his position. If he did it too early or too late, it would be interpreted as an unintentionally sloppy move by an opponent, and *that* would result in a horizontal hail of nine-millimeter slugs traveling at eight hundred miles an hour. Not a pretty picture, especially if you were on the business end of those slugs.

*Here goes.*

Nathan timed it perfectly. When the man swung toward his position, he leaned out from behind the tree and said, "Don't shoot." He said it loudly and forcefully, but not *too* loudly and not *too* forcefully—somewhere between a command and a request. Body language—it was all about body language. Nathan saw it instantly: A tense movement of shock and surprise raked the spotter's body, with a predictable result.

*Shit!* He ducked behind the ponderosa pine a split second before the spotter's gun erupted. With his back to the trunk, Nathan felt a continuous vibration through its thick form as dozens of bullets slammed home. Pulverized chunks of bark shot out from either side of the tree as if sprayed with a fire hose. When the buzz of bullets ceased, he knew he had mere seconds while the shooter ejected the spent magazine, slammed another home, and cycled the bolt.

"Hold your fire, damn it. I'm on your side."

"Bullshit." The unmistakable voice of a woman. When the human mind encountered something completely unexpected, it usually took a few seconds to process the information, formulate a response, and then execute the plan. Not so with Nathan McBride. He had the uncanny ability to react instantly, without thinking. He knew this spotter had already communicated with the rest of her team, and he figured he had less than thirty seconds to get control of the situation before being surrounded by angry FBI SWAT agents who were, as Harvey suggested, going to shoot first and ask questions later. What he said next was perfect for the situation he faced.

"You have nothing to prove here," he shouted. "My name is Nathan McBride. I'm not one of the bad guys. I fired that warning shot before the claymores went off."

"Bullshit," was the response again, but not as disbelieving this time. The tone had softened by a degree or two.

"It's *not* bullshit."

"How do I know you're telling the truth?"

"You've got a pair of field glasses?"

No response.

"Take a look at about two hundred yards to your five-o'clock position. My partner has a rifle trained on you. If we'd wanted you dead, we wouldn't be talking right now." He figured it would take about five seconds for the spotter to verify his claim. It happened faster than that. What the agent saw must have caused her some concern—actually, a lot of concern. Nathan imagined what peering through a pair of field glasses and seeing a sniper lined up on you felt like. Hell, he knew exactly what it felt like; he'd just seen it a few minutes ago.

"Okay. Very slowly, I want you to step out from behind that tree."

"You aren't going to shoot, are you?"

"That depends entirely on you."

"Okay, I'm coming out. I'm wearing a sidearm. Don't shoot or we *both* die." He slowly pivoted from behind the trunk and faced the spotter, holding his arms out to his sides. He watched her whisper something into the boom mike of her combat helmet and knew she was strung tight. He also knew she was now facing a large, menacing man in a woodland BDU, with his face and hands painted black, green, and brown, wearing a sidearm. In essence, a Special Forces soldier whose partner was training a sniper rifle on her. She needed to be careful—no, not just careful; she had to be delicate with her movements. Nothing sudden. Nothing threatening.

"Place your hands on top of your head and lace your fingers together. Please do it now."

She said *please*. A good sign. Nathan complied.

She whispered something into her boom mike again, probably responding to the other team members, who would quickly be on their way. Nathan glanced to the right and saw three camouflaged figures advancing in leapfrog progression again. He figured he had twenty seconds before being surrounded. "I need to give my partner the all-clear sign."

"Please don't move," she said, her tone a little more relaxed. She knew backup was seconds away, and security came with numbers.

Nathan moved his hands to the top of his head, interlocked his fingers, and turned to face the first man arriving. He was of medium build. Under his olive helmet and clear protective goggles was a four-part expression of pure intensity in his blue eyes—one part curiosity, three parts anger. His woodland BDU had turned gray from being blasted with dust and debris. Charred brown and black pine needles clung to his backpack. He'd been up front when the mines detonated. Had to be hell on earth. His MP5 aimed from the hip, the new arrival stopped ten feet away. With his left hand, red with blood, he issued a sharp, crisp signal for the others to advance. Two more SWAT figures appeared in front of Nathan, seemingly out of nowhere. They too were covered with dust and burned pine needles. A hand signal was given to the woman near the fallen tree branch, and she assumed a sentry's position again.

"Are you McBride?" the man asked.

That question spoke volumes. Ortega had gotten the word out. This man knew he would be here, but the woman who shot the hell out of the ponderosa hadn't.

Nathan nodded.

"All right. Let's do this delicately. I want you to ask Mr. Fontana to stand down."

"I need to give him a hand signal."

"Please do it slowly."

Nathan unlocked his fingers from the top of his head and turned to face Harvey's position. He slowly took his right hand, formed a fist, and placed it across his chest with the knuckles touching his right shoulder. He interlocked his fingers on top of his head again.

"Thank you," the man said.

"No problem. Your teams are top-notch, Commander," Nathan added. "The best I've ever seen."

The slightest hint of a smile formed on the man's lips, but vanished instantly. "You fire that warning shot?"

Nathan nodded.

"We've got three down, one dead," he said.

"I'm sorry," Nathan said.

"Took a fragment down through his shoulder close to his neck. Clipped an artery. He bled out in minutes. The toll could've been a lot worse."

Nathan looked at the man's bloody hands again. "There's probably another ring of claymores closer to the buildings."

"We're on hold for now. I'm Assistant Special Agent in Charge Larry Gifford, with the Sacramento Joint Terrorism Task Force." He closed the distance and held out his right hand.

Nathan shook it, ignoring the sticky feel of drying blood. "I'm real sorry about your man."

"Me too."

"How are the other two?"

"One has a concussion from a tree branch. Clocked him pretty good, but he'll be okay. His bucket saved his life. The other has a separated shoulder; at least his vest worked. I heard a shot a few seconds after the mines detonated, followed by several shots coming from the compound."

"I killed the man who detonated the mines. He was in a tree platform sighting in on your team with a scoped rifle when I nailed him. I'm damned sorry I didn't get him sooner."

"This isn't your fault. If our teams hadn't been on the ground when those claymores went off . . ." Gifford looked at Nathan's fatigues. "You're bleeding."

"Those shots you heard," Nathan offered. "The rock face

above our heads took a few impacts. The shooter was hoping for a cornering shot. Nearly got one."

"Do you need medical attention?"

Nathan shook his head. "Fragments."

"Please bring Mr. Fontana up."

He turned toward Harvey's invisible position and signaled him with a slight nod of his head. Two hundred yards distant, Harvey stood and began jogging toward them, weaving his way through the trees.

Harvey arrived thirty seconds later, barely breathing hard. Introductions were made.

"Nobody else knew we were here but you," Nathan said to Gifford.

"That's right." There was no apology in his voice.

"Understood. If you had told your team there were friendlies in the area, they might hesitate at the moment of truth, which could get them killed. They needed to know anyone not in a SWAT BDU was fair game. I would've played it the same way. Risky, to us."

"The price of admission, Mr. McBride. I wouldn't agree to your involvement any other way. I've also got a sniper team on the north rim of the canyon. They couldn't see the tree stand where you nailed the shooter, but they followed your movements the entire way, reporting only to me on a different frequency. You want to talk about top-notch—they said you two looked like part of the landscape."

"What now?" Nathan asked.

Gifford looked back in the direction of the compound. "We've got an explosives unit being flown in from Sierra Army Depot. Two Hueys are on their way from Amedee Field as we speak. Should be here within the hour. We run an explosives investigation unit out of there."

"The FBI does?" he asked.

Gifford nodded. He turned toward his other team members and pointed at Nathan and Harvey. "Collins, Dowdy, these

two were never here. I want the compound's perimeter secured out to a distance of two miles. Keep everyone well behind the first detonation ring. I want all the doors and
windows of the main building constantly watched; I don't
want anyone firing a shoulder-launched weapon at the approaching choppers."

The two agents hustled back toward the compound, the
lead man talking into his mike as he ran.

"I only saw three guys," Nathan said. "I got one of them,
but the other two are still in the main building. One of them
has a sniper rifle, and he's a shooter."

Gifford turned away and spoke quietly into his mike. He
turned back toward Nathan and Harvey. "I'll be honest: I was
resentful as all hell that you two were going to be here, but now
I'm glad you were. We would've made this a night raid if you
weren't. It's no secret who's missing. Frank Ortega still carries
considerable weight in D.C." Gifford issued a hand signal to the
woman SWAT member, and she hustled over to their position.
"Cover us." He addressed Nathan and Harvey. "You two,
you're with me." Gifford began walking deeper into the forest.

Nathan exchanged a glance with Harvey before following.
When they were fifty yards away, Gifford stopped and faced
them. He reached into his pocket and gave Nathan a slip of
paper with a handwritten phone number on it. "Call me in
six hours. If you're willing, I've got a very special job for you
tomorrow night."

# ⊕ Chapter Five

"A tunnel?" Senator Stone McBride's irritation couldn't be
concealed. Gripping the telephone too tightly, he continued,
"And nobody knew about it?"

Leaf Watson hesitated before answering. "I'm afraid not,

sir. I think it's fair to assume that if Special Agent Ortega had seen it, he would've reported it."

Stone had sent Watson out to California on a red-eye flight for a firsthand report. Now he couldn't help but wish he'd gone along with him.

"I have Assistant Special Agent in Charge Larry Gifford with me. We're on speaker, Senator."

Stone grunted acknowledgment. "Any sign of James Ortega?"

"Sadly, no," Watson said.

"I want the entire property searched. Bring in whatever resources you need. I want that compound torn apart. Dogs, whatever it takes. I want James Ortega found."

"Yes, sir. I'll see to it personally."

Stone rubbed his eyes. "What about the Semtex?"

"I'm looking at several pallets of wooden crates stacked head-high, with serial numbers written in Czech."

"How much?"

"Just over sixteen hundred pounds."

"Did we get all of it?"

"We're pretty sure ten crates are missing. About four hundred pounds' worth."

"So, let me get this straight," Stone said. "The raid nets nearly a ton of Semtex and the youngest Bridgestone brother, but in the process we lose one of your men, four hundred pounds of high explosives, and the operation's two ringleaders. Not a great trade-off, I'm afraid."

An uneasy silence hung on the other end.

Larry Gifford broke it. "It could've been a lot worse."

Waiting for Gifford to continue, Stone said nothing.

"We had a sniper team on the south rim of the canyon. They saw a compound member with a radio remote, put two and two together, and fired a shot out in front of my SWAT team. When the claymores blew we were on the ground. It saved I don't know how many of my men."

"Is that the official story?" Stone asked.

"Yes."

"Good, let's keep it that way." Stone knew the truth, and knew that both Gifford and Watson also knew the truth: It had been Stone's son who'd fired that warning shot. Chalk up another victory for cold-blooded snipers.

"Tell me about this damned tunnel."

Gifford continued, "Before storming the main building, we fired flash-bangs and tear gas, but they were long gone. On the inside west wall of the main building, the concrete had been saw-cut, then removed with a jackhammer. We found a ten-foot-square room below the slab reinforced with railroad ties. It connects to nearly a mile of thirty-inch-diameter concrete pipe. Must have cost a small fortune. They attached skateboard wheels to the undersides of water skis and used them like toboggans to traverse the tunnel."

"They didn't haul four hundred pounds of Semtex with them through that tunnel."

"No, sir, we think it was moved several days ago, just after Special Agent James Ortega went silent. The tunnel ended in the tree line to the west of the compound nearly a mile away. We followed footprints another half mile and found two canvas covers they'd used to protect off-road quad-runners. There were three more quads parked there, unused. The tire tracks extended to the west down the valley. We think someone met them on a logging road about fifteen miles away. The quad-runner tracks end there, in any case. They probably loaded 'em onto a trailer or hauled them into the bed of a truck. We're checking that angle, asking at gas stations and convenience stores in the area if anyone remembers seeing them, but it's a fairly common sight—quads in trailers, I mean. We're doing our best to piece together the chain of events."

"Keep after it." Stone paused a moment before asking, "Did you see my son during the raid?"

"Yes, sir," Gifford said. "He approached our teams after the claymores went off."

"What did you think of him?"

"I'm, ah, not sure what you're asking me."

"What was your impression of him?"

"He was definitely in his environment. He seemed comfortable in a high-stress situation. I'm glad he was on our side, that's for sure."

"Mm. That sounds like Nathan."

"He's an incredible soldier, *was* an incredible soldier. He's given a lot for his country, more than I'll ever know."

"That's true; he has."

"I, ah, offered him another job."

"Oh?"

"Yes, sir. I need someone to talk to the Bridgestones' cousins. Pair of lowlifes living on the outskirts of Sacramento. They've been in and out of jail most of their lives. A day before the raid we put their farmhouse under surveillance. They might know something, or the Bridgestones might call them or show up there. It's a long shot, but it's worth pursuing."

"So Nathan's to 'talk' to them?"

"Yes, a friendly fireside chat."

"Uh-huh. And I suppose he can 'talk' to these cousins in a way your people can't? Is that about the long and short of it?"

"Yes, sir. There are issues of deniability involved. And, of course, there's the Constitution."

"I see. Then this conversation we're having right now never took place."

"I think that would be best, Senator."

Stone issued a harsh laugh and shook his head. "I'm sure Nathan's your man, then. Anything you need, Special Agent Gifford, you talk to Leaf Watson directly. Make sure you get his cell number."

"Thank you, sir, I will."

Stone had one last question for Gifford: "Do you believe James Ortega is dead?" He waited through a brief silence.

"I want to believe he's still alive, but it's unlikely. The Bridgestones tried to frag my entire SWAT team. If James Ortega was discovered, they would've interrogated him and killed him outright. I can't see any reason they'd keep him alive. My people have searched every building within a five-mile radius of the compound, but he's nowhere. We've also set up road-blocks on every road leading in and out of there. We're bring-ing in cadaver dog teams tomorrow in case he's buried up here. Later today I'll have two FBI helicopters searching the area out to a twenty-mile radius, coordinating with CDF and Lassen County sheriff's horseback teams on the ground. We're doing everything possible to find him with the limited re-sources we have available."

"I'll call Sierra Army Depot's commander, see if he can muster a couple of platoons for you. Maybe a Huey or two."

"That would really help; the more people we have up here searching the woods, the better chance we have of finding him."

"If it's any consolation, Mr. Gifford, I'm going to nail those Bridgestone brothers to a cross."

"Thank you, sir," said Gifford. "Then I'll be there with the hammer."

It promised to be another long day for Nathan and Harvey. Yesterday, after the raid at the compound, they'd flown back to San Diego, arriving well after dark, and parted company for the night. Early this morning they had met with Frank and Greg Ortega at a coffee shop in Mission Valley and given them a complete update on the Freedom's Echo raid, includ-ing their latest phone updates from Assistant Special Agent in Charge Larry Gifford. Though the disappointment of both Ortegas showed in their voices and body language, they did seem encouraged by the assignment Nathan and Harvey had accepted from Gifford. After the meeting with the Ortegas, they again went their separate ways, agreeing to meet back at Montgomery Field at eighteen hundred hours for the return flight to Sacramento. Harvey told Nathan he needed to make a brief stop at the office and follow up on some potential contracts before heading home to say happy birthday to his oldest son.

Nathan needed more sleep than he'd been allowed. He could barely concentrate. One rule he'd taken to heart while in the Marine Corps—sleep when you can. He'd had less than six hours of shut-eye in the last two days, and he faced another long night. First, though, he needed to call Mara and find out if Toby had caused any more problems. He dialed her cell phone from memory.

"Any sign of our problem child?"

"No, nothing at all. I really think he's gone for good this time. Karen said to say thank-you for the money. A handyman's there now, fixing the walls and replacing the sliding glass door. Karen said she also wants to hire you to install a security system at the house."

"That's a good idea. Tell Karen we'll hook her up—with a special discount, of course."

"You're a gem."

"Take care, Mara."

"Bye, Nathan."

Maybe he'd read Toby right after all. A few miles later his phone rang. It was Harvey. "What's up?"

"I just had the damnedest conversation with Gavin."

"And . . ."

"She said a big guy came in and applied for a job yesterday. I believe she used the word *gorilla*. She said his right arm was in a cast, and he looked like he'd gone ten rounds with George Foreman. You know anything about him?"

"I might."

"You didn't . . ."

"I did." Nathan listened to the sigh on the other end.

"Think he can pass a background check?"

"I have no idea; probably not."

"You must really hate me."

"Consider it a personal challenge."

"All right. I'll run the check myself. You could've told me."

"Must have slipped my mind."

"Do me a favor and get some shut-eye. I don't want you falling asleep at the stick tonight. Waking your ass up is hazardous business, especially in a helicopter."

"It's called a cyclic, not a stick."

"Whatever."

"How was your son's birthday party?"

"I missed it. I was tied up with a national security issue up north in Lassen County."

"You know what I mean."

"Well, let's see. You want the long or short version?"

"Short."

"No surprise there," Harvey muttered. "I spent an hour removing toilet paper from the trees in my front yard. After that I drained the pool; it seems the water had mysteriously turned purple. But you know what the worst thing was?"

"Do tell."

"The little bastards had written 'Happy birthday, Lucas' with gasoline on the front lawn and lit it on fire. Can you believe that? It wasn't dangerous, but honestly. Today's youth . . ."

"Well, he *is* a teenager."

"Don't remind me. I'm making him replace all the burned grass. A pallet of sod's coming tomorrow morning. Should keep him busy for most of the day. Candace grounded him for a month."

Nathan chuckled.

"Oh, that's right, laugh it up. This is what happens when I turn my back for a few days."

"If that's the worst thing he ever does, consider yourself lucky."

"That's not very reassuring."

"What, you never did anything like that during *your* formative years?"

"Point taken. Now get some sleep, will ya?"

"I will. See you at Monty at eighteen hundred."

Nathan set the helicopter down at Sacramento Executive Airport in the exact same spot Harvey had. They were both suffering from major cases of flight fatigue and needed coffee and a pit stop. A plain four-door sedan was parked near the hangars to the south. It looked dark blue or black; Nathan couldn't tell which under the bland sodium lights. Its headlights flashed once.

"Our FBI friends," Harvey said, removing his flight helmet.

"Yep."

"You ready for this?"

"Not really."

"Come on; it'll be just like old times."

"That's what worries me."

While Nathan went through the shutdown procedure, Harvey retrieved their duffel bag and two smaller overnight bags from the rear seats. The duffel held their gun belts, spare ammunition, night-vision visors, two Fox USMC Predator knives in ankle sheaths, a roll of duct tape, and two Mini Maglite flashlights.

They climbed out, and Nathan gave the helicopter the obligatory pat on her fuselage before locking her up. A man and a woman slid out of the sedan and walked toward them. The man had been driving. *Probably means she's in charge*, Nathan thought. The male agent was perfectly tailored in a polo shirt, pressed slacks, and Italian shoes. He looked like a college preppy, the only thing missing a letter jacket. The woman was wearing new blue jeans, hiking boots, and a white button-down shirt. They both possessed Glock sidearms secured in waist holsters. She looked like the real deal, but her partner looked phony, like the picture of a fast-food burger on a menu board.

"Mr. McBride, Mr. Fontana? I'm Special Agent in Charge Holly Simpson of the Sacramento field office. This is Special

Agent Bruce Henning." Handshakes were made all around, and it was agreed to use first names. As they walked toward the sedan, Nathan evaluated his escorts. Holly Simpson was small and compact, but her demeanor said otherwise. She had a firm handshake and an aura of confidence surrounding her. Her black hair was shoulder length, not too long, not too short. It was . . . just right. When her hazel eyes had looked his face over, they hadn't reacted to the scars. Henning, on the other hand, had stared way too long, and Nathan got the distinct impression that he resented outsiders being involved in bureau business. An understandable attitude, but too damned bad. The guy was of medium height and build, with perfect, blow-dried sandy hair. Not a friggin' strand out of place. There was intensity in his dark eyes and something else, harder to pinpoint. . . . Nathan didn't like him.

"I'm very sorry about your man up at the compound," Nathan offered to Holly.

"I appreciate that," she said.

"What exactly are you authorized to do with the Bridgestones' cousins?" Henning asked.

Nathan stopped walking and faced the man. Henning's statement and tone were clearly designed to put him on the defensive. *Not on my watch, and not from the likes of you.* This was no time to show even the slightest hint of weakness or hesitation. Nathan leaned forward slightly and locked eyes.

"We're authorized to torture them, Bruce. Do you have a problem with that?"

Henning stared for a few seconds. "There's no evidence they had anything to do with Freedom's Echo. They're just a couple of hayseeds."

"Well, that's what we're here to find out."

"Look," Holly said, "the bureau owes you for firing that warning shot up at the compound. You saved a dozen lives, but you need to understand that we're uncomfortable with this kind of thing. The FBI doesn't condone it. It's a serious breach of ethics for us."

"That was you?" Henning asked. "*You* were the sniper at Freedom's Echo?"

"*We* were," Nathan said, nodding toward Harvey.

Harvey jumped in. "Look, we don't want to be here any more than you want us here. We've been retired for over a decade. We don't do this anymore. It's a personal favor for an old friend."

"Frank Ortega," Holly Simpson said.

Harvey nodded.

She issued Henning a glance. "Let's get going."

"Nice helicopter," Henning said. "Yours?"

Nathan ignored the question and tucked himself into the back of the sedan.

Henning muttered something and opened the sedan's trunk with a key. Harvey placed their bags inside and let Henning close the lid before climbing in next to Nathan.

"Can we stop somewhere for a pit stop and coffee?" Nathan asked.

From the driver's seat, Henning looked at Holly Simpson as if the request were a royal pain in the ass.

*We just spent four hours in a helicopter, you dumb ass.* Nathan was sorely tempted to smack the guy in the back of his head.

"We passed a Denny's about a mile from here," she said.

"That's fine."

Henning drove through the automatic gate of the airport's transient aircraft parking area and waited for the gate to close before leaving. Holly Simpson began briefing them on the Bridgestones' cousins' background, and the layout of their farmhouse. Basically, these guys were your garden-variety, petty-criminal losers. Through most of their adulthood they'd been in and out of jail—mostly in. Drunk driving. Drug possession. Soliciting prostitution. Petty larceny. Vagrancy. Poaching. Spitting on the sidewalk. You name it. Both of them were currently on parole and probably would be for the rest of their lives. A matched pair, Nathan thought. Give 'em a six-pack, some chicken wings, and a black-and-white TV, and they were happy as clams in mud. Currently they lived together on the outskirts of Sacramento and took odd jobs when they could—mostly as auto mechanics for mom-and-pop garages. Their father, Ben Bridgestone, was currently serving a life sentence in Soledad for his third strike.

Henning pulled into the Denny's parking lot and killed the engine. No one spoke. Nathan exchanged a glance with Harvey.

"Do you guys want anything?" Harvey asked.

"No, thank you," she said.

Hands not leaving the steering wheel, Henning stared straight ahead.

They slid out and walked the short distance to the Denny's entrance.

"Henning's an asshole," Nathan said.

"Don't bust his balls, okay?"

"Keep him out of my hair."

"I don't think he'll be a major problem. He just doesn't like outsiders being involved. If the situation were reversed, we'd probably feel the same way."

Nathan grunted. One of the fluorescent tubes over the entry was flickering with an annoying electronic buzz, a result of absent management. He caught the nasty smell of a Dumpster nearby. Once inside, Nathan hit the head while Harvey ordered two black coffees to go. Then Harvey used the restroom while Nathan paid for the coffee with a twenty-dollar bill, telling the server to keep the change. He knew graveyard shifts could be lean, and he, like Harvey, had a generous nature, even when in a foul mood.

Four minutes after stopping they were on the road again, heading east on Highway 50. The drive took just over thirty minutes, the last ten traveled in silence. The bright urban streets of the city gradually transformed into dark country roads defined by barbed-wire fencing. The foothills of the Sierra Nevada mountains. Horse and cattle country. To the west Nathan could see barns and small houses backlit by the orange glow of Sacramento. As the sedan slowed, Henning flashed his high beams twice, pulled behind a plain gray van parked on the shoulder of the road, and killed the engine.

"Please wait here," Holly said. She climbed out and approached the surveillance van. The rear doors opened, and she disappeared inside. Nathan had a brief look at the wall-to-wall black boxes and video monitors.

"The bureau doesn't condone this sort of . . . operation," Henning said.

"Actually, it just did." Nathan yawned. "And we aren't with the bureau."

"You know what I mean."

Nathan stared out the window, bored with the conversation. "You're following orders. Can we just leave it at that?"

"So that makes it okay? Just following orders? Sounds like Nuremburg to me."

Nathan ignored the comment.

"Who are you, McBride, some kind of has-been CIA interrogator? Some former burned-out spook for hire?"

"You're in the FBI; check me out for yourself."

"I already tried. Your service record is classified top-secret by the Department of Defense."

"And . . . ?"

"And I don't like not knowing who you are."

Nathan leaned forward and whispered, "We're legitimate businessmen with a successful security services firm. We can provide you with customer references if you feel you really need them."

"That's cute, McBride."

Nathan nudged Harv's leg.

"What exactly do you want to know about us," Harvey said, "and what would that information mean to you? Suppose we gave you our colorful background; then what? What would it mean to you? How are you better off knowing it?"

"For one, I'd like to know who I'm getting in bed with. I need to know I can trust you if the shit hits the fan out here."

"Did it occur to you that we might be wondering the same thing about you?" Harvey asked. "We're on the same side here, okay?"

"The hell we are."

Nathan sighed. The man lived in a fishbowl. If you weren't FBI, you weren't shit. In Nathan's limited experience with the bureau, he hadn't found that to be a common attitude. Every FBI agent he'd ever met—granted, there hadn't been that many—had been reserved and professional. Low-key. He supposed every law enforcement agency had its share of gung ho types, like Henning. But deep down he respected the FBI and what it stood for or he wouldn't be here, debt or no debt to the Ortega family.

"Aren't you forgetting something?" Nathan asked.

"And that would be?" Henning asked.

"Four hundred pounds of missing Semtex. Don't you want to recover it?"

Holly Simpson emerged from the back of the van and walked over to Nathan's window. He rolled it down.

"You're on," she said. "We haven't heard anything but snoring for the last two hours. We have bugs in every room. They're both crashed out in the living room just inside the front door."

As Nathan and Harvey climbed out, Henning opened the trunk and stepped back. Harvey grabbed their duffel bag, set it on the asphalt, and unzipped it. He removed two pistol belts and handed one to Nathan. Harvey strapped on a small black waist pack containing their Mini Maglite flashlights and two rolls of duct tape.

"Dogs?" Nathan asked.

"None," Holly answered. "I doubt they could handle the responsibility."

"I only have one condition," Nathan said. He retrieved two sets of night-vision visors from the duffel bag and handed one to Harvey.

"It's a little late for any conditions," she said.

"None of it gets recorded. I don't care if you listen in, but the black boxes aren't running. Deal?" He strapped his Predator knife to his ankle.

Harvey did the same.

Nathan placed his NV visor on his head. "I mean it. We'll have . . . unresolved issues otherwise."

"Are you threatening us?" Henning asked.

He ignored Henning and stared at Holly, his eyes unwavering. "Do we have a deal?"

Henning took a step forward. "Nobody threatens us."

Without taking his eyes from Holly, Nathan pointed at Henning's face.

"Get your finger out of my face."

"Holly? Do we have a deal?"

She looked at Henning, then back to Nathan. "Yes."

Nathan turned toward Harvey. "Let's go."

After they left, Holly faced Henning. "You're out of line, mister. I'm in charge of this operation. Are we crystal clear on that?"

"I just—"

"You just nothing. Don't ever test me again."

# ⊕ Chapter Six

As Nathan and Harvey walked toward the farmhouse, they lowered their night-vision scopes and turned them on. Their EX PVS14-D devices were state-of-the-art, third-generation design, the same model used by U.S. Special Forces. Their compact size allowed them to be mounted on a visor-type headgear that gave the user the option to pivot the monocular down to his eye, or up out of the way. Once activated, the device literally transformed night into day in the form of a tiny television screen. Internal lenses brought the miniature green image into focus. Both of them preferred to use their right eye for night vision while leaving their left eye uncovered. The world around them materialized. Although it was nearly pitch-black, they could plainly see the dividing stripes against the dark asphalt. On both sides of the shoulder, five strands of barbed wire paralleled their path, defining the sixty-foot-wide road easement. Cattle were lying down in the field off to their left, watching them. High in the stratosphere, wispy thin clouds reflected the glow of the city, which was all the light the devices needed.

They walked in silence for several dozen yards.

"We go in fast," Nathan said. "Shock attack. I'll cover the left side of the room; you take the right."

"How rough do we get?"

"We'll have to see. My best guess, light to moderate. They're just a couple of slobs who've drifted through life doing the minimum to survive. I'm not expecting anything different tonight. If they hold out, there'll be a damned good reason. We'll just have to wring it out of them."

Twenty yards ahead, Nathan saw the entrance to the property on the right side of the road, a makeshift gate with roadside litter piled a foot high at the posts. Two tire-worn impressions across the weedy ground pointed directly at the farmhouse. Nathan nodded to Harvey, and they drew their nine-millimeters. Invisible against the black backdrop behind them, both men transitioned into stealth mode and entered the property. From Holly Simpson's description he knew the house was located in the middle of a four-acre parcel with unused farmland surrounding it. A detached one-car garage was situated thirty yards to the north, its door facing the house. As they got closer, two older pickup trucks took shape. Both had numerous rust spots, dents and dings, broken taillights, and bald tires. Neither had current registration tags. At the far corner of the property, several hundred yards distant, some sort of big pipe extended a few feet above the ground. An old windmill sat atop its cylindrical form, and Nathan could see the outlines of a well pump and pressure tank. Its paint peeling, the house was on the small side, maybe seven hundred square feet. The grimy front door was flanked by two windows with bedsheets for curtains. Several wooden steps led up to a covered porch.

Nathan stopped and held his left hand up in a closed fist.

Behind him, Harvey brought his gun up and froze.

A string was stretched across the planks of the top step, its left side tied to the handrail's post. The other end wrapped around the opposite post and turned the corner toward the front door. The string terminated at a platoon of empty beer bottles, their Miller labels clearly readable through his NV scope. If the trip wire had been triggered, it would've pulled the rear bottle through the others, knocking them all down, making a shitload of noise. It was a dirt cheap and yet fairly reliable security mechanism, but it only worked against an intruder who didn't know what to look for.

Nathan turned toward Harvey, simulated pulling a string between his fingers, and pointed to the top step. Harvey acknowledged with a nod. Nathan pulled his knife from its ankle sheath, carefully cut the string, and tossed the loose line over the side of the steps. He tested the first step with a few pounds of pressure under his boot. No creaking. He slowly transferred his weight until he was completely standing on the first step. Nothing. No sound at all. So far, so good. While Harvey watched the windows, Nathan repeated the same procedure for the next two steps. No creaking. Once atop the landing he flattened himself against the wall between the left window and front door. The stack of bottles was on the opposite side of the door. He nodded to Harvey, who navigated the steps with equal care and stealth.

Nathan pivoted and faced the front door. "Infrared on," he whispered.

They reached up and turned knobs on their scopes. Small red dots could now be seen in the lower corners of their images, indicating that the infrared spots were activated. The front door instantly brightened, and Nathan's device automatically lowered the image's intensity to compensate.

Harvey tucked in close behind him.

A smile touched his lips. Here he was again—Nathan McBride, in his environment. Ready, willing, and able to kick ass.

He reared up with his right foot and stomped.

The door burst open in a crash of splintered wood and dust.

In the green images of their night vision, they could see everything.

Two men were present, caught in midsnore. The first lay back in an easy chair, the second in a fetal position on the couch. Simultaneously both pairs of eyes snapped open. Nathan stepped forward to the easy chair and clubbed its occupant with the butt of his gun. It wasn't hard enough to knock him unconscious, but it *was* hard enough to render him semidazed and groggy.

Harvey jammed the muzzle of his gun against the couch potato's forehead and said, "Don't move."

The guy tried to sit up. "What the fu—"

Harvey clocked him. With a grunt of pain the man slumped back into the stained fabric. With his free hand Harvey unzipped his waist pack and grabbed a roll of duct tape.

Nathan yanked his mark from the chair and rolled him onto his stomach. He reached over and grabbed the tape from Harvey, set his gun down, and secured the guy's hands behind his back with several loops of tape. He covered the man's mouth with a six-inch strip and tossed the roll to Harvey, who did the same to his man.

Within eight seconds of bursting through the door, Nathan and Harvey had overwhelmed and immobilized both targets. *Just like old times,* Nathan thought. "Check the rest of the house," he whispered.

In complete silence, Harvey disappeared down the hall and returned twenty seconds later. "Clear."

"Okay, let's get them situated."

Harvey grabbed a couple of chairs from the eating area. Nathan was hesitant to think of it as a dining room because these two didn't dine; they merely ate, and from the look of things, they didn't get all of it into their mouths. He removed his night-vision visor, turned it off, and reached into his pocket for the lens cap. "NV off?" he asked.

Harvey reached up, turned his unit off, and capped the lens. Nathan handed his visor to his partner, and both were placed on the front porch outside the door. Nathan flipped a switch on the wall, and a lamp with a bare bulb in the corner of the room came to life.

"Oh, man," he said. He hadn't expected to see Wayne Manor, but this . . . this place belonged in a Hall of Shame museum. He'd seen the mess in shades of green through the scope, but in Technicolor, the true nature of this pigsty took on a whole new dimension. The family room table consisted of three bald tires stacked on top of one another, topped off by half a sheet of painted plywood. Household trash was strewn everywhere. Beer bottles. Empty soup and chili cans. Milk cartons. Used paper towels. Apple cores. Peanut shells. Candy bar wrappers. Half-eaten hot dogs and hamburgers. Microwave popcorn bags. Dirty dishes. Crusty silverware and girlie magazines. Clothes were thrown on every available surface. Shoes. Work boots. Socks. Soiled T-shirts. Old blue jeans. Mechanic's overalls. Several cases of motor oil were sitting under the living room window. Cleared paths through the clutter and filth connected the various rooms like worn trails on college campus lawns. And the smell . . . it was like a landfill in here. Nathan shook his head.

"You should see the bathroom," Harvey said. "I don't know how people can live like this."

"That's just it; they don't live. They survive."

"I've never seen anything this disgusting before."

"Ever watch the show *Cops*? Let's clear an opening on the floor and set them up right here." Nathan kept his gun trained on them while Harvey went to work. After a minute or so he'd kicked enough crap out of the way to place two chairs about five feet apart. Harvey hauled the two men into sitting positions and wrapped several layers of duct tape around their chests and the backs of the chairs to keep them from slumping over. The guy on Nathan's left was thin and lanky, maybe one-fifty or -sixty. Blood was seeping through a gauze bandage taped on the triceps portion of his arm. That bandage looked uncharacteristically clean, Nathan thought. It didn't fit in this environment. Beneath the guy's shaved head was a narrow, pointed face with a mustache shaped like a horizontal butter knife. His brother, the couch potato, was compact and fit. He had a square face with strong cheekbones and short dishwater-blond hair that looked like he'd combed it straight up with bacon lard. This guy weighed in at close to two hundred and looked somewhat formidable.

"Knife and Fork," Nathan said, nodding toward them.

Harvey stepped back, stared for a few seconds, and smiled.

The Bridgestones' cousins were dressed in dirty blue jeans, white tank tops, and scuffed work boots. Their hands, arms, and faces were smudged with motor oil and grease. The bigger guy had a tattoo on his arm that looked like it had been etched with copper wire and a blowtorch. From prison, no doubt. It was impossible to tell who was older; they both looked twenty years past their actual age.

"Let's bring them around," Nathan said. He reached down, grabbed an empty beer can, and crumpled it in his palms. As if shooting a free throw in basketball, he tossed it at Fork. It bounced off Fork's forehead with a metallic clink. A few drops of stale beer splattered the man's nose and cheeks. His eyes fluttered open, then grew wide with terror.

"Nothin' but net," Harvey said, giving Knife a firm shaking. Knife's eyes registered fear, then changed to rage. He whipped his head back and forth, trying to dislodge the tape covering his mouth.

Nathan dragged a chair over and sat down. Without taking his eyes off Knife, he pulled a thin pair of black gloves from his front pocket and slowly pulled them on. Harvey did the same.

"Here's the deal," Nathan began. "We aren't going to play good cop, bad cop with you two miscreants. For one, we aren't cops, and for the other, we're both bad. We don't work for the FBI, CIA, NRA, PTA, or the ASPCA. We're . . ." He looked up at Harvey. "What are we?"

"Independent contractors."

"We're independent contractors, so your Miranda rights are not in play here. In fact, this is an anti-Miranda situation; you absolutely do *not* have the right to remain silent. Oh, and the Eighth Amendment of our beloved Constitution is hereby suspended until further notice. If you're curious, it has to do with cruel and unusual punishment being inflicted. Now, before we get started, is there anything you'd like to say?"

Knife began nodding furiously, but Fork stared straight ahead, refusing to make eye contact. Nathan leaned forward and yanked the tape from Knife's mouth. It tore loose with a raspy rip. Knife's mustache didn't fare so well. It had been reduced in thickness by a good ten percent. With an expression of revulsion, Nathan held the strip with his thumb and forefinger and tossed it aside like a plague bandage.

"You stupid motherfuckers," Knife hissed. "I want my phone call."

Nathan looked at Harvey. "He wants his phone call. Would you bring me the phone, please?"

Harvey walked into the kitchen and yanked the phone off the wall, cradle and all. Its cord dangling uselessly, he handed it to Nathan.

Without warning, Nathan swung the phone like an oversize palm sap.

"Oh, man," Harvey said. "I'm afraid that's going to leave a mark."

Blood began streaming from Knife's nose.

\* \* \*

Out in the surveillance van, Holly Simpson and the two techs looked at each other in the glow of the black boxes. They'd heard the impact. As promised, nothing was being recorded.

"Would you like to make another call?" Nathan asked.

"You son of a bitch. You broke my fuckin' nose!"

"In about ninety seconds, the mucous membrane of that pointed beak you *call* a nose is going to swell to twice its current size. Breathing through it will become difficult, if not impossible. If I have to tape your mouth again, you'll start choking on your own blood."

*"Fuck you!"*

Nathan sighed. "I am truly disappointed." He peeled another six-inch length of tape from the roll.

Cursing like a madman, Knife began whipping his head back and forth in a frenzy.

Harvey maneuvered behind Knife, while Nathan retrieved a filthy dishcloth from the kitchen counter. Harvey grabbed Knife by the ears and held his head still while Nathan wiped the blood from Knife's mouth and jammed another strip home. He held his wrist up in an exaggerated manner, looking at his watch.

Knife's face turned a bright shade of crimson and his chest began heaving for air. Nathan raised an eyebrow, silently saying, *I told you so*. Knife coughed behind the tape and was forced to inhale his own blood. His body wrenched in a violent spasm. "It's only going to get worse. Soon you'll be aspirating blood *and* vomit into your lungs. That's a bad situation for sure. You could get pneumonia, and after I've broken all your ribs, coughing is going to be a tad bit uncomfortable."

Fork's bladder quit. The liquid ran down the legs of his chair and soaked into the carpet. The pungent smell of urine drifted.

Knife's desperate wrenching reached a peak, and Nathan knew the guy was close to passing out. He yanked the tape free, reducing Knife's mustache down to eighty percent. Vomit spewed from Knife's mouth.

"Oh, man, that's disgusting." Nathan looked at Harvey. "Garden hose, please."

Harvey walked out the front door and returned a few seconds later dragging a green hose with him. He handed the business end to Nathan and stepped back outside. "Say when."

Nathan removed the glove from his right hand. "When," he called.

There was a faint squeak as the spigot turned.

Knife wrenched in his seat. "What the fuck're you doing?"

Nathan used his thumb to form a jet of water and summarily hosed the two men down like dogs. Water flew in every direction. As if washing off a driveway, he used the hose to spray the vomit in front of Knife's chair aside, then soaked the carpet under Fork's chair, diluting the urine. Knife shook his head back and forth, trying to clear his vision.

"Okay," Nathan yelled to Harvey. Another squeak. The stream of water ended.

Harvey returned from outside.

"Once again, here's the deal," Nathan said, keeping his tone even. "We have all night, and there's all kinds of things in an everyday household that are perfectly suitable for inflicting pain. Almost anything works. Take your pick. Scissors, screwdrivers, pliers, lamp cords . . . I once beat a guy senseless with a twelve-inch salami and then made myself a sandwich. Ever had your fingers inserted into a toaster? A frying pan is effective, too. You know, those heavy-duty cast-iron jobs? What we do is heat it up several hundred degrees and then lovingly place it in your lap for safekeeping. Let's see, what else works . . . ?"

"A grinder," Harvey said.

"Perfect. Go take a look in the garage; I'll bet they've got one."

Harvey took a step toward the door.

"Okay . . . okay. What the fuck do you want from me? I

don't know where they are. My cousins are crazy. I don't have nothing to do with them. I swear."

Without looking, Nathan reached over and yanked the tape from Fork's mouth. "Is there anything *you'd* like to add?"

"Tell him about the cabin!"

Nathan squinted at Knife. "What cabin?"

Knife twisted toward his brother. "You dumb shit."

Nathan asked again, slower, "What . . . cabin?"

"There's no cabin," Knife said.

Nathan picked up the phone and held it an inch from Fork's nose. "Would you like to make a call?"

"I don't know where it is. I swear I ain't been there."

There was fury in Knife's voice. "Shut the fuck up, Billy."

Nathan nodded to Knife. "He's been there?"

"Lots of times. He goes hunting up there. It belongs to our dad's sister, but it's really theirs. They don't want nobody knowin' about it."

Nathan tore another piece of tape from the roll and secured Fork's mouth. Avoiding the empty soup cans and milk jugs on the floor, he strolled into the kitchen and started rummaging around, opening cabinet doors, tossing pots and pans aside, purposefully making all kinds of noise. He found what he was looking for, set it on the front burner with an audible clang, and twisted the knob. The rapid clicking of the stove's igniter was followed by the distinctive whoosh of the gas catching.

He heard Harvey say, "Uh-oh."

"My cousins will kill me," Knife pleaded.

"He'll do it," Harvey said. "I've seen this before. It's pretty bad. It fuses the denim to your skin."

"They'll kill me!"

"Your concern should be more immediate."

After a minute or so, the odor of burned cooking oil drifted into the room.

"Son of a bitch," Knife spat. *"You motherfuckers!"*

"Warming up nicely," Nathan called from the kitchen.

"Son of a bitch, *son of a bitch!*"

"I'm going to tape your mouth. I just can't stand the sound of a grown man screaming." Harvey jammed the tape over Knife's mouth and removed his Predator from its ankle sheath.

Knife's eyes grew wide.

"Hold still," Harvey said, and cut a slit in the tape.

The tape hissed with each labored breath Knife took, lungs heaving.

Nathan entered the room, holding the frying pan with a potholder in one hand, and a small cup of water in the other. Blue-gray smoke belched from the pan's black surface like steam.

Knife began whipping back and forth, nearly toppling his chair.

Nathan stood in front of him and held the simmering pan six inches above his lap. He poured an ounce of water onto its flat surface. The liquid burst to life in a macabre dance of boiling rivulets that hissed and sizzled like tortured snakes.

Out in the van, Holly Simpson held her breath.

# ✛ Chapter Seven

"Last chance," Nathan said. "Are your cousins really worth it? Do you think they'd take this kind of pain for you?"

Knife violently shook his head. "Uhhh eerrr huhhh."

"Are you ready to talk about the cabin?"

He closed his eyes and nodded.

Nathan tossed the pan aside. It sizzled on the wet carpet, belching steam. He tore the tape from Knife's mouth. "Well?"

"It's three hours' drive from here. Up Highway 70 near Quincy."

"What's the address?"

"It don't have an address."

"You're going to show us where it is. Is there anything else we should know about?"

"That's it, man, I swear. I don't know nothing else."

Nathan usually knew when someone was lying to him. It was hard to describe; maybe it was in the eyes, or micro-changes in body language. Whichever it was, it didn't matter. This guy was holding something back, something he was willing to risk a great deal of pain over. Nathan stared at the man. Hard. It was time to screw with him.

"Okay," Nathan said. "This isn't personal; you understand that, right? I'm just doing my job here." He walked behind Knife's chair and began cutting the duct tape. He sensed the man relax a little. Good. Now take it away. He stopped cutting the tape and grunted, a puzzled sound as though something wasn't quite right. "What about the cash?" he whispered in Knife's ear.

Knife stiffened a little. "What cash?"

"*The* cash," Nathan said, watching Knife's reaction closely. Bull's-eye. A direct hit. Knife gave it away as clearly as a kid who looked down after peeing his pants. Cash. Emergency money. Probably lots of it, and without a doubt it was hands-off as far as these two mutts were concerned. It made perfect sense. The Bridgestones probably had stashes all over the place. The Bridgestones were many things, but stupid wasn't one of them. They hadn't been able to come here because the FBI stakeout had started before the raid on the compound.

"There's no cash," Knife said, but it sounded weak, unconvincing.

Nathan shook his head and looked at Fork, who was nodding furiously. "I think your brother has something to tell us."

Nathan yanked the tape from Fork's mouth.

"It's buried near the garage. Leonard told us if we ever touched it, he'd kill us."

"Billy, I swear to God. *I'm* going to kill you." Knife glared at his brother with pure hatred in his eyes.

"Your bro here sounds upset," Nathan said. "I'm a little disappointed you didn't mention it earlier, Billy."

"Look, man, I'm sorry. I wanted to; I really did. You don't understand; they said they'd kill us. Our cousins're crazy."

Nathan faced Knife. "It's simple, really. If anything happens to your beloved cousins—say . . . like life imprisonment or death—the cash would be yours, right? They'd be out of the picture, so it's easy money. There's no need to ask where your cousins are, because if you knew, you'd give them up; then the money would be yours. Right?"

Knife didn't respond.

Nathan looked at Billy. "Right?"

"I guess."

"You mean you hadn't thought of that? Your brother sure had."

"I swear to God, Billy. You're so fuckin' stupid."

"Easy now," Nathan said. "He saved you a boatload of pain. I would've wrung it out of you eventually. You might've needed a wheelchair and a colostomy bag for the rest of your life, but you would've told me. No doubt about it. In fact, I think you owe your brother a thank-you for sparing you all that pain."

Knife wouldn't look at his brother, but managed a hissed, "Thanks."

"That wasn't so bad, was it? Don't you feel better now?"

"Yeah, right, whatever."

"Billy is going to show me where the money is buried. You stay put, okay?"

Knife just stared. There was more than hatred in his eyes, something else, something harder to pinpoint. Fear? Anxiety?

Nathan winked at his partner. "If he even looks at you funny, give him another phone call."

Harvey answered in his best gangster voice, "You got it, boss."

"Cover us for a second."

Harvey pulled his SIG, triggered the laser, and pointed it at Billy's chest.

Billy looked down at the tiny rose of death. "Hey, man, take it easy, okay?"

Nathan cut the tape from Billy's torso. "Hands behind your back, Billy. Do it now." Nathan was all business again. Although he doubted Billy's blabbering cowardice had been an act, he wasn't willing to take any chances. He secured Billy's wrists behind his back with several layers of duct tape. "Outside. Let's go."

Holly Simpson was standing just outside the door when they stepped through. She had her standard-issue Glock twenty-two in her right hand and a flashlight in the other hand. "We need to get up to that cabin right away," she said.

"They aren't there," Nathan said.

"How can you be sure?"

"Because the cousins just gave the place up."

"You really think there's money buried out here?"

"I seen it," Billy said. "They got it stashed in fifty-caliber ammo cans right over there. Three of 'em."

"And you believe him?" Simpson asked.

Nathan shrugged.

"You'd better be right about this." She turned on her flashlight and shined it on Billy's chest. "Show us."

They followed Billy through a maze of junked cars, rusted farm equipment, and fifty-gallon drums full of Lord knew what, probably motor oil, from the smell of things. Backlit by the orange glow from Sacramento thirty miles distant, their dark forms cast eerie shadows from Holly's flashlight. Coming from every direction, the symphony of ten thousand crickets filled the night. Holly swept her flashlight back and forth through the jungle of Americana crap, gun held at the ready. Nathan knew she was looking for threats. This was a hell of a good place to get ambushed. Lots of hiding places.

Billy stopped at the corner of the garage, a simple

ten-by-twenty-foot box with a gable roof. The bottom of its
tan stucco walls were stained with reddish-brown mud from
rain splatter dripping off the eaves. "Right here," Billy said.
"I'm standing on them."

"How deep?" Holly asked.

"I don't know. A foot or so?"

"You got a shovel?"

"'Course I do."

"Well?"

"It's in there." He nodded toward the garage.

Holly Simpson tucked her flashlight under her arm, pulled
her radio, and thumbed the button. "Copy?"

"Copy," came the response.

"Hustle up here. We're at the garage, north of the farmhouse."

Henning acknowledged with a click. Thirty seconds later
he arrived, but stopped short about one hundred feet away.
He flashed his light twice. Holly pointed her flashlight in his
direction and issued three flashes in response. Henning's light
bounced as he closed the distance.

Nathan was impressed. A predetermined signal in case Simpson was being held hostage and forced to use her radio. If
Henning hadn't received the three flashes in return, he'd instantly know Simpson was in trouble. Breathing a little heavily from his run, he closed the distance and focused on Billy.

Holly glanced at Nathan, then back to Henning. "We're
going to open the garage door. You two okay?"

Both men nodded.

Henning crouched down at the opposite corner of the garage.

Holly did the same on her corner. "On the deck, Billy," she
said, "right here in front of me."

"In the dirt? I'm soakin' wet!"

"Do it now."

"It's just a friggin' garage," he muttered. Because Billy's
hands were secured behind his back, he had to drop to his

knees first, then slide his legs out from under himself. He plopped over with a grunt and lay still.

Holly nodded to Nathan. "Okay, lift it slowly."

Nathan pulled his gun and stepped to the middle of the garage door. He grabbed its galvanized handle and began lifting. "Watch for trip wires," he said.

Henning crouched lower and swept his flashlight in an arc across the garage floor, his gun tracking the beam.

"Clear," he said.

"Clear," Holly echoed.

"Check the rafters," Nathan said.

They both swept the ceiling area. Two more "clears" were issued.

Nathan raised the door the rest of the way. The single-car garage was mostly empty, its concrete floor cracked like a black widow spiderweb. A red Suzuki Enduro occupied one corner, looking like it had rarely been ridden. A small rack for storing gear was mounted above its rear wheel. In the opposite corner, several shovels, hoes, and rakes were secured in a linear bracket screwed into the wall. A workbench occupied the left side. Various household tools were hung on hooks. Saws. Hammers. Pliers. Screwdrivers. Wrenches. Everything was arranged by type and function; nothing was out of place. The opposite wall hosted power tools, all kinds of them, new-looking and well maintained. And yes, there was a grinder. Most of the empty power-tool boxes were neatly stacked against the rear wall of the garage. Nathan frowned. This didn't look right.

Henning stepped into the garage and was about to flip a light switch.

"Wait!" Nathan yelled. He looked at Holly.

She nodded her understanding. "It could be rigged."

Henning stared at the switch for several seconds before backing away from it.

"Okay," Holly said, returning her attention to Billy. "You stay put."

"Better let Billy dig up the ammo cans," Nathan offered. "They could be booby-trapped."

"Agreed."

"They aren't," Billy said.

"Your cousins tried to frag a dozen federal employees yesterday," Holly said. "We're a little short on trust right now."

Henning stepped forward and cut the tape binding Billy's hands. "On your feet, maggot. If you run, I'll shoot you in the back. Clear?"

"I ain't gunna run," Billy said, tearing the remaining tape from his wrists.

"Get the shovel," Holly said. She and Henning tracked him with their pistols across the garage floor and back.

"I'm going to check the perimeter of the farmhouse," Henning said. "Two minutes."

"Two minutes," Holly confirmed.

Henning disappeared into the darkness.

Tight and professional, Nathan thought, except for the "maggot" comment. That had been unnecessary.

Holly refocused on Billy. "Start digging."

Nathan and Holly backed away to a safe distance. It was close enough to plug Billy if he tried to bolt and hopefully far enough away from any sort of explosive booby trap the Bridgestones might have rigged. He looked at Holly again. She was really quite striking, even in the reflective glow of their flashlights. She had well-defined Slavic cheekbones and full lips. Her eyes were the color of dark honey. She was small and compact, maybe five-foot-three or -four. Confident. Self-assured. He liked her. A lot.

Holly kept her voice low. "I'm sorry about Henning's attitude."

"Already forgotten," Nathan said.

"I reviewed your classified file."

Nathan said nothing.

"I wouldn't agree to your involvement unless I knew exactly who you two were."

"Understood," Nathan said. "I would've played it the same way."

"Not many would've survived what you went through."

"I did the best I could under the circumstances."

They were silent for a few seconds. Billy's shovel clanked on metal.

"You don't have many friends," she said.

He kept his voice low so Billy couldn't hear him. "Just Harvey."

"I don't either. You didn't seriously hurt them in there, did you?"

"Not really."

"Did you want to?"

"No."

"We should get up to that cabin ASAP."

"Let's play this out. A few more minutes won't make or break things. James Ortega's been missing for over a week."

Henning retuned and joined them. "What have we got?"

"We're about to find out," she said.

Billy was just finishing the dig. On his knees, he cleared the last of the dirt away with his hands. He looked up.

Holly told him to pull the first one out slowly.

"Could be a gun in one or more of them," Nathan said.

"Agreed."

Billy did as he was told. He reached into the hole, tore the plastic garbage bag away, and tugged one of the handles. He hefted the ammo can out and set it on the ground. It was matte green, about the size of a large shoe box. Nathan read the five lines of yellow stenciled lettering and knew the can used to hold a disintegrating link of one hundred armor-piercing, incendiary, fifty-caliber rounds, with every fifth round being a tracer.

Billy looked up and squinted against the flashlight beams.

"Pull the others out," Holly said, "and place them five feet apart with their latches facing us. Now stand behind the one on your left, reach over the top, and pull its lid open. Do it slowly."

Nathan knew that wasn't going to work, but didn't say anything. To open an ammo can like that, especially one that had been buried, you had to hold the carrying handle below its latch with one hand and yank the latch cover with the other hand. Unless it was filled with ammunition weighing it down, it would take two hands. As predicted, Billy struggled with the can. Although he was able to unlatch the cover, every attempt he made to lift the hinged cover didn't work; the entire can lifted into the air. He wasn't getting the necessary leverage.

"May I?" Nathan asked.

She nodded.

"Step away, Billy," Nathan said as he holstered his gun. He walked forward and showed Billy the exact technique needed to open the can. "It takes both hands, like this." He grabbed the carrying handle with his left hand and the latch cover mechanism with his other. "You have to give it a quick tug in opposite directions." He stepped back and crouched down.

Holly and Henning followed suit. Billy grabbed the ammo can like he'd been shown and gave the latch a yank. The lip popped open. Billy stared straight down into its contents. "Oh, man."

"Open the others," Holly said.

Five seconds later all three ammo cans were open. Billy couldn't take his eyes off the contents.

"Move away, Billy," Holly said. "On the ground again."

Billy didn't comply; he just stood there, licking his lips.

"Back away, Billy, on the ground. Do it right now," she said more forcefully.

Billy did as instructed.

The three of them walked forward and looked down. Staring up at them were bundles of used bills. Lots of them. Stacked upright in two rows along each can's long axis, they were nearly a perfect fit. The distinctive smell of greenbacks wafted up to them.

Henning let out a low whistle.

Nathan crouched down and pulled a bundle from each can.

The middle can held stacks of one-hundred-dollar bills, and the other two cans held stacks of twenties. Each stack was about an inch thick, meaning it probably held one hundred bills. Nathan counted the bundles. There were twenty-two stacks of one-hundred-dollar bills and forty-four stacks of twenties. Nathan ran the calculation. "Two hundred twenty plus eighty-eight. That's . . . three hundred and eight grand," he said, "assuming that each of those stacks contains one hundred notes of the same denomination."

"Incredible," Holly whispered. "You think they have stashes like this in other locations?"

"Count on it," Nathan said. "I'm going to check on my partner." Ten feet from the farmhouse's front door, Nathan stopped and issued a low warbling whistle and heard the same whistle in return from the inside. He found Harvey sitting on the chair facing Knife.

"Billy wasn't lying about the money."

"How much?"

"Just over three hundred grand."

"Nice little stash."

"Yep."

"What now?"

Nathan looked at Knife. "After you and your brother change into dry clothes, you're going to take us up to that cabin."

Half an hour after the discovery of the buried cash, a caravan of three FBI sedans was ready to leave Sacramento and motor toward the Sierra Nevada mountains. The ammo cans had been locked in Holly's trunk. Larry Gifford and two SWAT team members had joined the party with two additional vehicles, one of them designed for transporting perps in custody. There was no way to know what to expect up there, so the extra firepower was a prudent call on Holly's part. The SWAT guys were dressed in black overalls, but they hadn't donned their SWAT gear yet; there was no need until they arrived at the cabin. Gifford was in blue jeans and a white polo-type shirt with no label showing. His gun belt held a standard-issue Glock twenty-two, two spare magazines, and a set of handcuffs. He looked a lot different out of SWAT gear, but he had the same intense blue eyes Nathan remembered when they'd first met at the Bridgestones' compound.

Nathan and Harvey shook hands with Larry Gifford and the two SWAT team members. Nathan was pretty sure the two SWAT guys were the same ones who had made the leap-frog approach to them yesterday. It made sense: They had already seen Nathan and Harvey and already knew of their involvement.

"Special Agents Collins and Dowdy, if I recall," Nathan said, pumping their hands, "but I don't know who's who."

Holly smiled.

Henning glared.

"We've got a long drive ahead of us; let's get moving," Holly said.

"Let's do it," Gifford agreed.

An awkward moment followed.

Nathan looked at Harvey for several seconds, but said nothing.

"I'll, ah, ride with Gifford," Harvey said. "If that's okay?"

Henning was about to protest, but bit his tongue.

*Taking one for the team*, Nathan thought. *Attaboy, Harv.*

"Come on, then," Gifford said to Harvey. The two SWAT guys exchanged a glance before sliding into the rear seats. Harvey climbed in next to Gifford.

Henning slid into the transport sedan, and Nathan eased in next to Holly Simpson. Ten seconds later all three vehicles were fired up, turned around, and headed down the road, with Henning and the Bridgestone cousins leading the pack. Holly and Nathan were in the last sedan to leave.

As Nathan and Holly settled in for the long drive into the mountains, he slid his seat back as far as it would go and reclined it slightly. He wasn't sure what to expect conversation-wise; she was, after all, a complete stranger. Might as well start with an observation.

"Henning's got a thing for you," he said.

"Is it that obvious?"

"It's the way he looks at you."

"I've done my best not to encourage it. I don't want to transfer him, but it may come to that. His wife works under my command. You probably saved her life up at the compound. She's the SWAT agent who tried to light you up behind that tree."

"She's Henning's wife?"

"Yes."

"Well, he's just bubbling over with gratitude."

"This situation is difficult for him. To be honest, for me too."

"Did you and Henning . . ."

"Absolutely not. He's married, and I don't have those kinds of feelings toward him. I never did. Don't get me wrong: Bruce Henning's a fine agent. He's honest and hardworking, and loyal as hell to the bureau, but he's a Boy Scout."

"And you don't date Boy Scouts."

She looked at him. "I don't date married men." They rode in silence for several minutes.

"I saw that glance you gave your partner just before everyone piled into the vehicles."

Nathan didn't respond.

She smiled. "You have the deepest blue eyes I've ever seen. They're almost purple."

"Thanks, I guess."

Following the other two sedans, Holly made the turn onto Highway 50, heading west toward Sacramento. "You handled Henning pretty well back at the airport," she said at last. "You didn't back down or go on the defensive. Calmly assertive, I think they call it."

"Exactly. You ever watch a television show called *Dog Whisperer*?"

"Hmm." She thought for a moment. "I've heard of it, but I've never watched it."

"Well, it's about this guy called Cesar Millan, and he has this uncanny ability with dogs. He's a dog psychologist of sorts, but he really councils people who have dog problems. He likes to say he rehabilitates dogs."

"Okay . . ."

Nathan knew she was wondering where this was going. "It's what you said about being calmly assertive. That's Cesar's philosophy. Be calm, but assertive."

"And you think the same approach works with people?"

"To a limited extent. The basic difference is that dogs live in the moment; people don't. Dogs don't hold grudges. People do. Everything is right here and right now with dogs. I really like them a lot. I own two giant schnauzers."

"I've heard of that breed."

"They're a little bigger than a German shepherd. Super smart. Bullheaded, though."

"Sounds familiar."

"Point taken."

"Not many people own giant schnauzers—or a helicopter," she said.

"The helicopter isn't a symbol of ego or financial status for me. It's about freedom. Too many people take it for granted."

"I'd have to agree with that." She paused for a moment. "May I ask you a personal question?"

"You can ask. . . ."

"What was it like . . . I mean, being a sniper?"

"That's quite a question, Holly. We hardly know each other." He fell silent for several miles. The road stripes slid under them in an endless procession of hypnotic yellow flashes. She didn't force the conversation, and he appreciated the silent interval to gather his thoughts. He wasn't sure how deep he wanted to go. There were demons down there.

"I can't speak for anyone else. For me, at the moment of truth, it's a feeling of intoxicating power."

Holly didn't respond.

"It's dangerous, Holly. Real dangerous, like an addictive drug. Only worse. A lot worse."

"I guess I never really thought about it like that before. I have snipers under my command. Two of them are in that sedan ahead of us. All our SWAT members are cross-trained."

"Don't ever ask them what you just asked me."

"Why not?"

"They'll resent it. Trust me on that."

"Do you resent it?"

"No, I don't work for you."

Holly said nothing.

"Your guys may have a totally different take on it. They don't do covert field ops where the exit from the SP is a concern."

"You won't like my next question."

He waited.

She looked over. "Did you like it?"

"Man . . . And I thought your first question was tough. May I assume you aren't just morbidly curious?"

"Yes, that's a fair assumption."

"Then the answer is both yes and no. But not in the way you're probably thinking."

"And that is . . . ?"

"That I liked everything but the actual killing. The trigger pull."

"Are you saying you liked it?"

"No, I didn't."

Holly remained silent.

Nathan knew she was waiting for him to explain his "yes and no" answer. "I loved the exit after the shot. The thrill of being chased. Of knowing the cat was out of the bag and everyone was hunting me."

"And that's the part you liked? It scares me just thinking about it."

"I'm afraid so. I never felt so alive . . . so, I don't know, exhilarated, I guess."

"Did Harvey feel the same way?"

"No, just the opposite. Harv hated the exit. He liked the insertion and tracking. But not the killing. Neither of us got off on that."

"You and Harvey are pretty close."

"Sometimes I think we share a single consciousness. He can read my mind, and I can read his. Like the look I gave him before we left. I didn't have to say a word; he just knew I wanted to ride with you alone."

"I envy you, being that close to someone."

They rode in silence for several minutes, the glow of Sacramento growing with each mile they traveled toward the city. In the dim moonlight, mature oaks loomed like giant mushrooms.

Holly broke the silence. "You think we'll find Ortega's grandson at the cabin?"

"I wouldn't be surprised. Or at least evidence of his interrogation there. They needed an isolated place for that. They couldn't use the compound knowing it was probably under surveillance."

"If he's there at least his family will get closure. It has to be horrible not knowing whether he's alive or dead."

"After meeting with Frank Ortega, I'm pretty sure he believes his grandson is dead. I saw it in his eyes."

"It takes a special kind of personality to work undercover. I don't know how they do it. The constant stress of being discovered. Having to act like one of them. It would be like waking up every morning with a gun pointed at your face. I couldn't handle it."

"Me either," he said.

"How do you think they made him?"

"He was probably seen by someone the Bridgestones had on the outside. A grocery store clerk or gas station attendant, someone like that. He or she probably reported seeing him use a pay phone or sending a fax from a local store. When he returned to the compound, they grabbed him."

"You're probably right. I doubt they could've tailed him without his knowledge."

"He blew his cover relaying the info because he knew how critical the situation had become. He's a hero in every sense of the word, Holly. I hate the idea of those dirtbags doing whatever they wanted to him. It's why I agreed to help Ortega. It really pisses me off thinking about it. I'm sure he held out for as long as he could. He bought time for you guys with pain."

"It must be horrible."

"It is."

"You and Harvey did a good job with the Bridgestones' cousins. I heard everything. Nothing was recorded, as promised."

"Thank you."

"I had all kinds of images in my head of what you'd do to them."

"It's rarely necessary."

"Then you've . . ."

"Been rough? Yes. You have to detach yourself from it," he said, answering her unspoken question. "You have to think of it like acting in a play or a musical."

"Do you like musicals?"

"Immensely, and thank you for changing the subject." In the amber light of the dashboard he saw her smile, and he admired the way it transformed her face. In a way he'd never felt toward Mara—or anyone else—he was definitely attracted to Special Agent in Charge Holly Simpson. *Mara . . .* He looked out the window and wondered if he should be pursuing this. Was he ready for this, whatever *this* was? Where could it go? But somewhere, deep down, where only the truth survived, it felt like something, something new and exciting. Maybe that was it—somehow Holly *felt* right. The ease he felt with this woman couldn't be denied. Standing on the edge of the precipice, he had a decision to make: jump off and hope the parachute opened, or back away. For now, he did neither.

"I wouldn't have figured you for a musical sort of guy. What's your favorite?"

"*The Music Man.* I've seen it half a dozen times at the Starlight Theatre in Balboa Park. It's an outdoor amphitheater that's directly under the flight path of Lindbergh Field. When the actors hear an oncoming jet, all the action stops. Everyone freezes in place, even the orchestra, as the jet roars overhead on its approach. After the jet's gone, everyone resumes as though nothing happened. It's the damnedest thing you've ever seen, but they make it work."

"I have to confess I've never seen a musical."

"You're missing out. It's a traditional form of entertainment. People dancing and singing on a stage. No special effects, just good old-fashioned live acting. If I hadn't joined the Marine Corps, who knows . . . ?"

"I just can't picture it. You as a stage actor?"

"I appreciate the discipline involved. I like ballets and symphonies too, although some operas can be a little heavy."

"Well, aren't you a cultured sort of fellow. What about sports?"

"Ice hockey."

"Me too, I've been to a couple Sharks games. It's a rough sport. If I'm not mistaken, it's the only sport that actually allows fighting, with a penalty, of course. Five minutes."

"Yep. Five for fighting."

"I wish I had more time for stuff like that."

"Fighting? Nah, it's overrated."

She laughed.

"You need to make time, Holly. You know what they say about too much work. . . ."

"Do you think I'm dull?"

"I didn't say that. What I'm saying is something you already know, but need to hear. You need downtime, time to reboot. Especially with a high-stress job like yours. It can't be easy running a field office along with all the resident agencies as well. You must have, what, five hundred people working under you?"

"I manage."

"But at what cost? Sooner or later you'll reach burnout."

"I haven't yet."

"It sneaks up on you. One day you'll just break down into tears over something small. It's your brain telling you you're on overload."

"You speaking from personal experience?"

"Absolutely. Take my advice and do something for yourself, something totally selfish. Go to Cancun or Bermuda. The Bahamas. Lie out at the pool. Give that lily white skin of yours a tan. The FBI will do just fine without you for a spell."

"Henning told me the same thing, except for the lily white skin part."

"I hate to agree with the guy, but he's right."

"I guess I do have pretty fair skin."

"You're a goddess."

"Come on . . ."

"Hey, I'm just calling it like I see it."

"Well, thank you. It's nice of you to say."

"Why don't we try dinner at a restaurant of your choice?"

"I'd like that."

Holly followed the caravan onto I-5 north and took the Highway 70 exit a few miles later. For the next thirty miles the landscape was totally flat. Farmland receded into the darkness on either side of the highway. When they reached the town of Marysville, it was deserted except for a few convenience store gas stations. They followed Highway 70 as it jogged through town before heading north again toward Oroville, some twenty-five miles distant. Off to the west, the black outline of the Buttes contrasted the distant glow from the Bay Area.

Holly kept the conversation lighthearted and told him about her family. Told him she came from a long lineage of law enforcement. Told him her father was a retired City of Sacramento detective. Told him her two brothers were cops, one in Dallas, one in Modesto, California. She talked about her college years at Boston University, about her childhood, and of their family pet, a toy poodle named Pierre who used to sleep under the covers with her. Nathan had to admit he was a little jealous of Pierre.

Either she hadn't made the connection with his last name, or she was being respectful of his privacy, but she hadn't asked about his father. Given her assertive and frank nature, it was likely she didn't know or she would've mentioned it. It was also fair to assume everyone in the FBI knew of the Committee on Domestic Terrorism, especially special agents in charge of field offices. The FBI was directly involved in the security of the nation, and domestic terrorism was high on its list of responsibilities. He knew sooner or later the subject would come up, so why not just get it out in the open and be done with it? Besides, she'd told him about her family; it seemed rude not to reciprocate.

"My father is Senator Matthew McBride."

She looked over at him, then back to the road. "You're joking, right?"

He said nothing.

"Stone 'Stonewall' McBride, chairman of the CDT?"

"The same."

"Well, aren't you full of surprises."

"I thought maybe you knew and were just being discreet."

"I hadn't made the connection with your name. It wasn't in your file. Is that why you're involved?"

"Honestly, I don't know. Probably. He and Ortega go way back; they served in the same unit in Korea. Harvey's close friends with Ortega's son, Greg. That's the personal favor he mentioned at the airport."

"As far as I'm concerned, it doesn't change anything between us. I'm glad you're on board, but it does add a bit of depth."

"We aren't close. I hardly know him."

"I'm sorry to hear that."

"He didn't approve of my career choice. His commanding officer was killed by a sniper. Deep down he knows I'm no different from any other soldier. The man was a battalion commander. He called in artillery and tank support. He gave orders that cost lives on both sides. Hell, *he* had snipers under *his* command."

"Then what's the real problem between you? In a single word."

"A single word?"

"It cuts to the chase, eliminates the BS."

Nathan thought about it for a few seconds, and one word came to mind. "Okay, a single word . . . absence."

"Okay . . ."

"Your turn. In a single word, why aren't you close to anyone?"

"That's brutal."

"Hey, it's your game."

She was silent for several miles, and Nathan started to think she wasn't going to answer. He thought her word would be *commitment*, or *dedication*, something along those lines. She was married to the FBI and she couldn't—or, more accurately, *wouldn't*—take time to form a meaningful relationship. Her answer surprised him.

"Fear," she said, staring straight ahead. "Maybe you'll change *your* mind about dinner tomorrow."

"Look at the bright side. Think of all the money we just saved," he said.

"Seeing expensive shrinks?"

He nodded.

"I think my word was a little more honest than yours."

"It was."

"Want to try again?" she asked.

"Honestly, no, but I believe in playing fair." When she didn't say anything, he took a deep breath and jumped off the precipice. "Okay . . . my word is resentment."

"Well, now we're getting somewhere. What's your best childhood memory of him?"

Nathan didn't hesitate with an answer, because it was one of the few memories he *did* have of his father—he could probably count them on one hand. "We were fishing—I don't remember where, some lake up near Yosemite. I reeled in a big one, or what seemed like a big one, you know, to a kid. He was so proud of me. I remember his smile." He turned toward the window, grateful for the dark interior. "You're way out of my league, Holly. After ten minutes you've hit the bull's-eye with me. Am I really that transparent?"

"Not at all. Just truthful."

"I guess. . . . This isn't easy to talk about."

"I appreciate your confiding in me. To be honest, I expected you to be all business."

"I had the same expectation about you. I thought all you'd want to talk about was the Bridgestones."

"I do want to talk about them, but it's a three-hour drive up to the cabin. I've never met anyone like you."

Nathan said nothing.

"It's a compliment."

"If you say so."

"How did you know about the buried money?"

"I didn't, not with absolute certainty, but I'm betting the Bridgestones have been dealing in Semtex for a while. They obviously don't take checks as payment, so they need to move huge amounts of cash around, and it's not easy to do without someone on the inside of a financial institution. They can't just fly overseas with suitcases full of cash. They need someone they really trust to launder it. They probably do it through bogus third-party loans, so they'd need someone to process the transactions. I wouldn't be surprised if they have numbered accounts in the Caymans or Switzerland or wherever. They've probably been making lots of smaller deposits over the years."

"So how do we catch them?"

"You probably won't."

"If we could, how would we do it?"

He thought about it for a few seconds. "Follow the money trail."

"It's a dead end; we've looked at it."

"You have to find their insider."

Holly thought about that for a while. "Any ideas who it might be?"

"I'd start with Leonard Bridgestone's military background. Someone he knew, a fellow NCO or grunt under his command, someone who's now working for a financial institution. Whoever it is, he's getting a percentage for his services. There would be signs. Someone who's living beyond his means. A huge house. Expensive cars. A stock portfolio, those kinds of things. Things that can't be explained by his reported salary. If nothing turns up, then do the same with Ernie."

"Good thoughts."

"Find their insider, and you'll have a better chance of finding them. If it's someone they're blackmailing or threatening, it'll be nearly impossible to find him. I suppose you could start with local branches, but it's likely they travel out of state to make the deposits. Probably Nevada, where large cash transactions are common. Harvey and I had a similar situation once. This woman was getting a divorce and suspected her husband was hiding money. His old college buddy had managed to launder just under three million dollars exactly as I described."

"I thought you guys ran a security company."

"We do, but we'll take on private investigative work too. It just depends."

"So how did it turn out?"

"We blackmailed him."

"You serious?"

"Yep. When we confronted him he was really belligerent—until Harvey showed him the error of his ways."

"Do I want to know what Harvey, you know . . . did to him?"

"Probably not. At any rate, he wrote a check for just over two million dollars to stay out of jail. He was worth ten times that on paper, but as they say—cash is king. She offered us ten percent, but we only accepted three."

"That was generous of you guys."

"We made money on the deal."

"Still, you turned down a hundred and forty thousand dollars."

He shrugged. "It didn't seem right taking that much. We were doing okay. Besides, she referred several clients our way, who in turn referred more. . . . It snowballed. We were turning down jobs because we didn't have the staff to keep up. There's another possibility with the Bridgestones," he said.

"What?"

"They'll come after *you*. Not you literally, but the FBI. Under your banner I killed their little brother. They can't be real happy about that."

"You think they'll try to avenge him."

"It's a possibility I wouldn't discount too much."

"Based on what those guys were peddling up there, that's a scary thought."

"If I were you, I'd double my security measures for a while. Maybe you *should* take that vacation. Get out of town for a while."

"If anything happened, I couldn't live with it; you know that."

"Yeah, I do, but I needed to say it anyway. They could be long gone. They might not give a damn. I suppose it comes down to two choices. Either they'll cut and run right away, or they'll cut and run after avenging their kid brother. There's no way to know which."

"Which do you think?"

He took a breath and sighed. "At the compound during the raid, one of the brothers—I'm pretty sure it was Ernie—made a mad dash across a hundred and fifty yards of open ground to rescue his little brother after he knew SWAT teams were present. I was about to light him up when the other brother took a few shots at us. Either that was the most reckless act of stupidity I've ever seen, or the most selfless act of bravery. I'm leaning toward bravery, but it's probably a little of both."

"Then you think they'll try something before they flee?"

"I'd say there's a good chance."

"Against us, the FBI?"

He nodded. "They aren't terrorists, Holly. They don't have some fanatical ideology of hatred driving them, like Al-Qaeda. It's all about money. If they try something, it won't be random. They won't bomb a city bus, or train station, or sporting event. They'll go after whoever hurt them. They don't have a lot of time, so they'll pick a target of opportunity, something that doesn't require prolonged surveillance. Who knows, they might already have something planned. It wouldn't surprise me if they did."

"What can we do?"

"That's just it; there isn't much you *can* do besides increase security. When it comes right down to it, we've always lived in a voluntary society. Chaos is only a major disaster away. You remember the New York City blackout in the late seventies?"

"Sort of."

"I was reading about it online recently. Rioting and looting were out of control. Over a thousand fires were lit; entire city blocks were torched. When it was all said and done, nearly four thousand people had been arrested, and three hundred million dollars' worth of damage had been done. There was no hurricane or earthquake or flood. The lights went out. Everybody was pointing fingers at the city, saying it should've been better prepared, should've done this, should've done that. The bottom line—it's impossible to protect society from itself. It's been proven over and over throughout time. If the Bridgestones are hell-bent on revenge, they'll get it unless we find them first."

"That's a pretty bleak picture."

"Don't get me wrong. If you do the math, only one in a thousand people acted disgracefully that night. It was a small minority of opportunistic criminal types that caused all the problems. The vast majority of the city's residents acted honorably, helping one another, lending candles and flashlight batteries to strangers. Disasters define character. I have no doubt you'd be at your best when things are at their worst."

"I'd like to believe that."

"Believe it. You didn't join the FBI for the money. There're a million jobs out there with better pay and fewer hours. Well, maybe not a million, but you know what I mean. You want to look back on your life someday and know that you made the world a better place. Hold on to it, Holly. Hold it close and never let it go."

"Like I said, I've never met anyone like you before."

"I was thinking the same thing about you."

"But you really are different. To be able to have that attitude after what you went through . . . ?"

"It's taken a long time. But I made a choice not to dwell in the past. Everyone has tragedy in his life at one time or another; it's how a person deals with it that defines them. I don't hate the Nicaraguan people for what happened to me. I used to, but I don't anymore. Should a rape victim hate all men for the rest of her life? Anger and bitterness are normal feelings, but they're like cancer if you can't control them."

"I've never been tested. I can't honestly say how I'd deal with it."

"No one can until it happens to them."

The rest of the ride from Oroville into the mountains went by quickly. Highway 70 followed a steep river canyon. They crossed trestle-type bridges and navigated through short tunnels blasted through solid granite. Areas of still water reflected the moonlight. On the opposite side of the canyon wall, railroad tracks paralleled the highway. Every so often they passed a small hydroelectric power plant, their square forms contrasting with the random shapes of the rocky terrain. Although he was tired from all the flying and lack of sleep, he found conversation with Holly relaxing. She had a good sense of humor and, despite the situation with Ortega's grandson, kept a positive outlook.

"This is a beautiful drive in daylight," Nathan said. "Harvey and I drove it the day of the raid."

"I've been up here a few times. It's a designated scenic highway."

The road continued a gradual climb into the mountains, winding its way up the rocky canyon into a pine forest. Her radio crackled. It was Henning. "We're coming up on the turn. We should kill our headlights."

"Copy," she said. All three vehicles went dark. Nathan watched the brake lights of the two sedans in front of them blink on. Henning, still in the lead, made a left turn at the intersection of a narrow dirt road that peeled off the highway to the north. There was no street sign associated with the road, just barbed-wire fencing on either side. Massive trees lining both sides of the track screened a half-moon low on the eastern horizon. After traveling about a hundred yards down the potholed road, the caravan came to a stop and everyone piled out. They formed a huddle next to Holly's sedan. Nathan noticed that the dome lights remained dark when the doors of the FBI vehicles were opened. Disabled, he knew. He watched Holly pull on a dark blue coat with large FBI letters on the back. Henning made sure to position himself between Holly and Nathan. *If you only knew,* he thought.

The surrounding forest was muted in eerie silence; the

symphony of crickets he'd heard back at the farmhouse was absent. The only sound present was the lonely whisper of wind filtering through the trees. It was cool up here, low fifties. Nathan guessed the elevation to be around seven thousand feet. He'd kept track of the Caltrans signposts on the way up. The last one they'd passed indicated six thousand feet, and they'd climbed for several miles after that.

He walked back to Holly's sedan, retrieved his coat from the backseat, and quietly closed the door.

Henning relayed what the Bridgestone cousins had told him. "According to our guests of honor, the entrance to the property's another thousand yards up the track. It's the first locked gate on the right-hand side. The cabin's another five hundred yards beyond the gate. The entire parcel is fenced with barbed wire. I recommend cutting it at the far corner and approaching from there."

Keeping her voice low, she addressed Collins and Dowdy. "Okay, I want a visual recon of the cabin from a safe distance first. Gear up. We'll sit tight until you report back to us."

They walked over to Gifford's sedan and popped the trunk.

"There could be more claymores out there," Nathan offered. "Make sure your guys watch closely for trip wires. With all the deer around it's unlikely, but you never know."

"Good thought," she said.

Gifford nodded, walked over to the SWAT agents, and spoke quietly to them. Several minutes later Collins and Dowdy were ready to go. Nathan saw that they had the same night-vision devices he and Harvey used, except theirs were mounted on their helmets in tandem. They'd have perfect depth perception using two scopes rather than one. The boom microphones extending from the sides of their helmets nearly touched their lips. Nathan felt a pang of envy; he wanted to go with them, but knew Holly would never allow it.

"Okay, recon only," Holly said. "Do not engage if anyone's there. Return fire only if fired upon."

Nathan watched the two SWAT agents walk down the track and vanish into the blackness.

Holly removed her handheld radio from her hip, turned the volume down, and keyed the button. "Dowdy, radio check."

"Copy."

"Collins?"

Another whispered, "Copy."

"Now we wait." She turned toward Henning. "Your guys say anything useful on the ride up here?"

"Not really. I tried them a couple times. I think they're really pissed about the cash. I'm sure they had plans for it."

"Beer money for the rest of their lives," she said.

Nathan listened to them, but his mind was elsewhere. Something was bugging him, gnawing at the back of his mind like a festering splinter. Something about the farmhouse. The garage. He couldn't place it. He also kept listening for the telltale blast of a claymore detonating out of the darkness. *Be careful out there, guys.*

"What do we do with our guests after this?" Henning asked.

"We take them back and release them. There's still a possibility their cousins will try to make contact. We keep watching them."

"Better let me have a chat with them first," Nathan said.

"Okay . . ." she said.

"I—or rather, we," he said, nodding toward Harvey, "need to convince them that reporting any of this would be a bad idea."

"We did bend the rules a little," Holly said.

"A little," Nathan echoed.

"Do you honestly think they'll keep quiet about this?" Henning asked.

"There are two hundred and six bones in the human body," Nathan said.

Henning glanced at Holly with a combined expression of revulsion and dismay.

"You could offer them some of the cash," Nathan said, "as compensation for their undivided cooperation tonight."

Holly didn't respond.

He shrugged. "What could it hurt? The money's unofficial so far. Give them four grand apiece; that leaves an even three hundred grand left over. A nice round number. No one would be the wiser. It kinda evens the score for them a little. Tell them if they say anything, you'll deny it. It's your word against theirs. All of this is."

"That's not an altogether bad idea. . . ."

In the dim light filtering through the trees, Henning looked as if he were ready to come unglued; his mouth was opening and closing as if he were choking on a chicken bone.

"Let's use this time wisely. Are you and Harvey up to giving those guys two hundred and six reasons to keep their mouths shut?"

When he heard that from his boss, Henning's jaw literally dropped.

The more time Nathan spent with Holly, the more he liked her. This woman was definitely with the program—on board for the big win. "Come on, Harvey. We've got an orthopedic lesson to give." He turned back to Holly. "Can we offer them the cash?"

She hesitated, then said, "Sure, why not."

Three minutes later Nathan and Harvey were back.

"Well?" she asked.

"They're A-plus students with beer money for a year," Nathan said.

Holly's radio came to life. It was Dowdy. He wasn't whispering anymore. "We've got a burned-out structure with one bound BBR inside."

*BBR*, Nathan told himself.

*Burned beyond recognition.*

James Ortega.

# ⊕ Chapter Eight

Fifteen minutes later two FBI vehicles left the scene, Nathan, Harvey, and Larry Gifford in one, Bruce Henning and the Bridgestone cousins in the other. Holly stayed behind with the two SWAT agents to secure the remains of the cabin until an FBI forensic team and the Sacramento County coroner arrived.

It was a somber, quiet ride down a granite canyon under a red-and-orange sunrise. Nobody felt like talking. It didn't take a microbiologist to guess whom they'd found up there.

Back in Sacramento, Gifford took the J Street exit for the Hyatt Regency, while Henning's vehicle kept going south on Interstate 5. Henning flashed his brake lights twice, and Gifford flashed his high beams in return.

*Good riddance*, thought Nathan. The Bridgestone cousins were the embodied definition of human debris. He still couldn't get over the condition of their farmhouse. It had literally been a dump, like an indoor landfill. Except in the garage, which he'd fully expected to be as filthy as the house. *Think, damn it.* He tried to clear his mind and concentrate on the garage, but it was no use. He couldn't bring whatever was bugging him forward. His mind was shutting down due to sleep deprivation. Sitting next to him, Harvey looked in roughly the same shape.

As if reading his thoughts, Gifford asked, "How much sleep have you guys had in the last forty-eight hours?"

"Not much," Nathan said.

"Do yourselves a favor and get some shut-eye at the hotel. You're no good to anyone in your present condition. We'll call you as soon as we know anything."

"Thanks, Larry."

Gifford dropped them off under the porte cochere of the Hyatt just after nine in the morning. As the bellman retrieved their bags from the trunk, they shook hands with Gifford and waved as he pulled away. They staggered up to the counter and checked into adjoining rooms on the sixth floor overlooking Capitol Park. At their rooms, Nathan slipped the bellman a twenty, dialed the operator, and asked to have their calls forwarded to voice mail.

Ten minutes later they were both asleep.

When Nathan awoke, the message light was blinking on the nightstand phone. He picked it up and hit the retrieve button. It was from Holly, asking for a return call. He dialed Harvey's room.

"Get any sleep?" Nathan asked.

"Four hours. You?"

"About the same. I've got a message to call Holly."

"Two minutes," Harvey said.

Nathan used the toilet, splashed some water on his face, and stared into the mirror. That damned garage—he'd awakened still thinking about it. For some reason he couldn't get it out of his head. What was bugging him? The tools? The toolboxes? *Think, damn it.*

Nathan answered the soft knock on the adjoining room door, and Harvey stepped through. Without sitting down Nathan punched nine, waited for the dial tone, and called Holly Simpson's cell.

"Holly Simpson."

"Holly, it's Nathan. I have you on speaker. Harvey's with me."

"The news is not good. It was James Ortega. The Sacramento County coroner confirmed his identity from dental records. I just found out ten minutes ago. He'd been subjected to severe blunt-force trauma. Six of his fingers were missing. They found smoke residue in his lungs." Her voice cracked. "Nathan, they burned him alive."

He squinted and looked at his partner. Harvey's jaw started working.

"You still there?" she asked.

"I'm really sorry, Holly."

"We wouldn't have found him this quickly without your help. I never thanked you guys last night."

"I really wanted a happy ending. I kept hoping we'd find him alive—dehydrated and hungry, but alive."

"Me too."

"We'll tell the family."

"I appreciate it. I have to go. It's a real mess over here. Call me later?"

"I will." He hung up and looked at Harvey. No words were necessary.

The situation had just turned personal. *This isn't over, you lousy shitbirds. This isn't over at all, not by a long shot.* He knew their call to Frank Ortega was going to be an emotional train wreck. Although Frank had suspected his grandson was dead, having it confirmed was another matter. Until you had absolute proof, there was always a small glimmer of hope. Now there was none. James Ortega, third-generation FBI, was dead, killed in the line of duty. No, not just killed—tortured, humiliated, and burned alive by two cold-blooded animals. It made Nathan sick to his stomach thinking about what James Ortega must have gone through. Wasn't there even the tiniest speck of humanity left in these guys? They could've easily killed him first. A hard blow to the head. A bullet to the temple. A slit throat. A plastic bag over his head. Anything. Why burn him alive? Why? It was a message, loud and clear, with no chance of being misunderstood: *Mess with us and you'll die badly.*

Nathan looked at Harvey. "We should call Ortega. Want me to do it?"

"No." Harvey reached into his pocket and pulled out a small piece of paper. He stared at the phone number.

"Harv?"

"I'm okay."

But Nathan knew his best and oldest friend *wasn't* okay. Far from it. Nathan walked into the bathroom and looked in the mirror. Icy blue eyes stared back. With his teeth clenched, he balled his hands into fists so tight they hurt from the pressure. Had James Ortega pleaded at the end? Had he begged to be killed first? Had the Bridgestones looked at each other in mock sympathy and then laughed at the request before tossing the match? Had they stayed and listened to his screams of agony?

Nathan drove his fist into the mirror.

It shattered into a thousand pieces, some sticking out of his knuckles.

He staggered back and sat on the edge of the tub. *Damn those assholes.*

Harvey appeared at the bathroom door. "Lemme see that hand."

Like an automaton Nathan held it up, allowing Harvey to remove the small shards of glass from his flesh. Blood was already running down his fingers and dripping onto the marble floor. Harvey wet a washcloth and dabbed the damaged skin before wiping the blood from the floor. "We'd better get you a couple butterflies. You okay?"

Nathan nodded.

"Sit tight."

From the bathroom Nathan listened as Harvey called the front desk and reported an accident. He asked for a first-aid kit, and a maintenance man for the broken mirror.

"Come on," Harvey said. "Let's get some chow in you. We haven't eaten in over eighteen hours. I'll order room service. The usual? Various hors d'oeuvres?"

Nathan nodded. "Sorry about the mirror."

Harvey forced a smile. "You beat me to it." He sat Nathan down on the bed and wrapped the washcloth around his friend's knuckles.

"We have to get those guys, Harv. No matter what it takes."

"Count on it. Any ideas where we should start?"

"Yeah, I'm thinking we follow the money—the cash we didn't already find. We'll start with the visitation logs from the Castle. I want to know who visited Ernie Bridgestone while he was in prison."

"An old girlfriend?"

"Maybe. I think these guys have been planning this operation of theirs for a long time. Years. Someone they've known and trusted a long time—that's who we're looking for. Anyone who could lead us to their money, so we'll know where they'll head next."

Harvey nodded, making notes.

"Let's also work on getting the names of the people Leonard worked with when he was stationed in northern Iraq. Fellow NCOs, grunts under his command. On the drive up to the cabin I told Holly he might even have someone on the inside of a financial institution to launder their money. We'll be looking for someone who's living beyond his means. Someone who's living within a one-day drive, maybe Reno or Vegas. Somewhere large cash deposits are fairly common."

"This will be a lot easier with some inside help," Harvey said. "Let's call General Hawthorne in the Pentagon, see if he'll help."

Gen. William "Thorny" Hawthorne was the Marine Corps commandant, the top man in the corps, and one of four Joint Chiefs of Staff. Hawthorne had been their commanding officer during their operations in Nicaragua, and their successful missions had helped boost his career by a star.

"Good thought," Nathan said. "I'll call first thing in the morning."

"Think he'll help us?"

"Yeah, I do. He won't have time to do it personally, but he'll assign us a liaison officer to dig into the DOD computers. I doubt he'll give us access."

"We're going to need some help up here for the legwork. There's no way we can do everything. I'll pull two of our guys up from San Diego. We'll set up our base of operations here. We'll need a secure fax line to send and receive transmissions. I'll make sure Lewey sets our guys up with an encrypted cell phone connected to a fax. Hawthorne will want assurances we're using secure lines for the data transfer back and forth."

Nathan was already feeling better. It felt good to be doing something, to have a plan and work toward a goal. And it was a worthy goal. The Bridgestones were going to be hunted down like the rabid dogs they were. A reckoning was coming, coming like a freight train with its engine roaring and horn blaring. Those two turds had no idea of the wrath they'd brought upon themselves.

Harvey ordered room service and asked for it to be delivered to Nathan's room. A moment later Harvey answered a soft knock at the door. Carrying a first-aid kit, the maintenance man strode into the room, tools hanging from his belt. At the bathroom door he saw the broken glass covering the countertop and floor, looked at Nathan sitting on the bed, noticed his bloody hand, looked at the damaged face it belonged to, and decided silence was the best course of action. He handed the first-aid kit to Harvey.

"How long do you need?" Harvey asked.

The maintenance man shrugged. "Maybe an hour."

Harvey pulled a couple of butterfly bandages out of the kit and applied them to Nathan's knuckles. He wrapped a couple layers of gauze around the wound and secured it with white tape on the palm side of Nathan's hand, opposite the cuts.

"Thanks," Nathan said.

"Think nothing of it."

With the maintenance man in the bathroom, Harvey transferred the duffel bag containing their SIG Sauer pistol belts, night-vision visors, and other tools into Nathan's room through the adjoining door.

After Harvey returned, Nathan said, "We'd better make that call to Ortega. The longer we wait, the harder it'll be."

"Yeah, I know. . . ."

"How do you do it, Harv? Keep your cool."

"Like I said, you beat me to it. That mirror was doomed from the day it was installed."

"I've never seen you break anything."

"That's just it; you've never *seen* it. . . . I once beat the living daylights out of a lawn mower with an aluminum baseball bat. It was gassed up and brand-new, right out of the box. But the damned thing wouldn't start. I must have pulled that cord a hundred times before I took the bat to it. Candace came out to the lawn and, without saying a word, handed me the instruction manual. She reached down and turned the gas shut-off valve to the 'on' position, winked at me, and then walked away."

Nathan half-laughed. "Yeah, that sounds like Candace."

"Yep. I have to admit it felt great smashing that mower. Come on; let's get this call over with."

"Harv, I'll make the call to Ortega."

"No. I should do it. You're in no shape to talk to Ortega right now. Honestly, it's my responsibility. I got us into this; I'll make the call."

Nathan reluctantly agreed, and had to admit Harv was right: He wasn't in the right mind-set to talk to Ortega. Nathan tried to clear his mind of the red fog blanketing his thoughts. He needed to focus, to see the situation from a calm perspective. He concentrated on the FBI's role in all of this. The farmhouse had been under surveillance before the raid. Okay, why? They obviously thought the Bridgestones might show up there. Still, no one had known about the tunnel at Freedom's Echo, or else the FBI would've been waiting at the other end to grab them. Did Holly Simpson truly believe he and Harvey represented the FBI's best chance of getting the information needed to catch the Bridgestones? However effective, it seemed unlikely and overly risky. Maybe Frank

Ortega had insisted they remain involved. That seemed more reasonable, but that scenario assumed Ortega had a level of influence with Director Lansing that he'd denied during their initial meeting in San Diego. So what was the truth? Nathan wasn't so sure anymore.

Setting that thought aside, he again envisioned the cousins' farmhouse. Immediately his thoughts returned to the garage. Something about it *had* been odd. He took a deep breath, closed his eyes, and pictured it in his head. Okay, it had a workbench on one side, tools on the other. The toolboxes were stacked against the far wall. There was a new Enduro motorcycle in the corner. Red, with a luggage rack. What did something like that cost? Four, maybe five grand? The Bridgestone cousins didn't seem like the type of guys able to afford something like that. It had looked fairly new and well maintained. Everything in that garage had. He pictured the wall of tools above the workbench, everything organized by type and use and hung on neatly organized eye rings and hooks. And the power tools on the opposite side of the garage: shiny and well maintained, again arranged by use and type. The empty power-tool boxes. Who saved the empty boxes? And why would a pair of idiots like those two need a trip wire on their front porch? How many people did that? He pictured the rigged stack of beer bottles. Were the two just paranoid? Maybe they thought Leonard and Ernie were going to drop by. Could they have anticipated the authorities' interest in them?

Nathan looked down at the bandage Harvey had applied to his hand and thought about the gauze bandage on cousin Billy's arm. There had been blood seeping through, and the white tape was crossed at the corners. It looked a lot like a field dressing. He held up his hand. A lot like this one. He thought back to his field medic training. *We were taught to cross the tape at the corners, just like Harv did right here.*

*Shit!*

He literally sprinted across the room and grabbed the phone

message from Holly. He punched the numbers into the night-stand phone and heard an annoying *beep-beep-beep*. Shit, he hadn't punched nine first. He stabbed the button and waited an eternity before hearing a dial tone. He forced himself to slow down, dialing Holly's cell number.

"Holly Simpson."

"Holly, listen to me very carefully. We blew it—blew it badly."

"Who is this? Nathan?"

"We blew it."

"What are you talking about?"

"The farmhouse. I think they were there last night, the Bridgestones, Leonard and Ernie."

"What? How? That's impossible."

"Get back out there, Holly. Get SWAT out there as fast as you can."

"Nathan—"

"Holly, please, just do it."

"But we've had the farmhouse under constant surveillance, even before the raid. Nobody's come or gone from there."

"Last night I saw what looked like a large-diameter pipe sticking up above the ground near the property corner under the windmill. I didn't think twice about it until now."

"Another tunnel," she whispered.

"Holly, be careful. Have your people check the garage again, the light switch."

"I will. I'll call you later."

Nathan began pacing back and forth across the room. "They played us, Harv. They put on a dog-and-pony show and we bought it—hook, line, and sinker. Son of a bitch. We had them."

"You could be wrong; they may not have been there."

"They were there."

"Nate, you can't know that for sure."

"I didn't put it all together; I should've. Their cousins could've lasted a lot longer than they did. They gave up the cabin and the cash to satisfy us, to make us think we'd gotten something valuable. They threw us a bone to get us out of there. I think they had this whole routine planned in case they were ever questioned by the FBI or police. That place was their safe house, by design, from the beginning."

Harvey said nothing.

"It was the garage. It kept bugging me. I thought to myself, 'No way. There's no way in hell this garage should look this neat and tidy. These guys are total slobs.'"

"What if you're wrong? Holly's risking a lot taking a SWAT team out there. Suppose they don't find anything?"

"Harv, you saw those guys; they were covered with oil and grease, especially their hands. The bandage on Billy's arm was clean. There should've been smudges on the tape from tearing it off the roll. It was the only thing in the entire house that *was* clean. I remember thinking it to myself."

"Bit of a stretch, don't you think?"

"If records could be found, I'm pretty sure not all the storm drain pipe they purchased can be accounted for up at the compound."

"Let's assume you're right and there was a tunnel and they were there. Why didn't the cousins give them up? The money would have been theirs."

"Maybe they were more afraid of them than us. Or maybe they were promised a bigger chunk for keeping quiet. Who the hell knows?"

"Okay, tell me this, then: Why were they there? What reason could they possibly have for going there?"

Nathan said nothing; he didn't have to.

"Semtex," Harvey said. "The missing crates from the compound."

Nathan nodded. "Yep."

"And the cousins?"

"Dead," Nathan said. "They wouldn't risk leaving them alive. Those two don't leave loose ends."

"If you're right, we have to tell Ortega."

"Not yet. Things might take a nasty twist for Holly Simpson. I don't want her becoming a scapegoat. I know how it works; crap flows downhill. If I have to, I'll take the heat for this."

"How? We weren't even supposed to be there."

"I'll threaten to expose this whole thing. The way I see it, crap is going to flow *uphill* if they try to throw Holly to the wolves. She's not taking the fall on this, Harv. It isn't right."

"Nathan, you can't blackmail the FBI."

"Watch me."

"No, I mean you can't do that to Ortega. I'm not on board with that."

Nathan stared out the window. "Then I want a conversation with FBI director Lansing. Tomorrow."

"There's no way Ortega will agree to that."

"It wasn't Holly's decision to involve us, Harv. It was Ortega's, with Director Lansing's foreknowledge, the 'don't ask, don't tell' business. Besides, I'm pretty sure I know who's behind all this cloak-and-dagger crap."

"Your father."

"Yep. Remember Ortega's answer when I asked if dear old Dad knew of our involvement?"

Harvey said nothing.

"He wants a political victory for his CDT, and he's willing to break the rules to get it. It's a mighty big feather in his cap if he pulls it off. It'll guarantee funding for the next five hundred years. It's front-page, headline-grabbing material."

"I think it's Occam's razor."

"All right, I'm listening."

Harvey lowered his voice. "Frank Ortega called your father. He's the one pulling the strings. He wanted his grandson found at any cost. If the civil rights of a couple dirtbags get violated in the process, so be it."

Nathan heard the pain in his partner's words and softened his tone. He stopped pacing. "Look, Harv, if it was you who'd gone missing, I would've done the same thing. You know that. Don't condemn the man for wanting closure. Think he'll level with you if you ask him? Will he tell you the truth?"

"Yeah, I think so."

"We need to know for sure. I want that call with Director Lansing. If we handle this right, everything will stay under wraps. If he doesn't already know the score, I'll tell Lansing the truth. All of it, from the beginning. No threats. I'll take full responsibility for the screwup."

"Come on, Nate, that's not fair to you, to *us*. There's plenty of blame to go around. It was the FBI's stakeout, for cryin' out loud."

"It was all there, right in front of me. I should've put it together. I want to make this right. *We* need to make this right."

"We have to protect ourselves."

"That's why I want the call with Lansing."

# ⊕ Chapter Nine

Several hours later, Nathan lay awake, staring at the ceiling, thinking about James Ortega. Nicaragua. The farmhouse. When the phone rang he glanced at the clock. Almost midnight.

"Nathan, it's Holly."

"Hi, Holly."

"Did I wake you?"

"No, I can't sleep."

"Me either. I'm five minutes away; can you meet me in the lobby?"

He hesitated, not sure he wanted company, but there was something in her voice. Something he recognized. "Yeah, sure, I'll be right down."

"You were right. About everything."

"I'll see you in a few minutes." He gently replaced the handset into its cradle. In the bathroom he brushed his teeth, rubbed a wet washcloth over his face, and made his way out to the elevators. About to press the button, he stopped. No cell phone. He went back for it. During the elevator's blinking countdown he thought about Holly, what her last twelve hours must have been like. He shook his head as the elevator dumped him into a deserted lobby. The clerk behind the counter smiled as he walked past. Holly Simpson entered the hotel three minutes later. Her white-collared shirt was tucked into blue jeans secured by a silver-and-turquoise Indian jewelry belt. She looked beautiful, but tired.

He stood as the automatic glass doors pulled open.

"Hello, Holly."

Her expression told all.

"Oh, man." He held his arms wide.

She moved forward and embraced him. Tightly.

"Rough day?" Nathan felt her nod and rested his chin on her head. He needed this hug as much as she did.

She wiped a tear aside. "What happened to your hand?"

"The bathroom mirror lost an argument."

"You okay?"

"Just embarrassed."

She released him and stepped back. "Look at me, crying like this—some professional I am."

"Nonsense, you're a human being with deep feelings."

She managed a smile. "Thanks for the hug. I really needed it."

"Me, too."

"You saved our lives at the farmhouse last night."

"The light switch."

"It was rigged to several claymores concealed in an empty toolbox. If Bruce had flipped it we would've been killed. He's really torn up over it, threatening to resign."

"Don't let him do that. I don't like the guy, but don't let him quit, okay?"

"I won't." They sat down, facing each other. "There's more: The Bridgestones killed our two techs in the surveillance van. Tortured them first, like Ortega. We found them in the farmhouse, both shot in the head. Everything was recorded. The machines were running when they grabbed them. It was horrible. . . . Their screams."

"I'm sorry, Holly."

"That's not all, Nathan. They know about you. They know you're the one who killed their little brother at the compound. They also know who your father is."

He just stared. *How the hell could they know that?* His mind raced with possibilities, all of them bad.

"We can protect you, put you in the witness protection program."

"Forget about it. I'm not hiding from those two mutts."

"But everything's changed. They know who you are."

"I'll be okay. Come on; let's get out of here."

Outside, under the porte cochere, she asked if he minded driving. He tucked her into the passenger seat and walked around the front of the SUV. Moving the driver's seat all the way back, he climbed in and reached for the keys. They weren't there.

"Sorry." She reached into her purse. "There's a piano bar not far from here. It's open for another hour."

"Sounds good. You go there often?"

"When I can't sleep. I live a couple miles from here. How did you know about the garage switch?"

"I didn't, for sure. It was just a feeling in my gut."

"Turn right at L, then left at the next signal. Based on what?"

"I'm not sure I can explain it."

"Will you try?"

He took a deep breath and let it out slowly. "It was a lot of things. Things that had been floating around in my head. Like the claymores at the compound. The trip wire on the porch steps of the farmhouse. The buried cash. It's hard to pinpoint."

"There was a trip wire?"

"It was rigged to a bunch of empty beer bottles. I cut the string before you got there."

"I saw the bottles, but I didn't think twice about them."

"They looked perfectly normal. Harv and I were a covert ops team. We're trained to look for stuff like that, to be suspicious of things that seem ordinary. I'm just glad the garage door itself wasn't rigged. That's why I asked you and Henning to look for a trip wire when I started lifting it."

"I'm just really glad you were there. To be honest, I resented your being involved. I didn't say anything at the airport. I didn't want to offend you."

"Larry Gifford told me the same thing at the compound, almost word for word."

"Larry's a good man."

"I like Gifford a lot," Nathan said. "He's the real deal."

"We're like a family, the FBI. We look out for one another. Sometimes I think we're dependent on one another to the point of being restrictive, arrogant even. We don't like asking for outside help."

"You're not alone. When Harv and I first accepted this assignment from Ortega, his son, Greg, wanted to come along. I told him flat-out no. Needless to say, he was rather upset. The situation's different, but the principle's the same."

"How can you sound so calm about all this? The Bridgestones know who you are."

"Like I said, all they have is my name."

"Turn left at the next signal. You can park anywhere; the bar's just up the street."

Nathan pulled over to the curb and climbed out quickly, but before he made it to Holly's side of the Explorer, she had her door open and was sliding out. He closed it for her.

"You don't have to do that."

"My mother's old-school."

They walked in silence down the sidewalk. A few cars still lingered about, but for the most part the downtown streets of

Sacramento were deserted. Nathan saw the entrance to the piano bar just ahead. A small black awning overhung its glass door. In the shape of a grand piano, a red neon sign lit the window next to the door. The opposite window had two blue neon signs shaped like cocktail glasses. He could hear muffled jazz coming from inside—a saxophone and, of course, a piano. It sounded good, even through the glass. He looked for black, flattened wads of gum on the sidewalk as a gauge of the bar's patrons and found none. The glass door was clean. No handprints or smudges.

Holly hesitated, letting him open the door. Once inside Nathan gave the place a quick scan; so did Holly. She scanned from left to right, while Nathan went right to left. Their surveillance met in the middle, and they smiled at each other, knowing they had both been doing the same thing. A linear bar stood to their left, with cocktail tables on the right. A small elevated stage on the far wall hosted the two musicians. Because the room was small and intimate enough for natural sound, the musicians weren't using a PA system. To Nathan's surprise he and Holly had the place to themselves. The bartender nodded, and they grabbed the first table on the right. Nathan pulled Holly's chair in for her, and she thanked him.

"You don't mind being this close to the door with your back facing it?" she asked.

"I prefer it."

She looked puzzled.

"If trouble comes in, I'm already behind it. Besides, you've got a small throwaway under your jeans in an ankle holster. Right side."

She rolled her eyes. "It's not a throwaway. It's a Glock thirty-nine."

"Correction: It's a small cannon. I'll bet it fits well in your hand. Forty-five ACP, single, double action. Six shots?"

"Seven, including one in the pipe. You know your guns."

"A hobby. I noticed the bulge."

"Is that all you noticed?"

"I, uh, tell you what: When a bad guy in a trench coat comes in, I'll duck. You shoot."

"It's a deal. You haven't asked about the Bridgestones' cousins."

"From the way you looked in the lobby, I didn't want to press."

"I guess I've finally reached that burnout you talked about. I broke down into tears. Sorry."

"Hey, don't apologize. This isn't something small. On the drive up to the cabin I was talking about a dropped dish or a burned steak." He instantly wished he hadn't said the "burned steak" part. "Sorry, bad choice of words."

"How could they do that, burn him alive like that?"

"I don't know, Holly. I honestly don't."

The bartender approached them, a short, thin, balding man with a bushy mustache, bow tie, and friendly smile. He placed a bowl of miniature pretzels on the table. "Can I get you folks something to drink?"

"What type of wine do you have by the glass tonight?" Holly asked.

"Tobin James cabernet sauvignon, vintage 2003."

"Is that a local winery?"

He issued a more-or-less gesture with his hand. "Paso Robles."

"That's perfect, thank you."

"You, sir?"

"O'Doul's, please."

"You don't drink alcohol?" she asked.

"I've been recovering for a long time."

"Good for you. Are you okay with me having some wine?"

"Not a problem."

Holly lowered her voice a little. "We found the entrance to the tunnel in the bedroom closet. They used a piece of plywood covered with dirty clothes to hide it. There was a small chamber with two bunk beds just under the slab. Probably took weeks to excavate by hand. It looked exactly like the setup at the compound. They used railroad ties for the walls, and water skis with skateboard wheels to travel the tunnel. As you suspected, the other side came up under the windmill at the property corner. We found marks in the dirt where they crawled across the neighboring property to a canyon that connects to another road."

"What about Billy and his brother?"

"SWAT found them. They'd been dragged fifty feet into the tunnel on the farmhouse side. Both had been shot in the back of the head, twenty-two caliber."

Nathan pursed his lips and shook his head.

"It isn't your fault, okay? We can't even be sure they were there at the same time we were."

"They were there," he whispered.

"You don't know that for sure. They could've shown up anytime yesterday. They could've been waiting there early this morning when Bruce dropped off their cousins. Bruce is lucky to be alive; he could've been killed too. In fact, I think it's fair to assume they weren't there, or he *would've* been killed. We also had the place bugged; we would've heard them talking."

"They probably suspected the bugs were there and communicated by written notes, who knows . . . ? I should've seen this coming. It was that damned garage. Other things too. Everything was right there in front of me, staring me in the face, and I didn't see it. I should've put it all together."

"Come on, that's not fair. We had no reason to believe Ernie and Leonard would be there. Bruce was right; their cousins were just a couple of hayseeds."

"Then why were they killed?"

Holly said nothing.

"It's because they knew something, maybe something about another safe house or hiding place or a contact. Something important. Was the motorcycle still in the garage?"

"No. We've got an APB out on it. City, state, and local law

enforcement are stopping anyone seen riding Enduros regardless of color. Maybe we'll catch a break."

"Let's hope so."

"We're doing everything possible to find them."

"I'm pretty sure I know why the Bridgestones went to the
farmhouse. I think they stashed the missing Semtex from the
compound there. Probably in the tunnel or the underground
room. Can your forensic people check for trace evidence of it?"

"Yes, but it's very difficult to detect. Semtex doesn't
leave—"

The bartender returned with their drinks. Nathan's
O'Doul's was served with a mug cloudy from frost. He poured
some and offered a silent toast. Under a spotlight onstage, the
musicians continued their jamming.

"Semtex doesn't leave much of itself behind," she continued, "even when it's exposed. It's not like gunpowder or TNT;
we can test for those compounds easily. If it was still sealed in
its crates, all bets are off."

"We should've spent a few minutes poking around out
there."

"I was the one who wanted to get up to that cabin ASAP."

"There's a bigger question here," he said. "A huge question.
If the missing Semtex *was* there, why did they want it?"

Holly stared. "I don't like that question."

"You shouldn't. I think it's fair to assume they weren't trying to complete a sale in progress, and I seriously doubt they
were selling individual crates. That'd be too risky. They'd
have a single buyer for all of it."

"Who do you think they were selling it to? Foreign terrorists? An Al-Qaeda cell operating within the United States?"

Nathan shook his head. "No, I don't think so. It was more
likely being sold to radical militia groups. They love the stuff.
It's way easier to use than fertilizer or TNT. The Bridgestones
are cold-blooded, but they aren't terrorists. Something tells
me they wouldn't sell to radical Islamic types. I just can't see

them doing that. It's all about money, not hatred of their country. I don't have anything to base that on but my gut instinct. If the Bridgestones could somehow be caught and interrogated, I think we'd find they've been doing business with militia groups, not terrorists."

"By strict interpretation, the Bridgestones already *are* terrorists," Holly said. "Look at what they've done so far."

"I can't deny they've committed some horrible crimes, but at the risk of sounding callous, not on a grand scale. Like I said on the drive up to the cabin, if they try something, it won't be a random target. They'll go after whoever hurt them. The FBI, and now me."

"Why do you think the Bridgestones showed their cousins where the money was hidden? I mean, they could've told them to get lost for a couple of hours while they buried it."

Nathan took a swallow. "I wondered the same thing myself. I think they had this routine planned from the beginning. It's a believable bone to throw. That much cash gets serious attention. You remember Henning's reaction to seeing it? If the cousins were ever questioned by the authorities, they could hold out for a while, then give up the cash and the cabin, making it seem like they caved."

"So you think the Bridgestones used the money as a distraction, a decoy? They sacrificed it?"

"It worked, didn't it? Once we had the cash and the info about the cabin, we were out of there in a hurry."

"I can't deny that."

"Listen, Holly, there's something you need to know, and I don't want to do it behind your back."

"Okay . . ."

"I've arranged a phone call with Director Lansing tomorrow."

She stared, her mind working. "May I ask why?"

"This whole thing reeks of my father's involvement. I asked Harv to call Frank Ortega and verify my suspicion. Ortega confirmed it. When we first met with him, Ortega told us

Director Lansing knew of our involvement before the raid. Ortega said he'd never do something like that behind the director's back. Lansing told Ortega he didn't want to know about it, kind of a 'don't ask, don't tell' thing, but Lansing didn't say no. I think Ortega called in a major favor to involve us. He knew we were a covert ops team, knew how we did things. I think he wanted his grandson found at any cost. I don't blame him for wanting closure."

"What do you hope to accomplish by talking with Lansing?"

"Holly, I've known Harv through life and death. I've never seen him like this before. It's tearing him up. He needs closure too, maybe more than he's willing to admit to me or himself. What they did to James Ortega, and now two more of your people . . . it can't go unanswered."

"You didn't answer my question."

"I want a green light to pursue the Bridgestones."

She shook her head. "Lansing will never agree to it."

"I'll give him our word we won't kill them or seriously hurt anyone in the process. Obviously we're aware the FBI needs them alive for questioning. You've seen us in action."

"It's what I haven't seen that concerns me."

He looked down, didn't respond.

"That wasn't fair to you."

"But it was honest."

"I didn't mean to judge you. It's just . . ." She reached across the table and squeezed his hand. "I'm sorry."

"No, you're right. We've done some horrible things, Harv and me. I've always felt what we did was justified in the name of national security, even though a little voice in the back of my head sometimes said otherwise. The night we accepted this assignment, Mrs. Ortega said something to me, something that rang true. She told me she didn't see the world through rose-colored glasses."

"I don't either."

"I wasn't suggesting you did. All I'm saying is, there's more at stake than justice for James Ortega and your two techs. You don't know how long those guys have been peddling Semtex. The FBI needs to find out who's been buying it and try to recover as much as it can."

"That's all true, but I can't see Lansing agreeing to your continued involvement. Why would he? He'll want containment at this point. Involving you further has serious consequences if it ever leaks to the press. Besides, he's got the resources of nearly thirty-one thousand employees under his command, and a budget of six billion dollars. In all honesty, he'll say he doesn't need you."

"Just like he didn't need us at the compound, or to find James Ortega?"

Holly said nothing.

"We'd prefer to have his blessing. But when it comes right down to it, we don't need his blessing. The stakes were raised when they found out who we are. One way or the other, the Bridgestones are going down."

"And you think you're the ones to do it?"

"Yeah, I do."

"Where will you look? This is a huge country; they could be anywhere."

"They're still here in Sacramento."

"You don't know that for sure," she said.

"They have unfinished business."

"Tell me you're not thinking of using yourself as bait."

"Actually, I am."

"Absolutely out of the question. You know what those guys are capable of. Suppose something went wrong and they managed to get ahold of you."

"I can take care of myself."

"I couldn't live with that on my conscience. Please promise me you won't do it. Give me your word you won't do it."

"Holly . . ."

"Your word."

He took a deep breath. "Okay, my word."

"Thank you."

"If Lansing isn't on board, will you help us? It would help if we had access to the FBI's NCIC database."

"You know I can't do that."

Nathan didn't respond.

"I'm willing to help you, but there's only so much I can do, so far I can go."

"It's okay. I understand."

She ate a pretzel and followed it with a sip of wine. "I suppose if you were to make an unofficial request, say . . . for some very specific information on a very specific individual within the NCIC system . . ."

He smiled. "Good enough."

"You understand that *officially* I said no, right?"

"Yes, absolutely. Officially you said no."

"Good. I'm glad we understand each other that I said no."

"Perfectly, the answer is no." They exchanged a smile.

"What's next?"

"Harvey and I are going to dig into the Bridgestones' backgrounds."

"May I ask what you're looking for?"

"I need access to Leonard's service record in the first Gulf War. I also want the visitation logs from the USDB at Fort Leavenworth, where Ernie served his sentence. The commandant of the Marine Corps, General Hawthorne, used to be my commanding officer."

"One of the Joint Chiefs. Wow, that's a good contact. Will he help you?"

"I think so. I've never asked him for anything before."

"How much are you going to tell him? I mean, there's still an issue with containment. The more people who know of your involvement, the more likely it is there could be a leak."

"Speaking of leaks, how *did* the Bridgestones find out about me, and about my father?"

She looked down at her glass of wine. "During their interrogation, the two techs from the van told the Bridgestones they overheard Gifford and Henning talking about you last night. They gave you up under torture, as anyone would in that situation. The Bridgestones knew everything was being recorded; they openly mocked the FBI during the torture."

He softened his tone. "Look, you've lost three people under your command: the SWAT agent at the compound and the two surveillance guys. Four, if you include James Ortega. I didn't mean to sound callous."

"It was horrible. I've never heard men scream in pain like that before."

"Holly, I'm really sorry about all of this."

"It's not your fault."

Nathan didn't respond.

She lowered her voice. "I don't want to be alone tonight. Do you?"

"Got a comfortable couch?"

"Very. I can't tell you how many times I've awoken on it in the morning still fully dressed."

"I don't doubt it," he said.

"Come on; let's get out of here."

"I should call Harv. He worries about me. I need to tell him the Bridgestones know about us. Do you mind?"

"No, of course not."

Nathan pulled his cell from his hip and the Hyatt's business card from his front pocket. "Room six twenty-seven, please . . . Thanks . . . Harv, it's me. . . . Yeah, I'm okay. . . . No, I'm with Holly. . . . Just down the street. The Bridgestones know about us, my father too. . . . They wrung it out of the two surveillance techs. The techs overheard Gifford and Henning talking about us last night. . . . Everything was recorded. The machines in the van were running when they grabbed them." Nathan mouthed the word *sorry* to Holly. She mouthed, *It's okay*, back. "Yeah, she's right here. Okay." Nathan pressed the speaker button and keyed the volume down to a whisper. "Okay, you're on speaker." Nathan set the phone down and they both leaned toward it.

"Hello, Holly."

"Hi, Harvey."

"Holly, I'm really sorry about this situation, with you losing two more of your people."

"Thank you."

"But I need to know exactly what the techs said."

"I listened to it; I can tell you."

"I need it word for word. I can't rely on your memory for something this important. I need *every word*."

Nathan mouthed *sorry* again. She shook her head at him. "Under the circumstances, I think it's a reasonable request. I'll make a copy for you."

"I need it fast. Tonight, if possible."

"Harv," Nathan said, "It's almost one in the morning. There's no one there to do it. I don't think we need to wake up one of Holly's gizmo nerds at one in the morning."

She mouthed, *Gizmo nerds?*

"First thing in the morning, okay?" Harvey said. "I don't have my laptop with me, so I'll need it in either cassette or CD format. I'll buy a player at Wal-Mart or somewhere. What time does your field office open?"

Holly leaned toward the phone. "I'll have it ready by six tomorrow morning. Will that work?"

"Yes, that works."

"I'll have it couriered to the Hyatt's front desk under your name."

Harvey didn't respond.

"Harvey?" Nathan asked. "You still there?"

"Let's, ah, just use my room number."

"Understood," Holly said.

"You'll label the envelope yourself?" Harvey asked.

"Scout's honor," she said.

Another mouthed *sorry* from Nathan.

"Okay, good," Harvey said. "Then things are okay. We're all set then."

He smiled at Holly and shrugged.

"I've got you covered," she said.

"That's good; that's real good. Okay. We're all set. I'll see you in the morning."

"I'll call you at oh six thirty. Good night, partner," Nathan said.

"Okay, that's it then. Good night."

"Sorry about that," Nathan said, closing the phone. "He's a cautious man."

"I can tell. Does he have a family, a wife and kids?"

"Yes. Three sons. He's been married for almost fifteen years, but he's not worried about his family. If I know Harv, he's already paging the office and arranging for two of our best guys to be here first thing in the morning. If I called back right now, the line would be busy."

"He's bringing in bodyguards?"

"He worries about me. Ever since our last mission he's been superprotective. To be perfectly honest, overly so, to the point of being annoying at times. Even though the Bridgestones have my name, there's no information on me in any computer system they could access. Even if they had a high-level contact in the DOD, they still couldn't access my file. I'm surprised you were able to get it. Speaking of, how *did* you get it?"

"I didn't; Larry Gifford did. I didn't ask how."

"I'll have to grill him about that. He must be a resourceful guy."

"He is. If I had to speculate, he probably used your father's influence."

"Yeah, that would do it," Nathan agreed. "Anyway, back to Harvey. I rarely give him a hard time about being overprotective, and when I do he shrugs it off. His picture's in the encyclopedia under *cloak-and-dagger*."

"It's his training; it'll always be with him. Yours, too."

"I'm afraid so."

"Would he be as concerned if there wasn't . . . interrogation involved? Torture?"

"Probably."

Despite Holly's protest, Nathan paid for their drinks. At her Explorer Nathan asked if she still wanted him to drive. Because of the glass of wine, she said yes. Legally she wasn't drunk, but because of her position in the FBI, discretion was the better part of valor. He agreed and tucked her into the passenger seat. Out of the corner of his eye he noticed that Holly kept checking her side mirror, looking for anyone who might be following them. As they wound their way through the deserted streets of downtown Sacramento, Nathan did the same using the rearview mirror. *Two peas in a pod*, he thought.

Holly's home was in a planned residential neighborhood with neatly landscaped yards. As he approached her driveway, she leaned across him and hit the button on the remote attached to the Explorer's visor. He held his breath as her left breast brushed across his chest. For a few seconds their faces were inches apart. *Oh, man . . . She did that on purpose.* There was plenty of room to avoid contact. Besides, he could've triggered the garage door opener; all she had to do was ask. . . . He pulled the SUV into her garage and killed the engine. This time Holly waited while he climbed out and opened her door. She punched a six-digit number into the keypad by the door, and the blinking red LED changed to solid green. Once inside, Holly rearmed the system and turned on some lights.

"Nice," Nathan said, looking around. Her kitchen was spotless, cleaner than his, which was saying a lot. Either she didn't spend a lot of time in here, or she was obsessive about tidiness. He suspected it was a combination of both. The blue granite countertops were a perfect complement to the dark cherry cabinets. In the family room, mission-style furniture was arranged at right angles to a big-screen television. Several limited-edition prints of Wyland's seascapes adorned the walls. He recognized one of them—a pod of orcas—because the original oil was in his La Jolla home. No need to mention that.

She set her purse down on the counter. "I don't have any

nonalcoholic beer, but I've got a pitcher of tea in the refrigerator. Glasses are in the upper cabinet on the right side of the dishwasher." She disappeared down a hall on the right. "I'll be right back."

"I like your home."

"Thank you. Make yourself comfortable. I'm going to check phone messages and e-mail."

*Married to the job*, he thought. He grabbed two glasses from the cabinet, the pitcher from the fridge, and poured himself and Holly some tea. He settled onto the couch in the living room and stared at the blank television screen. He closed his eyes. Sleep would come easily right now. He thought about Holly and her brush against him in the car. Had it been an overture, an invitation? He supposed it could've been a mistake, but in his experience women were acutely aware of that type of contact. It didn't take much to send the wrong signal to men. He wasn't presumptuous enough to believe she had given him a green light for anything more than a snooze on the couch, which was looking more and more likely the longer he sat here with his eyes closed.

What an incredible twenty-four hours it had been. He ran the events through his mind. The helicopter ride into Sacramento. The ride out to the farmhouse. Henning's challenging and arrogant attitude. The Bridgestones' cousins' dog-and-pony show under interrogation. The buried cash. The long ride into the mountains with Holly. James Ortega's charred body. The SWAT raid at the farmhouse. The second tunnel. The dead surveillance techs and cousins. And the Bridgestones' knowledge of Nathan's involvement. What else might they know? He sighed. The four hours of sleep he'd gotten earlier this afternoon seemed like decades ago. . . .

## Chapter Ten

"Nathan?" The voice seemed distant. Tinny. As if coming from an echo chamber. He looked around suddenly. Holly's living room. She was standing a few feet away, staring at him.

"How long?" he asked.

"Fifteen minutes."

"Fifteen minutes, not too deep. I guess I didn't realize how tired I was. Sorry."

"No need to apologize. I checked on you ten minutes ago and saw you'd dozed off. I didn't want to wake you. I have a spare bedroom if you want a real bed."

He waved a hand at the floor. "Do you care if I stretch out in here?"

"What, on the floor?"

He shrugged.

"Are you sure? It's no trouble setting you up in the spare bedroom."

"I'm good right here, thanks."

"At least let me put some blankets down; that wood is like concrete." She returned half a minute later with an armful of blankets and a quilt.

Nathan picked up the coffee table and moved it aside—he didn't want to drag it across the oak floor. He helped her spread the blankets out.

"Do you sleep on the floor very often?"

"I usually end up there by morning, so I may as well start there."

"Your dreams?"

He nodded. "It's just something I've gotten used to over the years. It's no big deal."

"I know I keep coming back to it, but I've never met anyone like you before."

"I'm just a guy."

"No, you aren't 'just a guy.' . . . Trust me on that."

"We had a hell of a day, didn't we?"

She took a step forward and took his hand. "Yes, we did. It
doesn't have to end just yet. . . ."

"No, I suppose it doesn't."

An hour later, after Nathan had fallen asleep, Holly staggered
up from the floor and gathered her strewn clothes. Her body
still tingling, she padded down the hall, being careful not to
make any noise. He looked so at peace. She wondered if he
was truly asleep. The screams of her surveillance techs still
fresh in her mind, she couldn't begin to imagine the horrors
he'd endured at the hands of his sadistic captors in Nicaragua.
When he'd removed his shirt, her breath had caught at seeing
the crisscrossing network of scars on his chest and back. Despite how he thought of himself, Nathan McBride *was* a truly
remarkable man. He'd been so aware of her needs during
their lovemaking. Granted, there hadn't been many others—
she could count them on one hand—but hands down, he'd
been the best lover she'd ever experienced, and she sensed he
hadn't been with many others either. Encouraged that they'd
connected on an emotional level, she hoped there might be a
future for them. But given their situations, their professions,
and the distance separating them, she doubted it could work
long-term. One or the other would have to relocate, and possibly give up the life he or she had built. She toyed with the
idea of transferring to San Diego, but she liked being a special
agent in charge of a major field office, and she was sure the
same opportunity would not be available in San Diego for
some time. Such openings were extremely rare, and she felt
fortunate to have been promoted to Sacramento's top position. *At least we'll always have something special between us*, she
thought, tucking herself into bed. Nathan was right; it *had*

been one hell of a day. She closed her eyes, and five minutes later she was gone.

Holly awoke with a start. What was that sound? Had an animal somehow gotten into the house? She reached for her gun, but her hand froze an inch from its cold form. She heard a muffled moan, followed by a hissing and spitting sound. No, not an animal. Human. She tore the sheets away and hurried down the hall. In the living room she dimmed the overhead light before flipping the switch. *Oh, dear Lord, Nathan!* His hair plastered to his head, he was covered in sweat, moaning and waving his hands in front of his face at invisible demons. He issued a howl that sent a shiver through her body. *He's there, in Nicaragua, being tortured.* She remembered something he'd said on the ride up to the cabin, that he'd put a girlfriend in the hospital for waking him up, but how could she let this go on? Would he wake up on his own? She took several steps back and called his name from the opposite side of the couch.

"Nathan." No response. She said it louder: "Nathan." Nothing. What should she do? She couldn't let this go on. Steeling herself, she yelled his name: *"Nathan!"*

His eyes snapped open and found her, wild with anger. He gritted his teeth, a growl escaping his lips. He jumped to his feet and assumed a low fighting stance, his hand clutching an invisible knife.

"Nathan, it's me!"

His eyes darted around the room and returned to hers. Her instincts told her to back away, but she held perfectly still. "Nathan?" Then his face changed to recognition. She rushed around the sofa and wrapped him up in her arms, ignoring the sticky feel of his skin. They held each other for several moments without speaking.

His voice cracked. "What time is it?"

"Just after four in the morning. You okay?"

He nodded. "I'm really thirsty."

"I'll get some water."

She returned a few seconds later and handed it to him. He downed it in a single pull. "The moths came for me again."

They settled onto the floor facing each other.

"Moths?"

"In Nicaragua they put a bright light in my face at night. The moths were attracted to it. My hands were tied. I couldn't bat them away."

"That's horrible."

"Thanks for the water."

She could see he was still trembling.

"I'm okay."

But he wasn't okay; an echo of terror was still etched on his face. She reached over and held his hand.

He half-chuckled. "I'm sorry you had to see that. I was hoping for a night off."

"Hey, there's no need to apologize about anything."

He looked down at himself. "I think I need a shower."

"Come on." She led him down the hall to the guest bathroom. "You want some company in there?"

"Is there a mustache in Mexico?"

She laughed, hardly believing how good it felt. "I'll take that for a yes."

After their shower, there wasn't any merit in trying to fall back asleep; even if they wanted to, neither of them could. Holly scrambled some eggs and made toast. After breakfast Holly rinsed the dishes and put them in the dishwasher. Nathan noticed the machine was empty, looking as though it had never been used. Lots of takeout, he suspected. After she retired to her bedroom to get dressed, Nathan folded the blankets from the living room floor and stacked them on the couch. Ten minutes later they were both ready to go.

She dropped Nathan off at the Hyatt just before five in the morning. "I'll make sure Harvey has a copy of the tape before six."

"You've got another long day ahead of you," he said.

"Will you keep me informed of your progress?"

"You know I will."

"Nathan . . . about this morning . . ."

"It's okay."

She smiled. "I'll call you later."

"Stay safe, Special Agent in Charge Holly Simpson."

She smiled again and pulled away from the curb. He waved when she looked in her mirror. With a spring in his step, he strode through the lobby and rode the elevator to floor six. Harvey would already be up, so he knocked quietly on his door. He saw the peephole darken just before the door swung inward.

"Mornin', partner," Nathan said, passing across the threshold. "Get much sleep?"

"A few hours." Harvey grinned. "You?"

"Almost none."

"Attaboy."

"Hey, it was all in the line of duty."

"Uh-huh."

"Holly just dropped me off; she's heading over to the office to make sure you have the tape by six."

"I hope I wasn't too, ah, you know, overbearing last night about wanting to hear the tape."

"You, overbearing?"

"I made some coffee. It's not too bad."

"So who are you bringing up from San Diego?"

Harvey handed him a cup. "You can't blame me. It's better to be safe than sorry."

He took a sip. "Hey, partner, I'm totally on board with it."

"We've got a long day ahead of us. It's after eight back east, so we should make that call to General Hawthorne. It might take him a few hours to get the visitation logs from the Castle. You still want that chat with FBI director Lansing?"

"Yeah, I do."

"I thought as much. He wasn't real happy about it, but

Ortega's arranged it for you. He sounded like he's worried about being blacklisted from the investigation. Now that James has been found, he probably will be. You've got a *very* brief window at ten hundred this morning." Harvey winked. "I've been instructed to tell you to lose the phone number after you make the call. It's a direct line to Lansing's secretary; she'll put you through to his cell phone. He's in New York City today."

"Good work."

"What do you hope to accomplish?"

"I want a get-out-of-jail-free card."

Harvey just stared.

"We're going after the Bridgestones," Nathan said, "with or without his blessing, and we don't operate within socially acceptable boundaries. Let's face it, Harv: We're no Ozzie-and-Harriet team. If we have to kick a few butts along the way, so be it. I just want the FBI to stay out of our way."

"Lansing will want us to stay out of *his* way. I don't think he'll agree to what you're asking."

"Since blackmailing him is out of the question, he definitely won't agree. I just don't want him running interference. Tailing us. Tapping our phones. You know the drill."

"You really think he'd do that?"

"Yeah, I do."

"What about Frank Ortega?" Harvey asked. "How much do we tell him about what we're doing?"

"As little as possible."

"Because of your father?"

"Yes."

"Ortega could still help us. I don't think he's been blacklisted yet, and Greg could access the NCIC database for us."

"I've already got that covered."

"Hasn't Holly risked enough for us? Why involve her further if we don't need to? Greg has access to nearly everything she does."

"*Nearly* being the operative word."

"Beyond access to the NCIC, what else would we need?"

Nathan sipped his coffee and said nothing.

"You want her to get the credit if we catch them."

Nathan didn't answer.

"The reverse is also true. She could take the fall if we screw up."

"We aren't going to screw up."

"A lot of things could go wrong, Nathan."

"Lansing's people are not going to collar the Bridgestones before we do. To steal a line from General Patton, I'm going to beat that gentleman to Messina."

## ⊕ Chapter Eleven

Several thousand yards from his destination, Leonard Bridgestone pulled an old gray pickup behind a supermarket and parked near its loading dock. As expected, the area was deserted. Ernie pulled the stolen UPS truck next to the pickup, and together they untied the tarp covering the pickup's bed.

Leonard helped Ernie haul the Enduro motorcycle out of the bed and get it upright on the asphalt. He checked the large ice chest strapped to its luggage rack atop the rear fender. All secure. He squinted as his brother gave the ice chest a soft caress before pulling a ten-foot-long, three-by-six piece of lumber from the bed of the pickup. Leonard followed him to the rear of the UPS truck and hoisted its roll-up door. Bound and unconscious, the driver was stripped down to his underwear. Although the driver's uniform didn't fit Leonard perfectly, it was close enough. Ernie slid the three-by-six in next to the driver. Shaped by a table saw, two of its squared edges were cut at forty-five-degree angles along its length so it could be easily driven over when the time came. The bottom of the three-by-six also had a V-shaped channel cut along its entire length.

"Are we sure about this?" Leonard asked. "It's not too late to call it off."

"Of course we're sure; they killed Sammy."

"This won't bring him back."

Ernie frowned. "What, you having second thoughts?"

"Getting out of the country is going to be a lot more difficult."

"Shit, we'll get out. Is that your only reason?"

Leonard didn't like the accusatory tone. "Do I have to spell it out for you? Use your fucking head, Ernie. This is a huge thing with huge consequences."

"Hey, take it easy. I didn't mean nothing by it."

"Once we do this, there's no turning back. You know that."

"I know," Ernie said.

"Do you really? Do you have any idea? I wonder. . . ."

"We already talked about this."

"Well, we're talking again."

"So talk."

Seeing it was hopeless, Leonard slammed the roll-up door down and latched it. "Let's just do this before I change my mind." He retrieved a helmet with a dark visor from the front seat of the pickup and handed it to his brother. Ernie pulled it on, swung his leg over the motorcycle, and pressed the starter button. Its four-stroke motor hummed to life in a deep-throated rumble. His brother nodded approval. Leonard climbed into the UPS truck, fired it up, and pulled away from the loading dock, heading for Kern Parkway. He was sorely tempted to drive in the opposite direction and never look back. He thought back to the raid at the compound and had to admit that seeing Sammy's lifeless eyes staring into space had hammered him. His youngest brother, someone he'd sworn to insulate and protect, was dead. Murdered by a sniper—and a damned good one at that. Leonard hadn't wanted to involve Sammy in the first place, but Ernie had talked him into it. He should've known better, should've known something like this would happen. And now they were about to raise the stakes a thousandfold.

Forcing his mind back to the task at hand, he merged into traffic. In the side mirror he watched his brother gun the motorcycle's engine to keep up. Leonard scanned the traffic in both directions, looking for cops. Where was a cop when you really needed one? he mused. At Kirkland Avenue he made a right turn smoothly—not too fast, not too slow. At Delano Avenue he turned right again and slowed, paralleling a multistory concrete block–and–glass building about the size of a football field. Behind him, Ernie pulled over to the curb and stopped. At the far end of Delano Avenue Leonard maneuvered the brown delivery truck into a driveway and rolled to a stop at a guard shack with an automatic gate.

His hand on the butt of his gun, a security guard, sharply dressed in a blue uniform, came out of the shack and approached the UPS truck.

"Where's Malcolm?" the guard asked. Then he smiled. "Too many beers last night?"

"Couldn't say," Leonard said, smiling. "Probably got a case of the flu."

"Yeah, it's been going around lately. Since I've never seen you before, I'll have to ask for some ID."

"No problem, glad to do it." Keeping his head down so the bill of his cap covered his face, Leonard climbed out and walked around the front of the truck. A few more paces and he'd be out of the camera's line of sight. Before the guard could react, he pulled a forty-five automatic from his jacket and pressed it into the guard's belly. "Open the gate and you'll live to see another day." In one smooth movement he removed the guard's gun, shoved him back toward the shack's entrance, and pushed him through its open door. Staggering backward, the guard lost his balance and fell with a grunt.

Leonard jammed the barrel of his automatic into the guard's mouth and pushed until the man's head met the cabinet under the counter. "Open the gate right now."

When the guard didn't move, Leonard stomped on the guard's left hand with the heel of his boot. Fingers crunched. The guard howled and bit down on the blue steel lodged in his mouth.

Chips of teeth flew.

"Open the gate."

"Uurr cuhh ohhhnen itth rohh heer."

Leonard yanked the gun from the guard's mouth and pressed it against his forehead.

"I can't open it from here; they have to do it from inside!"

Leonard's mind raced with possibilities, all of them bad. Precious seconds were ticking by. "Tell them there's a UPS delivery out here with a package for Special Agent in Charge Holly Simpson. I'll blow your brains out the back of your head if you try anything cute." He nodded to the picture sitting on the counter of two girls in pigtails. They looked like twins, around six or seven years old. "Nice-looking girls," Leonard said. "Yours?"

That message got through loud and clear. As if a switch had been thrown, the guard struggled to his feet and picked up the phone. He waited a few seconds. "UPS," he said, but that was *all* he said.

Leonard squinted.

The guard held up his good hand, indicating *Wait, don't shoot.* After a few more seconds the guard replaced the handset into its cradle. Leonard heard the whine of an electric motor. Through the shack's rear window he saw Ernie's motorcycle pull behind the UPS truck. He knew his brother was retrieving the three-by-six piece of lumber from the back. The heavy iron gate began rolling along a large inverted-V-shaped track bolted down to the concrete. As it opened, Leonard knocked the guard unconscious with a blow to the head. Then he pulled a folded envelope from his pocket and placed it on the counter.

Being careful to stay out of the camera's line of sight, he walked around the back of the truck, where Ernie already had the three-by-six in hand. Without looking at his brother, Leonard climbed back into his seat and pulled the truck forward just inside the gate, where it blocked the camera from seeing the motorcycle behind its rear bumper. With the gate fully open, he knew Ernie was setting the three-by-six down on top of the gate's V track. He gave his brother a few more seconds to climb back on the bike before driving down the driveway toward the building's front entrance. Not too fast. Not too slow. Just right. In his side mirror Leonard watched the gate attempt to close, but when it hit the three-by-six blocking its path, it stopped, seemed to ponder its situation, and opened again. Its electronic brain would repeat this process indefinitely until the obstruction was removed.

Leonard pulled the truck over to the curb in front of the building's glass facade and stopped. *Come on, Ernie; move it!*

At the main entrance Ernie coasted the bike up the curb's wheelchair ramp, killed the engine three feet from the glass doors, and lowered the motorcycle's kickstand.

*Are we really doing this?* Leonard thought. He was tempted to yell for his brother to stop, but knew Ernie would ignore him. He watched his brother slide off the bike, remove the bungee cords securing the lid, and open the ice chest. Leonard knew he was flipping the arming switch and cranking the egg timer to fifteen seconds.

*Come on, Ernie. Come on!*

Slowly Ernie walked away from the bike and climbed into the van's passenger seat. Fighting the urge to peel rubber, Leonard pulled away from the curb and started back out the driveway.

Eleven seconds.

Barely a minute had passed since their UPS truck had first appeared at the guard shack. Trembling from adrenaline, Leonard remembered to breathe. He sucked in a huge lungful of air and audibly blew it out. Quite literally, there was no turning back now.

Seven seconds.

Unconsciously Leonard pressed the gas pedal a little harder than he needed to. The truck's engine roared as he accelerated down the driveway. Out of the corner of his eye, he watched Ernie remove his helmet, lean forward slightly, and stare into the side mirror.

Three seconds.

*Mother of God, what are we doing?* In his own side mirror, Leonard saw a man in a business suit step through the glass doors. The man looked at the motorcycle, then scanned the area for its rider.

"Adios amigo," Ernie said.

The man vanished in a blinding flash.

One second he was there.

The next, he wasn't.

Forty pounds of Semtex quite literally vaporized him.

A huge mushroom of fire and smoke roiled skyward, looking as though a small nuke had detonated.

The blast wave accelerated through the glass facade with hideous results.

Traveling at five miles per second, superheated carbon oxide gas separated human flesh from bone, instantly incinerating both. Within twenty feet, the force tore arms and legs from torsos. At thirty feet entire bodies flew. Necks snapped. Eardrums ruptured. Skin peeled. At forty feet, people were slammed into the walls of their cubicles like rag dolls, knocked lifeless from the force of the shock wave. And at fifty feet those who weren't dead were dying.

A chilling silence ensued, broken only by the hiss of a few fire sprinklers, the crackling of flames, and the soft moans of those still clinging to life.

Flat on her back, a woman with no sense of her body stared at the charred ceiling tiles as a fine mist rained down on her. She tried to move her right arm to cover her eyes, but it wasn't there. Her life ended thirty seconds later.

Choking and coughing, a man in a shredded business suit crawled on his hands and knees across the debris field, heading for the far end of the building, where children were screaming in the day-care area.

# ⊕ Chapter Twelve

Nathan glanced at Harvey while his call went through.

"Director Lansing's office."

"Hello, this is Nathan McBride. The director's expecting my call."

"One moment please, Mr. McBride. I'll put you through."

The line went silent, totally and utterly silent. No clicks, no electronic buzz, no crackling. Nothing. He was about to hang up, thinking he'd been disconnected, when a man's voice came on the line.

"This is FBI director Ethan Lansing; am I speaking with Nathan McBride?"

"Yes."

"What can I do for you, Mr. McBride?"

"I have you on speaker, Director Lansing. Harvey Fontana is with me. Are we being recorded?"

"Yes."

"Will you reconsider, please?"

"I'll tell you what, Mr. McBride. Because of who your father is, and because he's also a friend of mine, I'll agree to keep this conversation off the record. Hold the line, please."

Once again Nathan found himself listening to complete silence. Coming through the hotel room's window he heard the muffled whine of a siren, followed by the staccato blast of a fire truck's air horn. A few seconds later Director Lansing was back.

"Now that we're off the record, I'll also agree to keep this conversation private because you and Mr. Fontana saved the lives of a dozen of our Joint Terrorism Task Force SWAT team agents. You're owed a debt of gratitude for that. I'll also thank both of you for your military service to our country."

Nathan knew he was being buttered up. "I appreciate your saying that. May I ask how much you know of our past?"

"All of it."

"I assumed as much. . . . I know you're a busy man, so I'll get to the point. We want a green light to pursue the Bridge-stone brothers."

"I see. As private citizens, you're entitled to do that provided you conduct yourselves within the confines of the law."

"Director Lansing, may I speak freely?"

"You may."

Nathan frowned at a second siren outside. From the window Harvey shrugged. "Circumstances may dictate a certain amount of flexibility. You're aware of how we found Frank Ortega's grandson?"

"Yes, I've had a complete briefing."

"I'm asking for a temporary extension of that flexibility."

"If I understand what you're asking for, then you must know that as a sworn law enforcement officer, I can't agree to it. I did not approve the interrogation of those individuals at the farmhouse outside Sacramento, and I'm disappointed it took place."

"Director Lansing, I'm not recording this call either; you have my word. No one was seriously hurt at the farmhouse."

"That's beside the point, Mr. McBride. This isn't Nicaragua or the former Soviet Union, and you aren't part of a covert ops team anymore. You're a civilian now, governed by the laws of our land. The Constitution isn't just a piece of paper; it's a fundamental building block of who we are as a society. It defines us."

*The man's a politician,* Nathan thought. *Of course he is—he has to be; it goes with the territory.* Forcing himself to relax his grip on the phone, Nathan continued. "Frank Ortega's wife said something to me, and I agreed with it. She told me she doesn't look at the world through rose-colored glasses."

"Diane is a fine woman, and I don't disagree with her from a philosophical perspective. But what you're talking about is a very slippery slope. One digression could be regarded as a mistake; two is a pattern. I want containment at this point; involving you further has considerable risks. Can you imagine the fallout if this ever leaked? The FBI can't afford that kind of coverage from the media. We're already under the microscope with the presidential-powers issue of wiretapping suspected Al-Qaeda operatives."

"Based on everything you know about my past, I'm asking you to trust me, to trust my judgment. I'm not indiscriminate."

"For what it's worth, I do trust you, but that's also beside the point. I'm sorry, but I can't agree to what you're asking. I cannot, and will not, sanction your continued involvement. Don't get me wrong—I'm grateful for your help to this point, but that's as far as it goes. You're a smart man; you know why I've taken this position." There was a pause on the other end. "Hold the line, Mr. McBride."

Nathan looked at Harvey. "What's going on out there?"

"Something big. I just saw another fire truck speed through an intersection, followed by two police cruisers."

Lansing came back on the line. "I've got to go, Mr. Bride. We've got an emergency situation."

"What's happening?"

"There's been an explosion at our Sacramento field office." The line went dead.

*Oh, please, dear Lord, no. Not the missing Semtex!* Nathan's thoughts went to Holly. A horrible image flashed through his mind: Was she dead? Worse than dead? He saw her burned, broken, and bleeding body. He grabbed the note with Holly's phone number from the nightstand and dialed. It was ringing! More than once. That was enough to give him hope that she hadn't been there, that she might be okay.

*Come on. Come on. Answer. Answer the phone!*

The line connected and a man's voice spoke. "Hello?"

"This is Special Agent Nathan McBride calling for Special Agent in Charge Holly Simpson." Nathan heard the whine of a siren in the background.

"We didn't know her identity. She's unconscious. She's en route to Sutter's emergency room."

"What's her condition?"

"Critical. She's got multiple fractures to her legs, one compound. She's got second- and third-degree burns. Probably bleeding internally. Both her shoulders are separated. We've got her stabilized, but her head trauma is our biggest concern. Who is this again? We'll need to notify her family."

"I'll take care of it." Nathan hung up the phone. He turned toward Harvey. "She's being taken to Sutter's emergency room in critical condition."

"I'm sorry, Nathan."

"Can you handle our guys when they arrive from San Diego? Get them set up?"

"Yeah, no problem."

"Will you call the bell desk and make sure there's a cab ready at the curb?"

"No problem."

"I'm sorry to dump this on you, Harv."

"I got you covered. Go on, get out of here."

Special Agent Bruce Henning's expression turned dark as Nathan strode into Sutter's emergency room. The man wasn't immaculate anymore, far from it. He looked like he'd been dragged by rope down a dirt road.

"What the hell are *you* doing here, McBride?"

"Where's Holly?"

Henning didn't answer.

Nathan took a step toward him. "Where is she?"

"Upstairs in ICU. Hey, where're you going?"

"I don't have time for you, Henning."

"You can't go up there."

"Watch me." He approached a nurse who was running toward the ER doors.

"Where's ICU?" Nathan asked.

"Third floor." The nurse pushed through the dual swinging doors. Nathan had a brief look inside. Doctors. Nurses. Blood.

"Damn it, McBride. Wait!"

"You coming, Special Agent Henning?"

The fed stepped into the elevator. "You've got a lot a nerve barging in here like this."

"Save your resentment for someone who gives a shit."

"I should arrest your sorry ass."

Nathan squared with him. "You're welcome to try."

At the third floor the elevator chimed, and the doors opened to a horrific scene. Directly ahead was the nurses' station—abandoned. Several dozen gurneys containing the wounded lined the perimeter of the room. The floor was tracked and smudged with blood. What was normally a quiet place had been transformed into a battlefield triage unit. Physicians, paramedics, and nurses were hovering over the injured, and from the look of things, many of them were critical. It was plainly evident that there weren't enough doctors and nurses to deal with the situation. The moans of pain, mixed with the electronic beeping of the monitoring machines, sounded forlorn and eerie. A uniformed officer stationed just inside the room looked ashen, his expression grim. He stepped toward Nathan and Henning, but when the FBI man flashed his badge, the officer nodded and turned away.

On the far side of the room a doctor leaning over a wounded woman looked over his shoulder and yelled, "I need help over here."

No one came; clearly no one was free.

Nathan sprinted across the vinyl floor. "What do you need?" He looked at the woman's arm where a twelve-inch gash had laid it open, exposing muscle and tendons. The skin surrounding the wound was charred and blistered. Blood was pooling on the sheets of the gurney.

"Who are you?" In his mid-fifties and balding, the doctor wore protective goggles over rimless eyeglasses. Nathan towered over him by a good twelve inches.

"I've got field medic training; tell me what you need."

"Throw on some gloves. Behind you on the counter. Nurses' station."

Nathan ran over and grabbed a pair of light green latex gloves from the box and pulled them on.

"When I pull the biceps aside, I need you to clamp the brachial artery as close to the tear as you can. The tear's just above the radial and ulnar branch. I'm pinching it closed right now." The doctor looked at the mobile table containing instruments. "Shit, use the hemostats; they're all I've got. You'll need to sponge the blood first. Ready?"

"Yes," Nathan said.

With his free hand the doctor reached into the woman's arm just above the elbow, grabbed a handful of muscle, and pulled it aside. "Sponge," he said.

Aware of Henning's presence behind him, Nathan pressed the sponges into the opening and watched the blood soak into them. He knew he had mere seconds to get the artery clamped before more blood would overflow the sponges and fill the cavity. "I see it," he said, opening the hemostats. He inserted the tool into the wound and applied the needlelike pliers just above the tear in the artery.

"Not too tight," the doctor said. "One click."

"One click," Nathan repeated. He pinched the hemostat to its first locking setting.

The doctor released the muscle from his thumb-and-forefinger grip. "Good job."

Nathan removed the sponges without being told and set them on the table.

The doctor let the muscle slide back into place overlying the pinching end of the hemostat. He removed the tourniquet. "That artery will have to be repaired where it's clamped. Crushing it with a hemostat makes it susceptible to clotting at the crush point, but it's the lesser of two evils. It's better to damage the artery and repair it later than for her to lose the arm."

"How long can you leave it that way?" Nathan asked.

"Not very long; alchemic time for muscle is two hours, max. We have to add the tourniquet time to the clamp time, so she'll need a vascular surgeon within ninety minutes at the outside. Problem is, she's tied up downstairs in the ER. We need to repeat this procedure for the other end of the tear to prevent back-bleeding from collateral artery pressure. You ready?"

"Yes."

"Okay, I'm going to pull the biceps aside again. Use another pair of hemostats on the other side of the tear. Clamp it as close to the tear as you can. Get ready with a sponge again. Here we go."

Nathan had no trouble clamping the lower end of the tear—the bleeding was much less severe—but as the doctor had known, the lower end of the tear had been oozing blood from back pressure.

"Okay. I need you to wrap up this wound with gauze fairly tight, but not too tight. Don't worry about the hemostats. Just leave them where they are and work around them. Shave the area around her head wound, clean it up, and lay gauze over it, untaped. Try to keep her hair out of the cut. Keep an eye on her IV. She'll need another bag of saline in a few minutes. Can you stick around until more of our people arrive?"

"You got it. No problem."

"I appreciate your help." The doctor looked Nathan's face over. "Looks like you've had some trauma yourself."

"A little bit."

"Do you know how to hook up an intracranial pressure monitor?"

"I'm afraid not."

"Don't worry about it. Just do what you can." As the doctor moved on to the next gurney, Nathan went to work wrapping her arm.

"That's Special Agent Ashley Banks," Henning whispered.
"Find me a bag of saline."

The man didn't move.

"Henning!"

"Yeah . . . okay, I'll be right back."

For the next twenty minutes Nathan went through a dozen pairs of gloves assisting other doctors, nurses, and EMTs. He and Henning spent most of their time acting as gofers, bringing monitoring machines, medical instruments, and bandages to the doctors and nurses who called for them. He kept looking for Holly, but she wasn't there. She must be undergoing emergency surgery. *Yeah, that has to be it. They're operating on her right now, at this very moment.* He wasn't willing to distract anyone by asking. Now wasn't the time, and no one up here would know her status anyway. *Stay busy*, he told himself. *Stay focused.*

As each minute passed, more of the hospital's staff arrived. By the time Nathan felt some sense of sanity had returned to the room, the ICU had close to fifty doctors and nurses attending the wounded. Nathan deeply respected the dedicated people working there. Although he'd been helping for only a short time, he felt drained, as though hours had passed, not minutes. Most of the victims were burned to one degree or another, some severely, and the smell of charred flesh permeated the room. Nathan was no stranger to the sight of blood—he'd seen plenty—but Henning was another matter. All things considered, the fed had managed to hold himself together pretty well.

Senator Stonewall McBride was on the phone in his office when he heard a knock. He covered the mouthpiece. "Come in."

Heidi, his secretary, entered and handed him a note: *Leaf Watson holding on line two: SUPER URGENT.* He nodded and she left the room, closing the door behind her.

Stone continued with his call. "Look, Scott, I can't promise a yea vote yet. I haven't read the entire bill. As long as the bacon's not raw, I don't see a major problem. Give me another day or two. What are the latest poll numbers on it? . . . Well, that's something. Listen, I've got to go. Two days, max . . . Okay, let's do lunch soon. . . . Take care." *Lobbyists*, he thought. He punched line two. "Hello, Leaf."

"Turn on your television."

"Which channel?"

"Any of them."

A knot wrenched his stomach. He grabbed the remote, swiveled around in his chair, and pressed the power button. The FOX News Channel filled the screen. The image was taken from a helicopter orbiting high overhead. Dozens of emergency vehicles, with their red and blue lights flashing, lined the streets surrounding a two-story building with a gaping hole in its side. Smoke belched from the opening. Above the damaged structure, a black column climbed a mile into the sky. Booms from ladder trucks were spraying jets of water into the open gash and onto the rooftop.

Stone turned up the volume.

He caught Shepard Smith in midsentence: ". . . know so far. A bomb has been detonated in the Sacramento field office of the FBI. We have no information on the number of people killed or wounded. From what local authorities have indicated, this is clearly an act of terrorism and not an accidental explosion. We don't know if it's Al-Qaeda- or Hezbollah-related. We do know the bomb was detonated very close to ten a.m., Pacific time. . . ."

"Get everyone in here right now," Stone said.

"They're already on the way."

Heidi knocked again and entered without waiting for an invitation.

"It's the president," she said. "Line three."

"Leaf, I want a chemical analysis on the material we seized in California. Find out if it matches this new bombing. Make it happen fast. I'll call Quantico and tell them to expect your call." Stone disconnected by punching the button for his other line. "Mr. President."

"Stone, I need a briefing as soon as you have anything."

"Yes, Mr. President, you'll get it."

"What's your initial assessment. Is it Al-Qaeda or Hezbollah?"

"I don't think so. I have no way of confirming it, but my instincts tell me it's related to the raid we made in California several days ago. I don't think it's a coincidence the FBI was targeted, or that the bombing occurred in Sacramento. I think this is revenge-driven, sir."

"Anything you need?"

"Time. My people are doing a bomb-residue analysis as we speak. I think we'll find it's a match to the seized cache of Semtex."

"When will you know for sure if it's a match?"

One thing Stone knew when dealing with the president— never, *ever* bullshit the man. If you didn't know, say so. "I don't know."

"I don't need to tell you the repercussions of this, Stone, especially after our press conference regarding the Semtex raid yesterday. This is getting wall-to-wall coverage on every major network."

"No, Mr. President, you don't. I'm on it."

"Call me as soon as you know for sure; I'll make sure you're put through. We need to be one hundred percent sure."

"Understood."

The president never said good-bye in the conventional sense. When the conversation was over he'd just hang up. Well, this conversation was over, because the line went dead.

Stone punched the intercom button. "Heidi, put me through to Kevin Ramsland at Quantico's materials lab right away. If he's not in his office, have him paged and hold on the line until they find him. See if you can get FBI director Lansing on the phone, but the Ramsland call takes priority."

Stone frowned. Larry Gifford worked in the Sacramento field office. Stone's frown deepened when he realized Nathan also remained in the area. Though seldom used, his son's phone number was one of his twenty-five speed-dial presets.

Just before he dialed Nathan's number, Heidi's voice came through the intercom. "I have Kevin Ramsland on line one."

Stone punched the line and picked up the handset. "Mr. Ramsland, thank you for taking my call."

"No problem, Senator."

"My man Leaf Watson needs a bomb-residue analysis ASAP. Can you see to it personally?"

"Yes, absolutely. I've already called down to the lab. We're just waiting for the trace to arrive."

"How long will it take once you have it?"

"For the best result, we'll detonate a small sample and compare it to the trace from Sacramento. It shouldn't take more than an hour once we have it. Can you get someone to fly the samples out here personally? That would save a bunch of time."

"I'll get to work on it right away."

"Who did this, Senator?"

"I'm not one hundred percent sure, but I've got a pretty good idea."

"I'm beyond angry."

"Channel the anger, Mr. Ramsland. Stay focused. I'll call you back about the courier."

"We're ready over here."

Stone hit the intercom button. "Any luck reaching Lansing?"

"He's on the phone," Heidi answered. "His secretary promised a callback within fifteen minutes."

"Okay, that's good. Call Leaf back. Ask him to get a copy of any security video taken from the Sacramento field office. Tell him to have a sample of the Semtex recovered at Freedom's Echo and a sample of the bomb residue from the Sacramento field office flown over to Quantico by an FBI courier right away. First available flight. I want those Semtex samples flown directly into Quantico's airfield within five hours. I don't care if the courier has to be strapped into the backseat of an Air National Guard F-15E Strike Eagle and refueled in midair, if that's what it takes."

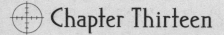 # Chapter Thirteen

Nathan's cell woke him. He immediately scanned his surroundings, unsure where he was. The ER's waiting room. Having confirmed that Holly had survived but remained in surgery, Nathan had planted himself and promptly fallen asleep. He glanced at his watch. Four hours. Sitting directly across from him, Bruce Henning had also dozed off, but Nathan's phone had awakened him as well. The LCD indicated a restricted number.

"Hello?"

"Mr. McBride?"

"Who's calling?"

"This is FBI director Ethan Lansing."

Nathan didn't respond.

"Are you there, Mr. McBride?"

"Yes."

"You've got your green light. Don't do anything until we talk again."

"Understood."

The line went dead.

Henning stretched. "Holly came to. She needed emergency surgery to relieve pressure on her brain. She asked to talk to you when you woke up."

"How is she?"

"Not so good. She's been in and out of consciousness for the last hour. They've got her pumped full of morphine."

"Her burns, how severe are they?"

"How do you know about that?"

"I called her cell phone. The paramedic answered it on the way to the hospital."

"They're mostly on her legs and back. Not too bad, considering where she was. The doctors think something large struck her head, a piece of a desk or chair, could've been anything."

"Where were you when it detonated?" Nathan thought it strange that he hadn't asked this until now.

"Second floor, far side of the building. The air . . . it seemed to shimmer for an instant."

"The compression wave. How are your ears?"

"Still ringing. I hope it goes away."

"It should. Might take a day or two. Can you take me up to see her?"

"Yeah, sure. I didn't want to wake you. You know, I, ah, never thanked you the other night for saving my wife's life up at the compound." Henning attempted a smile. "I hear she tried to kill you."

"*Tried* being the operative word. Is she okay? Was she in the building?"

"No, she was training at Sierra Army Depot."

"I'm glad to hear that. Believe it or not, I really am on your side."

Henning nodded. "I know that now. I'm sorry about being rude the other night."

"Yeah, me too."

"Will you keep your visit with her brief? She needs to sleep."

"No problem." Nathan followed him through the emergency room's foyer, past two seated Sacramento police officers, and down a narrow hall lit with fluorescent lights.

At a bank of elevators, Henning pressed the button and took a step back. "We've got seventeen dead, fifty-eight with serious injuries. Four critical. They aren't expected to make it."

Nathan said nothing.

"It's not hard to guess who did this. You going after them?"

"Big-time."

"I want to help. What can I do?"

Nathan turned and faced him. "You're a hardworking and honest public servant, Henning. Holly . . . SAC Simpson told me as much on the drive up to the cabin. Don't blow everything you've worked for over this. It's too high a price to pay."

"*Fuck* that. As far as I'm concerned, the gloves are off." A soft chime announced the elevator's arrival. They stepped in and waited for the stainless-steel doors to close. "We take care of our own." Henning stabbed the third-floor button harder than he needed to.

Being careful not to sound condescending, Nathan said, "That's not how you felt the other night. Look, I'm dirty when it comes to this sort of thing. I'll admit that. I don't give a rat's ass about the Constitution when the stakes are high enough. Only a fool plays by the rules when the other side doesn't. If we're going to find these guys, things may have to get nasty. And I mean *nasty*."

"Just tell me what you need, and I'll make sure you get it."

"For starters, I'll need access to the NCIC database, and I'll need license plates run, addresses, phone numbers. Those kinds of things."

Henning pulled out his wallet and removed a business card; he wrote a phone number on the back. "This is my cell phone number. I keep it with me all the time, twenty-four/seven."

"You're risking a lot by helping me."

"I have to sleep at night."

"This doesn't go any further than you, Henning, and me, unless you want Holly to know. It's your call. Given the circumstances, I don't think she'll object."

The elevator opened onto the third-floor ICU where they had assisted with the wounded several hours ago. All was calm. The nurses' station was remanned. The gurneys gone. The blood mopped. The smell of charred flesh cleaned from the air. Henning nodded to the uniformed police officer sitting to the left. Nathan followed Henning to the nurses' station, where they identified themselves and signed the log sheet. Holly Simpson was in room three twelve. As they walked through the ICU, Nathan considered telling Henning about his conversation with Holly in the piano bar, how she'd agreed to help in much the same way, but dismissed the thought. He didn't want to betray the trust she'd given him. It wasn't Nathan's place, nor his nature, to disclose anything he and Holly had talked about. If Holly told Henning, that was fine. And he wasn't going to betray Director Lansing's trust either. As far as Holly was concerned, Lansing's call giving Nathan a green light never happened. And what exactly was a green light? What did it mean? He wasn't sure. For now, he couldn't worry about it. He'd do things his way and let the chips fall where they might, although he was reasonably sure the old adage, *Kill 'em all and let God sort 'em out,* didn't apply.

"What are you thinking about?" Henning asked.

"My next moves."

"And those are?"

They stopped at Holly's room. Her door was closed.

Keeping his voice low, Nathan continued. "I'm going to find people connected with the Bridgestones. With your help, it should be easier."

"Where will you start?"

"With Ernie Bridgestone. I'm going to look at the visitation logs from his prison term in Fort Leavenworth. There might be a contact there. An old girlfriend or drinking buddy. I'm also going to look into Leonard Bridgestone's military contacts when he was stationed on the Iraq–Syria border. I think that's where this Semtex business started. Also, the brothers almost surely have someone on the inside of a financial institution laundering the cash from their operation. I'm betting it was a fellow officer or a grunt under his command, but it could be anyone associated with either of them. Someone they'd trust. That's where you come in. I give you names; you give me everything the FBI has on them."

"You got it." Henning opened the door and stepped aside. In a whisper he said, "Keep it brief in there, under five minutes, okay?"

What Nathan saw next nearly brought him to tears.

Holly Simpson lay on her back. The top of her shaved head was completely wrapped in gauze. Both shoulders were secured by harnesses designed to keep the dislocated joints from moving. Her legs, from the hips down, were braced with some sort of external steel casts designed to minimize contact with her skin, which was also wrapped in gauze. Burns, Nathan knew. Seeping through in areas, reddish-yellow stains contrasted with the white gauze. Two IVs were dripping fluids into veins in both her wrists. The soft beeping of her heart monitor was the only sound present.

Her eyes opened when she heard a visitor, and she turned her head. "I guess they found us."

"Hey, kiddo."

"I must look like a real mess."

"Oh, Holly, I'm so sorry."

"Can you get me a drink of water, please?"

Nathan approached the bed and guided the cup's straw to her lips.

She pulled a small amount into her mouth and tried to smile. "Thanks."

"More?"

She nodded.

Nathan let her have as much as she wanted. "What time is it?" she asked.

"Just after fourteen thirty."

"Can you elevate my bed a little?"

"Sure." Nathan reached for the controller and hit the button. The electric motor whined softly. She did her best to conceal it, but her face tensed with pain.

"That's good, thanks. There's no TV in here; I haven't seen any coverage. How many?"

"Seventeen. Four more may not make it."

Her eyes welled with tears. "I should've taken better security measures, had more guards at the gate."

"Holly, don't do this. They would've been killed where they stood. Don't second-guess yourself."

"Director Lansing called me."

Nathan waited.

"He asked me lots of questions, all of them about you, mostly about what kind of person you are."

"I'm in trouble."

She managed a smile. "He told me about your call, what you want to do. We both agreed we want you aboard."

"I didn't want to betray his trust, but now that you know, he called a little while ago and gave me a green light."

She gave the slightest nod. "Nathan, I'm sorry. Director Lansing told me Larry Gifford was killed."

He shook his head and forced himself to relax his hands. *Damn those Bridgestones*. "I liked him a lot."

"Me too. Is Bruce here?"

"Just outside."

"Can you bring him in, please?"

Nathan walked over to the door and opened it. Henning was standing a respectful distance away. Nathan knew he didn't want to appear as though he'd been eavesdropping. "She wants you to come in."

With both men at her bedside, Holly continued. "Last night I promised to help Nathan. That's on you now, Bruce. Are you two okay?"

Henning nodded. "We're on the same page now."

"That's good. I don't want you to be directly involved with his"—her face tensed with pain—"investigation. But I want you to give him NCIC database information when he asks for it. Okay?"

"No problem. I'm glad to do it."

"I've cleared it with Director Lansing; he's having a Lear flown out from D.C. It's at Nathan's disposal, okay? Anywhere he wants to go. You go with him, but I don't want you directly involved."

"Understood," Henning said.

"The Bridgestones left a note in the guard shack. Five words: 'Expect more of the same.'"

Nathan shook his head.

"Our document people are . . . checking it out, trying to determine what kind of paper and printer were used. We might catch a break there." Holly took a deep breath and let it out slowly, her face masked in pain. "Director Lansing's beefed up security at every field office and resident agency."

Holly closed her eyes for so long that Nathan wondered if she'd dozed off.

Eyes still closed, she said, "Find them, Nathan. We can't let this . . . happen to anyone else."

"You can count on it, Special Agent in Charge Simpson."

She smiled, and gradually her features went slack. This time she really had dozed off.

During the elevator ride down to the lobby, Henning did his best to hide the fury he was feeling, but Nathan felt it emanating from the man like heat from an oven.

Outside Henning asked, "What kind of animals would do this? I don't get it."

"There's no easy answer to that, except that the safety mechanisms that keep most of us in check are absent in those two. They've justified the bombing as revenge for the death of their kid brother."

"You think they'll try to hit another field office?"

"I don't know, maybe. The note's more likely a diversion, drawing attention away from their true target."

"What true target?"

"Me."

At the Hyatt, Bruce Henning pulled his sedan up to the curb and killed the engine. Rather than simply dropping Nathan off, he stepped out and shook his hand.

"I'll call you as soon as the Lear arrives," Henning said. "Is there anywhere you want to go right away?"

"The USDB at Fort Leavenworth, Kansas."

"USDB?"

"United States Disciplinary Barracks. I hadn't planned on going out there because of the time it would take flying commercial airlines. With the Lear we can go immediately and land right at the fort. I want to speak to the psychiatrist who counseled Ernie Bridgestone. Ernie was nearly beaten to death in there. To get over something like that he probably needed support from the prison shrink. He might have valuable insight into Ernie's psyche, as well as his personal life. I'm looking for any lead we can get. I just hope the man's willing to talk and doesn't pull some doctor-patient-confidentiality crap on me."

"Given the circumstances, I hope he shares whatever he has." The fed grinned. "You could always visit him after hours if he doesn't."

"You know, Henning, I'm beginning to think you really *are* with the program."

"Listen, I want to thank you for helping out in the ICU with our wounded."

"I was glad to do it."

"I'll call if there's any change in Holly's condition."

"Get some sleep. We had a basic rule in the Marine Corps: Sleep when you can."

Henning took in a deep breath and let it out slowly. "I've got a long report to write, but it can wait. Now that you mention it, I *am* pretty exhausted. I hope you're right about this damned ringing in my ears; it's driving me crazy." He climbed back into the sedan and rolled his window down.

"I mean it, Henning, get some shut-eye. I'd like to be in Fort Leavenworth sometime after midnight."

Inside his room, Nathan plopped down on the bed and groaned.

"That you?" Harvey called from the connecting room.

Nathan stared at the ceiling. "Yeah." He sensed Harvey's presence at the adjoining door, and answered his unspoken question. "She took a brutal beating, but she's gonna pull through. They've got her doped up on morphine for eight broken bones, a fractured skull, and second-degree burns, but she should be okay in the long run. No spinal or nerve damage."

"I guess that's great news, considering the alternative. . . ."

"Amen to that. The Bridgestones left a note in the guard shack telling the FBI to expect more of the same."

"Think they're serious?"

"Hard to say. I told Henning it was probably a diversion to tie up resources."

"It makes sense. A lot's happened while you were gone. I've got our two techs checked into a room down the hall. They've got our secure fax line up and running. I took the liberty of contacting General Hawthorne while you were gone. He promised to fax us the visitation logs for Ernie Bridgestone by twenty hundred tonight."

"Good work. How's old Thorny doing?"

"He sounded busy. He asked about you, though."

"What'd you tell him?"

"I told him I still needed to wake your ass up with a ten-foot pole."

"That's nice, Harv."

"He's also gonna get us that list of Leonard's military contacts."

Nathan sat up. "Director Lansing called me back. Gave us the go-ahead. I guess the bombing changed some attitudes.

We even get an FBI Lear at our disposal. It's being flown out from D.C. as we speak."

"No kidding?"

"Nope. Lansing talked to Holly about it, and they agreed on everything. They're strongly motivated to find the Bridgestones. Even *Henning's* in our court."

"Talk about a change from a few nights ago. This is a pretty strong statement of trust."

"It's not absolute. I fully expect Henning to be Lansing's eyes and ears."

"Lansing's just covering his ass by having Henning tag along. I wouldn't read too much into it. What's your first stop, then?" Harvey asked.

"The Castle."

"We should have the visitation logs tonight; why go there in person?"

"A hunch. I want an insight into Ernie Bridgestone's head."

"The prison shrink?"

"Yep."

"You could do it by phone."

"I'd rather have a face-to-face."

"Understood. I'll coordinate things from here. I need to follow up on Leonard's military contacts—Ernie's too. Like you said, maybe we get lucky and one of them's working for a bank or financial institution."

Nathan lay back on the bed. "I'm going to catch a few hours of sleep. Wake me up in three hours, okay?"

"Will do. I'm going down the hall to check on our boys."

Fifteen minutes later Nathan fell into a dreamless void.

Nathan's eyes snapped open, and for the second time that day he felt disoriented, unsure where he was. As the room came into focus, he saw that Harvey stood a comfortable distance away, next to the small coffeemaker on the table near the window.

"How long?" Nathan asked.

"Three hours on the button." Harvey switched on the machine and settled into a chair.

Nathan sat up and stretched his arms over his head. He walked into the bathroom, brushed his teeth, and splashed some water on his face.

"I took the liberty of taking your phone into my room. Henning called about an hour ago, said the Lear will be here by twenty-three hundred. He wants you to call him back."

"You get the logs from the Castle?"

"Yep, and it seems Ernie had a frequent visitor, besides his brother. His ex-wife from Pensacola when he was a DI at the NAS. Her name's Amber Mills Sheldon. She came up to Kansas several times a year while he was inside. Worth pursuing."

"Definitely. You get an address? Phone number?"

"Just what she wrote in the log, but it's six years old. Our guys are checking it out. We should see if she's in the NCIC database. If she is, we'll get the most current info on her."

"I'll ask Henning to run her. Anybody else visit him?"

"Not a soul."

"Why am I not surprised? Did Thorny get you anything on Leonard's contacts yet?"

Harvey shook his head. "I don't expect to hear from him until tomorrow morning."

"I should be back by midday then."

"With a little luck, we'll have a starting place to hunt these guys down."

"Agreed." Nathan's cell phone bleeped to life from a restricted number. He hit send. "Hello?"

"Nathan?"

"Dad," Nathan said. Harvey gestured, asking if he should leave the room. Nathan shook his head.

"Am I calling at a bad time?"

"No. You're working late tonight."

"Goes with the territory. We need to talk."

Nathan said nothing.

"I hear you've been busy out there."

Was this an attempt at a thank-you? "Yes, I have. *We* have, Harvey and I."

"You saved a bunch of lives with that warning shot you fired at the compound. I'm glad you were there."

"Frank Ortega asked us to keep an eye on things. He had a feeling things could go south."

"I know; he told me. He also told me you want to speak to FBI director Lansing."

"I have spoken with him." *And you already know that.*

"May I ask what you talked about?"

"Harvey and I are going after the Bridgestones."

"I see. Is there any way you'll reconsider that course of action?"

"They beat James Ortega to a bloody pulp, cut six of his fingers off, and then burned him alive." Nathan waited through an uncomfortable silence. "You still there?"

"Yes, I'm here."

"Frank didn't tell you that part?"

"No, Nathan, he didn't tell me *that part*, and I didn't ask."

More silence. He knew his father was wondering why he hadn't been told. In Washington, D.C.'s inner circles, information was king—especially if that information was personal. "Look, these guys have to be found and interrogated. You want every ounce of that Semtex accounted for, don't you? Especially after today."

"The FBI has its own people for that. They don't need you."

Nathan sighed. "What do *you* need?"

"I need you to back off and let the FBI handle things from here. I can't . . ."

"You can't what?"

"All right . . . I can't protect you if you continue down this road of vengeance."

"It's not vengeance, and I don't need your protection."

"You're not in the CIA working on foreign soil anymore.

This is the United States of America. You can't just grab people off the street and interrogate them."

"Watch me."

"*Damn* it, Nathan. This isn't Nazi Germany. Your brutal methods are illegal and insidious. Let it go. This isn't your fight."

"The hell it isn't. One way or the other, the Bridgestones are going down. If the FBI finds them before I do, that's fine with me. So you called to warn me off, is that it?"

"If you persist with this manhunt of yours, you could go to prison, and I won't be able to help you."

"Like you helped me in Nicaragua?"

"That's a hateful thing to say. I had no idea where you were being . . . held."

"You can say it, Dad. It's just a word. *Tortured*. You had no idea where I was being tortured . . . for three weeks."

"They . . . I couldn't find you."

"Oh? Harvey found me."

No response.

"And guess how he did it? He grabbed people off the street and interrogated—"

"I know how he did it," Stone interrupted.

"Yeah, well, there's a big difference between you and Frank Ortega. Frank Ortega did everything possible to find his missing grandson, even bending the precious Constitutional rights of a couple dirtbags in the process. I don't need you to lecture me on violating human rights; I've had firsthand experience with it."

"Clearly it was a mistake to call."

"*Clearly*. One last thing. I debated telling you, but what the hell. The Bridgestones know I was the shooter who killed their little brother. They also know you're my father. That makes us both targets. So you watch yourself, *Senator*, because *clearly* this isn't over."

Nathan snapped his cell phone shut and sat on the edge of the bed. He closed his eyes and used the safety catch he'd shared with Toby. He arrested his breathing, tilted his head back, and imagined the leaves fluttering past his body. He was vaguely aware of Harvey shifting his weight in the chair near the window. After a good minute of silence, Nathan said, "I guess I didn't handle that very well."

"No, you didn't."

"I let him get under my skin. I should've known better."

"Yes, you should've."

Nathan half-chuckled. "Well, aren't you just overflowing with good advice."

Harvey grinned at him. "Did you know your ears turn red when you're angry?"

"You know, I honestly didn't."

"Well, they do. Go take a look in the mirror—and don't break it, okay?"

"Cute, Harv, really cute." Humoring his partner, Nathan walked into the bathroom and flipped the switch. He looked at himself in the newly replaced mirror, turning his head from side to side, getting a good look. "I'll be damned," he muttered. He splashed some water on his face and rested his weight on the counter.

"Make sure you wet your ears," Harvey called from the other room. "I wouldn't want you to burst a blood vessel. Those damned cauliflowers are ugly enough."

## ⊕ Chapter Fourteen

Three thousand miles away, Stone McBride replaced the handset into its cradle and shook his head. How the *hell* did the Bridgestones know Nathan was the shooter, and why hadn't Frank told him what they'd done to James? Stone wondered what else he hadn't been told. . . . *What a friggin' mess* . . . As if his life and this Semtex business weren't complicated enough already. He hit the intercom button. "Heidi,

I need to speak to FBI director Lansing again right away; I also need Kevin Ramsland on the line."

Nathan's attitude wasn't about to change, and it was obvious his son still held bitter feelings about what had happened in Nicaragua—and rightfully so. But Stone knew those feelings were misdirected.

Despite what Nathan thought, he *had* made a genuine effort to find his son. He'd called CIA director Bartholomew dozens of times, asking for updates, asking if there was anything he could do that wasn't already being done, and he'd gotten the same answer every time. Stone was essentially told the situation was "delicate in nature" and that "we're doing everything possible to find your son."

To some degree, he'd understood the director's position. The presence of a covert CIA sniper team working in Nicaragua would've been a major scandal, and sending in a Special Forces team to get Nathan out—if he were even still alive—involved considerable risk of exposing that scandal. Containment could've been lost. So why hadn't it been a scandal? They had Nathan. Surely they must have known he was CIA; they'd had three weeks to wring it out of him. And they *had* tortured him—tortured him to the brink of death. Stone didn't like thinking about it; it sent a shiver through his body every time he did.

Stone shook his head, trying to clear his mind. This wasn't the time to rattle this cage. If his son wanted to blame him for what happened, so be it; there was nothing he could do about it. But for now, he had more important things to worry about. If Nathan pursued this reckless manhunt of the Bridgestones, and broke laws in the process, he was on his own.

Impatient, he hit the intercom button again; Heidi informed him she was still waiting for return calls from Lansing and Ramsland.

"That's fine. I need you to call Commissioner Bob Price of the Capitol Police immediately. I want extra security patrolling all the senate and house buildings. If he gives you a hard time about it, put him through to me. And needless to say, no one talks to the media. I'll personally skin anyone who even looks at a reporter."

"Yes, Senator. I'll see to everything right away."

On impulse, Stone picked up the phone and called Frank Ortega.

"Hello."

"Frank, it's Stone."

No answer.

"You okay?"

"No, I'm not okay. Why would I be *okay*?"

Stone didn't respond; all he heard was the chime of Frank's clock in the background.

Finally Frank spoke. "Why didn't your people know about the tunnel?"

The question caught Stone by surprise, and he resented the accusatory tone of it. Clearly they weren't *his* people; the FBI had conducted all aspects of the operation. Maybe it was better if he ended this call as soon as possible. "Look, I just wanted to see how you were doing. We'll talk later, okay?"

The line went dead. Frank Ortega had hung up without a good-bye. Stone felt as if he'd been sucker punched. Frank Ortega, a man he'd known for forty years, had just sounded like a complete stranger. For the first time in his life Stone felt like an intruder to Frank, not a close friend. *Maybe he just needs time*, he reasoned. This was the second time tragedy had struck Frank's family: first his daughter, now his grandson. It had to be tearing him up. In all likelihood Frank would call back in a week or so and apologize for being so abrupt, and all would be forgiven and forgotten, regardless of the outcome of the manhunt. That was what true friendships were all about.

Stone pivoted back to the muted television and shook his head at the endless parade of talking heads analyzing the bombing from every conceivable angle. The nation's first big terrorist attack since September 11, and it wasn't even from Al-Qaeda. Domestic terrorism now occupied center stage, and the negative political fallout was going to fall squarely on his shoulders, especially after his press conference with the president trumpeting the seizure of a huge stockpile of illegal Semtex. To make matters worse, his Committee on Domestic Terrorism had been created to prevent this very thing. Why hadn't he seen this coming? In his defense, nothing Stone had read in the file about the Bridgestones had led him to believe they were capable of such a cold-blooded act. So why had they done it?

Deep down, part of him hoped his son would find them before the FBI did. Not even the Lord Almighty could help them then.

Nathan had been on a Lear before, and he felt a little underdressed in his blue jeans and white polo shirt. The sixty-foot Learjet 60XR was spacious, offering stand-up headroom. Two rows of single tan leather seats lined both sides of the fuselage, half of them opposing one another. The rear third of the jet was set up like a small office, with a table and two opposing seats facing it. Near the back, a small door opened into the head, a little cramped for a man Nathan's size, but manageable. The pilot and copilot introduced themselves as special agents Jenkins and Williamson, respectively. Jenkins wore captain's shoulder boards with four chevrons, while Williamson, the first officer, wore three chevrons. Nathan guessed they were both ex-military, navy or air force. As they studied their new VIP's face, both men betrayed surprise at what they saw.

"I, ah, lost an argument with a chain saw," Nathan said, lightening the tension.

"That was some argument," Jenkins said. "Where are we going?"

"The airfield at Fort Leavenworth, Kansas."

The two pilots exchanged a quick glance.

"I'll check it out," Williamson said. He disappeared into the cockpit and returned twenty seconds later with a black binder. He started thumbing through the pages. "Here we are . . . Sherman Army Airfield . . . Looks like it's a joint-use military and civilian airfield. Runway's fifty-nine hundred feet. We're good to go; gives us five hundred feet to spare for our takeoff roll." He smiled. "Shouldn't be a problem."

"Make yourselves comfortable." Jenkins waved a hand around the interior. "As you can see, there's no flight attendant, so you're on your own for beverage service. I trust you'll be able to find what you need?"

"We'll manage," Nathan said. "What's our flight time?"

"Around three hours, depending on the winds aloft."

"Hell of a job you've got here," Henning added.

"We like it. To be honest, it's nice to ferry someone other than the director for a change." He lowered his voice and looked around in fake secrecy. "He's not real personable."

"So I've heard," Nathan said.

"We aren't strict enforcers of seat belt rules, but it's best if you're strapped in for takeoffs and landings."

"Shouldn't you at least brief us on emergency procedures?" Nathan joked. "You know, emergency exits, that kind of stuff?"

"Naw," Jenkins said. "If we crash, there will be lots of exits."

Nathan smiled, deciding he liked these guys.

"Nathan's a helicopter pilot," Henning added. "He owns a Bell JetRanger."

"No kidding?"

Nathan shrugged.

"I've always wanted to learn helicopters."

"Is your father really Stone McBride?" Williamson asked.

Jenkins bumped him. "We aren't supposed to know that."

"Oh, yeah, that's right. Can you, uh, forget I just asked that?"

These two were real characters. Nathan hoped they took their flying more seriously. "To answer the question, yes, he's my father."

The first officer nudged his captain. "Shouldn't we salute him or something?"

Shaking his head, Nathan took a seat facing forward and fastened his belt.

Jenkins mouthed the word *sorry* to Nathan and pivoted toward the cockpit, but before disappearing behind the cockpit door he turned back, his expression serious. "Listen, it might seem like we're indifferent about what happened today. We aren't. We use humor to relieve stress. We're as angry as the next man, but that anger doesn't belong in here."

"Understood," Nathan said.

"We've got to file our flight plan into Fort Leavenworth; it'll take a few minutes." Jenkins studied him for a few seconds. "Did Lansing bring you in to find whoever bombed us?"

Nathan wasn't sure how to respond, wasn't sure how much he could share without violating Lansing's or Holly's trust. He hadn't been introduced as Special Agent Nathan McBride, so they knew he wasn't with the bureau. They probably figured him as some kind of VIP bounty hunter. He sensed Henning tense behind him. Walking a tightrope, Nathan used only his eyes, moving them up and down in a nod.

Jenkins got the message. Definitely ex-military . . .

Twenty minutes later, during the takeoff roll, Nathan let his head press against the seat as the Lear's wings bit into the midnight air. Behind him Henning was silent. He'd been rather subdued on the short drive to the airport. Perhaps the horror of today's events had finally soaked in. Whatever the reason, Nathan welcomed the silence. Despite the catnaps he'd been taking over the last four days—a few hours here, a few hours there—a deep fatigue had crippled him. He was sluggish, both physically and mentally, and it bothered him to be less than one hundred percent. He gauged his operational readiness at fifty percent. Not good. Unacceptable in military terms. Sooner or later, preferably sooner, he'd need uninterrupted slumber of at least eight hours. But for now, another catnap would have to do. *Sleep when you can.* . . . He reclined his seat, extended the leg rest, and closed his eyes. He hoped his personal demons would take the night off, especially in front of Henning.

The jet's PA system woke him just after zero five thirty East Coast time. "Good morning, campers," Jenkins's voice announced. "We hope you enjoyed the ride. We'll be on the ground in ten minutes. We called ahead for a taxi; should be there by the time we touch down."

Nathan looked out the window and saw the faint glow from Kansas City to the east. Directly below, a few scattered lights here and there were the only indicators that something other than an empty black void was down there. Kansas. The heartland of America. Somewhere, amidst the endless wheat-fields and buffalo ranches, was a giant ball of twine. He'd seen a picture of it, but couldn't remember where—perhaps a travel magazine in his dentist's office.

Jenkins greased the landing, making the smoothest touchdown Nathan had ever felt. The thrust reversers deployed, and Jenkins gunned the engine, gently applying the brakes at the same time. At the end of the runway the jet turned onto the taxiway and rolled back toward the hangars. After the engines had spooled down, First Officer Williamson appeared and opened the fuselage door. He lowered the steps into place. Cool, damp air carrying burned jet fuel greeted them. Nathan inhaled deeply; he liked the smell.

"Here's our ride," Williamson offered.

Nathan looked in the direction of the hangars and saw a taxi approaching. It stopped about a hundred feet away. The driver, a Middle Eastern–looking man, exited the vehicle, but out of respect or apprehension, or both, didn't approach the jet.

Williamson continued. "We need a few minutes to shut down and secure the aircraft. We'll be out in a few."

Nathan complimented the first officer on the landing before

grabbing his overnight bag from the rear luggage compartment. Henning also retrieved his two carry-ons, an overnight bag, and, from the look of the other, a laptop computer. Nathan let Henning take the lead exiting the aircraft. They walked over to the cab and, as expected, the cabdriver took a little too long looking at Nathan's face.

"We need a motel," Henning said. He hadn't said *hello*, or *how are you*, or *thank you for coming*, or offered any other pleasantry.

If the cabbie was insulted by Henning's lack of courtesy, he hid it well. "The Days Inn is only a few minutes from here."

"That's fine," Henning said. The driver popped the trunk, and Henning placed his two carry-ons inside. Nathan dropped his bag next to Henning's and stepped to the front passenger seat. He wanted the front, which offered considerably more legroom. He glanced at the Lear, admiring its sleek form. It had no markings identifying it as an FBI bird, which for some reason surprised him. On the way back to Sacramento, he planned to peek over the crew's shoulders and ask a few pilot-to-pilot questions. What little he'd seen of the avionics package had impressed him. He wouldn't mind switching seats with the copilot for a spell, if they'd let him.

At the motel, Nathan gave the cabbie a fifty and told him to keep the change. Everyone retrieved their bags and briefcases from the trunk. Hoping to make up for Henning's lack of social skills at the airport, Nathan addressed the cabbie in Arabic.

"Thank you for the ride, my friend."

Henning's head turned quickly when he heard Nathan speak Arabic. Williamson, the copilot, didn't react at all, which in itself *was* a reaction.

The driver's eyes grew a little. "You speak Arabic."

"I do. Please excuse my friend's abruptness at the airport. We are all very tired."

"It is okay. I understand."

"Stay safe and go with God."

The driver pumped Nathan's hand and smiled. "You too, my friend."

After the cab pulled away, Henning stepped forward. "What did you just say to him?"

Nathan shrugged. "I thanked him for the ride and told him we're all very tired."

"Well, aren't you just full of surprises. What's next—you going to pilot that Lear back to Sacramento?"

"As a matter of fact . . ." He looked at Jenkins, who gladly joined in.

"Sure, why not? It practically flies itself."

"No way," Henning protested. "That's not happening, not on my watch. You may be able to shoot a tennis ball at a thousand yards, land a helicopter in a palm tree, perform emergency surgery, find buried treasure, *and* speak Arabic, but you are *not* going to fly that jet back to Sacramento. Not while *I'm* on board."

"You left out master sushi chef," Nathan added.

Jenkins came to the rescue. "Maybe we should, uh, get checked in?"

Ten minutes later they were all settled into their respective rooms. The first thing Jenkins did was dial his first officer's room. "Is that really what McBride said to the cabdriver?"

"Yeah, but he left something out," Williamson said.

"What?"

"He apologized for Henning's behavior. Apparently Henning had been abrupt with the driver."

"Who *is* this guy?"

"Haven't the slightest."

"Think he's one of us?"

"No, I'm betting he's a spook. CIA or NSA."

"How many languages do you speak?"

"Including English, five."

"Think I should let him into the cockpit?" Jenkins asked.

"If you're asking me if he's dangerous, I'd have to say no."

"Think he bought our act?"

"Not for a second."

"Well, until Lansing changes his mind, we stick to the plan and fly him wherever he wants."

Nathan considered calling Harvey but decided against it. It was almost three in the morning in Sacramento. He set his overnight bag on the small table next to the bed and dug out his toothbrush, toothpaste, and phone charger. In the bathroom he washed his face, brushed his teeth, and plugged in his phone. He stripped down to his underwear, climbed into bed, and set the alarm clock for zero seven hundred, a whopping one hour away. Staring at the ceiling, he rehearsed the questions he planned for the Castle's shrink, hoping this little jaunt would be worthwhile. His mind moved to the pilots. When he'd spoken Arabic to the cabbie, Nathan had been certain First Officer Williamson had understood every word. He'd seen it in his eyes, an unmistakable twinkle of recognition. What were the odds that one of the pilots assigned to ferry him around spoke Arabic? Astronomical. It seemed Lansing's trust did indeed have its limitations.

Too tired to worry about it, Nathan rolled onto his side. Another long tomorrow loomed. Actually, he realized with a sigh, tomorrow was already here.

Despite his exhaustion, Nathan awoke before the alarm sounded. He cracked the curtains and scanned the parking lot where a smattering of pickups, sedans, and SUVs waited beneath a red Kansas sky. He estimated the motel's occupancy at fifty percent. At the opposite end of the room, he made a miniature pot of coffee.

After a quick shower and shave, Nathan called Henning's room.

"How'd you sleep?" Henning asked.

"Not too well. You?"

"About the same. Hungry?"

"Yeah."

"I called the front desk. There are several coffee shops within walking distance."

"What about our flight crew?" Nathan asked.

"I didn't want to wake them."

"Five minutes," Nathan said, and hung up.

Over breakfast Henning asked about Nathan's background. Although the FBI agent understood Nathan's need for secrecy regarding his past, there was a touch of resentment nevertheless. Nathan couldn't worry about it; he wasn't here to pacify Henning's curiosity. As they walked back to the motel, Nathan's cell phone rang. He looked at the screen. Harvey.

"How was your flight?"

"First-class. It's a nice ride."

"No doubt. Listen, I took the liberty of arranging your meeting with the Castle's shrink. I've been on the phone all morning trying to reach him, finally did. It took a bit of coaxing, but I think I convinced him of the urgency of the situation. He's seen the television coverage of the bombing, and knows his former patient is responsible. His name is Dr. Harold Fitzgerald, and yes, that's really his name. He's agreed to meet with you at the officers' mess at ten hundred."

"Great work, Harv. What's your read on him? Will he talk to us?"

"I honestly don't know. My gut says yes, but I could've read him wrong. Our call was pretty brief. I'm sure he'll want any conversation with you off the record."

"I'm really hoping to learn something, anything, that might give us a starting point for tracking Ernie Bridgestone. I still need to run his girlfriend in the NCIC database. Did our guys find anything from the visitation log info?"

"Maybe. The address she used on the log sheet was a dead end. We called the phone number and got a changed-number recording, so it's a fairly recent change. The new number is a five-five-nine area code in Fresno. When I had Mason pretend to be a telemarketer and call the number, he thought the woman who answered hadn't been honest. Mason said she hesitated for an instant before saying he had the wrong number. It might have been a girlfriend or a sister, or it might have been our mark herself."

"It's possible Bridgestone has already warned her she might get a call like that," Nathan said.

"If he still has any contact with her at all, he probably *has* warned her—or more accurately, threatened her. She might go underground. Maybe we should've waited on the call."

"I wouldn't worry about it too much; telemarketers call all the time. Listen, we just finished breakfast; we're walking back to the motel. I'll call you after we've met with Fitzgerald."

Nathan tucked his phone away and filled Henning in on what he'd learned about Ernie's old girlfriend and the fake telemarketer call.

"That might have been her," Henning said.

"It's possible; we won't know until we talk to her."

"And if she won't talk to us?"

"She'll talk."

The entrance to Fort Leavenworth looked like a hundred other military base entries. A small guard shack divided the road. MPs in urban BDUs with sidearms approached the taxi and asked for everyone's identification. Their taxi had been expected, so the security procedure went smoothly. As instructed, the driver placed the bright yellow temporary vehicle pass on the dashboard. He was given a small map of the base showing the location of the officers' mess.

Nathan thought the fort had a college campus feel to it— lots of green, open spaces, mature trees, and historic buildings. The driver had no trouble finding the officers' mess—no doubt he'd been here before. At the curb, Henning asked— told, really—the driver to wait for them. A mix of army officers filtered in and out from the mess, some of them in more formal dress uniforms, while the majority wore BDUs. A man in civilian clothes stepped out and approached them—Fitzgerald, no doubt. The man looked nothing like the stereotype of a shrink. No Freudian glasses, bald pate, or goatee. No white coat. He looked more like an aging California surfer than a prison psychiatrist. Dressed in tan slacks and an aloha shirt, he was in his mid- to late forties, with sandy-colored hair, broad shoulders, and a pleasant smile.

Nathan offered his hand. "Dr. Fitzgerald, I presume?"

"The one and only."

"Nathan McBride. Thank you for meeting with us. This is Special Agent Bruce Henning from the Sacramento field office." Henning and Fitzgerald shook hands.

"I'm very sorry for the loss of your colleagues."

"Thank you, Doctor," Henning said. "I appreciate it."

"I'd prefer we talk out here," Fitzgerald said. "The less we're seen together, the better. I know a nice spot under some trees. I eat lunch there all the time."

At the curb, the cabdriver was looking at them. Nathan issued him *a stay there* gesture. The three men began walking down the sidewalk. After several hundred yards they veered over to a group of oaks. There wasn't any place to sit except on the grass, so that was what they did. The meeting instantly became cordial, as though they were there for a picnic, not a discussion of national security.

"This okay?" Fitzgerald asked.

"Perfect," Nathan answered. "You know why we're here."

"I do."

"I appreciate your meeting with us on such short notice."

"You realize I'm hanging my tail out on a limb talking to you."

"You have my word as a former Marine Corps officer that it doesn't go any further than us. We need to find Ernie Bridgestone and his brother, Doctor. Find them fast."

"I'm not sure what I can do to help."

"There are a couple of things. First, I'm looking for any insight into his head, how he thinks."

Fitzgerald took a deep breath and let it out slowly. "I've counseled hundreds of troubled souls, but he possesses a pathology we don't see very often."

Nathan waited while the doctor gathered his thoughts.

"He's what I'd consider a borderline devoid."

"Devoid?" Henning asked.

"I'll try to explain by using an example. A mother has a child—a little boy, for our purposes. As the child matures, his mother starts to notice he isn't like other boys. He doesn't smile or laugh or cry or show any type of emotion at all. He's picked on by other children. They think he's stupid because he doesn't laugh when they do, and it's made worse when he doesn't react to their ridicule. So imagine the mother sitting the little boy down and explaining that when he sees other children laugh, he should do the same thing. She teaches him to curve his lips up in a smile and show his teeth and make a heh-heh-heh sound, like the other children do."

"That is seriously messed-up," Henning said.

"That's right, Agent Henning. Just as some children are born with a childhood disease that cripples parts of their bodies, others are either born or molded into masking emotions. That's why I consider him a borderline case. I believe his emotional responses are suppressed, not missing altogether, although I can't be certain of that diagnosis."

"I'm assuming guilt would be missing as well?" Nathan asked.

"Definitely. As a child he would've had a hard time distinguishing between right and wrong. What all of us instinctively know as being wrong—say, mistreating an animal—is missing or, more accurately stated, short-circuited in Bridgestone. The safety mechanism is bypassed, or it's missing altogether. He wouldn't feel any regret for the Sacramento bombing. None."

Henning visibly stiffened a little.

"What about his brother Leonard?" Nathan asked. "What would Ernie feel toward him?"

"Loyalty isn't clearly defined as an emotion; in fact, I don't think it's an emotional state of mind, per se. I mention it because Ernie Bridgestone is extremely loyal to his older brother. He talked about Leonard often."

"In what way?" Nathan asked.

"Mostly about their childhood. Their father was abusive. Brutally so, I'm afraid, and their mother didn't intervene. A common belief among psychiatrists is that the first year of a baby's life is perhaps the most important. I wouldn't be surprised if Ernie had also been neglected for long periods of time. Try to imagine it: An infant cries because it's hungry or lonely, but there's no one there to feed it or comfort it, to give it the tactile feedback it needs to feel secure and loved. Think of it: an infant screaming into the dark, isolated and alone, for hours, maybe even days." Fitzgerald shook his head. "It's cruel beyond comprehension. I truly believe Ernie is the product of such an environment. Leonard is a few years older, so he might have filled in for Ernie where their mother didn't. It would explain the strong family bond Ernie feels toward Leonard."

"Isn't it reasonable to assume Leonard was subjected to the same neglect?" Henning asked. "And wouldn't he then have the same condition?"

"Yes and no. I believe he was, but some people can overcome such trauma through intellect. My own father, for example. He was from a broken and abusive home, but he became a valuable member of society, putting himself through medical school and becoming a naval flight surgeon. He was also a loving father to me and my sisters. He broke the cycle. Some can; some can't—or, more accurately, some won't. They justify their negative behavior by blaming someone else. This act of blaming, of being a victim, if you will, becomes part of their pathology."

Nathan nodded his understanding. "Would Ernie have been able to form a meaningful relationship with anyone other than his brother? We know he was married. . . ."

"The answer is yes, but it depends on what you mean by meaningful."

"Love, would he be capable of love?"

"I'd have to say no. At least, not in the way we think of it. His love would be based on actions, not emotion. I'll give you an example. Let's say Ernie comes home from work and his girl-friend hasn't cleaned up the kitchen from breakfast. She's tired or having a bad day or whatever. Ernie would interpret the dirty dishes in the sink as a sign that she didn't love him. Follow?"

Nathan nodded. "Tough situation. She'd never be able to do enough to prove her love."

"That's exactly right. A relationship like that is doomed from the start. No matter what she did, it would never be good enough, because the emotional bond is missing. When people are truly in love with each other, small things are for-given and forgotten. Not so with a devoid. Seeing those dirty dishes would be like a slap in the face. He wouldn't look at the dishes with compassion and ask her if anything's wrong; he'd just see them as an indication she didn't love him. Living with a devoid would be the ultimate walk on eggshells."

"Why would someone stay with a person like that?" Henning asked.

"The simplest answer is love. She loves him and she's will-ing to put up with his shortcomings. There are other reasons. She might have nowhere else to go, or she's convinced she can change him if she only did this or that, but the tragic reality is, unless Ernie gets comprehensive psychiatric help, he'll never change. He'll never come to terms with who and what he is. I was beginning to make some real progress with him just before he was released. You have to remember that, on some level, these people instinctively know there's something wrong with them. They just don't know what it is, or how it happened.

"To use a simplistic example, take cats. If kittens are exposed to human love and affection within the first few weeks of their lives, they become pets. If not, they're feral. Of course, it's not that simple with humans, but the principle's basically the same. Unless an infant receives the stimuli needed to feel safe and secure, it's guaranteed to grow up with emotional problems to one degree or another."

"What's his prognosis?"

"Unless he receives comprehensive therapy, hopeless. He won't change. He can't. To use a metaphor, he'll spend the rest of his life barking at the moon."

"What did you talk about?" Nathan asked. "I mean generally. You know, what did Ernie think his problems were?"

"That's easy," said Fitzgerald. "It was the drunk-driving incident that landed him here. He claimed he was railroaded."

"Was he?"

"I reviewed the police reports and eyewitness accounts. There's no question Ernie was legally drunk, but from everything I remember reading, it wasn't truly his fault. The woman walked out from between two parked cars. Even if he hadn't been drinking, he still would've hit her. She was quite drunk herself."

"But 'railroaded'?" Nathan asked. "It sounds like you actually give that some credence."

"I do give it some credence. *Some*, mind you." Fitzgerald paused, trying to remember. "I don't recall her name, but I think she was from a family of some influence. Justice acted swiftly in the case; that's for sure. I kept copies of the newspaper articles in Ernie's file. He griped about it a lot, to the point of being obsessive, swore to get revenge someday. He also never believed he got a fair court-martial."

"That's what they all say," Henning said. "They're all innocent."

"Point taken," Fitzgerald said. "But if the circumstances had been slightly different, there may not have been any charges leveled at all."

"We'll check it out," Nathan said. "If you could, please send us everything you have on Ernie's DUI conviction, all right?"

"Will do."

Nathan stood, shook hands, and gave Dr. Fitzgerald a business card with his cell and fax numbers handwritten on the back. Henning did the same. "I really appreciate your talking to us."

"To be honest, it wasn't my decision. I got a call from the USDB's commanding officer, who got a call from the fort's commanding officer, who had received a call from the chief of staff of the army."

*Good old Thorny*, Nathan thought. "Well, I still appreciate it."

"One last thing," Fitzgerald said. "Watch yourselves. They don't come any more vicious than Ernie Bridgestone."

# ⊕ Chapter Fifteen

On the short ride out of the fort, Nathan and Henning rode in silence. They didn't want to discuss anything in front of the driver. At the motel Nathan paid the cabbie and gave him a generous tip.

As they walked through the lobby, Nathan asked, "So, what do you think?"

Henning shook his head. "That business about teaching a kid to smile was just plain creepy."

"Yeah, it's weird, all right."

"What do *you* think?"

"What I think," Nathan said, "is that wherever we go next, we should rent a car. It'd be better than taking taxis all over creation."

They shared a nod, releasing a good bit of the tension that had built while discussing nothing but Ernie Bridgestone.

"So," Henning said, back to business, "where do we go next?"

"Fresno, to pay Amber Sheldon a visit." Nathan looked at his watch. "I want to keep moving. When we find her we won't have time to conduct a prolonged surveillance. We'll take the direct approach and knock on her door."

"Just like that?"

"Do you have a better idea?"

"Not really."

"We need to run her through the NCIC. Can you access the database from the motel's LAN port on your laptop?"

"Yeah, I should be able to."

"Maybe we'll catch a break; if she's in the system we'll have a current address, even better if she's on parole or probation. If she's not at home when we show up, her PO will have her employment info."

"What do you hope to learn from her?" asked Henning. "I mean, besides the obvious, Ernie's whereabouts."

"I'm not sure yet. I won't know until I talk to her. We might be able to use her."

"Use her? You mean, like bait?"

"I don't have it figured out yet. A lot depends on what I learn from her." Nathan needed to change the subject; he didn't want to pursue this train of thought aloud. "We should call and check on your SAC, see how she's doing and give her an update."

"I was thinking the same thing."

"I'll swing by your room in ten minutes."

Back in his room, Nathan brushed his teeth and washed his face. He thought about Amber Mills Sheldon. Interrogating a woman involved different techniques and psychology. In truth, he hoped it wouldn't be necessary. He'd interrogated women before and in some regards found them to be more resilient than men. Despite what was commonly believed, interrogation was a mind game more than anything else. To be effective, the victim's spirit must be broken, and along with it, the will to resist. Physical discomfort, while effective, wasn't the best method unless the interrogator was under time constraints, which was often the case. Information was often time-sensitive, like a loaf of bread.

He dried his face, wishing he had a female interrogator available. The psychology of having a woman present, looking on with emotional detachment and a complete lack of sympathy, worked well toward breaking a female's spirit. Having a woman present was especially effective against men. Nathan figured it was the macho syndrome. Men didn't like to appear weak and vulnerable in front of women, especially when naked. Once again, it was all about mind games. Unless the victim had counterinterrogation training, it usually didn't take long to wring information out of them. If that held true, Amber Sheldon would be an easy nut to crack.

He gave Henning a few extra minutes before knocking on his door.

"It's not locked," Henning said.

Nathan stepped in and left the door partly open. Sitting at a small desk, Henning was typing on his laptop's keyboard.

"What've we got?" Nathan asked.

"Looks like we've got that break we were looking for. Amber Sheldon is currently on probation for drunk and disorderly conduct, disturbing the peace, and driving while intoxicated. Here, take a look; I didn't bring a printer along. Probably should've."

Nathan looked over Henning's shoulder while he scrolled down to Amber Sheldon's color mug shot. As usual with mug shots, she didn't look real happy. She had stringy blonde hair, blue eyes, and a hollow, sullen-looking face, probably from using. She looked hard, a *summa cum laude* graduate of the school of hard knocks. When the picture was taken, she'd definitely fit the description of *rode hard and put away wet*. The photo was a year old.

"She's got a fairly long sheet," Henning continued. "Nothing too serious. We have a current address, phone number, and place of employment. She does indeed live in Fresno, California. Works at an establishment called Pete's Truck Palace. Let's see . . . after her arrest in 2006, her driver's license was revoked for six months. Based on her background and the trouble she's had with the law over the years, I'm not expecting her to be real friendly. Let's make that call to Holly—SAC Simpson. I think she'll want you present for the call."

Henning pulled out his cell phone and scrolled down the numbers stored in memory. When he found the number he wanted, he hit send. He didn't put it on speaker yet. Nathan waited.

"Hi, SAC, how are you feeling? . . . Yes, he's here. . . . Okay." Henning pressed the speaker button. "You're on speaker."

"Hi, Nathan."

Nathan sat on the bed. "Hey, there." He didn't ask how she was feeling; he already knew.

"How are things going out there?"

"Good. The meeting with the Castle's shrink was helpful."

"What did you find out?"

Nathan went over the salient points of their discussion. He finished with what they found on Amber Sheldon in the NCIC.

"That's good," Holly said. "You heading to Fresno, then?"

Nathan nodded for Henning to take over.

"Yes," Henning said. "We're planning to rent a car, rather than call the Fresno resident agency for transportation. I'm trying to minimize Nathan's exposure."

"Hold off on that," Holly said. "Fresno's ASAC, John Pallamary, is a good friend of mine. We went through the academy together. I'll give him a call."

"We're hoping to be in the air within the next half hour," Henning said.

"Good. What's your plan once you get there?"

"We have her current address. We'll head over there and see if she'll talk to us."

"If she isn't forthcoming, let Nathan take over. Understood?"

"Yes," he said tightly.

"Nathan, use your best judgment when questioning her."

Translation: *Don't get rough unless you absolutely have to.* "No problem," he said.

Holly continued. "We've copied all the video from the bombing and sent it back east to your father's committee. They're trying to glean as much as they can. We've implemented the largest manhunt in the history of the bureau. Hundreds of agents are on the case. Three more of our people died last night; the rest are probably going to make it. Six of them will never walk again."

"I'm sorry, Holly."

"This isn't your fault. I've had a lot of time to think about it."

"Maybe I didn't have to kill their little brother. Maybe I should've only wounded him. I could've—"

"Nathan, listen to me. I've read all the reports. Don't do this. Sammy Bridgestone was aiming a sniper rifle at our SWAT teams. You took the proper action for the situation as it existed at the time. If our sniper team had seen him before you, they would've done exactly the same thing. Any law enforcement officer in America would shoot to kill in that situation. Don't second-guess yourself. None of this is your fault. Clear?"

"Clear," he said.

"Okay. We've set up a hotline. Tips are coming in by the hundreds with possible sightings. We're checking them out. John Walsh is going to air an entire episode of *America's Most Wanted* the day after tomorrow. He's had good success with the show. ASAC Perry Breckensen is in temporary command until I get out of here. Nathan?"

"I'm here."

"Despite all the manpower we've got, I think you're our best chance at finding them."

Nathan said nothing.

"I'm glad you're aboard with us. I've got to go; my nurse just came in. Will you ask Harvey to share anything he finds with Breckensen?"

"Sure, Holly. No problem."

"Bruce, remember, you're a sworn law enforcement officer. Where Nathan is concerned, it's 'don't ask, don't tell.'"

"Understood," he said quietly.

"If you haven't heard back from me before you leave Fresno, call me from the air."

"I will," Henning said.

"I've got to go." The cell went dead.

"She's an amazing woman," Nathan said. "Henning, listen. I know you and—" He cut himself off. "She's going to be okay."

Henning reached for his laptop. "Let's pack up and get going."

Back in his room, Nathan called Harvey and told him how Thorny had forced Fitzgerald's cooperation, and what the shrink had said about Ernie Bridgestone. Harvey agreed to follow up and get the drunk-driving news clippings and any other documents Fitzgerald had to send. Harvey also told him Thorny had come through with Leonard's contacts from his deployment in Iraq.

"We just talked to Holly."

"How's she doing?" Harvey asked.

"She sounded tired, but otherwise not too bad, all things considered."

"Listen, I got that tape of the Bridgestones torturing the two FBI surveillance techs. It's pretty ugly stuff, but I didn't hear anything we didn't already know."

"Okay . . ."

"All the techs could tell them was your name and that your father was Stone McBride. Incidentally, our personal info isn't available; I had Mason try to dig it out. You know—DMV, Social Security, IRS. He couldn't come up with anything. I think we're okay. They'd need someone on the inside of the DOD with high-level passwords to access anything on us, and I don't see that happening. Your father's a different matter. I don't know how protected his personal information is."

"Me either," Nathan said.

"If they're heading back east, it's possible they could tail him from one of his public appearances. We should warn him to stay under the radar for the time being and hire some personal security guards."

"I told him what could happen. He'll have to take care of himself. He always has. Keep checking out Leonard's contacts. I have a feeling one of them is our financial insider. We're looking for someone within one day's drive, two max."

"The list is pretty long, several hundred. And that's a lot of territory to cover, basically the western third of the country."

"You might need to call ASAC Breckensen and ask for some help."

"I definitely will."

"Does the FBI have a temporary field office up and running yet?"

"I don't know. I'll find out. Their building isn't a total loss, but there's no way they can operate out of there in its present condition. What about you? What's next?"

"Fresno. We'll be airborne in half an hour. I'll call once we know something."

Fifteen minutes later everyone was boarding the Lear. As Nathan climbed the stairs, he looked at First Officer Williamson and decided to play his hand. Time for this covert bullshit to end. Nathan spoke in Arabic. "We are on the same side, okay? I have no agenda other than finding the Bridgestones."

Williamson narrowed his eyes, but the spark of recognition

in his expression couldn't be hidden. Nathan knew he was considering his options. There were two: Continue playing the game or come clean.

From the rear luggage compartment, Henning turned at hearing Bridgestone's name in a sentence spoken in Arabic.

Williamson came clean. "Understood," he answered in Arabic. "I am just doing my job. For what it is worth, I am not happy about it."

Nathan continued in Arabic. "I am an open book. If you have questions, just ask. I will answer them truthfully."

"Good enough. What happened to you? Those scars."

Very few people had ever asked him about his face. They were either too intimidated, too polite, or just plain didn't give a damn. Most people were neatly tucked into the too-intimidated category, the "let sleeping dogs lie" crowd. Nathan believed Williamson's curiosity was born more out of respect than anything else, and he actually admired the man for asking. Underneath the act the man had put on, Nathan knew Williamson was a no-nonsense guy. Whatever his actual vocation, he had the cool, low-key demeanor of a military aviator.

"A botched mission." Nathan was already saying more than he should. But those three words were enough for any intelligent person to figure it out.

The two men shook hands and the tension vanished. Williamson nodded and headed for the cockpit.

"What did you say to him?" Henning asked.

"I told him the same thing I told you the first time we met—that we're on the same side and my only goal is to find the Bridgestones."

Henning's expression was genuinely puzzled, and Nathan now believed he didn't know Williamson had been assigned as a watchdog. He hadn't been sure before.

"How did you know he spoke Arabic?"

"When I spoke to the cabdriver early this morning, I didn't

see any reaction from Williamson at all. None. Most people show some degree of surprise."

Henning lowered his voice. "You think Lansing brought him on board to keep an eye on things? To spy on you?"

"Yeah, I do."

"Why bring in someone who speaks Arabic? Al-Qaeda isn't involved with the Sacramento bombing. It doesn't make sense."

"It does if you consider that Harvey also speaks Arabic."

"Good grief," Henning said. "Sometimes I think there's no limit to the cloak-and-dagger bullshit in this business."

"Don't worry about it; it's a safe play on Lansing's part. There's a lot at stake. He was concerned I might speak in a foreign language with Harvey to hide things we discover about the Bridgestones. I'd be willing to bet Williamson also speaks Russian. Probably Spanish too. We aren't going to conceal anything from you guys. If your people find the Bridgestones before we do, that's fine with me. Don't get me wrong: We'd love some quality time with them, but finding them is the primary goal."

In the cockpit, Williamson lowered his voice. "He knows."

"Is it going to be a problem?" Jenkins asked.

"He seemed okay about it. He's a big boy; he knows the score."

Jenkins was flipping avionics switches from a checklist as he spoke. "As far as I'm concerned, nothing's changed. We keep reporting to Lansing as ordered."

"Do we tell Lansing he knows?"

"Not unless we want egg on our faces," Jenkins said. "He'd view McBride's discovery as a screwup on our part."

"Yeah, you're right about that. McBride seems like a decent guy." Williamson didn't mention Nathan's comment about the botched mission out of respect for the man, but he could hint about it. "It's not hard to guess how he got those scars on his face. They aren't random, and he sure didn't get them from any chain saw accident."

Jenkins started the engines, keeping his eyes on the gauges. "I think you're right; he's a spook. Someone carved him during an interrogation. Had to be hell."

"Yeah, no shit."

Twenty minutes into the flight, Henning used the air phone to call Holly again. Nathan looked over, but there was no way to put the call on speaker. After a brief conversation he hung up.

"She made contact with ASAC Pallamary from the Fresno resident agency. An agent's going to meet us at the airport."

"You okay with that?" Nathan asked.

"Sure, why not? You're the one who wanted to stop taking taxis."

"You know that's not what I meant."

"Not my call. I just follow orders."

Nathan heard the frustration in Henning's voice. "Don't read anything into it. Like I said, there's a lot at stake."

Henning didn't respond; he just leaned back and stared straight ahead. Nathan felt for the guy, but knew the extra measures being taken by the bureau weren't a reflection on Henning's competence or loyalty. Although Nathan wasn't familiar with FBI methods of operation, he figured it was probably standard procedure to double up on field assets whenever possible to ensure the best chance of success. Even though he preferred working alone, Nathan would play along for now. The FBI Lear was too big an asset to turn down. He figured having a federal ball and chain in the form of Bruce Henning was the price of admission, but he couldn't in all honesty discount the help he'd received from Henning so far. If the time came to cut ties with his FBI friends, he'd do it, but for now he was comfortable with the status quo.

The Lear touched down in Fresno a little after noon, local

time. As it taxied to the general aviation transient parking area, Nathan admired the F-16C Falcons parked next to the Air National Guard hangar. They were beautiful machines. Pure in both form and function. Although he couldn't imagine it, he wondered if flying them ever got old.

After Jenkins parked the Lear, Nathan spotted a man standing next to a plain sedan in front of a long hangar building. The FBI contact. He was reasonably sure the agent assigned to them would've been briefed on their objective and the rules of engagement. Nathan had no expectations about the agent's attitude, but he hoped it wouldn't be a repeat of a few nights ago when he'd first met Bruce Henning. Because the director of the FBI had given him the use of a Lear, he hoped this new agent would show some discretion. Nathan had to admit there was a definite feeling of importance associated with traveling by Lear. He could definitely get used to this.

As the Lear's engines wound down to idle, First Officer Williamson appeared and opened the fuselage door. Unlike Fort Leavenworth, the air was dry. A bright afternoon greeted Nathan as he followed Henning onto the tarmac. Several dozen smaller planes were parked off to their right, a mix of single- and twin-engine turboprops.

Dressed in tan slacks and a dark blue Windbreaker to conceal his sidearm, their FBI contact began walking toward them. In his mid-forties, he had cropped, thinning hair with a touch of gray at the temples. Ex-cop or -military, Nathan thought. The guy would never make it as an undercover. Their new arrival identified himself as Special Agent Paul Andrews. He looked Nathan over from head to toe before smiling and offering his hand—an unexpectedly welcome start.

Located in the northeast area of Fresno, a mixed neighborhood of residential and commercial properties, Amber Sheldon's apartment was part of a larger complex of identical structures laid out in pairs, back-to-back, with parking on both sides. Second-story walkways ran their entire lengths, accessed by prefab concrete stairs on each end. Several hundred yards to the north, the metal river of Highway 41 could be heard but not seen. Andrews parked the sedan at the west end of the buildings, where it wouldn't be noticed from the target's apartment. According to the NCIC file, Sheldon lived in apartment number forty-six.

"If she's not there and has a roommate, we're blown," Henning said. "It's fair to assume the roommate will call her and tell her the FBI came knocking at her door."

"We don't have much choice," Nathan said. "We don't have time for a prolonged stakeout. If she's not there we'll ask where she works; that way the roommate will think we don't know." Nathan turned toward Andrews. "Do you know where Pete's Truck Palace is?"

"It's off Highway 99, about twenty miles south of the city. I've never stopped there, but I've passed it quite a few times."

"Okay," Henning said. "It's probably better if only two of us knock on her door. Andrews, you cover the stairwells and watch our backs in case the Bridgestones are around. Shoot first and ask questions later."

"You got it."

They followed a concrete sidewalk paralleling the building, then cut across the grass over to the west stairs. Apartment forty-six was on the second floor. This had to be a nicer neighborhood, because a Big Wheel tricycle as well as several children's bikes were leaning against the building, unlocked. A smattering of litter was present, nothing serious enough to suggest it was a low-life establishment. Licking its paws, a calico cat sat on the midlevel landing of the stairwell. She squinted in friendship as they moved past her. The windows on either side of Sheldon's door were screened by closed curtains. Nathan and Henning paused and listened to the buzz of a muffled television set.

Nathan kept his voice just above a whisper. "Bridgestone could be in there. I'll go left; you go right."

Henning nodded and put his hand on the butt of his gun.

Keeping to the side of the door, he knocked twice. The sound of the television went silent, followed by a forceful, "Who is it?"

"FBI, ma'am. We're just here to ask you a few questions; no one's in any trouble, okay?"

The curtains parted, revealing a slightly overweight, dark-haired woman in her late teens or early twenties. Her yellow tank top revealed more than it should have.

"My mom's got nothin' to do with that man no more." From what Nathan could hear through the window, Amber Sheldon's daughter had retained—post-Pensacola—most of her Southern drawl.

"May we come in, please?" Henning asked.

"Y'all got some ID?"

"Yes, ma'am." Henning held up his FBI badge.

"Lemme see your gun too. All you FBI guys carry guns, right?"

"That's affirmative, ma'am." Henning pulled his Wind-breaker open.

"Okay, just a sec."

They listened to the dead bolt clicking back and the slide chain being removed from its slot. The door opened and the smell of cinnamon greeted them.

Gun drawn, Henning rushed into the room and pivoted to the right.

"Hey!" the girl protested, "what the hell y'all doing?"

Nathan dashed into the kitchen and checked behind the counter. "Clear!"

Henning checked the bathroom, a hall closet, and both bedrooms. "Clear," he called, and returned to the living room. "I'm sorry for doing that, ma'am, but we had to be sure you weren't being held against your will. We're looking for a very danger-ous man."

"You could've just asked me."

Both thinking the same thing, Nathan and Henning exchanged a glance.

"I apologize again, ma'am," offered Henning.

Nathan surveyed his surroundings. Although the living room wasn't a complete mess, it could've been neater. Some clothes were strewn on the furniture here and there, and a few dishes were out of place, but overall it looked reasonably presentable. Nathan watched her freeze when she took in his face.

"What the hell happened to *you*?" she asked.

*Nothing like a little tact*, he thought. "Industrial accident."

She whipped her waist-long hair to the side. Along with her tank top she wore blue jeans—tight in all the wrong places—and fuzzy pink slippers. Her ankles were swollen. She introduced herself as Janey "not Jane" Sheldon.

Henning asked if her mother was expected anytime soon.

"No, and I don't know where she is."

*He didn't ask you that*, Nathan thought.

"Does she have a cell phone?"

*Tactical question. Good job, Henning.*

"Hardly—we can barely pay the rent around here. They just raised it on us by fifty bucks."

"We really need to talk with her."

Janey's face clouded. "She's a good mom and all, but she's got a problem, you know . . . with drinking."

"I'm sorry to hear that. Is there someplace she goes regularly?"

She cocked her head. "Probably, but it isn't around here. I've already looked in all the close places."

As Nathan watched her body language closely, Henning continued. "Has anyone called her lately?"

"You mean that *dangerous man* you mentioned?"

"Yes, ma'am."

"I can't say it was him for sure, but she did get a call the other night. She was upset afterward, got really drunk and passed out on the floor right about where you're standing."

"Did you hear any of the call?"

"Not really. I was watchin' *American Idol*."

Nathan took a closer look at Janey's eyes. Piercing pale blue . . . He ran the calculation of her age through his head.

"What time does she go to work?"

"Eight p.m. She works the graveyard shift."

"Does she usually come back here before going to work?"

"Sometimes. Not always, though."

Henning turned to Nathan. "Anything more?"

"That *dangerous man* is your father."

Henning visibly flinched at Nathan's comment.

Janey narrowed her eyes, disgust stealing over her face. "I think you should get out."

"You're a lousy liar, Janey."

"I said *get out*."

Nathan took a step forward. "And if we don't?"

"I'll call the police."

"We *are* the police."

"I'll still call."

Nathan took another step toward her. "That's going to be rather difficult after I've broken your jaw in three places." He quickly scanned the room for a phone; it was in the kitchen.

"Listen, asshole. You can't come in here and threaten me like this."

Nathan spoke over his shoulder to Henning. "Why don't you wait outside?"

Henning opened his mouth to respond, but hesitated, not sure what to do. "Yeah, I guess maybe I'd better," he said. The FBI agent stepped through the door and closed it behind him.

When they were alone, Janey glanced at the phone behind Nathan. Her lower lip trembled when she spoke. "What do you want from me?" She was close to tears.

"The truth," Nathan said. He moved between Janey and the kitchen phone, trapping her in the living room. She crossed her arms over her chest as a tear rolled down her cheek, but she said nothing.

"It's like this, Janey. I believe you about your mother having a drinking problem, and I believe your life has been difficult because of it. I also believe that when you went looking for her, you found her at a local bar. And I also believe that's where she is right now."

"You don't understand; she hates cops. If you go in there, she'll freak out."

"Listen to me very carefully, Janey. I don't blame you for what your father did. You didn't ask for any of this; it just landed in your lap. It's a raw deal, but that's the hand life has dealt you." Nathan pointed to his face. "I've had a raw deal too. Life goes on. The bomb in Sacramento was made of forty pounds of Czech-made plastic explosive. We think Ernie still has three hundred pounds of it. He murdered twenty-four people and wounded fifty-three others; six of them will never walk again. They'll spend the rest of their lives in wheelchairs. The blast wave blew people's arms and legs clean off, and the heat from the explosion was so intense it peeled the skin from their bodies like barbecued chicken. Have you ever seen a third-degree burn victim, Janey? Smelled one?"

She was openly crying now. "Why are you telling me this?"

"You know why."

"She'll kill me."

"Maybe it's time you were on your own. Don't you want to get out of this place?"

She nodded.

"Do the right thing, Janey. Break the cycle. Make something of your life."

"The Parrot's Nest. She hangs out there before going to work."

"Will you show us where it is?"

"What, right now?"

"Yes. Right now."

Henning was visibly surprised at seeing Nathan emerge from the apartment with Janey in tow. She had changed into more respectable attire, wearing a formal white button-down shirt with pressed jeans. Her fuzzy pink slippers had been replaced with tan walking shoes.

"Janey's had a change of heart," Nathan said. "She's going to show us where her mother is."

"Did he hurt you?" Henning asked.

"No."

"Then why are you helping us?"

She practically yelled at him. "Because I'm not like my father, okay?"

Henning held up his arms defensively. "Okay, okay . . ."

Nathan winked at Henning and shook his head, his meaning obvious: *Let it go.*

From the look of things, the Parrot's Nest wasn't in the best part of town. Most cities the size of Fresno had a bona fide skid-row district, and this area of downtown definitely qualified. Part of an abandoned five-story building made of brick, the Parrot's Nest should've been called the Rat's Nest. The small parking lot was lousy with trash, broken glass, dented pickups, run-down Hogs, and various other beaters that looked like they might or might not start when their owners finally staggered out to them, assuming they could even find their keys.

"Is that your mother's car?" Nathan asked, "the red Sentra?"

"Yes."

Henning frowned.

Reading his mind, Nathan said, "It was in her NCIC file."

Andrews parked on the curb in a red zone.

"Maybe I should go in with you," Henning offered. "It looks like a rough joint."

"They'll make you right away. Just cover the rear door. Andrews, you stay with Janey."

Andrews looked at Henning, then back to Nathan. His expression neutral, he nodded.

Nathan climbed out and walked toward the main entrance while Henning traversed the parking lot, heading for the rear of the building. The cracked sidewalk was peppered with hundreds of black gum wads—poor man's silver dollars. A staccato thump of bass emanated from within. Although it was the middle of the afternoon, the street was devoid of traffic. Most of the coin-hungry parking meters had been vandalized, their half-moon windows broken.

At the door, Nathan sucked in a lungful of fresh air and stepped inside

## ⊕ Chapter Sixteen

Nathan's entrance ended up as clichéd as any cheesy B movie. Every head turned. Beer mugs froze in midair. The pool game stopped. He strolled over to the bar and avoided touching the grimy brass rails.

Huge, with hands like catcher's mitts, the bartender scowled and pointedly ignored him. *Okay* . . . Nathan used the time to study the place in the mirror behind the bar and spotted his mark right away—a tall, stringy blonde sitting at a table with three guys in sweatshirts, jeans, and stained ball caps. Scattered around the room, twenty or so other patrons stared in ape-faced silence. Aside from the bartender, who looked formidable, Nathan didn't see any threats. Half a minute later, the bartender had made it plainly obvious he had no intention of serving someone who'd come in to case the joint.

Without looking at the bartender, Nathan walked over to the jukebox, grabbed its power cord, and yanked it free.

The machine went dark. Charlie Daniels went silent. All heads turned.

A few obscene grumbles spewed from dark corners.

"I'd like a Shirley Temple, if it isn't too much trouble."

The bartender shot Nathan a dirty look, came out from behind the bar, and plugged the jukebox back in. With his right hand he pumped in a quarter and punched up another shit-kicker song. The music boomed again. Nathan waited for him to return to his hole, made eye contact, and pulled the plug again. The tension in the room instantly doubled, with all eyes now focused on the battle of wills unfolding. With an irritated expression, the bartender started back over.

A smile touched Nathan's lips. Nathan McBride in his environment—ready, willing, and able to kick ass.

He observed the bartender closely. Right-handed. Six-three or -four. Two hundred seventy-five plus. Weak left eye. Something was strapped to his ankle under his left pant leg, a knife or small gun. *This gorilla probably runs the dive with an iron fist.* As the bartender approached, Nathan saw a black nylon cord encircling his right wrist, and the man's hand seemed to be half-closed around something, like a magician concealing a playing card. Using his *left* hand this time, he reached down to plug the machine back in.

"Don't do it," Nathan warned.

The meaty hand froze before being retracted. The bartender straightened up, issued a *give me a break* smirk, and then swung for Nathan's jaw with an open right hand.

Nathan saw it a split second before ducking. A palm sap.

If that blow had made contact Nathan would be unconscious, or maybe even dead. Deep-rooted anger flared as he glimpsed James Ortega, bound and helpless, screaming in agony.

It happened so fast no one in the room actually saw it, although half the room heard it. In less than a second Nathan stomped down on the man's right leg just above the ankle. The crunch of ligaments sounded like uncooked spaghetti breaking.

Howling, the bartender went down.

Nathan pounced on the downed man and rendered him

inert with a right knee to the jaw. Several teeth flew. Nathan removed the man's small semiautomatic handgun from its ankle holster and jammed it into his own front pocket. Half the occupants scattered for the exits, gone in seconds, bar tabs unpaid—no doubt parolees who didn't want to be caught in one another's company when the cops arrived. Two men at a corner table caught Nathan's attention. A little too clean-cut for this shabby crowd, they looked out of place. He ignored them. For now.

Amber Sheldon hadn't moved. In fact, she appeared to be enjoying the show—not unlike a kid with a magnifying glass poised over an anthill.

Nathan addressed the silent room. "Anyone else?" When no one made a move, he approached the table where Amber Sheldon was seated. Although her smile had somewhat faded at his arrival, it wasn't completely gone. He addressed the three men seated with her. "Would you gentlemen please excuse yourselves from the table?"

The politeness in Nathan's voice took them by surprise, but all three left the table. One of them bent over the bartender; the other two grabbed stools at the bar and helped themselves to free draft beer.

Amber removed a cigarette from the pack sitting on the table and fired it up with a wooden match. Through a slit in her lips, she blew the smoke up and away and nodded to a vacant chair. "Have a seat, cowboy."

Nathan sat down facing the center of the room. He caught the two men he'd noticed earlier watching him. He winked and they looked away.

She studied his damaged face for several seconds. "Been in a few fights?"

"A few."

"What do you want?"

"My own private jet."

"Cute. What do you want with me?"

"That's much more specific, but you already know why I'm here, don't you?"

"I got a pretty good idea. You a cop?"

"No."

She took another deep drag and blew it out slowly.

Nathan leaned forward slightly. "What did he say to you on the phone the other night?"

Her face showed instant understanding. "That little slut—what did she tell you?"

"I'm asking the questions from now on."

"The *fuck* you are. I don't have to tell you jack." She blew smoke in his face and smiled.

In a lightning-fast move, Nathan snatched the cigarette from her fingers and flicked it at her. In a shower of red sparks it bounced off her forehead.

"Hey, asshole! Who *the fuck* do you think you are?"

He engaged Amber's stare. "I'm the one who's asking the questions. You're the one who's going to answer them." Nathan softened his tone. "It doesn't have to get rough. It's entirely up to you. We can talk like mature adults right here and now, or you can be tortured in a soundproof room, screaming your lungs out in agony. I'm okay either way."

"Some cop you are."

"I'm not a cop."

"Who are you?"

"A vested third party."

"A bounty hunter?"

"Not entirely accurate, but essentially, yes."

"Ernie told me someone like you might come around asking about him."

"Go on."

"He said if I talked, he'd kill me and Janey."

"Does he know she's his daughter?"

"Hell, no."

"Do you know where he is?"

"No."

Nathan watched her reaction closely.

"I don't," she said. "I'd give his ass up if I did. He's a piece a' shit."

She wasn't lying. "Tell me about his old hangouts, places he liked to go, people he knew. Anything that might help me find him."

Sheldon half-laughed. "Places? He liked to play pool for money, but he wouldn't be doing that now, would he? The only people he knew besides me were his brothers."

"Why'd you visit him when he was locked up?"

She considered the question for a moment before answering. "Don't get me wrong—Ernie's a first-class jackass, but he still got a raw deal. The DUI thing? His court-martial?"

"What about it?"

"That dumb broad walked right in front of his car. I know, 'cause I was there, sitting next to him when it happened. It wasn't his fault. We weren't even speeding, and he wasn't really drunk. He got railroaded 'cause she was some sort of big-shot lawyer from a rich beaner family."

Nathan leaned forward. "I find the word *beaner* extremely offensive. Don't use it with me again."

"Okay, whatever. No need to get pissed off. Anyway, her dad was some big government guy. She was the one hammered that night, not Ernie."

"That may be true, but the law only recognizes the legal limit, and Ernie was beyond it. He had a long history of insubordination and alcoholism."

"He still got screwed. He was real bitter about the whole thing. It's all he ever talked about. He swore to get revenge someday. I told him he should just forget about it and move on. After he hooked up with his older brother, I never heard from him again until his call the other night."

"Did you believe him about getting revenge?"

"Yeah, I did. Still do. One thing about Ernie: He don't forget about shit like that. At the time I felt sorry for him. I don't now, but I did back then."

"So what changed?"

"I did. I decided I wasn't going to put up with his shit any-more. After he got out he was worse than ever. He was always yelling and screaming. I could never do anything right. Noth-ing was ever good enough for that man."

Nathan didn't want to pursue this line; he already knew about Ernie Bridgestone's pathology. "Is there anything else you can think of that might help us find him?"

"Not really."

"Do you mind if we put a trace on your phone, in case he calls again?"

"Knock yourself out."

Nathan grabbed a pen from his shirt pocket and wrote his name and cell number on a napkin. "If Ernie calls you again for any reason, tell him Nathan McBride is looking for him. Remember it. Nathan McBride."

"I'll remember, but I pray I never hear from that piece a' shit again."

"I need your help."

"Forget about it. I'm not doing nothing to put me or Janey in danger."

"There's a million-dollar reward." That got her attention. Then he took a few minutes to lay out his plan—and her part in it.

"I don't like it," she said, "even with the money you're of-fering me over and above the reward I might or might not get."

"If it doesn't work, you still keep my fifty grand; if it works, you're a million dollars richer."

"I'll think about it."

Nathan stood. "He's murdered twenty-four people."

She lit another cigarette. "I said I'll think about it."

"Remember, if he calls, don't talk to him on your work or home number. Drive a few miles down the road and find a pay phone. Make sure you're not followed. Write the number down and arrange a time for him to call you back. After he calls, wait a few minutes before calling me. And be sure you mention my name, Nathan McBride."

"What so damned important about that?"

"He'll recognize it. Nathan McBride."

She squinted her eyes and took another hit on the cigarette.

"Also, if he calls, tell him that Janey's his daughter."

"I don't like that either."

"Think about it, Amber. Put the pieces together."

She was quiet for a few seconds. "You're thinking he'll want to see her."

"That's right."

"What makes you think he'll give a damn? He never has before."

"That's true, but he doesn't know about Janey."

She didn't respond.

"Janey's outside. Don't give her a hard time for talking to me; I didn't give her a choice. She's just trying to do the right thing. I hope you will too. Let her drive you home. If you get behind the wheel, those two over to my left will probably arrest you."

She glanced in the direction of the clean-cut guys who still held the corner table. "Thanks for the heads-up."

Nathan left her sitting there and walked over to the clean-cut guys. "It's a little warm in here for Windbreakers."

They didn't reply.

"She doesn't know where he is."

No response.

"You feds? Or local?"

Keeping his eyes squarely on Nathan, the man sitting on the left slid his right hand from the table into his waist pack. "We don't want any trouble."

"You're dressed right, but your hair and clothes are too clean. They make you stand out in a place like this."

They glanced at each other, their expressions guardedly neutral.

Nathan continued through the bar, waved to the now-toothless bartender, and received a middle-finger salute in return.

Outside, he found Henning with his Glock drawn. All six patrons who'd bolted out the rear door were neatly lying face-down in the alley, arms out to their sides. "Looks like an undersize catch," Nathan said. "I'd throw them all back."

"How'd it go in there?"

"About like I expected. Sheldon doesn't know where he is. She confirmed he called, though. Gave us permission to tap her phone in case he calls back."

"Well, that's something."

They started across the parking lot.

"What about us?" one of the barflies asked from the concrete.

Henning turned back. "Take off."

Watching them scramble in every direction, Nathan was reminded for the second time in as many days of a real-life *Cops* episode. Back at the sedan, Nathan opened the door and let Janey Sheldon out. "Your mother needs a ride home. Don't let her drive, okay?"

"What happened in there?"

He lowered his voice to a whisper. "Watch what you say in your apartment. Big Brother's listening."

"What?"

"Just don't let your mom get behind the wheel."

"That's it? You're just gonna leave me here?"

Nathan slid into the backseat. "Yep."

Something occurred to him as Special Agent Andrews started the engine and pulled away from the curb: Amber Sheldon hadn't asked for any sort of protection against Ernie.

The drive back to Fresno's airport was somewhat hushed. Nathan answered a few questions from Henning and Andrews, but he couldn't stop thinking about the presence of the two undercover cops in the bar. It didn't pass the smell test. In fact, it stank to high heaven. He didn't want to think about the implications, didn't want to believe what he suspected was true: that Holly Simpson had told Director Lansing of his plans, and Lansing had beaten him to finding Amber Sheldon. Why else would those two undercovers have been in there?

The odds against any other explanation were astronomical. That left Nathan with a decision to make: Should he continue to share information with Holly? He found it difficult to believe Holly would knowingly betray him and act behind his back. It was more likely that she had simply reported his plans to Lansing, and Lansing had acted independently. Even if Holly *had* reported his activities to Lansing, she hadn't done anything wrong. It was her job—and indeed her obligation—to report her activities to her boss.

One thing was certain: He wanted to talk to her alone, wanted the truth.

Starting with Lansing, he began to analyze and question everything. So Lansing had placed a multilingual agent on the Lear to keep an eye on his activities. Okay, that was an understandable move, given what was at stake, but was it really necessary? If Lansing wanted a watchdog, he already had one in the form of Bruce Henning. So why the doubled asset? An asset who not only spoke Arabic, but probably Russian as well? Did Lansing possess that level of mistrust? Did he really think Nathan would speak to Harvey in a foreign language to hide information? No, it didn't make sense. There had to be something else going on, something a lot deeper in play here. But what was it? What was Lansing hiding?

The more Nathan thought about it, the uneasier he became. Had Lansing given him the use of the Lear strictly as a way to monitor and control Nathan's activities? He thought back to Holly's comment in the piano bar. She'd said Lansing didn't need him. Why would he? He had thirty-one thousand employees under his command. She'd also said Lansing would want containment at this point, and further involving him in the investigation would have serious consequences if it ever leaked. So why had Lansing caved and brought Nathan in? Granted, the bombing in Sacramento had changed the equation, but did Lansing truly believe Nathan McBride was the FBI's best bet for capturing the Bridgestone brothers? The Godfather's adage flashed through his head: *Keep your friends close and your enemies even closer.* Was Nathan the enemy? If so, why? What was Lansing afraid of? In the piano bar Nathan had made it quite clear to Holly that he and Harvey were going to pursue the Bridgestones with or without the FBI's blessing. Had Lansing allowed him into the investigation only to monitor his every move?

Nathan took a deep breath and tried to clear his mind. He rewound to the beginning of his involvement in the operation. Freedom's Echo and Semtex. James Ortega discovered while undercover. The raid at the compound. The FBI's field office being bombed. Semtex being used. Semtex still missing. Semtex. *Semtex.* He closed his eyes and let his head rest against the seat back. Aside from the dead FBI agents, the stakes of this case *were* Semtex. How easy would it be to get the stuff? Even if Leonard Bridgestone had made contact with a Syrian official in northern Iraq, there was still a language barrier. Unless Bridgestone spoke Arabic, which he doubted, someone would've been needed to translate conversations. He made a mental note to check whether Leonard spoke Arabic. Then, if a deal were struck, the Semtex would have to be smuggled out of Syria, but not without at least a partial payment— more likely the entire payment. Did Leonard have that kind of money back then? Nathan doubted it. So how had the deal gone down? Assuming Leonard had managed to find a translator, and assuming he'd made a deal with a foreign national— probably a complete stranger—and assuming he had the financial wherewithal to purchase the Semtex in advance, why wouldn't the Syrian official just keep his money and never deliver the Semtex? Leonard was one man, working alone, and without significant leverage in the deal. It wasn't like he could've gone to court and sued the guy for not keeping his end of the contract. And how was the Semtex smuggled out of Syria? That country was high on the NSA's watch list of terrorist states. Smuggling Semtex to a neighboring country like Lebanon was probably difficult enough, but smuggling it into the United States had to be a million times harder. It would involve lots of people. People to create fake documents and falsify cargo manifests. People to remove the Semtex from its stockpiled location. People to pack the Semtex into disguised crates. People to transport the disguised crates down to the shipping terminal. People to load the crates into a cargo container.

Nathan couldn't remember ever seeing any type of product that had a label stating, MADE IN SYRIA. He knew Syria exported textiles and clothing, olive oil, and, of course, crude oil. But anything leaving Syria on a direct path to the United States would be under much closer scrutiny than from other exporting countries. It was unlikely the Semtex could be sent directly by container ship, so that meant the disguised crates would probably be sent to another country first, then transferred to another cargo container before being loaded onto a ship bound for the United States. Virtually all cargo containers were monitored and controlled by computerized inventory programs that both identified and tracked them as they were loaded and unloaded from ships. He supposed the Semtex could've been transported by a smaller private ship that met yet another ship out at sea and transferred the Semtex that way, but how likely was that? And, again, how many people would be involved? Dozens? It simply couldn't be done by two or three people. And it would be expensive. Nathan had no idea what a ton of Semtex sold for on the black market, but whatever the number was, he doubted it would be economical, based on the scenario he'd just worked out.

The Syrian connection, now that he'd had time to think it through, was looking more and more unlikely. Okay, so if the Bridgestones hadn't gotten it from Syria, where *did* they get it? Someone within Freedom's Echo had a connection? If so, who? Was the FBI even looking at the other members? Surely they had to be. The bureau would be asking the same questions as Nathan: Where *did* the Bridgestones get the Semtex?

Maybe there was no Syrian connection. Maybe the Bridgestones had purchased their Semtex here, from someone inside the United States. The big question was: Who?

# ⊕ Chapter Seventeen

With the smell of Italian food still lingering in the air, Frank Ortega sat at his desk waiting for his phone to ring, his gut burning with growing irritation. When the phone finally bleeped to life, he glanced at his Chelsea ship's bell clock. Right on time. He pivoted his wheelchair and stabbed the speaker button.

"What the hell is going on out there?" he asked. Not *hello*, or *good afternoon*, or *how are things in D.C.*

"We're trying to sort it out."

"Trying to sort it out? What kind of answer is that? They burned my grandson alive."

"Frank, I'm as angry as you are. He was your grandson, but he was also my employee."

"There's a big difference."

"Damn it, Frank. I know that. Your grandson isn't the only casualty. I've got twenty-one more unhappy letters to sign."

"Look, I'm sorry. I haven't been sleeping well. I'm . . . I'm so *damned angry*, I just want to kill someone."

"I wish I could bring him back, unwind the clock and start over. I'd do a lot of things differently."

"Let me be clear, Ethan: I don't blame you for any of this."

"Well, it's eating me too. Maybe bringing McBride aboard wasn't such a good idea. He complicates things."

"Why? He's under your control, isn't he? He found my grandson."

"Yes, and he also killed the Bridgestones' kid brother. That was an unexpected twist with unexpected consequences."

Frank tried to keep his voice calm. "He did exactly what I asked of him. You'd have a dozen dead SWAT agents if he hadn't been there. I asked him to back you guys up, and that's what he did, to the letter."

"You know I'm grateful for that. But the problem's different now. It's bigger, more public. What am I saying? Public? It's worldwide news. We still have over three hundred pounds of Semtex missing."

Ortega pinched the bridge of his nose, trying to keep the conversation on track. "All the more reason to have McBride on their trail, then."

"It was that damned tunnel. If they'd shown it to James, he would've told us. As far as we knew, the Bridgestones had no way to get the Semtex out of there. Or themselves, for that matter. We had that compound under constant surveillance. This whole thing would be over if it weren't for that *damned tunnel*. Hell, I don't know. . . . Maybe I should've anticipated something like this. Maybe I should've had choppers orbiting just over the ridgeline. I could've—"

"It's not your fault, Ethan. I don't mean to interrupt, but let's stay on track. . . . Do we keep McBride aboard?"

"At this point, I suppose we don't have much choice. It's all I can do to contain him. If he finds the brothers before we do, that's great. But I don't see it happening."

"What's he doing now?" Frank asked.

"He checked Ernie Bridgestone's visitation logs at Fort Leavenworth. Then he made contact with Amber Sheldon in Fresno, but she doesn't know where Bridgestone is."

Frank paused. When he spoke, there was a hard edge to his voice. "What did Sheldon tell him? Did she—"

"Frank, I don't know. McBride's been tight-lipped. He spotted a couple of my agents watching her, but he doesn't know for sure they're mine."

"Don't kid yourself. He knows." Frank wheeled around

and looked at the photographs on his wall. "Maybe we *should* cut ties with McBride."

"No. I hate to admit it, but you're right. McBride's probably our best shot. Despite what we think of his methods, he gets the job done. He thinks the Bridgestones might go after his father next. He told my SAC he thinks the Sacramento bombing is probably a diversion."

"Some diversion."

"And on our consciences."

"The hell it is," said Frank. "We didn't make those bastards do anything. Their lousy kid brother deserved to die. He was about to shoot your SWAT teams."

"You know what I mean. Look, if McBride's as good as I think he is, he'll eliminate the problem and we'll close the book on this."

"Let's hope so."

Three thousand miles away, FBI director Ethan Lansing hung up the phone, leaned back in his leather office chair, and sighed. He needed to go home to his wife and kids. Hell, if containment weren't forthcoming, he'd be spending a lot more time there, which, when he thought about it, wasn't an altogether bad idea.

Leaving Fresno behind, the FBI Lear climbed into the clear afternoon air. Nathan pulled out his cell phone and called Harvey.

"You on your way?" Harvey asked.

"Yes, we're just leaving Fresno."

"We've come up with squat on the financial insider."

"There may not be one. I'm beginning to think they've been stockpiling cash. They probably have a huge stash buried somewhere."

"That's beginning to make the most sense, but it's also going to make it a lot harder to find them."

"I know." Nathan lowered his voice. "Bear with me, Harv. I'm playing a hunch."

"Okay . . ."

"I left my name and number with Amber Sheldon. I told her if Ernie calls back she's to tell him I came looking for him. I asked her to specifically mention me by name."

Silence from Harvey.

"There's more. Amber's got a seventeen-year-old daughter. Guess who the father is?"

"No way."

"Yep, Amber never told him."

Harvey paused, thinking about this new twist. "You're thinking if he discovers he's got a long-lost daughter he'll want to see her before he bugs out."

"Yep."

"Then everything depends on Ernie calling her again. What if he doesn't call?"

"I've got that covered."

"What's your plan?"

"Five by one," Nathan said.

"Understood. Want me to pick you up at Sac International?"

"No, Henning's got a vehicle there. I'll see you at the hotel in about an hour."

"Stay safe, partner."

Nathan settled in for the short flight back to Sacramento. He needed to talk with Holly Simpson. Alone. Everything hinged on her being honest with him. At a minimum he was going to need the full media power of the FBI to pull off his plan for trapping Ernie; beyond that, he'd just have to wait and see how his conversation with Holly went. Despite everything he suspected about Director Lansing, he still felt Holly could be trusted. They'd connected on an emotional level, and he didn't think she would willingly betray him. *Willingly* being the operative word.

He turned toward Henning, who was looking at him. "I'd like to visit with SAC Simpson tonight. Alone, if you're okay with that."

"It's up to her. Want me to call her?"

"I'd appreciate it."

Henning pulled his phone and dialed the hospital. He asked to be connected to Simpson's room. "Hi, SAC," he said. "How are you feeling? . . . Yes, we're on our way, should be landing in about twenty minutes. . . . Nathan McBride wants to stop by. . . . Yes, tonight . . . Okay. We should be there in about an hour, plus or minus. Okay . . . See you then."

"Thanks," Nathan said.

"No problem. May I ask what it's about?"

"The truth."

"I don't blame you for being suspicious. There hasn't been a lot of trust around here."

"I'm an unproven asset. It's a safe call on Lansing's part."

"If Lansing had seen you in action at Sutter Hospital, he'd probably feel differently."

"For what it's worth, I've got no problem with you. I mean, I trust you."

"Well, at least that's something. What does 'five by one' mean? I heard you say it to your partner."

"Since we're talking the truth here, it was code—meaning I'm uneasy with the current situation and I didn't want to discuss the subject out loud. I have a plan, but I want to run it by SAC Simpson first."

"Why not run it by me too? Since you trust me and all . . ."

"I will when I'm able. I *can* tell you this much: My plan's risky and I'm going to need some luck to pull it off, but it's all I've got."

"I want to help."

"It'll be Simpson's call. You and I have worked well together. I'll ask for your continued involvement."

"Well, that's good enough for me."

The first things Nathan noticed when he entered Holly's hospital room were the flowers and heart-shaped helium balloons.

Despite the monitoring machines and IV stands, the room looked colorful and bright. Holly was sitting up in bed with an FBI file in her lap. She set the file on the table next to the bed.

"Thank you for the flowers and balloons," she said.

He paused, but recovered quickly. *Harvey*. "You're welcome. Feeling a little better?"

"Tons."

The top of her shaved head was still wrapped in gauze. The external splints on her legs were also still there, suspended by a cable system of stainless-steel supports that looked like jungle-gym bars. Some of the balloons were attached to them, swaying gently in the processed air. The room had conflicting odors, antiseptic versus floral. Nathan thought she did look better. Her eyes were brighter and more alert. When he'd first visited she'd looked like death warmed over.

He dragged a chair over from the corner and sat facing her. "Director Lansing beat me to finding Amber Sheldon. When I arrived at the bar, two of his people were already in there watching her."

Holly stared, her mind working. "Are you sure they were ours?"

"Am I one hundred percent positive? No."

"Then why do you think they were?"

"Lansing put an agent on the Lear with me, the copilot. He came clean and told me he was reporting directly to Lansing on my activities."

"Nathan, I didn't know."

"I know that. Look, I'm not trying to be confrontational. I think it's a safe play on his part, but before I go any further, I need to know who I can trust and who I can't. And right now, Lansing's in the negative column."

"Of course I told Director Lansing where you were going and what you planned to do, but I didn't know he'd take this kind of action without telling me."

"He's in the hot seat for any political fallout. He has to be cautious."

"Overly so, it seems."

"I have a decision to make, and I wanted to talk with you first. If we're going to catch these guys, we can't be working against each other. If Amber had made those undercovers in the bar the entire dynamic would've been different; she might not have talked to me. You understand where I'm going with this."

"Yes."

"Because I don't want you to compromise your position with Lansing, I'm reluctant to continue with the status quo. If you feel you have to report everything I'm doing, then maybe we should part company."

"I don't want to do that."

"I don't either. I absolutely need the FBI for the next phase of my plan."

"If I'd known what Director Lansing was planning, I would've tried to stop it. And I certainly would've told you."

"Like I said, I'm not blaming you or your boss, but the surveillance needs to stop."

She reached out and grasped his hand. "I'll find out what the hell's going on. That's a promise."

"Don't compromise your relationship with him over this. You and me, kiddo? We're still good."

"I'm glad to hear that." She released his hand. "You mentioned the next phase?"

"I'll be honest: It's a long shot, but it's all I've got. I need Ernie Bridgestone to call Amber again."

"He already called her?"

Nathan had told her about the first call. Once again, he credited her memory lapse to the heavy drugs in her system. Surgical anesthetics had a certain amount of amnesia associated with their use. He wasn't worried about her yet. . . . "Yeah, he called and told her not to talk to the authorities or he'd kill her. I'm going to tap into that; here's my plan."

Holly listened while Nathan laid it out. It took several minutes.

"It's a good plan," Holly said, "but you're making a huge assumption about Bridgestone's character."

"It's all I've got. And aside from Leonard, Janey's all Ernie's got in terms of family. If we set this up right, I think there's at least a chance Ernie will feel compelled to call. I told Amber not to talk with him on her home or work numbers. I told her to have Ernie call back on a pay phone. I think it's fair to assume her phones are being monitored, especially since she gave me—or the FBI—permission to bug them."

"No doubt they are."

"She's also being shadowed; let's hope Lansing's people aren't using rifle mikes on her every move."

"It's a little cruel, what you're planning."

"To pull this off it has to be spontaneous. She can't know it's coming. We can't worry about her feelings getting hurt; in fact, I'm hoping she *will* be angry about it."

"Why?"

"Because I broke my promise."

"What promise? What are you talking about?"

"Remember our conversation in the piano bar? The part about me not making myself a target?"

"Nathan, what did you do?"

"I added an insurance policy. During my interview with Dr. Fitzgerald at the Castle, he said Ernie was obsessed with revenge for being railroaded. I'm hoping to tap into his tendency toward revenge, this time for his little brother, Sammy. If Ernie calls Amber, I told her to specifically mention my name, that a guy named Nathan McBride came around looking for him."

"I really wish you hadn't done that."

"I'm sorry. I know I told you I wouldn't, but things have changed. I made that promise before they bombed your field office. This isn't a simple manhunt anymore. It's a fight to the death. The FBI is now the hunted, not the hunter. If the family-loyalty angle doesn't work, I'm hoping Ernie's desire for revenge will. Think about it: They could've taken their cash and bugged out, but they chose to stay and avenge their kid brother. Although they don't know it yet, they didn't kill the person directly responsible. After they find out I'm still alive, it probably won't sit well with them. If I can just get Ernie to call Sheldon again, things will fall into place."

"In any case, we need to protect you. You know what they're capable of."

"Don't worry about me; I can take care of myself. After all, I'm in the security business."

"And, Nathan?"

He waited.

"Thank Harvey for me, for the balloons and flowers."

Nathan shook his head and laughed. "You don't miss much."

"Well, after all, I am in the investigation business."

# ⊕ Chapter Eighteen

Nathan entered his hotel room and collapsed on the bed. He knew Harvey would hear him.

"That you, Nate?"

"Yep."

"How's Holly doing?"

"Better. And thanks for sending the balloons and flowers. Her room looked nice."

"I figured it might brighten things up a little."

"I need a shower and some chow. Have you eaten?"

"Not yet, I had an early lunch. Let's grab a bite down in the restaurant. Dr. Fitzgerald promised to fax everything he has on Ernie Bridgestone's drunk-driving accident. We don't have it yet, but it might be here by the time we finish dinner."

Nathan rubbed his face. "I keep having this feeling. . . . Doesn't it seem like there's something's missing? Something we're not seeing? I mean, think about it—Lansing's gone to a lot of trouble to monitor my every move. The agent on the Lear, the two agents in the bar. I wouldn't be surprised if he's tapped our phones. They're probably listening to us right now."

Harvey nodded. "Whatever the case, we should probably go stealth from now on."

"Agreed. Also, I was thinking about Frank Ortega. When was the last time you talked with him?"

"I called him early this afternoon."

"How's he doing?"

"Hard to say. He seemed calm. He was very curious about your trip out to the Castle and your chat with Fitzgerald. He was especially interested in your meeting with Amber Sheldon. He really grilled me over it."

"Grilled you? What about?"

Harvey pointed at the ceiling. "I'll tell you on the way to dinner."

"Let's go then; I'm starved." In the elevator Nathan resumed their conversation. "What did Ortega want to know about Amber Sheldon?"

"Everything. He wanted to know what you two talked about. Word for word."

"What did you tell him?"

"I thought it best not to get too specific. I basically told him you asked Amber about Ernie's background, anything she could share that might help us find him. Said she didn't have anything. I didn't say a word about Janey being his daughter."

"Good thinking. We need to keep that under wraps."

"I'm uncomfortable withholding information from him."

"I'm not. Something tells me Lansing and Ortega are closer pals than we realize. I've been thinking about that too. How much clout would you need to involve a couple of outsiders like us in top-secret bureau business?"

"A lot."

"Exactly. Ortega's been cashing in a big debt Lansing owes him. I wish we could find out what it is."

"With all due respect, Nate, why would we care? We don't need to know."

Nathan sighed. "I suppose you're right. I guess all this cloak-and-dagger crap is getting to me."

Neither of the Hyatt's restaurants were open yet, so they walked a few blocks to the Hard Rock Café. It was still a bit early for dinner, so the place wasn't crowded yet, which suited them just fine. They were escorted to a corner table by a hostess who looked sixteen years old; in reality she was probably in her mid-twenties. *I must be getting old*, Nathan thought as he watched her walk back to her station. He had to admit she had a nice walk. When the server came, he ordered a Caesar salad with the dressing on the side. Harvey ordered a teriyaki-stick platter, pot stickers, a shrimp cocktail, a bowl of New England clam chowder, a calamari steak sandwich—with fries—and a chocolate milk shake.

Nathan just stared.

"What?" Harvey said.

"You got a hollow leg or something?"

"I'm hungry. What about it?"

"I'll bet you fifty bucks you can't eat all that."

"You're on."

Forty minutes later Nathan fished out his wallet.

On the walk back to the Hyatt, Nathan shook his head. "You amaze me."

"I know."

Nathan switched to Russian. "You spot the two agents watching us in there?"

"Yes," Harvey answered in Russian. "Opposite side of the room. Male/female combo sitting at the bar. They were good. I thought maybe you had missed them."

"What are we going to do about them?" Nathan asked.

"You want to mess with them?"

"It is tempting, is it not? Did you see them while I was out of town with Henning?"

"No."

"Means they are watching me, not you."

"Probably, but I could've missed them."

"You are better at this than me."

As they chatted in Russian, they passed a homeless man sitting against the brick wall of a liquor store. "Gol-darned for-ners," he muttered.

Nathan smiled at the comment, removed his wallet, and fished out a twenty-dollar bill. The guy nodded a thank-you. "Don't spend it all in the same place," Nathan said in English. He used the opportunity to glance back to the Hard Rock's entrance. The male/female combo was just walking out the door. They turned and started down the sidewalk, holding hands. *Yeah, right* . . .

Harvey kept walking without turning. "They coming?" he asked in Russian.

"Yes. I will divert over to the registration desk and let them catch up. You head into the bar and order a glass of wine. I will head up to the room. Give me three minutes; then come up."

"What are you going to do?"

"Waste some taxpayers' money."

At the registration desk, Nathan spoke softly to the woman behind the counter. She was in her mid-thirties and slightly overweight. Her dark hair was in a bun. Her name tag said, YOLONDA. Below that it said, POWAY, CALIFORNIA. As did most, she did a double take at Nathan's face, but recovered quickly and forced a smile.

Nathan leaned forward and spoke quietly. "There's a man and a woman following me. When they come through the doors, give me a nod. Okay?"

"You want me to call the police?"

"No, just nod when they come in. They work for an insurance company; they're harmless."

Ten seconds later she gave Nathan his nod.

"Thanks," he said.

"You're welcome."

Nathan strolled over to the bank of elevators and pressed the call button. At the sixth floor he hurried to his room and let himself in with the electronic key card. He grabbed his nine-millimeter from the duffel bag and unloaded it. After opening the door on his side of the adjoining room's doorway, he placed an ear against the second door. Sure enough, he heard the room's hallway door open and close. With a smile, he stepped back, raised his foot, and kicked the door with all his strength. The door splintered away from its jamb, flew open, and smacked the dresser hard.

Nathan burst through, gun-first, just as the woman he'd seen in the Hard Rock was setting her purse down on the bed.

She was alone and made a move for her gun, but Nathan pointed his SIG at her chest. "Don't."

She held her hands up. "FBI special agent."

"I know that. Where's your partner?"

She hesitated. "In the lobby, watching Mr. Fontana."

Nathan held his gun up. "Do I need this?"

"No."

"I've got your word on that?"

"Yes."

"Good, 'cause it's not loaded."

"When did you spot us?"

He tucked the gun behind his back. "In the Hard Rock. Your partner kept using the mirror behind the bar to watch us." He smiled, but it wasn't returned. He gave her a closer look. She was actually quite attractive. Stunningly beautiful, really. Around the same age as Nathan, she wore jeans and a white silk shirt under a black leather jacket. Her blonde hair was cut shoulder-length, and she had piercing blue eyes in a Slavic face.

Nathan glanced around the room at all the surveillance

equipment. Half a dozen black boxes were stacked on the dresser next to the door, all of them connected to a digital recorder.

"Okay, Special Agent . . ."

"Grangeland."

"How do you want to play this out? We have a couple of options. The first is, I smash every piece of equipment in this room and you'll have to explain its destruction to whomever you're reporting to, presumably Lansing. The second is, we maintain the status quo. Harvey and I will be careful what we say, and no one needs to be the wiser. I'll tell the hotel staff I lost my footing and fell against the door."

She crossed her arms. "What makes you think I'd allow you to break all this equipment?"

"Because I outweigh you by a hundred pounds."

She thought about her options, and a smile touched her lips. "I have a counterproposal. You and me. Right here. Right now. The winner decides the outcome." She slipped off her coat, unclipped her gun holster from her belt, and tossed it onto the bed.

Nathan stared, not sure he'd heard right. Was she challenging him to a physical contest? He'd make mincemeat of her. He narrowed his eyes. "May I assume there will be no closed fists or head blows?"

"Sure, why not?"

Nathan tossed his gun on the bed next to hers.

It happened fast.

One second she was six feet away; the next she was on him. He parried her palm punch aimed at his solar plexus and realized his mistake too late. Before he could react, she had dropped down and swept his legs out from under him. He went down hard, landing on his butt with a grunt. Two seconds later he found it difficult to breathe. Pinned against the base of the bed, he tried to register what had happened, but his vision was already graying. He was pretty sure he felt her left forearm across the back of his neck and her right hand squeezing his throat, but he couldn't be sure. Somewhere in the growing black tunnel he heard her whisper in his ear, "You can cry uncle anytime, big boy."

Nathan would've responded with a witty retort, except he sat immobilized and close to passing out in a half nelson executed by an opponent half his weight. He braced his legs against the base of the bed and thrust out, flipping them both onto their backs. Now underneath him, Grangeland didn't loosen her grip on his throat. Nathan's mind was fading fast. He figured he had mere seconds to break the hold or be rendered unconscious. If they hadn't agreed to no head blows, he could easily drive the back of his head into her face and smash her nose, but that wasn't an option, even if it meant losing this match.

With what little air he had left in his lungs, he issued a half chuckle, and then realized he had an opportunity to break her hold. Yeah, it could work. Using the space between the bed and the dresser, Nathan rolled to his side and braced his feet against the bed. With his free right hand, he reached behind her back and grabbed her belt above her butt. With Grangeland still clinging to his back, he began simultaneously pulling her jeans up while starting a crushing leg press. As he'd planned, all one hundred and ten pounds of Special Agent Grangeland ended up pinned between himself and the dresser. He was hoping the intrusive distraction of her jeans coupled with the pressure on her torso would drive the air from her lungs. Feeling his mind begin its plummet into the void, he both pushed and pulled harder, giving it all he had in a last-ditch, hydraulic-force effort to break free. It worked. He felt a hiss of air escape her lungs on the back of his neck. Her arms loosened, giving him just enough room to wrench his head sideways. When her grip on his windpipe failed, he jerked his head free and sucked in a precious lungful of air.

Red faced and panting like a dog, he gasped, "Let's call it a draw." He managed to gain his hands and knees just before his Caesar salad came up in projectile fashion. When he finished vomiting his dinner, he wiped his mouth and half-laughed. "*Damn it*, woman, that was some trick."

She rolled onto her back, her legs bent at the knees. "You cheated. I had you."

"The hell you did."

"No doubt you enjoyed that little stunt with my pants."

"You think? Well, now you'll never know." They both looked up at the same instant. Harvey was pointing his SIG at a man who was pointing his Glock at Nathan's head—the four of them frozen in time like waxwork figures.

"It's a good thing you showed up when you did," Nathan said. "I might have killed her."

Grangeland held up a hand. "Stand down, Agent Ferris. This isn't what it looks like."

Somewhat reluctantly, Ferris holstered his gun and looked at Harvey.

Harvey tucked his gun into the small of his back and looked at Nathan, then at the woman, then at the pool of vomit. "I see you two have been properly introduced."

Still breathing heavily, Nathan said, "Special Agent Grangeland, meet Harvey Fontana."

Harvey shook his head. "What is it with you, Nathan? Didn't your mama hold you enough as a baby?"

"Hey, it was her idea."

"Uh-huh."

"Well?" Nathan asked her.

With a grimace, Grangeland sat up. "I guess we'll keep the status quo."

"Good choice," Nathan said.

"Would someone please tell me what the *hell* is going on?" Ferris asked. He looked at the splintered doorjamb, then back at Nathan. "Looks like a clear case of breaking and entering to me."

"Tell me about it," Grangeland said. She staggered to her feet, walked bowlegged into the bathroom, and closed the door.

Nathan rubbed his throat. "She'll be okay; she's just got a really nasty wedgie." Even though Ferris was formidable-looking, Nathan towered over him. In his mid-forties, Ferris had the same intensity in his eyes that Henning had shown several nights ago. He was clean-cut, dressed in tan Docker-type slacks with a long-sleeved button-down shirt. Nathan knew Ferris didn't like the idea of his partner rolling around on the floor with a complete stranger.

"Sorry about the mess," Nathan said. "Tell me something: Where'd she learn to wrestle like that?"

"Alternate for the 2000 Olympic team."

"No shit," Nathan said. "You ever go a round with her?"

"Once."

"And?" Nathan prompted.

"Got my ass kicked in five seconds. She's also holds black belts in aikido and tae kwon do."

"I'm in love," Nathan said. He looked at the processed romaine lettuce on the carpet. "Want me to call house-keeping?"

Ferris just stared.

Harvey grabbed Nathan's handgun from the bed. "Come on, Nathan; let's get the hell out of here." Harvey turned toward Ferris, then pointed at the electronic surveillance equipment. "This is bullshit."

"Easy, partner; don't shoot the messenger."

"Why not?" Harvey said. "We've been open and honest." He waved a hand at the black boxes. "And this is the thanks we get?"

"It's just business," Nathan said.

Harvey grunted and walked out of the room.

Nathan addressed Ferris. "This doesn't have to go any further than the four of us. We'll let you save face with Lansing, but we're on to you now. If you want to know what we're up to, just ask." Nathan joined Harvey and closed the door behind him. Still rubbing his throat, he sat on the edge of the bed.

Harvey was standing at the window, staring at the State Capitol building. "I'm sorry I snapped at you." He turned and smiled. "Your mother held you a lot; you were an only child."

"No, you're right; I acted childishly in there. I didn't have to spar with her. I could've said no."

"Why didn't you?"

"Not sure. I guess I wanted to test myself. I'll tell you what: She's tough as nails."

There was a soft knock at the door. They both turned at the same time. Half-expecting to see the hotel manager standing in the hall, Nathan went to the door and peered through the peephole. It was one of their own security guards. Nathan opened the door, and the tech handed him a fax. It was from Dr. Fitzgerald at Fort Leavenworth.

"Let's see what we've got." Nathan sat down at the desk while Harvey looked over his shoulder. The first piece of paper was a copy of a Pensacola Police Department's incident report. Ernie Bridgestone had been going the speed limit; the skid marks on the road verified it. From what they could glean from the report, a woman had entered the street from between two parked cars. The right bumper of Ernie's Camaro had clipped her, sending her head over heels. She died nearly instantly from a broken neck. Her BAC, or blood alcohol concentration, had been point-three-five, over four times the legal limit of point-zero-eight. Ernie's BAC had been point-one-zero. Just as Amber Sheldon had said, he hadn't been truly drunk, but he'd been over the legal limit, and that was all that mattered. The responding officer had written in his notes that Ernie had been extremely indignant, stating over and over that he wasn't drunk and that it wasn't his fault. He'd used profane and derogatory language about the dead victim's ethnicity, which was Hispanic. Things quickly turned ugly. After resisting arrest, he'd been Tasered by a backup officer and booked for felony drunk driving. His bail was set at ten thousand dollars.

The next documents in the file concerned Ernie's civil court matters. His driver's license had been revoked for eighteen months, and he'd been fined two thousand dollars, the maximum allowed by law. Because Ernie had been in the military, Nathan knew his troubles were only beginning. As an active member of the United States Armed Forces, Ernie had been subject to the Uniform Code of Military Justice, no matter where the accident had happened, on or off base, it didn't matter. He'd been surrendered to the Military Police of Pensacola Naval Air Station and placed in the brig. Notes from the transporting MPs also indicated that Ernie had been belligerent, profane, and generally uncooperative. In the court-martial that followed, the presiding military judge lowered the hammer on Ernie. Had he possessed an outstanding military record with no prior offenses, things might have been different. But Ernie had a long history of insubordination. The bottom line was, the Marine Corps made an example out of him, sentencing him to five years in the USDB at Fort Leavenworth, Kansas, after which he would be dishonorably discharged. Basically it was the Marine Corps version of *Good riddance, dirtbag.* The final sheet of paper was a copy of a newspaper clipping, complete with a photograph of the victim. Nathan's eyes grew as he stared at the low-resolution photocopy.

"I've seen this face," he said.

Behind him Harvey whispered, "No, it can't be."

Nathan rewound his mind, trying to place it. In a moment he had it. Staring up at him from the lifeless sheet of paper was an image he'd seen for the first time only days ago.

The face of Frank Ortega's daughter.

## Chapter Nineteen

Harvey barely managed a whisper, "Do you know who that is?"

Nathan nodded.

"Do you know what this means?"

"Yes."

"I've never felt so . . . used," Harvey said. "This whole thing, it's . . . it's . . ."

"Dirty," Nathan finished for him.

Neither of them spoke for several seconds, each running the events of the past week through his mind.

"We risked our lives for Frank Ortega at the Freedom's Echo compound. We could've been killed—almost were killed. Nathan, I'm so sorry."

"Harv, this isn't your fault."

"How could—" Harvey cut himself off and pointed to the door interconnecting the rooms.

Nathan nodded.

Without saying another word, they both left the room. In the elevator Harvey said, "How could the Ortegas have done this to me, to us?"

"Blood is thicker than water," Nathan said quietly. "A lot thicker, it would seem."

"Greg and I go back fifteen years. *Fifteen years.* We spent night after night together looking at satellite imagery when you were missing. I knew Frank's daughter had been killed, but Greg never talked about it. I never knew the circumstances."

"How deep does this go, Harv?"

"You mean Lansing? Ortega must have cashed in that IOU

earlier than we imagined. Getting his grandson assigned to the Bridgestone operation . . ." Harvey gave Nathan a double take. "Oh, you mean your *dad* knowing? I can't fathom him betraying you like this."

"I can," Nathan said. The elevator dumped them into the lobby. Nathan kept his voice low. "We'll take a cab over to Sutter Hospital. Holly needs to know about this."

"Nate . . . she could be involved."

He shook his head. "She's not. I can't explain it, but I'm sure. No way."

After the bellman called the cab, it took several minutes for it to arrive. Their moods identical, neither of them spoke during the ride through rush-hour traffic.

Nathan sensed Harvey's anger mounting. Anger *and* pain—the pain of being used and betrayed by a trusted friend. Nathan grasped Harvey's arm. "We'll get through this, okay?"

Harvey shook his head, eyes closed. "I'm so damned angry, Nate. I . . . I can't . . . ." His throat choked up, words failing him.

Nathan squeezed his arm. "We're going to turn this around on them, Harv. You hear me? We own their asses now."

Nathan knocked on Holly's door.

"Come in." Her cheery tone ended the moment she saw the expressions on their faces. "What happened? Did they hit us again?"

"No," Nathan said. He pulled a chair over from the corner; Harvey did the same.

"You two look like you've seen a ghost."

"We have."

"What? What's happened?"

"Ernie Bridgestone killed Frank Ortega's daughter."

"Oh, no. When?"

"Eighteen years ago."

"Eighteen years?"

"Drunk-driving accident. It's why he went to prison. This whole thing's about revenge."

"No, I don't believe that. I can't believe it."

"It's true, Holly. Everything makes sense now."

"Director Lansing?" she asked.

"Right in the middle of it."

"Are you *absolutely* sure about this? Is there any possibility you could be wrong?"

"None."

"Do you know what this means? What it means for the FBI? For my field office, for my agents?"

"Holly, listen to me. Harvey and I aren't going to do anything that would compromise or embarrass the FBI. We aren't whistle-blowers. You have our word."

"Nathan, I—"

"Just listen for a sec. We've been thinking about this, working it out. Strictly speaking, what Lansing and Ortega did wasn't illegal. But it raises some other questions. What exactly were the Bridgestones doing prior to dealing in Semtex?"

She sat up a little. "Where are you going with this?"

"Stay with me here. Think back: What did the Bridgestones do initially to get the attention of the FBI?"

"I can't remember exactly, but I'm sure I got a call from Director Lansing to begin surveillance up there."

"Is that normally how things work? The call from Lansing?"

"No. My boss is in the Los Angeles field office; he's an assistant director. The call should've come from him."

"Right, but it didn't; it came from Lansing himself. It would be like a brigadier general giving an order to a battalion commander, bypassing the regiment commander. He bypassed the chain of command, left your assistant director out of the loop."

She nodded again.

"Do you remember what he said?"

"Vaguely. Something about a new militia-type group he wanted to watch."

"Do you see where I'm going with this?"

"No, I honestly don't."

Nathan looked at Harvey, then back to Holly. "We read the file on the Bridgestones' operation. Frank Ortega gave it to us prior to the raid. Freedom's Echo was tiny, way under the radar compared to other militia groups in Montana, Idaho, Ohio, you name it. Those big groups have hundreds, sometimes thousands of members. The Bridgestones were small potatoes. They dealt mostly in small-arms conversions, semi-automatic to full auto. It wasn't until the last few months that they started dealing in bigger things."

Nathan watched a light flick on behind Holly's eyes. "You're saying James Ortega wasn't just undercover; *he* was their contact for the Semtex."

Nathan nodded. "Yes. It was more than a deep-cover operation; it was a sting, like Abscam, the FBI acting as both the seller *and* the buyer of the Semtex." He paused to make sure she was absorbing it all. "Ortega and Lansing set the Bridgestones up for a fall for a very personal reason. They thought they had it all under control until two things went wrong: First, the Bridgestones made James Ortega. Second, when the raid came, the FBI had no idea about the tunnel. No matter what happened to James Ortega, the Bridgestones should've been cooked. But with the tunnel, the targets escaped with a bunch of the Semtex, leaving Lansing and Frank Ortega with a nightmare scenario—their personal little war gone amok."

Holly's face had gone sheet white; she was following perfectly well.

"There's more," Nathan said. "We have to assume James Ortega cracked under the torture and spilled his guts. I don't fault him for it." He looked down at the floor. "In Nicaragua I told my interrogators more than I should've. I'm not proud of it, but I'm only human. After a certain point you just can't take it anymore."

"So he told them *everything*."

"That's right. The brothers found out about Frank Orte-ga's plan to bring them down. James caved under the torture and told them who he was and who his grandfather was. Think about it, Holly. How angry would Ernie Bridgestone be at finding out who the FBI had sent to bring him down? The grandson of the man who railroaded him eighteen years ago. How angry would he be? Would he be angry enough to bomb your field office and kill over twenty of your people? Suppose it hadn't been James Ortega? What if it had been any other agent? Would the Bridgestones have let it go? Would they have just taken their money and run?"

"It's more complicated than that," Harvey said. "We also killed their little brother; that may have been the last straw. Could've been the deciding factor."

"That's absolutely possible," Nathan agreed. "We may never know the truth. But here's what we *do* know: After he got out of prison, Ernie Bridgestone had thirteen years to avenge what he claims was an unfair imprisonment for killing Frank Ortega's daughter. But he didn't. I think it's fair to assume he'd let it go, put it behind him. My point is this: It was very bad judgment to use James Ortega at Freedom's Echo against the Bridgestones. Undercover agents are always facing the threat of discovery and interrogation. Frank Ortega should've known that if his grandson were ever captured, he'd reveal his identity under duress. He had to know that would trigger Ernie Bridgestone's old vendetta."

"You'd think so," Holly said. "He just never thought they'd fail—that the brothers might get away. This whole thing . . ." She paused, shaking her head. "It's dirty. And stupid. There are stings, and there are stings. But giving those people Semtex? You may be right, Nathan; from a legal perspective Director Lansing's clean. Ethically it's a different matter. It was a severe conflict of interest to involve James Ortega. And giving them Semtex, then losing it? Then my field office gets bombed? That's a career ender. The real question, I guess, is what we're going to do about it."

"Nothing," Nathan said.

"Nothing?"

"I don't see anything constructive in blowing this wide-open right now, or ever, for that matter. As much as I resent being used as a pawn, it doesn't compare to the pain Frank Ortega has endured. He's lost both a daughter and a grandson to the Bridgestones."

"You amaze me, Nathan. I would be far less forgiving in your shoes."

"This isn't about me or Harvey. It's about justice. Justice for the dead SWAT agent, for James Ortega and the twenty-one other slain FBI employees. I'm not above using the information to keep Lansing off my back, though."

"Then we stick to the plan," she said.

"We stick to the plan," Nathan said. "We've got a big day ahead of us tomorrow."

"Nathan, I'm sorry about Director Lansing and Ortega."

"It's not a reflection on you. You and me, we're still good."

"I appreciate your trust, especially after all the BS you've been through."

"I don't need to tell you this, but I will anyway: Be careful, Holly. Watch what you say." He squeezed her hand and got up. "The walls have ears."

Under a flawless one-o'clock sky, the press conference was staged on the steps of Sacramento's Capitol building. The podium held over two dozen microphones, six of them from foreign countries. The Bridgestones' bombing of the Sacramento field office had made international news. The reporters and cameramen were set up in ten rows of semicircular seating fifteen feet away from the podium. Assistant Special Agent in Charge Perry Breckensen was being introduced by Governor Schwarzenegger. The ASAC looked sharp and focused, his tailored suit gleaming in the afternoon sun. He shook hands with the governor and took the podium.

Leonard and Ernie Bridgestone were still holed up in the same cabin they'd broken into after the raid on their compound. While charting their next moves, they'd been watching the near-constant news coverage of their handiwork, compliments of the cabin owner's satellite dish. For now, they'd agreed, their best course of action was no action. They needed to let things cool down before heading up north, but when they did depart it would be for good. Reaching the location of their hidden money cache in northern Montana concerned Leonard greatly and had been the topic of many conversations.

Their plan was to travel caravan-style, Leonard in the lead in the cabin owners' hot-wired Jeep. Ernie would follow a half mile back in the truck, with the remaining Semtex and blasting caps. The question was when to leave. As much as Leonard wanted to bolt immediately, he knew the best tactic was to let the authorities believe they'd already left northern California long ago. The more time that passed, the bigger the search radius became, leading to thinner and thinner resources for the feds. The longer he and Ernie stayed put, the better chance they'd have of quietly slipping through the net. Leonard found it ironic that he was the antsy one, while Ernie seemed content to watch twenty-four-hour-a-day media speculation on the whereabouts of the infamous Bridgestone brothers.

Ernie sat forward in his chair. "This oughta be good."

As the FBI's press conference was about to start, Ernie's quick search with the remote showed that all the news channels and networks were cutting away from normal programming, going with live coverage in Sacramento.

"We aren't out of the woods yet, Ern."

"Shit, these feebs couldn't find their own ass with a mirror on a stick." Ernie cranked the volume and sat back.

ASAC Breckensen's face filled the screen. "Thank you, Governor Schwarzenegger. I'd also like to thank the press for attending on such short notice. As you know, on October seventeenth, our field office was bombed, with catastrophic results. The blast killed twenty people and injured fifty-eight others, many with career-ending injuries. Our thoughts and prayers go out to all of our affected employees and their families."

"Breaks my fuckin' heart," Ernie said.

Leonard leaned forward and turned the volume up.

Breckensen continued, outlining the chain of events leading up to and following the bombing, which was nothing new to the cable junkies. The summary took nearly ten minutes. "One of the reasons we called this conference was to make a plea to the general public to come forward with any information, no matter how insignificant it might seem. As an example, I'd like to introduce Ms. Amber Mills Sheldon." He gestured off-camera to his right. "Ms. Sheldon."

Ernie jumped up from the sofa. "What the fuck?" Then he yelled at Leonard. "What the *fuck* is this?"

His mind already working, Leonard squinted and said nothing.

The camera followed a small, thin woman in her mid- to late forties as she stepped up to the podium. The makeup artists had earned their pay, Leonard thought. She actually looked good. She placed a piece of paper on the podium and thanked Governor Schwarzenegger and Breckensen. She looked visibly nervous. Reading from a prepared statement, she began.

"My name is Amber Sheldon. I was married to Ernie Bridgestone in Pensacola, Florida, where he worked as a drill instructor training naval aviator candidates at the NAS. I am both shocked and horrified at the bombing of the FBI's field office. I would not have thought him capable of such an act."

Sheldon looked up and stared into the camera for several

seconds with the haunted look of a woman in emotional pain. "I wish to express my deepest sorrow and condolences to the colleagues, friends, and families of the slain FBI employees. I have fully cooperated with the FBI . . . ." Her lip quivered, and a tear rolled down her cheek. She wiped it away and looked off-camera.

Breckensen stepped up to the podium and put his arm around her.

"Look at that son of a bitch," Ernie hissed. "He wants a piece of that. I can't believe this shit."

"Shut up, Ernie," Leonard said. "He's just comforting her."

"Yeah, right."

Breckensen leaned in toward the microphones. "Ms. Sheldon has agreed to take a few questions." He pointed to a reporter seated in the middle of the first row.

"Ms. Sheldon, have you had any contact with Ernie since the raid at Freedom's Echo?"

"No," she said.

The same reporter fired a second question: "When was the last time you spoke with him?"

She looked at Breckensen, silently asking if it was okay to answer. He nodded. "Years ago. After he was released from the disciplinary barracks at Fort Leavenworth. I haven't heard from him since."

Breckensen pointed to another reporter.

"Ms. Sheldon, is there anything from Ernie's past that might've led up to this?"

"Not really. He was very angry about his court-martial, but that happened a long time ago. I don't think this is about that."

Just as Breckensen was about to point to a third reporter, a question boomed out from one of the back rows. "Have you told Ernie Bridgestone that he's the father of your daughter, Janey Sheldon?"

The sudden anger in Amber's face couldn't be hidden. "That's none of your *damned* business." She twisted away from

Breckensen and stormed from the podium. The camera showed Governor Schwarzenegger running to catch her.

Leonard looked at his brother, who was staring at the television with his mouth hanging open. "Ernie? You okay, man?"

"She never told me. How could she never fucking tell me?" He hurled the TV remote across the room.

Leonard didn't know what to say. He didn't want to provoke Ernie, who seemed dangerously unbalanced at the moment.

"She never told me. I knew she had a daughter, but I didn't know she was mine. She said she got knocked up by accident in my first year in the Castle."

"Hey, man, it doesn't matter, okay?"

"It doesn't matter? Doesn't *matter*? She lied to me about my own flesh and blood! What do you mean, it *doesn't matter*?"

"Take it easy, Ern."

"I had a right to know."

"I'm not disagreeing with you, but we can't let this change anything. We've got too much to lose."

"I can't fucking believe this shit. I'm gonna kill that bitch."

"Ernie, you can't do that."

"Why the hell not?"

"This isn't a coincidence, Ern. Can't you see this whole thing is staged? They're trying to bait us, to flush us out. It could be bullshit."

"I can't believe this."

"She may not be your daughter."

"I saw her. Her eyes. When she was four years old."

"But you didn't know it, right? It wasn't that obvious, was it?"

"Shit, I don't know. Maybe. I guess I didn't want to believe it; it was easier that way. She never talked about it, and I never asked."

"It's a trap; they're baiting us. You know that."

"Yeah, I know. Shit. This really sucks."

"What can you do about it? Do you honestly think she's going to welcome you into her life with open arms? She doesn't even know you, other than what she's seen on TV, and that hasn't exactly been favorable lately. Think about it, Ern. You were out of Amber's life. She wanted a divorce and you agreed. You must know Janey can never be a part of your life. Let's not blow everything we've worked for over this."

Ernie nodded, but didn't respond.

Leonard walked into the kitchen and poured himself a glass of water. On the television, Breckensen was wrapping up the press conference. He watched his brother closely. What a disaster . . . He had to admit it, though, it was a brilliant move on the FBI's part. But it only worked if Ernie took the bait.

And, God help him, that was exactly what Ernie wanted to do.

Leonard thought through his own options. It might be wise to put some distance between himself and Ernie, fast. But he'd need to do it carefully, so it didn't seem obvious. He wasn't willing to lose everything they'd earned over this. Still, as much as he hated thinking about it—for many reasons—he'd cut ties with Ernie if he had to. He didn't plan on rotting on death row over a long-lost niece he neither knew nor cared about. No friggin' way. If Ernie became a liability over this, he'd be on his own.

Leonard went back to the TV room. "We might want to accelerate our plans. Are you okay for a few hours? I'm gonna get our cash near Quincy. We're gonna need it. We'll pick up the big stash on our trip up north."

"Want me to go with you?"

"Safer if you don't, honestly. We shouldn't be seen together, even in disguise." He came over and patted Ernie on the shoulder. "I know you've got a lot to think about. I'll be back by sundown. If you haven't heard from me, don't assume the worst; just head up north to the rendezvous point. We'll meet there. How much time do you have left on your cell phone?"

"I don't know, a few hours."

"Me too. I may not call, depending on the situation. Keep your cool, okay?"

"I will."

He looked Ernie in the eyes. "I know you want to call Amber. I'm not even gonna tell you not to. But be careful when you do it. Make sure she calls you back from a pay phone to your cell phone. Don't use the phone in here. Keep your conversation under thirty seconds. Don't do anything until we've had a chance to work out a plan. I'm serious, Ernie; stay put. Everything's going to be fine if you keep your cool. I'll see you in a few hours."

Ernie nodded.

"One more thing."

"What?"

"If the owners of this place show up, don't kill them."

"Yeah, yeah . . . I won't."

As Leonard drove away from the cabin, he looked in the rearview mirror and wondered if he'd ever see his little brother again.

# ⊕ Chapter Twenty

Rather than order room service, Nathan and Harvey decided to head downstairs to Dawson's American Bistro, a nice place with a classy atmosphere. The hostess seated them in a corner table big enough for four people. The rich hardwood paneling was accented by original oil paintings lit from ceiling spots. A few couples were seated at tables, engaged in quiet conversation underneath smooth jazz background music.

They hadn't talked much, each of them evaluating the chain of events that had landed them here in Sacramento, and each of them feeling betrayed. As Nathan took a swig of iced tea, he again wondered why Frank Ortega hadn't told them the truth.

Had Ortega thought they wouldn't take the assignment? The truth was, they *would* have agreed to help him find his grandson, no matter what his motivation had been. None of this deception had been necessary. He really felt bad for Harv.

Nathan set his glass down. "You okay, partner?"

"Yeah, I'm okay. Just embarrassed I got us into this mess."

"Harv, forget about it."

"I can't. I've known the Ortegas for nearly twenty years. Maybe I should've seen this coming."

"Be careful; you're starting to sound like me."

Harvey raised his glass in a toast. "I consider that a compliment."

Nathan smiled and clinked his glass. "Everything's in place; we've done what we can. Let's hope Ernie takes the bait."

"He probably knows it's a trap."

"No doubt."

They both turned at the same time and saw their two FBI agents enter the restaurant. When Grangeland noticed them sitting across the room, she seemed to hesitate. At this point Nathan was sure they weren't here to keep an eye on them; that game was over. No, they'd probably come in for the same reason: dinner. He motioned them over with a nod. Somewhat reluctantly, they approached. Harvey switched sides and sat next to Nathan.

"Will you join us?" Nathan asked.

Grangeland managed a smile. "Are you sure? We don't want to impose."

"Not at all." Both he and Harvey stood as Grangeland slipped into her chair.

"Such gentlemen," she said.

Ferris seemed all business, purposely avoiding a smile. *To each his own.* Nathan addressed Grangeland. "Are you okay? No broken ribs or, ah, other damage?"

"I'm not a china vase. But to answer your question, yes, I'm fine. I was raised with three older brothers who sometimes fought dirty. I'll live."

Nathan thought Grangeland looked stunning. Her red cock-tail dress was cut low and tight. Below her blonde hair, half-carat diamond studs adorned her ears. Nathan grinned. "I was, ah, just wondering where your piece is concealed."

She leaned forward and whispered, "It's a secret."

"I'll bet it is."

"Do you want Ferris and me to leave?" Harvey asked.

"No," Nathan said quickly. "That would be dangerous."

"Agreed," Grangeland added.

Harvey looked at Ferris. "I apologize for snapping at you up there."

"Already forgotten."

"So . . ." Nathan continued, "Ferris here said you were an alternate for the 2000 Olympic team. I'm assuming it wasn't for synchronized swimming?"

"Yes, that's a fair assumption."

"Look, I know we didn't get off to a good start. I'm sorry for busting in on you like that. I was frustrated by the surveillance. Not a very good excuse, I know."

Grangeland dropped her napkin in her lap. "Understandable, given the circumstances."

"Were you guys in the building when it blew?" Harvey asked.

Ferris shook his head. "No, we're from the Fresno resident agency."

"We've been under a lot of stress too," said Grangeland. "I feel like I wake up every morning with a gun in my face. I guess that's why I challenged you. I shouldn't have done that. At least there's one saving grace to all this," she said, looking around. "This hotel's first-class. We've stayed in some real fleabags before."

"I can imagine," Nathan said.

Their server arrived and took their orders for dinner. Grangeland and Ferris ordered iced tea. Officially, they were on duty.

"Harvey and I discussed it, and although we don't think

very highly of Director Lansing's tactics, we don't extend that resentment to you. We'd like to work with you, if you're willing."

"What do you have in mind?" Grangeland asked.

"We've set a trap for Ernie Bridgestone. If he calls Amber Sheldon again, I specifically told her to mention my name. She doesn't know why that was so important. Do you?"

Grangeland glanced at Ferris, then back to Nathan. "No, should we?"

"During the Freedom's Echo SWAT raid, we killed their little brother."

"You were there, at the compound, when the claymores went off?"

"We were backup," Harvey said. "Sammy Bridgestone was seconds away from sniping the SWAT team when we nailed him."

"I see."

Nathan leaned forward slightly. "We can't tell you everything that's happened, but we can tell you this: We're going to need your help if my plan is going to work."

"To avenge his little brother, you're thinking Ernie Bridgestone will use Amber to set you guys up."

"That's right."

"It sounds like another SWAT job. Why use us?" Ferris asked.

"Because we don't know who we can trust anymore."

"But you can trust us?" Grangeland asked.

"I don't know. Can we?"

An awkward silence settled over the table. No one spoke for several seconds.

Grangeland broke the silence. "You're already working with one of our agents, Bruce Henning. Why involve us?"

"Because five is better than three. Simple as that."

"I'm not sure we can do this without clearance. I'm assuming you don't want Director Lansing to know."

"You assume correctly."

She shook her head. "We could get in serious trouble."

"Yes, you could. Would it help if SAC Simpson gave you a green light? You're technically under her command, aren't you?"

"Technically, yes."

Nathan waited.

"I suppose that would give us some cover," she said, "but we have orders from Director Lansing to report only to him."

"Doesn't that strike you as odd?" Harvey asked.

"It's not protocol, but when the big man gives you an assignment, you do it without question."

"So you should," Nathan said. "Let me ask you something. What's the ultimate goal here? To capture the Bridgestone brothers and recover the missing Semtex, right? What if you were in on it? It wouldn't look too bad on your résumés if you helped collar both men at the top of the FBI's most-wanted list."

"No argument there," she said.

"Needless to say, it's going to be dangerous. Vest work for sure. Shots will probably be fired."

"When do you think it's going down?"

"I'm hoping tonight," Nathan said.

She and Ferris exchanged glances. "We're in," she said, "but we're not doing anything without SAC Simpson's orders."

Nathan smiled and opened his cell phone.

As much as she'd mentally prepared herself for it, Amber Sheldon wasn't ready for Ernie's call when it came. She must have gone over what'd she'd say dozens of times, and yet she found herself totally unprepared. When Ernie called her at work a little after eight thirty p.m., she told him to call her back in ten minutes at a number she gave him. With irritation in his voice, Ernie had agreed and seemed to understand the need for it. Earlier, on her way to work, she'd stopped at a

McDonald's several miles north of Pete's Truck Palace. Pretending to use a pay phone, she'd written its number down.

Amber was many things, but stupid wasn't one of them. She'd seen the sedan following her and assumed it was the FBI. Who else could it be? Both she and Janey had driven to Pete's Truck Palace together, parked in a dark area of the parking lot, and walked into the restaurant. Janey had a large purse slung over her shoulder. She scanned the area, not sure what she was looking for. In the truck staging area, close to fifty trucks were parked. Several dozen had their motors idling to keep their compressors supplying refrigerant to their cargo boxes. Diesel fumes hung in the air like fog. To her left, the fueling area was brightly lit by mercury vapor lights suspended under a flat metal canopy.

She closed her eyes and took a breath. It was time to take Ernie's call.

Its occupants sipping black coffee, a plain four-door sedan lurked in the northwest corner of the complex facing the restaurant. The two FBI agents had watched Amber park her car and walk into the restaurant.

"Looks like her daughter's with her."

"Yep."

"Now we wait."

"Yep."

Their wait wasn't long. Five minutes later Amber Sheldon marched across the parking lot and slid into her car.

"Here we go; she's on the move." At a safe distance, they followed her onto Highway 99 heading south. After three miles or so she used her turn signal and exited the highway at a convenience store gas station. Screened by mature eucalyptus trees, they stopped on the exit ramp. The driver watched through field glasses as Amber pulled into the gas station's parking lot and climbed out. She walked over to a pay phone on the side of the building and stood there, as if waiting for a call. Like a bad actress trying to look impatient, she kept glancing at her watch every few seconds. The agent on the passenger side pointed a clear, eighteen-inch parabolic rifle mike at Sheldon's location and donned a headset.

"She's waiting for a call," the driver said.

"Yep."

Somewhat irritated, the driver asked, "You ever say anything other than 'yep'?"

"Nope."

"Funny. Real funny."

"What the hell?" the driver said. He watched Amber Sheldon reach up to her head and pull off a blonde wig, exposing dark brown hair. She held it high in the air and waved it like a flag. "Shit! We've been had. That's not Sheldon; it's her daughter!"

*Will the real Amber Sheldon please stand up?* Driving her supervisor's car, Amber grinned as she pulled into the McDonald's driveway seven miles north of Pete's Truck Palace. Her smile faded as she realized this trick worked only once. She kept telling herself she wasn't doing any of this for herself; she was doing it for Janey. But she was already spending McBride's money in her head. Even if she never got the million-dollar reward for Leonard and Ernie, McBride's money wasn't peanuts—fifty thousand bucks could go a long way. Had it not been for Janey, she would've told Nathan McBride and his FBI pals to stuff it where it didn't shine. With a little luck, this would all be over tonight, and she believed in her heart that she was taking the right steps to ensure it. When the pay phone rang, she quickly picked up the receiver.

"Ernie?"

"Yeah, it's me."

"Thanks a lot for everything. My life's turned to shit."

"Why didn't you tell me about Janey?"

"I can't believe you're asking me that. Were you a part of my life? Were you ever going to be? You never gave a shit about me; it was always about you, what *you* wanted."

"I had a right to know."

"The hell you did."

No answer.

Amber continued. "You disappeared after you got out of prison. I can count on one hand the number of times you called to ask how I was."

"You're the one who called it off."

"Can you blame me? Yeah, I guess you can. Nothing is ever your fault, right? It's always my fault. *I* made you get behind the wheel that night; *I* made you resist arrest. Pull your head outta your ass and take a look in the mirror."

"You gotta lot of nerve talking like that. You think I can't get to you?"

"I'm not afraid of you anymore. It's you who should be afraid."

He laughed. "Afraid of what? The FBI? You?"

"Of Nathan McBride."

There was silence on the other end for several seconds. "How do you know that name?"

"He stopped by, and we had little chat about you."

There was venom in his voice. *"What did you tell him?"*

"What do you think? I told him you're a piece of shit."

"That cocksucker killed Sammy."

"What're you talking about?"

*"Sammy!"* Ernie screamed into the phone. "You know, my little brother?"

Amber froze, suddenly understanding why Nathan McBride had insisted she use his name. She'd been used again. Anger flared. "Well, he didn't tell me that. Must have slipped his mind."

"He's a dead man. . . ."

"Yeah." She laughed bitterly as she put it together. "He set me up. *They* set me up. That whole press conference thing, the question about Janey. It was all staged. Total bullshit."

"And you were dumb enough to buy it?"

"I needed the money."

"What money?"

"McBride offered me money to do the press conference."

"How much?"

"Ten thousand," she lied.

On the other end, Ernie chuckled. "Ten thousand?"

"It's a lot of money; I'm not exactly swimming in green-backs, Ern."

"It's peanuts."

"Peanuts? Who do you think you are, Donald Trump?"

"Shit, I could give you ten times that much. In cash."

Amber was silent.

"You still there?" Ernie asked.

"There's no such thing as a free lunch. What do you want?"

"I want to kill Nathan McBride."

"Well, good luck with that. I wouldn't mess with him. That's what he wants. In fact, I'm supposed to call him after I talk with you. He gave me his cell number."

"Give it to me."

"It's your funeral." She pulled the cocktail napkin from her jeans and read the number. "I'm sure he'd love to hear from you. Now, good-bye."

"Wait, here's what you're going to do."

"Screw that. I ain't doing shit for you anymore."

Ernie was silent for a moment. Amber knew she should hang up, but didn't.

"I'm serious about the money," Ernie said. "Leonard and me are buggin' out. We don't have much time. If you want the dough, here's what you're gonna do."

"I don't want your money. It's dirty."

"It's not for *you*; it's for Janey."

"Yeah, right, like you care."

"This can go one of two ways. The first, you and Janey can live happily ever after. The second, you don't."

"Don't threaten me."

"Oh, it's not a threat, sweet Amber; it's a promise, and you know I'll make good on it. What does this asshole look like?"

Amber gave him Nathan's description, ending with, "I wouldn't mess with him if I were you."

"Yeah, right. Now shut the fuck up and listen. Here's what you're going to say to McBride."

Nathan couldn't formulate a plan to collar Ernie until after Amber called, if she called at all. Until he knew Ernie had taken the bait, all he could do was wait. Nathan hated waiting. It grated on his nerves like a headache. As a sniper team, he and Harvey had been masters at waiting, often for days at a time until their mark materialized, but this was different.

Harvey preferred to stay busy during downtime. Currently he had all their equipment laid out on the hotel room's bed, and was checking and double-checking everything. He'd broken down their SIG Sauers and thoroughly cleaned and oiled their actions. He'd replaced the batteries in their night-vision scopes, their DAR-3 radio-frequency detector, their DRS Technologies handheld thermal imager, and their radios. In silence, Harvey used a lens cloth to clean their field glasses. Although it wasn't necessary, he pulled their Predator knives from their sheaths and checked their sharpness. He applied a fine coat of gun oil to their menacing surfaces and resheathed them with more force than needed.

When he noticed Nathan staring at him, he asked, "What?"

Nathan held up his hands. "I didn't say anything."

"I'm just making sure they're sharp."

Nathan's cell phone rang. He picked it up and looked at the number on the LCD screen. It was a number neither of them recognized. Nathan flipped it open and hit the speaker button. "Hello?"

"Well, well, well, if it isn't old Scarface himself."

Nathan knew instantly who it was. "Am I speaking with the loosest ass from cell block D?"

"Fuck you, McBride."

"Come on, Ernie, can't you think of anything more original

than that? Do me a favor and put Leonard on the phone. I'd rather talk to him. He's the brains of your operation. You're the . . . well, you know what you are."

"Yeah, I'm the guy who's going to kill you real slowly."

"That's going to be rather difficult after I've severed all your fingers."

No response.

"Tell me something: Did your baby brother die right off, or did he squeal on the ground like a little girl?"

"We'll see who does the squealing."

The line went dead.

The coldness and lack of emotion sent a shiver through Nathan. He slowly closed his phone and turned toward Harv. "Well, at least this confirms that he called Amber. She gave him my cell number. I love it when a plan comes together."

Two minutes later his phone rang again. It was a 559 area code. Probably Amber Sheldon. He took the call. "Don't say anything. Give me the number you're calling from."

She rattled off the number.

"Sit tight. I'll call you back in five minutes." He ended the call. "Let's go find a pay phone a few blocks away. I don't trust the ones in the lobby."

Nathan rapped on the door adjoining his room with the two FBI agents' and opened it. Grangeland and Ferris were waiting for him. They'd obviously heard everything said. "We're going out to call Amber Sheldon from a pay phone. We'll be back in a few minutes. Cross your fingers; with a little luck we'll be able to formulate a plan." He closed the door. They took the elevator down to the lobby and diverted over to the registration desk to get some quarters. Once outside, they walked the opposite direction from the Hard Rock and found a pay phone outside a liquor store. Ignoring the green wad of gum jammed into the receiver, Nathan dialed the number.

"It's me again," he said. "How did it go?"

"About like I expected." There was sarcasm in her voice. "He wants to give me and Janey some money. He said it's his way of making up for all the shit he's put us through over the years."

"Do you believe him?"

"Ernie's done plenty of bad things, but yeah, I believe him."

"How much money?"

"Twenty thousand."

"How're you supposed to get it?"

"He said he'd leave it in a paper bag in a trash can at the gas pump island at Pete's."

"Which one?"

"He didn't say. We have eight islands, if you include the commercial diesel pumps. I guess I'll have to rummage through all of them."

"When?"

"He said the money'd be there sometime before one a.m."

"Listen to me very carefully, Amber: Don't do anything. *Do not* approach the trash cans. Understood? I mean it; stay away from them."

"I will."

"What else did he say?"

"He said he's bugging out with Leonard and that I'd never hear from him again."

"Okay, good job. Sit tight. You won't see us, but we'll be there. Don't do anything."

"I won't."

Nathan replaced the cradle and turned to Harvey. "He took the bait; we're on."

"It's a trap. He told her what to say. You know that, right?"

"Yep."

"And you're taking the bait."

He smiled. "Wrong. *We're* taking the bait."

Harvey stopped cleaning their field glasses and shook his head. "Why do I get the feeling I'm going to regret this?"

"Relax, Harv. I've got everything under control."

"I was afraid you'd say that."

It would be a two-and-a-half-hour drive down to Fresno. For tonight's action, both Nathan and Harvey were dressed in woodland fatigue pants, combat boots, and black T-shirts. Nathan considered using his helicopter, and would have, except that he didn't want to separate from his backup of Henning, Grangeland, and Ferris, all three of whom were following their rented Ford Expedition in an FBI Crown Victoria. As usual, Harvey was driving. Nathan knew that until they surveyed Pete's Truck Palace, they couldn't plan anything in detail. One thing was certain; If Ernie Bridgestone was already there and waiting, he'd have a tremendous advantage over them. It'd be even worse if Ernie had a night-vision scope mounted on a sniper rifle, a very real possibility.

Nathan knew Harvey was right: Amber Sheldon hadn't been completely honest with him. It had been the money question. When he'd asked how much Ernie had offered, a slight change in her tone gave it away. Twenty thousand dollars wasn't chump change, but he was certain Ernie had offered more than that. How much, he didn't know or care. All that mattered was her dishonesty. And if she was lying about the money, what else was she lying about? For all Nathan knew, Amber was doing this under duress, with Ernie's knife at her throat. He couldn't worry about it right now.

Prior to beginning the drive to Fresno, Nathan had given Henning one of his radios in case they needed to stop for any reason. As they descended the on-ramp onto Highway 99 south from Highway 50, Nathan keyed the radio. "Radio check."

"Five by five," came Henning's response.

"Hey, you're catching on. We're going to exceed the speed

limit. I trust you'll use your FBI credentials if we're stopped by the CHP?"

"No problem."

Nathan set the radio on the seat and settled in for the drive. "I miss my giant schnauzers," he said. "When this is over I'm going to spend some quality time with them."

"Yeah," said Harvey. "I know what you mean. I miss my family too. Have you talked to Angelica lately?"

Angelica was Nathan's live-in housekeeper at his La Jolla home. She was a matronly lady in her mid-sixties who thought of Nathan as the son she never had. "No, remind me to call her tomorrow. My mother too."

"Will do." Harvey moved into the fast lane and accclerated up to ninety miles an hour, leaving the remainder of the obvious response unspoken.

*If we see tomorrow . . .*

## ⊕ Chapter Twenty-one

On the drive south they'd been forced to slow down through patches of fog, some of them several miles long. Twenty-five miles south of Fresno, Nathan spotted the sixty-foot sign for Pete's Truck Palace. Harv coasted down the off-ramp and turned right, away from their target. Anyone coming down the off-ramp at this hour would probably turn left, heading to Pete's. Harvey drove another hundred yards and killed the headlights. Nathan craned his neck and saw that they were obscured from Pete's by the Highway 99 overpass berm. Harvey pulled the Expedition onto the shoulder and slowed to a stop. The Crown Victoria pulled in behind them.

Nathan keyed the radio. "All right, it's fair to assume Amber gave a description of me to Ernie, so Harvey will conduct a site reconnaissance report back to us. I'll wait in your vehicle until he returns."

"Copy," Henning said.

"Okay, Harv, you're on. Locate all the trash cans at the islands. Fill the gas tank and check out the restaurant and convenience store. You know the drill; make a mental picture of everything. Look for places Ernie can ambush us from." Nathan opened the door and stepped out.

"Ten minutes," Harvey said.

Nathan watched his partner execute a U-turn and head east under the freeway overpass. He climbed into the backseat with Henning and glanced at his watch. As he'd suspected, the dome light in the Crown Victoria had been disabled.

Harvey was back in just over eight minutes and pulled in behind the Crown Vic. Making room for Harvey, Nathan slid into the middle of the backseat. Harvey climbed in and asked for a notepad and pen. Grangeland passed back a legal pad from her briefcase. Ferris held a small penlight to illuminate the pad as Harvey drew a quick sketch of the site, circling areas of potential threats. There were five: the transient truck parking area, the roof of the main building, the customer parking area, the truck washing bays, and a warehouse-type building across the street to the north. Harvey believed the greatest threat came from the truck parking area because it was dimly lit and noisy. It would be easy for Ernie to hide between the rigs.

"All right," Nathan said. "We have a juggling act to perform. We have to cover one another without looking like we're covering one another. If Ernie's already here, he's looking for plainclothes undercover agents. Essentially, us. Grangeland and Ferris will act like a couple and take up a position inside the restaurant. You guys will watch Amber's every move and report anything she does besides her restaurant duties. Henning will drive the SUV in case Ernie's already seen Harvey come and go. Harvey will be in the front seat; I'll be ducked down in the back. Henning will pull up to a fuel island, pretend to fill the tank, and then park in the customer parking area and go in for a cup of coffee and return a few minutes later. We'll disable the dome light in the SUV to keep the interior dark when the doors open. We're at a distinct disadvantage here; we don't know when or where Ernie will show, if he shows at all. If nothing's happened by zero thirty hours, I'll make an appearance to draw him out."

"Whoa," said Harvey. "I don't like that. He might have night-vision. He'd light you right up."

"It's a chance I'll just have to take. I'll be relying on you guys to cover my back."

"Nathan, we can't watch every square foot of that place. It's spread out over ten acres. It's impossible."

"I hope it doesn't come to that, but we have to force this to a head. Amber told me he's bugging out tonight. That's the one thing I *did* believe. If we don't get him, we may not get another chance. Grangeland and Ferris, you go in first; we'll follow in a few minutes. Use the radio if Amber makes a move. One last thing: Lansing had a couple of agents watching Amber; they're probably still around. Let's try not to get killed by friendly fire. Good luck, everyone."

"You too," she said.

Henning, Harvey, and Nathan got out of the Crown Vic and piled into the SUV. Grangeland made a U-turn and drove under the overpass. In the backseat, Nathan popped the plastic cover off the dome light and removed the bulb. "There are two more dome lights up there," Nathan said. Henning disabled the driver's side, while Harvey got the passenger's side.

Grangeland and Ferris pulled into a parking stall facing the southwest corner of the restaurant. The air was cold and damp, so the light coats they wore to conceal their sidearms didn't look out of place. They held hands as they strolled toward the restaurant's entrance. Even though it was close to midnight, two vehicles were fueling at the islands. Without turning their heads, they scanned the area with their eyes. Ferris opened the restaurant's door for Grangeland and they stepped through. A server behind the counter told them they could seat themselves, so they grabbed a table by the window overlooking the gas pumps and parking area.

They spotted Amber Sheldon right away. A few tables away, she was warming a truck driver's coffee. "I'll be right with you," she said to them. "You folks want coffee?"

"Please," Ferris replied.

Amber stepped behind the counter, grabbed a couple cups, and brought them over to their table. She filled them and took their orders for dinner. As she walked away, she glanced at her watch and muttered something.

Harvey started the Expedition's engine and made a U-turn. Thirty seconds later he parked the SUV in the northeast corner of the property, several hundred feet from Grangeland's Crown Vic. Nathan could see that Harv had been right: The place encompassed a huge area. The restaurant where Amber worked was in the same building as the convenience store. There were three gas pump islands for noncommercial traffic, and four diesel islands designed to handle large commercial trucks. The truck washing bays occupied the southeastern corner of the property. Just north of the washing bays was the transient truck parking area. Dozens of trucks were lined up in rows, many of them with their engines idling, the collective drone of their motors rumbling across the asphalt.

Per the plan, Henning stepped out and walked into the convenience store and served himself a cup of coffee. He returned two minutes later. "It's all quiet in there. I was the only customer. We might have a problem: Amber's daughter's in the restaurant. I saw her when I walked past the connecting doors."

"Did she see you?" Nathan asked.

"No, she was looking in the other direction, toward the gas pumps."

"This could complicate things," Nathan said.

"What now?"

"Now we wait."

Amber, also waiting, grew more and more annoyed by the minute. Although she'd been watching the gas pump islands as best she could, it was impossible to keep a constant eye on them. Between seating new customers, waiting and bussing tables, and acting as the cashier, she was earning her pay. When a lull in her duties surfaced, she asked her supervisor if she could take a break. He reluctantly agreed, giving her five minutes. She walked over to Janey's table, informed her she was going out for a smoke, and told her daughter to stay put.

Nathan's radio earpiece crackled to life. It was Grangeland. "Sheldon's on the move; she's walking out the front door."

"Copy," Nathan said into the miniaturized microphone boom.

"You see her?"

"She's lighting a cigarette and walking toward the rear of the building," Nathan said. "I've lost sight of her. Can you pick her up?"

"No, she might make us."

"Can you make it look like you're using the bathroom?"

"No," Grangeland replied, "it's in the wrong direction."

"Okay, go through the convenience store in case Janey's watching. Go the opposite way around the building. Watch yourself; Ernie might be back there."

"Copy."

Nathan watched Grangeland exit the convenience store and turn right. She disappeared from his line of sight. "Grangeland, report."

Five seconds went by. Silence.

"Grangeland, do you copy?"

A few seconds later, her whispered voice came through the radio. "She's leaning against the rear wall smoking. She's alone."

"Okay, hang back and stay in the shadow of the building."

"If anyone pulls into the main driveway, their headlights will light me up."

"Get out of there then. Harvey will take over from this side. He can use the landscaping and block wall for cover. Wait thirty seconds, then head back into the restaurant."

"Copy," she said.

Nathan estimated that the light fog had reduced visibility to just under two hundred yards. It was thinner in some areas and thicker in others. He knew that as the dew point and temperature closed in on each other, it would only get worse. Harvey slid out of the passenger seat and, staying low amid the parked cars, worked his way to the north edge of the property. He dashed across the driveway and vanished in the shadows of a head-high concrete-block wall screened by mature oleander bushes.

"Harvey, report," Nathan said.

"I can smell her cigarette; wait one."

Nathan waited through a long fifteen seconds of silence.

"She's leaning against the rear wall of the restaurant with her arms crossed, smoking. She keeps looking left and right."

"Okay, Harv, stay with her. Grangeland?"

"I'm back inside with Ferris. Her daughter hasn't moved."

"Copy that," Nathan said.

"She's on her way back," Harvey reported. "Grangeland, I'll lose sight of her as she rounds the corner. Let me know if you don't see her within the next five seconds."

"Copy," Grangeland confirmed. "I've got her. She's reentering the restaurant through the convenience store."

"Copy," Nathan said. Using field glasses, he watched Grangeland approach the convenience store checkout counter. She was purchasing something to cover her absence from the table—a DVD or a paperback book, he couldn't tell which.

Nathan conducted a three hundred sixty-degree sweep of his surroundings with the handheld thermal imager, a device that looked like green binoculars with a single lens in front.

It could pick up the heat signature from a vehicle at over twenty-two hundred yards, or a man-sized target at eight hundred yards. The HHTI used in tandem with night-vision became an extremely effective combination. Although a person or animal could hide from the night-vision scope, they couldn't hide their heat signature. The HHTI nailed them every time. Sure enough, it had no problem seeing through the light fog obscuring the area. The truck parking area shone extremely bright from all the heat signatures of the semi engines. In the open field behind Nathan it picked up eight to ten cattle lying several hundred yards distant. As he turned the device off, he keyed the radio.

"Harv, you on your way back?"

"Affirm."

"Grangeland, what's Sheldon doing? It looks like she's just standing at the door."

"She keeps looking at her watch. She seems irritated. Wait. She's going back outside. You see her?"

"Affirm. Where the hell's she going? Oh, shit, she's heading for the trash can at the island. Grangeland, Ferris, stop her! Don't let her approach that island."

Amber Sheldon was thoroughly pissed off, more at herself than anyone else. She felt like such an idiot. Ernie Bridgestone would never give her any cash, let alone a hundred thousand dollars as payment for setting up Nathan McBride. She must've been out of her mind to believe anything that jackass had said. The lure of money had clearly blinded her. The one thing she did believe was Ernie's desire to kill Nathan McBride. He'd made that quite clear. An image of the devastation in Sacramento flashed in her mind. She shivered. Coming anywhere near this damned place tonight was stupid. Stupid *and* crazy.

It was time to leave.

Ignoring the trash can, she marched across the gas pump island on the way to her car, but suddenly remembered Janey

was with her. She started toward the restaurant, across the island.

Grangeland stepped through the restaurant's door at the same
time Amber reached the island.

Nathan's voice buzzed from her radio. "Grangeland! Get
down! *Now!*"

She dropped to the concrete.

Amber Mills Sheldon disappeared in a bright flash.

For an instant, time froze. Grangeland's mind registered
the explosion and something else, something hideous. Charred
and smoking, Sheldon's upper torso smashed into the brick
wall right next to her.

Every window along the storefront shattered inward, shower-
ing the occupants in a horizontal hail of glass. Car alarms
sounded from every corner of the property. The SUV fueling
at the northern part of the island was lifted into the air and
flipped onto its roof. Its gas tank exploded two seconds later.
A huge mushroom of burning gasoline roiled into the air.

"Son of a bitch," Henning hissed as the Expedition's windows
shattered inward.

Then Nathan heard something, something chilling.

Children screaming.

The burning SUV had children in it.

Nathan dashed across the pavement, tearing off his shirt as
he ran. He wrapped it around his hand and used it on the door
handle of the overturned SUV. After two hard yanks, the rear
passenger door opened. Hanging upside down, two small girls
were strapped into car seats in the backseat, screaming bloody
murder as flames licked at their skin. Nathan reached into the
inferno and singed his arms unclipping the seat belt holding
the first girl's car seat. It fell into his grasp, and he yanked it out
of the flames.

Harvey and Henning sprinted over.

"Get the other side!" Nathan yelled as he hauled the car seat away from the burning wreck. He set the child down and rushed back to the SUV. Ferris was running from the convenience store with a fire extinguisher. He pulled its pin and flooded the interior of the SUV with carbon dioxide gas. Harvey reached into the cloudy discharge and freed the second car seat. When Harvey pulled back from the interior of the SUV, his shirt was smoldering. Ferris nailed him with another whooshing discharge of $CO_2$. Grangeland ran around the island and grabbed the first car seat. She sprinted for the restaurant and disappeared inside. A few seconds later she returned for the second little girl and ran her into the restaurant. Nathan glanced around for the SUV's owners but didn't see them. He suddenly realized he hadn't checked the front seats.

Nathan yelled over the crackling of flames, "Ferris, nail the front seats!" Ferris stepped forward, stuck the nozzle through the broken driver's-side window, and pulled the trigger. White, cloudy gas filled the cab, starving the flames of oxygen. The reddish-orange glow from the interior winked out. Nathan grabbed his shirt and used it on the door handle. It wouldn't move. With a roar of anger he pulled with all his strength, and the door screeched open. A woman was crumpled into a ball on the SUV's ceiling, which was now the floor. Her clothes and hair were burned and smoking. Fortunately, her skin wasn't too bad. As Nathan and Harvey dragged her away from the SUV, she cried out for her daughters.

"We got them out," Nathan yelled. "They're okay."

Running from window to window, Ferris continued to spray the SUV's interior.

"Ferris, get the tires."

Ferris aimed high and doused the flaming tires. He hurried to the opposite side and sprayed those tires as well.

Nathan glanced up and saw the blacktop moving all around him. No, not the blacktop. SWAT teams. What the hell were they doing here? *Lansing, that son of a bitch!*

MP5s at their hips, at least ten SWAT agents were advancing toward their position, some of them fanning out to cover the property's exterior boundaries.

Nathan heard the report of a rifle a split second before his right arm jumped. "Harvey," he screamed, "sniper! Take cover."

Harvey scooped the woman up from the pavement and dashed for the restaurant.

Grangeland, Ferris, and Henning ducked, but they were out in the open.

Nathan dived for the cover of the smoldering SUV as another shot cracked through the air. The bullet skipped off the asphalt three inches from his head. From just above his elbow, warm liquid began running down the bare skin of his arm.

The entire SWAT team had hit the deck. "Dowdy, Collins," he yelled, "did you see a muzzle flash?"

"Behind you," came the answer. "Five o'clock, plus thirty."

"Give me some cover fire. On the count of three. One. Two. Three."

Bursts of MP5 fire hammered the air as Nathan scrambled up and dashed for the restaurant. A giant bullwhip cracked again as a supersonic bullet whizzed past him. He sensed it miss his torso by less than an inch as he passed across the threshold of the restaurant's door. The floor was littered with broken glass. Janey was screaming. The other server cringed behind the counter, shaking glass out of her hair. Harvey knelt near the rear wall, tending to the injured mother and her little girls. Nathan looked back and saw Henning, Grangeland, and Ferris running in a full sprint for the door.

A fourth rifle report echoed across the pavement.

Twenty feet from safety, Henning tumbled.

Nathan ran back toward the door. "Henning's down!" He passed Grangeland and Ferris as they rushed inside.

"Nathan, wait!" Harvey screamed. "I'll get him."

"No time," he said. Steeling himself for the bullet that

would end his life, he dashed across the asphalt, bent down, and hoisted Henning's two-hundred-pound body over his shoulder. "Cover fire!" he yelled.

More bursts of SWAT MP5 fire echoed off the surrounding trucks and buildings. A fifth shot tore the air. This one found its mark. Shit! His right calf jerked with the impact, but he kept his balance and made it through the door. Harvey took Henning from Nathan's shoulder and laid the man against the rear wall with the other wounded. Grangeland had grabbed a first-aid kit from the convenience store and was about to apply a large bandage to the flesh wound on Nathan's arm.

"Later," he said.

"You're bleeding badly."

"There's no time; we have to get Bridgestone."

"You've got two gunshot wounds; you may not *have* time."

"I'll live. Ferris, can you handle Henning?"

"He's gut shot. The bullet missed his lungs, but he's in a bad way."

The convenience store's supervisor crouched down. "I called nine-one-one," he said. "An ambulance is on the way."

"Harv, Grangeland," Nathan said. "Bridgestone's on the roof of the building north of the property. We'll use the rear exit and stay against the perimeter wall for cover. When we get to the driveway, Harv'll retrieve the SUV. Ferris, let the SWAT teams know what we're doing. Tell them to hold their fire until we're in the SUV."

"Copy," he said.

"We've got to hurry; let's move."

They passed through a stockroom and burst through the rear door facing the freeway. They hugged the wall as they traversed around the northwest corner of the property. All of them heard it: an engine starting, then the squeal of tires as a vehicle took off toward the east. Nathan was limping, but kept up with Harvey and Grangeland as they sprinted toward the SUV fifty yards ahead. Blood had already soaked his sock and shoe. "Harv, you drive. Grangeland, follow us in the Crown Vic. Let's move it!"

Just as Nathan closed the passenger door to the SUV another deafening explosion rocked the night.

The island under the diesel gas pumps vanished in a yellow-white flash. The freight truck parked at the island was blown ten feet back from the force of the blast, lying on its side. Nearly one hundred gallons of diesel fuel in its cab tanks ignited, sending a fiery mushroom up to the bottom of the metal canopy covering the islands. Reddish-orange fire snaked along the underside of the canopy and shot skyward at the edges. Some of the truckers parked in the transient area began driving their rigs out of the danger zone. Men and machines were going in every direction. People were screaming and running for cover. Like black ants against a red background, the SWAT team was sprinting for the protection of the convenience store, two of them dragging a wounded comrade.

Harvey squealed the tires and shot out of the parking lot. With the windows of the SUV gone, they could hear the roaring headers of Ernie's retreating vehicle. It was running east with its lights out.

"That's him," Nathan said. "Punch it, Harv." He flipped on the thermal imager and immediately saw the heat signature of the fleeing vehicle's exhaust. "Straight ahead, four or five hundred yards." He was flung into his seat back as the Expedition's engine answered the call. Within ten seconds they were doing eighty miles an hour. Harvey stomped the accelerator and brought their speed up to one hundred ten miles an hour. "Stay with him, Harv. Wait one. He's slowing, turning south. I've still got him. We're coming up on the turn in three hundred yards."

"Nate, put the NV visor on my head; we should go dark."

Nathan reached into the duffel bag on the seat between them, grabbed the night-vision visor, and saw the blood covering his forearm. He turned the NV on, removed the lens cap, and placed it on Harvey's head before pivoting the scope down to his partner's eye.

Harvey made a slight adjustment, then said, "Good to go."

Nathan keyed the radio. "Grangeland, we're switching to night-vision. Hang back a little. We're going dark."

"Copy."

Harvey killed the headlights, and the road disappeared into blackness. Behind them Grangeland also went dark.

"Turn here, to the right," Nathan said. Confirming what he already knew, fresh skid marks marred the pavement where Bridgestone had made a four-wheel slide around the corner. They were now paralleling a sandy dry wash on the eastern side of the road, thick with oak trees and underbrush.

"How you doing, Nate?"

"I'm okay. Stay with him."

Nathan glanced over his shoulder and saw Grangeland make the turn. Through the thin fog he saw several other vehicles leaving the driveway from Pete's Truck Palace to join the pursuit. *Bring it on. The more the merrier.* The cold wind rushing in the windows against his bare skin was becoming a problem. Compounded by his blood acting like water, Nathan was losing body heat quickly. He fought back a shiver and leaned forward as much as he could to avoid the worst of the wind.

"You okay?" Harvey asked.

"Never better," he lied. "Keep closing, Harv. We'll intercept him in thirty seconds."

"I'm on it."

# ⊕ Chapter Twenty-two

Ernie Bridgestone whooped in triumph when he lost sight of the headlights pursuing him. He'd lost them. "Fuckin' pussies," he said aloud. "Now who's doing the squealing?"

He was sure he'd scored at least one hit, maybe two on McBride, the big man with the scars on his face. With a little luck they'd be fatal shots. *Bleed out slowly, you piece of shit.*

Leonard had been wrong about his getting caught, after all. Sometimes he wondered if his older brother truly had the balls for this type of thing, ex-Ranger or not. He'd been conveniently missing when the time came to head down here and take care of business. Ernie shook his head. He'd actually enjoyed blowing Amber to smithereens. The lousy bitch. She'd betrayed him for the last time. He'd easily spotted the two FBI agents tailing her. Besides, she had it coming for lying to him all these years. Hell, Janey was an adult; she could take care of herself. He wasn't worried about her at all. In fact, she was better off without that sleazy—"What the fuck?"

Nathan pulled his SIG 226 nine-millimeter and hung out the window. When Harvey closed to within twenty-five yards, Nathan took aim with both hands and emptied a fifteen-round magazine at the fleeing pickup truck. Each shot he fired illuminated the hood of the SUV in stroboscopic flashes. He aimed low and right, hoping for a skipping shot off the asphalt into the rear tire. He didn't want to shoot the cab because they needed Ernie alive; he couldn't risk a lucky head shot. He had an appointment with Ernie's fingers—an appointment he intended to keep.

Nathan passed the empty gun to Harvey and was handed a

fully loaded weapon in return. The chill on his exposed skin felt like a million ice picks. He hardened his mind, ignored the hideous sensation, and took careful aim. Ernie had begun to swerve back and forth in the road, which actually improved Nathan's odds of blowing out a tire. Harvey held the Expedition dead straight down the centerline of the road. Nathan let loose with another full magazine. *Got it!* Rubber began to peel away from the punctured tire. A baseball-sized piece whizzed past his head, and he pulled himself back into the interior. Shredded chunks of rubber thumped off the Expedition's shattered windshield.

"Good shooting," Harvey said.

Ernie's truck swerved right, then back to the left before he regained control. It skidded to a stop on the left shoulder. Ernie jumped out and took off into the dry wash. Harvey braked hard and pulled in behind the truck.

"He's wearing a sidearm, Harv. Looked like a 1911."

"I saw it."

Nathan was in no shape for a foot chase. Although not life-threatening, his calf wound was bleeding at a damned unhealthy clip. "Get him, Harv; we could lose him in there. Take the thermal imager. I'll be right behind you with my NV visor."

Harvey didn't have time to strap on his holster, so he jammed four magazines into his front pockets. "His ass is mine."

Nathan watched him disappear into the blackness. *Be careful, old friend.*

Grangeland saw the brake lights and knew the car chase had ended. She pulled in behind the SUV and killed the engine. She rushed to the passenger door and saw Nathan donning a night-vision visor.

"No way," she said. "Give that to me. You're in no shape to go out there. Your color's nearly gone, and you're shaking like a leaf."

"Damn it." She was right. He wasn't in good shape; in fact,

he was in terrible shape. The blood loss combined with the
shock and adrenaline wearing off had hammered him. He
handed her the visor. "Harvey's got a ten-second head start;
he's got a thermal imager and night-vision with him. We
need Bridgestone alive, understood?"

"Clearly," she said. Three seconds later she vanished into
the moonless void.

Nathan gathered as much strength as he could and shouted,
"Grangeland's coming, Harv, not me." He didn't expect an
answer and didn't get one.

He limped to the Crown Vic and found Ferris's coat in the
backseat. The flesh wound on his arm just below the elbow
was burning and throbbing. He was pretty sure the bullet had
passed clean through without hitting any bones or major blood
vessels, but he wasn't positive. His lower calf wound was a different story. He was tempted to take a look with a flashlight,
but decided against it. It was better if he didn't know. He'd
have time to lick his wounds later. He returned to the SUV
and looked for something to slow the bleeding on his leg. Settling for Harvey's Windbreaker on the front seat, he wound it
up like a towel about to be used for a prank whipping in a
locker room. Ignoring the pain, he wrapped it around his
lower calf and tied a knot. Tight. He also needed something
for his arm. He scanned the backseat of the SUV and saw his
shirt he'd removed at the truck stop. Although Nathan had no
memory of it, Harvey must've picked it up on their way back
to the SUV after the explosions. Using his teeth on one end,
Nathan tied it around the wound on his arm. Next, he
strapped on his gun belt, pulled the SIG, and jacked a round
into the chamber. He holstered the weapon and checked to
make sure his spare magazines were secure in their slots. Finally, he turned off his cell phone and clipped it on the gun
belt.

He limped over to Ernie's truck. The dome light from the
open door revealed an HK 91 .308 assault rifle with a night-
vision weapon scope on the floor of the passenger's side. He

wondered why Ernie hadn't taken it with him. *Panicked*, he thought. *He's probably regretting leaving it behind. Too bad for old Ernie.* He leaned in, grabbed the weapon, removed the magazine, and cycled the bolt. A live round flew from the breech and landed on the pavement. He picked it up, pushed it back into the magazine, and inserted the magazine into the receiver. He cycled the bolt, shouldered the weapon, and looked through the scope. *Friggin' beautiful with a capital B.* The Bridgestones were many things, but cheap with their weaponry wasn't one of them. The night-vision scope was state-of-the-art. Third-generation. He used it to survey the wash and saw Harvey picking his way through the underbrush like a Halloween wraith. Every so often Harv would bring the thermal imager up and scan the area in front of him before moving forward. In the image of the night-vision scope, the glow from the thermal imager lit Harvey's face like a spotlight. *Attaboy, Harv. Get some, baby! Just like old times.*

Through the scope, Nathan could see that the dry wash gradually turned toward the west several hundred yards farther up the road. It went under a bridge and continued wrapping around to the north. Wide-open fields lay on both sides. If Ernie left the cover of the underbrush, he'd be in plain sight and vulnerable. Nathan pulled on Ferris's coat and started across the field in a northwesterly direction, heading for a copse of mature oaks. With a little hustle, he'd get there before Ernie.

The FBI vehicles in pursuit had missed the turn where Ernie made his four-wheel slide, and were heading east. He heard the distant whine of approaching sirens on Highway 99 and the telltale bleating of fire engine air horns. Directly to the west, nearly a mile away, the red glow from the inferno at Pete's Truck Palace backlit the oaks he was limping toward. They looked like giant mushrooms against a sunset sky. Every so often he'd bring the weapon scope up and sweep the wash, but he saw no movement. The pain in his calf was distracting, but when he thought about Ernie's bomb at the gas pump island, and the screams of the little girls trapped in the burning SUV, he hardened his resolve and kept pushing forward.

Halfway across the open field, Nathan heard two shots off to his left. He recognized them as the distinctive reports of a large-caliber handgun. They came in rapid succession. *Boomboom.* A few seconds later two more shots rang out. Ernie was shooting at either Harvey or Grangeland or both. No fire was returned. Bridgestone was probably shooting blindly, gambling on a lucky shot. At least, that was what Nathan hoped. He quickened his pace, doing his best not to fall down on the mounds of the plowed field. He estimated he'd be at the copse of oaks within two minutes. Once there, he'd lie low and wait for Harvey and Grangeland to drive Ernie into his position. He needed to be careful; getting blown away by friendly fire would definitely ruin his evening. The saving grace? Harvey and Grangeland had night-vision; Bridgestone didn't. *Advantage, good guys.*

By the time Nathan made it to the stand of oaks, his lower calf was really throbbing. He was pretty sure the bleeding had slowed, but his sock and shoe were soaking wet. He worked his way over a barbed-wire fence and crouched down beside the top of the wash. At this location, the wash was about fifty feet wide and five feet lower than the elevation of the surrounding plowed fields. Islands of thick brush were scattered all throughout the dry riverbed. Fallout from the oaks had littered the ground with dead leaves. The moisture in the air had settled onto the mat of leaves, making it silent when stepped on. He shouldered the weapon, then swept the sandy expanse in the direction Ernie should be coming from. Nothing. No movement at all.

The area flared bright green in the scope, as though a camera flash had gone off. A second later the thump of Ernie's report reached him. Nathan knew sound traveled at close to one thousand feet per second, which meant Ernie was roughly three hundred yards away. He tried to spot Harvey or Grangeland, but couldn't see them.

Directly in front of him, a long strip of brush would make a perfect ambush location. It dawned on him like a slap in the face: He hadn't removed the keys from his SUV or Grangeland's Crown Vic. If Ernie circled back . . . He silently cursed himself for being so careless, and scanned the plowed field between his position and the parked vehicles. No sign of Ernie. If Nathan positioned himself down in the wash, he wouldn't be able to see the vehicles. He gambled that Harvey had Bridgestone in sight, either with the NV visor or the thermal imager. If Bridgestone made a beeline for their SUV, Harvey would intercept him. He slid down the sandy bank, limped in a crouch over to the strip of brush, and shouldered Ernie's Heckler & Koch.

"Got you," he whispered. Ernie Bridgestone was running along the eastern bank of the wash, ducking for cover every so often and pointing his gun back at his pursuers. Nathan spotted Harvey about fifty yards behind Bridgestone, advancing in leapfrog formation with Grangeland. It looked like they were trying to flank him. He had to let Harvey know he was here. He stepped out from the cover of the brush and shouldered his weapon. He saw Harvey bring the thermal imager up.

Harvey dived for the ground. So did Grangeland. *Shit!* Nathan knew that all Harvey saw was someone, possibly Leonard Bridgestone, pointing a rifle at him. Nathan dropped the rifle to his hip and, with his good arm, made a fist and brought it up to his right shoulder. He kept repeating the gesture for ten seconds. When he shouldered the weapon again and peered through the scope, he saw Harvey standing up, waving in recognition. Nathan returned the wave and pointed to the place he was hiding. Harvey waved again. He watched Harvey turn his head toward Grangeland's position, and she closed the distance. They huddled in a crouch for a few seconds before Grangeland sprinted to the western side of the wash, where she began working her way forward through the underbrush. Two more flashes lit the landscape. Grangeland dived again, but Harvey didn't move. *The man's got nerves of steel*, Nathan thought. Although Ernie was firing blindly, he could still score a lucky hit.

In a two-story farmhouse five hundred yards to the west, the porch lights snapped on. The locals were responding to the gunfire. It was only a matter of time before sheriff's deputies and/or the FBI SWAT team from Pete's Truck Palace arrived. When they did, the situation could get sticky. Friendly fire would become a very real problem. As if sensing Nathan's thoughts, Harvey let loose with three quick shots. Through the NV scope, Nathan watched Bridgestone duck for cover, then begin a full sprint toward Nathan's position. Harvey fired again. *Pop-pop-pop.*

*Attaboy, Harv, drive him home.*

If Ernie kept his current pace, he'd close on Nathan in about twenty seconds.

*That's it. Keep coming.*

Nathan squinted and steadied himself.

It wasn't cinematic. It didn't have to be.

Just as Bridgestone reached Nathan's position at the island of underbrush, Nathan stuck out his foot. Simple. Elegant. Effective.

Arms pinwheeling, Bridgestone fell flat on his face. Nathan pounced on the man's back, grabbed his wrist, and wrenched it up all the way to his neck. The handgun fell from Ernie's grasp and thumped onto the sand. Nathan both felt and heard Ernie's shoulder dislocate. Ernie cried out and tried to roll over, but Nathan kept his entire weight on the prone man's back. "Well, well, well, if it isn't the cell-block sweetie himself."

Harvey and Grangeland arrived ten seconds later and joined the restraint. Harvey forced Bridgestone's other wrist behind his back, and Grangeland handcuffed him.

"You stupid *motherfuckers*," Ernie hissed. "You're dead; you're all *fucking dead*."

"Oh, we'll be fine," Nathan said. "But *you*, Ernie, old boy? You're going to wish you were dead. Trust me on that."

"Fuck you."

"Sorry, you're not my type, but I'll get Doc Fitzgerald to call up some of your old inmate buddies, if you like."

"I'm not afraid of you."

"You will be," Nathan said. *"You will be."* He held his own hand up and started counting. "I count fourteen knuckles, Harv. Sound about right?"

"Fourteen on each hand," Harvey corrected.

"Brutal. Think he can take it?"

"Don't know. Only one way to find out."

"What are you guys talking about?" Grangeland asked. Like Harvey, she was breathing hard from the sprint up the sandy wash.

"I'm going to start cutting this asshole's fingers off. One knuckle at a time."

"The hell you are, McBride. The FBI doesn't torture its prisoners."

"We aren't with the FBI."

"I want my fucking phone call," Ernie said.

"That's what your cousins said. Before you killed them." Harvey shoved Bridgestone's face into the sand.

"You are *not* torturing this man," Grangeland said.

"Special Agent Grangeland, take a walk with me. You got him, Harv?"

"Oh, I got him, all right." Harvey kept his knee on Bridgestone's back and leaned on the dislocated shoulder. Ernie grunted and spit out sand.

Nathan led Grangeland fifty yards up the sandy wash and stopped. "I need the truth. Is my cell phone being tapped?"

"No," she said.

He unclipped it, turned it on, and dialed a Washington, D.C., number from memory. Holly Simpson had given him Director Lansing's cell number earlier this evening.

It rang four times. The voice answering was sleepy and a little annoyed. "This had better be good."

"It's good," Nathan said.

"Who is this?"

"Nathan McBride."

There was a pause. "How did you get this number? Never mind, I don't want to know. Now, do you mind telling me why you're calling at . . . four in the morning?"

"I've got Ernie Bridgestone in custody."

"Right now? You have him in custody *right now*?"

"That's right."

"Damned good news, Mr. McBride."

"I need to interrogate him."

"I see."

"I'm not sure you do. I mean *interrogate* him."

"If I understand what you're implying, we don't do things that way."

"Oh? I think you'll make an exception."

"And why would I do that?"

"Because I know about the Ortega/Bridgestone connection, that's why."

Lansing said nothing.

"And the Ortega/Bridgestone Semtex sting."

More silence.

"You still there?" asked Nathan.

"Yes, I'm here."

"Are we on the same page now?"

"Yes."

"Why was an FBI SWAT team at Pete's Truck Palace?"

"Amber Sheldon wanted the reward money. There's a one-million-dollar reward on the brothers. Half a million each. She called and told us all about tonight's money drop."

Nathan shook his head at the double double cross Sheldon had pulled off. "Well, I guess that money belongs to Harvey and me now."

"What about Sheldon?"

"Bridgestone turned her into red mist."

"Then yes, the money's yours. You collared him. It's yours."

"One of your field agents is with us." Nathan handed the phone to Grangeland. She took it, walked a few paces away, and kept her back to Nathan, but he could still hear her end of the conversation.

"This is Special Agent Grangeland from the Fresno residency," she said.

After a few seconds Grangeland tensed, as if she wanted to object to what she was hearing. "Yes, sir. Understood." She handed the phone back to Nathan.

"You've got one hour, Mr. McBride."

"I don't need that long. One more thing, Director Lansing."

"What?"

"Keep this under wraps. Tell absolutely no one we have Ernie until we've got his brother. Leonard can't know we have Ernie. If it leaks, he'll bolt and we'll never catch him. Play along and you'll get your front-page headline, and no one will be the wiser. You have my word on it."

"All right, agreed. I want you to call me back when you've got something to report."

"Will you put Special Agent Grangeland under my command for the remainder of this operation?"

"Yes."

"She'll need to hear it from you." Nathan handed her the phone again.

She listened for several seconds, then said, "Yes, sir."

She handed Nathan the phone back.

"Thank you," he said.

"No mutilations, McBride."

"We'll see." Nathan snapped the phone shut. "You're welcome to stay, if you think you've got the stomach for it."

"I'll stay."

"Suit yourself, Grangeland, but I don't want any interference. Are we crystal clear on that? No matter what you see, don't interfere."

She nodded tightly.

They hustled back to Harvey's position.

"Are you ready, Mr. Bridgestone?"

# ⊕ Chapter Twenty-three

There are moments in life in which you find yourself totally unprepared. This was such a moment for Special Agent Grangeland. Nothing in her FBI training or competitive athletic background could've prepared her for the horror unfolding before her. She found it difficult to watch, but more difficult not to watch. Ernie Bridgestone lay facedown in the sand. Harvey had dragged a large piece of wood over from the bank and placed it between the man's cuffed hands and his back. He dragged a second piece over and placed it under Bridgestone's chin so he wouldn't inhale the sand and choke. She watched in horror as Harvey removed a menacing knife from his ankle sheath and handed it to Nathan. Harvey then placed a knee on Bridgestone's upper back and applied his full weight. Facing Harvey, Nathan sat on Bridgestone's legs and grabbed one of his hands. Bridgestone tried to resist, thrashing about and swearing like a madman, but he was pinned and couldn't get any leverage. She watched in abject disbelief as Nathan forced the tip of the knife into Bridgestone's ring-finger knuckle and shoved—rocking it back and forth as if cutting through a tough piece of steak. She'd never heard a grown man scream bloody murder, and it left her jaw clenched so tightly her head began to throb. Although Nathan wasn't actually severing Bridgestone's fingers, it was damned close to it. Bile rose in her throat as she tried to separate her mind from her body, but the two kept clashing back together like a thunderclap. How could she allow this to continue? Surely Director Lansing hadn't approved what she was watching, had he? What kind of men were these? How could they brutally torture another human being with such casual indifference? Was it worth her job, a lifetime's worth of achievement, to put a stop to this? How could she live with herself, knowing she could've stopped this and didn't? She looked down in shock and disgust as they started again on the next knuckle up.

"How does it feel, you piece of shit?" Nathan hissed. "Did you enjoy cutting James Ortega's fingers off as much as I'm enjoying this? Well, *did you*?"

In truth, he wasn't angry, and in truth, he didn't enjoy it, but he wanted Ernie to think he did. He actually found it repulsive, but he needed Ernie to believe otherwise. He hadn't asked Ernie any questions; nor did he intend to. It was all part of the mind game he was playing.

Nathan pushed the knife.

Bridgestone shrieked in agony. Blood flew from his mouth where he'd bitten his tongue. He whipped his head back and forth, tearing his cheeks on the splintered log.

Nathan removed the knife after going halfway through the knuckle, and on the same finger started on the final knuckle. Within two minutes Bridgestone had been reduced to a sobbing wretch. He was crying like a child and begging for Nathan to stop. He promised to tell Nathan anything he wanted if he'd stop cutting his fingers.

Nathan looked up at Harvey. "What do you think?"

"I think he's full of shit. We've got twenty-five knuckles to go. Let's see how he feels in, say . . . twenty minutes or so."

Nathan reached down and grabbed Ernie's hand again.

"*Stop!*" Ernie screamed. "I'll tell you whatever you want, man."

"What makes you think we want any information?" Nathan asked. "This isn't about information; it's about payback for James Ortega."

"The Ortegas fucked me in Pensacola," Bridgestone wailed. "It wasn't my fault. I did my time. I was willing to let it go, but they fucked me again. Ortega set us up. His grandson sold us the Semtex."

"Is that why you burned him? *Alive?*"

"It was an accident; we didn't mean to, I swear."

"Save it for someone who gives a rat's ass."

"Leonard . . . I'll tell you where he is—just don't cut my fingers anymore. He took off for Montana around six o'clock tonight. I'm supposed to meet him up there tomorrow night."

"We already know where he is; he's being arrested right now. Do you think we're stupid?" Nathan looked up at Grangeland. "He thinks we're stupid." Nathan grabbed his hand and forced it against the wood.

"*Wait!* There's money. Over three million. In cash."

"I'm worth twenty times that. I don't need your lousy money."

"It's cash, man! Buried in ammo cans near the Canadian border."

Nathan looked at Harvey. "What do you think; do you believe him?"

"Hell, no."

"I don't either." Nathan jammed the knife into the first knuckle of finger number two. Ernie screamed again, rawer this time. His voice was going.

Grangeland turned away and threw up. Falling to her knees, she retched in violent spasms. With her back turned she said, "For God's sake, Bridgestone. Tell them the truth."

"It *is* the truth," he cried. "I swear to God."

"God has taken the night off. It's just you and me. I've been granted an hour with you. We've only been chatting for"—Nathan glanced at his watch—"three minutes."

"Please, fucking *please,* man."

Nathan grabbed Ernie's hair and yanked his head back. "Where's the rest of the Semtex?"

Panting like a dog, he said, "My truck. The toolbox. Leonard has the rest."

"How much is 'the rest'?"

"Ten bricks. That's it, man. I swear."

"Does he have blasting caps?"

"Yes."

Nathan looked up. "Grangeland, let your people know Leonard's got ten bricks of Semtex."

She didn't respond.

"Grangeland!"

"Yeah, yeah, okay." She pulled out her cell phone.

*This is it,* Nathan thought. *She's either with the program or she's going to blow it.* He couldn't risk it. "Give me the phone."

"What?"

*"Give me the phone."*

She wiped her mouth and stepped forward. When she was close enough to see his face clearly, he winked at her.

She nodded in understanding. "They're under my command. I'll make the call."

"Then do it," Nathan said. "Now."

She punched some bogus numbers into her phone, but didn't hit send, then looked to Nathan. He nodded that she was doing the right thing.

"It's Grangeland." She paused, doing a pretty good job of faking it. "Yeah, he's talking. He said Leonard's got ten bricks of Semtex and blasting caps." She paused again. "Where?" Another pause, longer this time. "Don't approach him, understood? Wait for SWAT. I say again, *do not* approach him. . . . All right, good work, I'll call you in ten minutes."

*Perfect.* Nathan couldn't have played it better himself. Ernie had soaked up every word. Now that he believed his brother was being captured, he'd have no reason to hold back.

Nathan pulled Ernie's head back again. "Where's the money?"

"It's buried near an abandoned ranch in Montana near the Canadian border."

"Montana's a big state; that doesn't tell me squat." He reached for Ernie's hand.

"Wait! I got GPS coordinates."

"Well?" Nathan asked.

Ernie rattled off the numbers. Grangeland pulled a penlight, secured it in her mouth, and wrote the coordinates down on a small pad of paper.

"If you're lying to me about this, we're moving on to tin snips and a plumber's torch to cauterize the wounds. I've got fifty-seven more minutes with you, and trust me, I'll use every last second."

"I'm not lying, I swear."

Nathan got off of Ernie's legs and stood up. "Harv, keep him company for a minute."

"No problem."

"Grangeland, let's take another walk." He led her across the sand, working his way through the islands of underbrush. After a hundred feet he stopped and kept his voice low. "Like I told Lansing, we have to keep Ernie's capture under wraps. It's vital it doesn't leak. If Leonard believes Ernie escaped, he'll head for the cash; I'm sure of it. Maybe even wait for him there for a time."

She pointed to the red glow from Pete's Truck Palace. "There's no way to keep all that under wraps. It's probably on the news already."

"Here's what we do: We leak to the press that all we got from the scene was Ernie's cell phone and his sniper rifle, that Ernie's still at large, and that your people are analyzing the cell phone carrier's call logs."

"Leonard will think Ernie's phone has been compromised and he'll ditch his own phone. They'll have no way to communicate."

Nathan nodded. "You got it."

"What's next?"

"I'm going to take custody of Ernie until we have his brother."

"What? That wasn't part of the deal with Lansing. I—"

"Think about it, Grangeland. You, me, Harvey, and Director Lansing are the only people in the world who know Ernie's in custody. He's number one on your most wanted list. How long could something like that stay under wraps? People talk; the walls have ears. We can't risk it. Don't worry: I'll make sure you get the credit for the collar."

"I'm not worried about getting the credit; I'm worried about getting fired, or worse."

"Director Lansing put you under my command, so I'm giving you a direct order. Ernie stays with us until we've got Leonard."

She wanted to protest, but nodded tightly.

"We need to get up to those coordinates ASAP. Just the four of us: me, Harvey, you, and Bridgestone. We'll take my helicopter."

"You own a *helicopter*?"

"Bell 407."

"I guess you weren't kidding when you said you're worth twenty times that much."

"We need to get out of here before the cavalry arrives. By the way, you did a great job with the fake telephone call. I wanted to kiss you."

"Let's just keep it professional."

They started back to Harvey's position. "Bridgestone might need a hospital. And you certainly do," Grangeland said.

"Harvey will take care of me once we've made it back to Sacramento. With a little luck, I'll only need some stitches and antibiotics."

They closed the distance, and Grangeland grabbed Ernie's forty-five automatic, shook the sand out of the barrel, and stuffed it in the small of her back. Harvey took charge of their prisoner and started marching him toward the vehicles. Five minutes later they were back at the SUV. Just as Ernie had said, they found nearly three hundred pounds of Semtex and several dozen blasting caps hidden in the oversized toolbox of his truck. The orange-colored bricks had been packed into cardboard boxes the size of milk crates. The blasting caps were in a smaller box. Harvey transferred the boxes of Semtex and the blasting caps into the trunk of the Crown Vic. Nathan laid Ernie's assault rifle on top of them. Grangeland retrieved the first-aid kit from the trunk, pulled on a pair of latex gloves, and told Ernie to hold still. The cuts on Ernie's knuckles were streaming blood and needed to be wrapped to stanch the flow. Holding the penlight in her mouth, she applied several tight layers of gauze around Ernie's two mangled fingers and secured them with white tape. Ernie grunted from the pressure.

"You'll live," she said.

Nathan kept a close eye on their captive as Grangeland tucked him into the backseat of the Crown Vic and closed the door. Ernie seemed subdued during all of this. Maybe it was shock. Maybe it was the false news about his brother's capture. More likely it was the reality of his fate sinking in. He was headed back to prison, only this time to death row. Depending on how cooperative he was on their trip up north to Montana, Nathan might give him an alternative to the hell awaiting him. *We'll see*, he thought.

Nathan reluctantly agreed to let Grangeland look at his wounds. He shucked off Ferris's coat and held out his arm. Once again holding the penlight in her mouth, she pulled on a fresh pair of gloves. When the beam swept across his chest, she gasped at seeing the network of crisscrossing scars. She obviously hadn't noticed them earlier, when the truck stop went up in flames.

He winked at her. "I lost an argument."

"Must've been some argument."

"It was." He let her remove the blood-soaked shirt and apply a dozen wraps of gauze around the torn flesh and secure it with tape.

"Better let me see that leg too."

He put his foot on the lip of the open trunk and pulled his blood-soaked fatigues up.

"Did you have a knife sheath like Harvey's?" she asked.

"Yeah, why?"

"Take a look." She shone the penlight on the wound.

"I'll be damned," he said. An angry bruised outline of the sheath's shape was visible on his bloody skin. The bullet had hit the thick metal handle and fragmented outward, shredding the flesh with shrapnel. The knife and sheaf were long gone. All the bleeding had been from torn skin, not a bullet hole. "Luck favors the well prepared," he said. After Grangeland wrapped the wound, he turned toward Harvey. "Let's take a walk. Grangeland, you've got Ernie."

"No problem," she said.

They walked a good fifty feet down the road.

"Based on what Ernie told us, I figure Leonard's got a six- to seven-hour head start on us," Nathan said. "We should assume seven. That has him arriving at the money drop in Montana by three in the afternoon tomorrow at the earliest. I can't see him driving there any faster than that. He'll drive the speed limit to avoid being pulled over. Whatever disguise he's using, it's probably good enough to fool the average law enforcement officer. Colored contacts, facial hair, whatever. He's got fake IDs too. We should assume he'll make it up to the drop. I've driven through that area of I-15; it's remote as all hell. You could drive for hundreds of miles without seeing a state patrol cruiser."

"You're thinking he'll drive straight through?"

"No doubt about it. He wants to recover the money ASAP. He'll pump himself full of over-the-counter caffeine pills for the drive. We need to be one hundred percent certain we arrive there first."

"We'll also need satellite images of the area." Harvey paused meaningfully.

"Damn it, Harv, he could be involved in all of this."

"Do you honestly believe that? Deep down."

Nathan didn't answer right away. "No, I guess not." Harvey was right; they did need satellite images. Without them they'd be going in blind, without knowing the terrain. Although she could arrange it, he couldn't risk asking Holly to get them, because quite frankly he didn't trust the FBI—or more accurately, he didn't trust Director Lansing. He didn't want to arrive up there and find three dozen FBI SWAT agents crawling all over the place. Leonard would spot them and bolt for sure.

"I know you don't want to ask, but we could really use his help. It could make or break this operation."

Nathan said nothing.

"Do you want me to make the call?"

Nathan sighed. "No, he's my father. I'll make the call. You realize we'll have to tell him everything."

"Nate, it's me, okay? I know you've been wanting to patch things up for a long time. Here's your opportunity. Give the man a chance."

"He's a politician."

"Has he ever lied to you?"

"No, I can honestly say he hasn't." His cell phone rang. Nathan unclipped it from his belt. He recognized the phone number on the LCD; it was Holly Simpson. "Hi, Holly."

"Nathan, thank God. The truck stop is all over the news. Every network's covering it."

"Holly, I can't talk right now."

"Are you okay? Special Agent Ferris just told me you were shot twice."

"I'm okay. I'll call you back in a few minutes."

"Nathan—"

"A few minutes, Holly, I promise." He snapped the phone shut. He looked at Harvey. "The cat's out of the bag. It's a good bet Leonard's heard about this on the radio news by now."

"He'll avoid the money cache until he hears from Ernie."

"I've got that covered. We're going to leak to the press that

Ernie got away and all we recovered from the scene was his sniper rifle and his busted cell phone. We'll also leak that we're analyzing the cell company's call logs. I'm betting that will make Leonard ditch his phone."

"They must have some contingency meeting location if they're separated for a long period of time."

"No doubt they do."

"Leonard could lie low awhile. He might wait a week or even a month before he approaches the money drop."

"That's a real possibility, but I'm betting his love of money will force his hand. For Leonard, this whole thing is about money, not revenge; it never was. As long as Leonard believes his brother's on the run, we've got a chance to nail him."

"Bringing Ernie along complicates things."

"We'll put Grangeland in charge of him."

"She'll love that. How's the arm?"

"Better than the leg." Nathan winked. "I'm fine. I should probably get some stitches, but we don't have time for more than that right now. When we get back to Sacramento, can you preflight the chopper while I get our gear from the Hyatt and clean myself up a little?"

"Not a problem."

"I'll drop you guys off at Sac Exec Airport and make the call to my father on the way over to the Hyatt. Oh—I'd better call Holly back." He dialed the number from memory and quickly recapped the events at the truck stop leading up to his current situation. She kept turning the conversation to his gunshot wounds, and he kept reassuring her he was okay. He told her about his call to Lansing after collaring Ernie.

"Lansing knows I know about Ortega and the failed sting," he said. "I used it to persuade him I needed some quality time with Ernie."

"Be careful, Nathan. Lansing can be a formidable enemy."

"We made a deal. He looks the other way for a spell and I keep quiet about the Semtex screwup. It's a good arrangement for him; he knows what's at stake if this ever leaks."

"Yeah, his job."

"He put Grangeland under my command, and she's okay with it."

"Nathan, I could get you SWAT backup. You don't have to do this alone."

"No. Harvey and I can handle it. I don't want the situation complicated by having friendlies in the area. It's a shoot-to-kill situation now."

"I don't like the sound of that."

"Neither do I, but frankly it's easier than trying to capture him alive."

She had no response for that.

"We tricked Ernie into believing we have Leonard in custody and that all we're doing is going up there to recover the cash."

"Smart move."

"I need your help again. I need your office to leak some information to the press right away. Tonight. Right now, if you can. Leonard *has* to believe Ernie is still on the run or he'll never show at the money drop. You need to leak that Ernie got away and is on the run, and all we recovered from the truck stop was his sniper rifle and his cell phone, and that the bureau's analyzing the call logs from the carrier. Leonard will ditch his phone. He won't risk the FBI tracking it."

"That's good. ASAC Breckensen is dating an anchor at News Ten. I'll take care of this right away."

"Needless to say, don't tell Breckensen the truth."

"He won't like it when he finds out."

"We can't worry about that right now. Leonard has to believe Ernie escaped. If it leaks that he's in custody we can kiss Leonard good-bye. He'll disappear. This is probably our only chance of catching him. We won't get another opportunity. Ever."

"Nathan, we lost another SWAT agent at the truck stop. Three civilians too."

"I'm sorry, Holly."

"I didn't know SWAT was going to be there or I would've told you. ASAC Breckensen was under direct orders from Lansing. They left me out of the loop again."

"The beat goes on. . . ."

"End this, Nathan, before anyone else gets killed."

"Oh, you can count on it." Nathan closed the phone and clipped it to his belt. "We need to get moving." He pointed to the west, where several sheriff's cruisers were racing down the road with their light bars flashing blue and red. "We've got less than a minute to clear the area. You get everything out of the SUV?"

"Yes."

They hurried back to the vehicles. Nathan was thankful the Crown Vic's windows had survived the blast. He was in no condition for a freezing two-and-half-hour drive back to Sacramento. Grangeland took the rear seat next to Bridgestone, while Nathan slid into the front. Harvey left the headlights off as he pulled onto the road. He flipped the night-vision scope down to his eye and stomped the accelerator.

"All the roads in this area are laid out at ninety degrees to one another," Grangeland said. "Take a right at the first major road we come to. That should take us back to the freeway or its frontage road."

After another mile or so, Harvey turned right and said, "Shit."

The northbound lanes of the freeway were stopped. A string of headlights stretched to the south for at least a mile. Emergency vehicles were using the shoulder to advance. The inferno at Pete's Truck Palace must have closed down the freeway.

"Keep going under the freeway," Grangeland said. "We'll take a parallel road until we're past this."

They had to go several miles until Harvey could make a right turn. Farmland lined either side of the road as Harvey brought the sedan up to seventy miles an hour. Other drivers had the same idea. The once-quiet country road now looked like a prime artery. Following the pack, Harvey made a right heading north and saw the same string of bumper-to-bumper headlights in the southbound lanes. After another right turn heading east, they passed under the freeway and accelerated up the northbound on-ramp.

Ernie remained silent. Nathan knew how he felt. Hell, he'd lived it. Immediately after being captured in Nicaragua, he'd been beaten senseless and thrown in the back of a truck under armed guard. Angry faces had sneered down at him; some spit. The drive through the jungle had seemed endless.

Nathan turned his head and addressed Ernie. "Why don't you give us the *real* GPS coordinates now?"

"What are you talking about?" Ernie said.

"I'll be honest with you. You've got a nasty ten years ahead of you before you get the needle. Think about it, death row at San Quentin with Scott Peterson, your brother, and the rest of the tattooed mutts. How long do you think you'll last in there before Big Bubba makes you his wife and swaps you with all his friends?"

"Shut the fuck up, McBride."

"Give me the real GPS coordinates and I'll give you another option."

"What other option?"

"A bullet to the head."

Ernie said nothing, which meant he was considering it.

"See, it's like this," Nathan continued. "I'm not turning you over to the FBI just yet. I've decided you're coming with us to the coordinates, and if you're lying about them, we'll start over. I've still got a fifty-seven-minute reserve with you." He glanced at Grangeland, who seemed to be biting her tongue. "You got something to say?"

"Only that I'm not sanctioning what you're talking about here. I'm a sworn law enforcement officer. What you're talking about is extremely *un*lawful."

"So is torturing a prisoner. You're already hip-deep."

Harvey jumped in. "It costs the State of California a million dollars to go through the appeals process. Isn't that money better spent somewhere else?"

"I can't argue with that," she said, "but I need to be insulated."

"Special Agent Grangeland, consider yourself insulated. I don't care how you deal with it. Plug your nose, look the other way, take a walk, whatever works." She still didn't look happy. Nathan wasn't sure if she was acting or not. If so, she was damned good.

"I've got your word you won't take me in?" Ernie asked, closing the deal.

"Marine to marine. Now give me the real coordinates."

## ⊕ Chapter Twenty-four

After dropping Harvey, Grangeland, and Bridgestone at Sacramento Executive Airport, Nathan pulled out his cell phone and glanced at his watch. It would be a little after zero seven hundred Eastern time. He dialed his father's mobile number.

"Hello?"

"Hi, Dad."

"Nathan."

"I need to talk to you."

"Okay . . ."

"Look, I, ah, know we haven't always seen eye-to-eye. For what it's worth, I feel like it's my fault. I have trouble trusting people. Trusting you."

"Nonsense. You're my son. Just because we don't always agree on things doesn't mean we can't trust each other."

"I need to trust you. Now more than ever."

"Okay . . ."

"What I'm about to tell you can't go any further. Tell no one; absolutely no one else must know. It's life and death, Dad. My life, and Harvey's."

"What's happened? Is this about Fresno? It's all over the news."

"I need your word."

"You don't have to ask for that."

*"Your word."*

He heard his dad sigh. "All right, I give you my word."

It took five minutes for Nathan to tell the story and describe the plan going forward. He knew with certainty that the news of the Ortega conspiracy to entrap the Bridgestones by selling them Semtex shocked and angered his father. The only thing that surprised Nathan was how good it felt to know his dad hadn't been in on it.

"Are you absolutely sure about this?" Stone asked when Nathan had finished. "I mean absolutely sure?"

"Yes, I'm absolutely sure."

"You think you know someone. Frank and I were in Korea together, fought side by side. We go back over forty years. I can't believe this whole thing is about revenge against Ernie Bridgestone."

"It hurts, I know. Harvey feels betrayed too. There *is* some good news. We recovered most of the missing Semtex. Nearly three hundred pounds."

"That *is* good news."

"Leonard still has ten bricks and some blasting caps."

"What can I do to help? Name it."

"We need satellite images of the location where they stashed their cash."

"I'll get to work on it right away. Do you have exact coordinates?"

Nathan rattled them off. "I need twenty-four-by-twenty-four-inch prints at three meters per inch, ten meters per inch, and one hundred meters per inch. Radial from point zero. Did you copy that?"

"Yes, I'm writing it down."

"Get me a fourth print at five hundred meters per inch. We'll be airborne within the hour. Communication will be critical. My cell phone's tied into the NavCom of my helicopter. It usually works over urban areas, but in the more remote locations all bets are off."

"Nathan, it'll be hard to keep this under wraps. Once the military's involved . . ."

Nathan didn't respond.

"Don't worry; I'll think of something."

"Do your best, Dad; that's all I can ask. I think Malmstrom Air Force Base in Montana is our best bet to download the images."

"I know Malmstrom well. We put our first Minuteman silos up there."

"Listen, I've got to go. We've got a long flight ahead of us."

"Nathan, thank you for trusting me. I'm sorry for the things I said to you the other night."

"Me too."

"I'll call you as soon as I have something to report."

"Tell Mom I love her, okay?"

"You can tell her yourself when this is over."

Nathan said nothing. He didn't have to.

"I'll tell her," Stone said.

Nathan arrived back at Sacramento Executive Airport thirty minutes after dropping Harvey, Grangeland, and Bridgestone off. His headlights found them standing next to the helicopter. Grangeland looked a little cold and a little concerned, but she looked better than Ernie did.

She asked about his arm. He told a white lie, handed her the medical supplies he'd picked up on the way over, and patted the fuselage. "She ready to go?"

"Ready," Harvey said.

"This is everyone's last chance for a pit stop. We'll be in the air for several hours."

Grangeland glanced around in an exaggerated manner. "Hmm, no restroom."

Nathan nodded to the hangar buildings. "We won't watch."

"You'd better not; I'm armed." She jogged over to the hangars and disappeared around the corner.

Nathan turned toward Ernie. "What about you?"

He shook his head.

Harvey removed the duffel bags from the Crown Vic's trunk and secured them in the rear-facing seats behind the cockpit's bulkhead.

"Listen up, Ernie," Nathan said. "I'm willing to cuff your hands in front for the flight, provided you behave yourself. Do we have an understanding?"

"I ain't gonna make no trouble," he said softly.

Without being asked, Harvey pulled his SIG and pointed it at Ernie's chest. Using the handcuff key Grangeland had given him, Nathan recuffed Ernie's hands from behind his back to in front of his stomach. Even though he had it coming, leaving the condemned man's wounded hands cuffed behind his back for the long flight seemed cruel, especially with Bridgestone's dislocated shoulder and finger wounds. Harvey tucked Bridgestone into the right rear seat, behind the pilot's position. He fastened Ernie's seat belt and shoulder strap and locked the door from the outside with a key.

Once Grangeland returned from her business, Nathan pulled her aside and kept his voice low. "I cuffed Ernie's hands in front for the flight. Guard your weapon closely, okay? My rifle and two handguns are in the duffel bags directly across from you."

She nodded and strapped herself into the left rear seat.

"What about the Crown Vic?" Harvey asked.

"Yeah," Nathan agreed. "Park it over by the hangars with the other vehicles."

"What about the Semtex in the trunk?" Harvey asked.

"We'll have to risk that no one steals the car within the next twenty-four hours. As a precaution, we'll take the blasting caps with us."

"Good thought."

When Harvey returned from parking the sedan, he secured the blasting caps into a duffel bag and handed Grangeland a Bose headset with a boom mike. He plugged it into the console over her right shoulder. Bridgestone didn't receive a headset. Although engine and slipstream noise would be loud, it wouldn't be overly so, but more important, it allowed Grangeland, Harvey, and Nathan to communicate without being overheard, which was far more important than worrying about Bridgestone's eardrums. Besides, he wouldn't need them much longer anyway.

While Nathan went through the startup checklist, Harvey connected Nathan's cell phone into the audio interface unit that would allow them to patch the phone communication through their flight helmets. Harvey entered the GPS coordinates Ernie had given them into the Garmin G600 Nav-Com. The glass avionics in Nathan's helicopter were state-of-the-art. Along with flight control data on the left screen, the G600 employed built-in terrain and navigation databases on the right screen, providing a precise moving map of where they were at any given time and where they were going. With the GDL-A data link receiver, they could access high-resolution weather information anywhere within the United States.

"While you were at the hotel, I did some rough flight planning," Harvey said. "It's a three-leg trip: Winnemucca, Nevada; Idaho Falls, Idaho; then into Great Falls, Montana. Our destination coordinates are close to a town called Dupuyer on Highway 89. We'll fuel up in Great Falls. I checked the airport listing binder. At each airport, self-service pumps are available if the flight service centers are closed. All of them have Jet A available, night or day."

"Good job. We might be landing at Malmstrom Air Force Base instead of Great Falls."

Harvey consulted the charts. "That's . . . no problem. It's only a few miles to the east."

Within two minutes of starting the engine, Nathan had the two-and-a-half-ton Bell in a stable hover.

"Clear on the left?" Nathan asked.

"Clear," Harvey answered.

They were on their way.

⊕ Chapter Twenty-five

Minutes after their stop in Winnemucca, Nevada, Nathan's cell phone rang. It was close to seven a.m. Harvey patched it through the NavCom.

It was Stone McBride. "I've got the satellite intel all set up for you."

"Great work, Dad. Thanks."

"I'm glad to do it. When you get within one hundred miles of Malmstrom, change to this frequency and announce your call sign as Civilian Delta." Stone rattled off the numbers, and Harvey programmed the frequency into the ninth preset on the NavCom unit.

"Got it," Nathan said.

"An air force Huey will intercept you and escort you onto the base. It would be useful if I could tell them when to expect you up there."

"Wait one," Harvey said. He began scrolling through menus on the G600 NavCom. "We'll be crossing Interstate 90 in approximately . . . four hours, assuming our fuel stop in Idaho Falls goes as expected."

"Got it," Stone said. "Once you're at Malmstrom, they'll fuel you up and give you the latest photos of the area. They'll probably be twenty to thirty minutes old by then, but that's the best they can do. Also, if anyone shows up at the location after you leave Malmstrom, they'll radio you."

"Perfect," Nathan said.

"Major General Mansfield is the base commander. I told

him this is a classified operation on a need-to-know basis. The number of people involved is minimal. He assured me there will be no leaks or, quote, 'heads will roll.' Don't take any unnecessary risks. Bridgestone isn't worth your life, or Harvey's."

"Thanks for your help, Dad. I'll call you later."

"Be careful, Nathan."

After a quick refuel and bathroom break in Idaho Falls, they were on their way north again. The weather was perfect, not a cloud in the sky, and it looked good all the way to the Canadian border. Nothing was forecast for the next forty-eight hours. Nathan wondered why he hadn't flown up this way before. It was truly beautiful territory. He made a mental note to go camping up here. River-washed valleys and rocky canyons dominated the landscape. In the distance, off to the west, snowcapped peaks lined the horizon.

Harvey worked the NavCom computer. "We'll be coming up on Interstate 90 in about twenty minutes. That would be a good point to call for our air force escort."

"Sounds good."

"How's the arm?" Harvey asked.

"A little sore, but the bleeding has almost stopped. Thanks for the TLC, Grangeland." She'd insisted on changing his bandages at each fuel stop.

"You're welcome. I wish I could do more."

"How's our passenger doing?"

"About the same," she said. "He's been staring out the window the whole time."

Not surprising, considering what lay ahead for him. One way or another, this was a one-way trip for Ernie Bridgestone.

At Interstate 90, Harvey pressed the ninth preset button for the frequency Nathan's father had given them. He toggled the transmit trigger on the cyclic control. "This is Civilian Delta on heading zero–one–zero crossing Interstate 90 at eight thousand five hundred."

The response came back immediately. "Civilian Delta, squawk three–two–two–five and ident."

Harvey repeated the instructions, entered the numbers into their transponder, and pressed the ident button.

The metallic voice came back. "Civilian Delta, radar contact confirmed. Maintain current heading and speed and await further instructions."

They flew for another ten minutes before the controller came back. "Civilian Delta, your escort is five miles at one o'clock. Maintain heading and speed. Advise upon visual contact."

Harvey repeated the instructions. "You got him yet?" he asked Nathan.

"No, but we're closing fast; we should see him in the next minute or two."

"There he is," Harvey said. "One o'clock high."

Harvey's eyes were better than Nathan's. It took him another ten seconds to find the tiny black speck. "Got him," Nathan said.

Harvey called in the visual contact, and for the third time they were told to maintain heading and speed. The black speck grew into the recognizable shape of a camouflage green–and–gray air force UH-1N Huey. It began a sweeping one–hundred–eighty–degree turn, dropping altitude as it formed up off their port side.

"Impressive sight," Harvey said.

Grangeland leaned forward to look out Ernie's window. "He's awfully close to us," she said.

Nathan glanced over at the Huey. "He's just looking us over, making sure he likes what he sees." Their escort was about one hundred feet away, matching their airspeed and altitude. Harvey gave the air force pilot a crisp salute, which was returned.

A different voice came through their flight helmets. "Civilian Delta, this is Air Force Escort One. Welcome to Montana. Maintain position off our starboard side." Its pilot waved.

Harvey waved back.

This was the first time Nathan had ever flown in formation with another helicopter. He liked it. It gave him a sense of belonging and power he hadn't felt for many years, since his service in the Marine Corps. Forty minutes later, with Great Falls off their port side, they were approaching Malmstrom Air Force Base. Their escort handled all the radio communication with Malmstrom's tower, and they were given clearance to land. The two helicopters made a straight-in approach from the south. Malmstrom's huge runway ran diagonally from the southwest to the northeast. They crossed it and settled into controlled hovers over a large expanse of concrete near some off-white hangar buildings. Once on the tarmac, Nathan went through the shutdown procedure, flipping switches and turning off avionics. After the engine had cooled he shut it down. Harvey opened Grangeland's door and she climbed out, keeping her attention sharply focused on Ernie.

An air force sedan pulled up between the two helicopters, and a major climbed out to meet them. The pilot's door of their escort Huey swung open, and a two-star in flight fatigues began walking toward them. Major General Mansfield, no doubt about it. Out of habit, Nathan and Harvey issued salutes. Mansfield, a six-footer with cropped gray hair and pronounced crow's-feet at the edges of his hazel eyes, returned their salutes. "At ease, gentlemen. Welcome to Malmstrom." The general introduced his aide as Major Reid, and handshakes were made all around.

Nathan looked at the Huey and then back to Mansfield.

Mansfield smiled. "Would you like to give her a test drive?"

"Oh, man," Nathan said. The Huey wasn't significantly bigger than his own ship, but it was far more powerful. He'd love to strap her on for a spell. "We're in a time-critical situation, sir. May I have a rain check?"

"That's a promise. Your father's a good friend to the military. He fights for every red cent we get."

Nathan nodded.

Mansfield addressed his aide. "Top off Major McBride's fuel tanks." He looked back at Nathan. "Jet A?"

"Yes, sir, thank you." Nathan asked if Grangeland would guard Ernie for a few minutes. She nodded, eyes never leaving their prisoner.

"Who's your passenger in the backseat?" Mansfield asked. "He doesn't look real happy to be here."

"For your ears only?" Nathan asked.

"My ears only."

"Ernie Bridgestone."

"You're kidding. He's been all over the news for a week. I heard he escaped from the Fresno truck stop. That was some show. The live news clips showed the underground fuel tanks exploding. Looked like a napalm attack." Mansfield looked over to Nathan's helicopter and then to his aide. "Major Reid, you didn't hear any of this."

"Hear what, sir?"

"The FBI leaked his escape to the press," Nathan said. "We're hoping to collar his brother Leonard. That's why we're here. Leonard needs to think Ernie got away. We think they're planning to meet at the coordinates my father gave you. We figure he'll be arriving in about two to three hours or so."

Mansfield noticed the blood soaking through Nathan's shirtsleeve. "What happened to your arm?"

"I took one at the truck stop."

"You were shot? You flew six hours with a bullet wound to your stick arm?"

"It's not bad. It went clean through."

"Major Reid, get a medic over here double-time."

"Yes, sir." The aide climbed into the driver's seat and made a radio call.

"General, I'm fine. Really."

Mansfield held up a hand. "Don't argue with me, son."

Nathan zipped it. You didn't argue with a two-star. Ever.

Mansfield pulled a large envelope from the passenger seat of his gray sedan. He spread the color photos on the hood. They were oblique shots taken from the south. "These are fifteen minutes old. I had my aide look them over. As far as we can tell, there's no one in the area. We didn't spot any vehicles or any engine or human heat signatures on the infrareds. It's harder to detect them during the day, but sometimes we can. They sure chose a remote location. These coordinates are just south of the Blackfeet Indian Reservation. They were wise to stay off tribal territory. The Blackfeet are protective of their land." Mansfield pointed to a dirt road. "This is Dutch Creek Road; it connects to Highway 89 several miles to the east. This track up here is Sweet Dam Road; it also connects to Highway 89. It's probably why they chose this location. They could approach the coordinates from the north or south. It also gives them two possible routes of escape."

"This is perfect, General. Just what we need."

Mansfield bent over the photos a little. "Point zero looks like some sort of spirelike rock formation on the south wall of the canyon; you can see its shadow here." He stabbed a finger on the most detailed photo, the image at ten meters per inch.

"It's easily recognized from the ground," Harvey said, studying the other photos. Nathan knew his partner was scoping potential shooting locations and looking for an LZ to set their chopper down.

"What else can I do to help?" Mansfield asked.

"Just keep us updated if anyone approaches the coordinates."

"We're on that. Right now we're checking with NORAD to see what birds we've got overhead. There might be some dark intervals. In all honesty, we won't be able to reposition any of them. They're needed over the Gulf."

"We'll make do, General."

"Ernie Bridgestone," he said slowly. "Public enemy number

one. I'm glad you caught the son of a bitch. That Sacramento bombing was cold-blooded."

"Yes, sir, it was. Special Agent Grangeland probably needs a pit stop. We all do. Harvey and I need to change into our BDUs. Can we trouble you for some chow and coffee?"

"It's no trouble."

As they walked back over to Nathan's helicopter, he was acutely aware of the passage of time. Although he didn't think Leonard could get up here in less than twenty-two hours, he wasn't one hundred percent sure. A sense of urgency seized him. Did they really have time for this? He forced himself to slow his breathing and relax his hands. If Ernie had lied about Leonard's departure time from California, it could cost them their lives. Although the satellite images were void of human activity, it didn't mean Leonard wasn't already there—cash in hand, planting Semtex charges and laying trip wires, waiting for Ernie to arrive. How long would he wait, a few hours? Longer? Or would he wait at all? The Canadian border would be whispering his name.

A gray aviation fuel truck pulled up to Nathan's helicopter, and the driver climbed out and attached the ground wire to a skid. Nathan made sure Jet A was being fed to his machine by asking the driver directly.

Mansfield told Reid to round up some turkey sandwiches and brown water from the officer's mess—on the double. Reid jogged back to the sedan and sped away.

"Should be about ten minutes."

"That's fine, General, thank you."

Mansfield nodded over his shoulder. "There's a head and locker room in the hangar."

Harvey and Nathan helped Grangeland extract Ernie from the Bell and followed Mansfield to the hangar, the general graciously carrying Nathan's duffel for him. Inside, Mansfield's medic had Nathan sit on a lunch table while he received eighteen stitches in his arm. Nathan refused a local anesthetic, claiming he didn't want any part of his body numb. Occasionally wincing, he took the tightly spaced stitches while eating a turkey sandwich. He was thankful the medic didn't comment on the crisscrossing network of scars on Nathan's torso, even after doing a fairly shocked double take. When Nathan noticed Grangeland staring at him, he feigned innocence and asked, "What?"

She rolled her eyes, trying not to smile.

A change of clothes later, General Mansfield walked them back out to Nathan's chopper and asked, "Are you sure you don't want any backup out there?"

"Positive, General," Nathan said. "We prefer to work alone."

"All right, then. Monitor the frequency we gave you. We'll keep you apprised of any activity at the coordinates. And I'll keep a squad standing by just in case you give us a nine-one-one call."

Ten miles southeast of Dupuyer, Nathan dropped the helicopter down to one hundred feet. "Watch for power lines," Nathan told Harvey. "Did you find an LZ on the photos?"

"I think so; we'll have to check it out. It's about a mile and a half northwest from ground zero. It's an island of trees in our canyon. It's kinda horseshoe-shaped. It screens the chopper from three directions."

"I'm dropping down to fifty feet. Keep your eyes peeled." Nathan lowered the nose. Ten seconds later they were skimming the grassy landscape at nearly one hundred forty miles an hour. The ground rush was intoxicating. As dangerous as it was, Nathan loved flying low and fast.

Harvey worked the NavCom screen. "Adjust heading to three-four-five."

"Three-four-five," Nathan echoed.

"Guys?" It was Grangeland, groaning more than speaking. Harvey whirled in alarm as Nathan asked, "You okay?"

"Uh, we're fine back here," she said, sounding anything

but. "I hate to be the weak link, but do we have to fly this low? I don't feel so good."

"Sorry, but yeah, we do," Harvey said. "Look straight ahead; don't look out your window, okay?"

She grunted an acknowledgment.

A small herd of elk dashed underneath them. The animals tried to stay in a group, but several peeled off in a different direction.

"Keep an eye out for birds, Harv. Striking an eagle at this speed will definitely ruin our day." Nathan's brow furrowed in concentration. "Do you see any transmission or antenna towers?"

"Negative. We're good to go."

"Let's call Malmstrom and ask for an update."

General Mansfield himself answered the radio and reported that all was quiet except for the thermal image of their exhaust. He informed them that in ten minutes they'd experience a thirty-minute blackout as the current surveillance satellite dropped below the western horizon.

Harvey had the five-hundred-meter-per-inch photo in his lap. "I seriously doubt Leonard has arrived yet. To get here before us, he'd have to drive eighty miles an hour the entire way, straight through. There's no way he could do it, and he certainly wouldn't risk getting pulled over."

"Agreed," Nathan said, though he shared Harvey's apprehension. "He wouldn't want to risk getting pulled over by state troopers. If what Ernie said is right, then we're beating him here by at least one hour, possibly as many as three."

"*If* . . . What's your gut on what Ernie told us?" Harv asked.

"Obviously he can't know for sure, but I don't think he was lying. He would've sold his mother into prostitution to save his fingers. Still . . ."

"We assume nothing," Harvey said.

"Right."

"Think Leonard will have an RF detector?"

"Hard to say, but I doubt it. If he does, he'll pick up our handhelds for sure, but unless it's a state-of-the-art device he won't have signal strength or direction; he'll just know there's radio chatter in the area. There's not much we can do about it, unless you want to bag the radios. Since our handhelds can't interface with the NavCom, I'm thinking we keep Grangeland with Ernie at the chopper. We'll need her to relay anything Mansfield sees from the surveillance birds. I'd say using the radios outweighs being blind out here. Lesser of two evils."

"Booby traps?" asked Harvey.

"I've thought about that too. I think it's unlikely they'd have any kind of long-term trip wires or pressure-triggered devices because of all the wildlife in the area. They wouldn't want a random accident to call attention to their cache. They might have something at the actual location of the buried money, though. If he does, it'll be a bomb-disposal job. Can your people handle it, Grangeland?" Nathan already knew the answer; he just wanted to distract her from her airsickness.

No answer.

"Grangeland?"

"Yeah, I think so," she said tightly.

"You okay back there?"

"I'm feeling really woozy."

"Hang in there. Harv, how far to Dutch Creek Road?"

"Maybe four thousand yards." He looked down at the satellite image. "Adjust heading to three-four-zero. That should take us pretty close to the LZ."

Nathan pushed the cyclic slightly to the left and watched the LCD screen's digital compass rotate. "Copy . . . three-four-zero." He sneaked a look out the port window. The snow-capped peaks of the Flathead Range were a damned beautiful sight. *Where the mountains meet the prairies,* he thought. Buffalo and Blackfoot territory.

"Should we risk a visual pass down the canyon to the money drop and back?" Harvey asked.

"It won't help us that much. For the kind of detail we'd need, we'd have to move slightly faster than a hover. Let's set her down ASAP, for Grangeland's sake."

"You'll have my"—she swallowed hard, suppressing a gag—"undying gratitude."

"Reduce speed to sixty knots," Harvey said.

"Sixty knots." Nathan lowered the collective, pressed the right antitorque pedal, and pulled back on the cyclic control. Maintaining its altitude, the helicopter flared and rapidly bled off airspeed.

"Oh, shit," Grangeland moaned.

"Hang in there," Harvey encouraged her.

"I think I'm gonna be sick."

"We're ninety seconds from being on the ground."

She didn't make it.

Nathan heard violent retching sounds as Grangeland leaned forward and lost her lunch. The distinctive odor of vomit filled the cockpit.

"Don't worry about it," Nathan told her. "Happens to all of us. Keep track of your weapon; Ernie might try something." She didn't respond. "Harv, what's happening back there?"

Harvey whipped around.

Her Glock still trained on Ernie, Grangeland was wiping her mouth.

"She's okay," Harvey said. "Crossing Dutch Creek Road. Slow to thirty knots."

A dirt track passed beneath them no more than twenty feet below their skids. Sixty seconds later the landscape suddenly dropped off as they cleared the canyon's southern ridgeline.

"Set her down inside that copse of trees at two o'clock," Harvey said.

"Power lines?" Nathan asked.

Harvey scanned the area. "Clear."

Twenty seconds later, sand and leaves cartwheeled away

from the LZ as Nathan set the chopper down. "Shutting down," he said. "Any bullet holes in us yet?"

Harvey grinned. "The afternoon's still young."

Grangeland heartily agreed with being delegated to guard duty. The nausea had left her weak and in no condition for physical exertion, let alone stealth. And her equilibrium remained screwed up. With Harvey covering, she handcuffed Ernie to the skid support just below the rear door and sat down in the sand facing him. Her headset was still plugged into the cockpit's bulkhead so she could relay anything General Mansfield reported to Nathan and Harvey.

Dressed exactly as they had been at Freedom's Echo in their ghillie suits, Nathan and Harvey parted company with Grangeland and headed east along the northern edge of the canyon's stream bed. Nathan estimated the canyon's width at three hundred yards, tighter in places, wider in others. Because the north wall of the canyon caught more sunlight, the underbrush was thicker and there were more trees for cover. In the middle of the canyon, a small amount of water still flowed toward the east. The canyon's seventy-foot limestone walls were steep in places, and shallow in others where smaller streams fed the main creek. In hundreds of places, striated layers of rock were exposed in a series of ten- and twenty-foot ledges, like giant steps. Dark recesses in the rock formations created ideal shooting positions for a potential sniper.

They moved quickly along the tree-lined bank of the sandy wash, stopping every three minutes or so to scan the area in front of and behind them with their field glasses.

"Ground zero is on the south side of the wash about·thirty feet above the bank," Harvey said. "In the oblique shot, it looked like a giant stack of flat boulders."

"How far?"

"Another thousand yards or so. We should be able to see it once we clear the next bend in the wash. I don't like being down low like this with the sun in our faces."

"That's affirmative; neither would Leonard. But don't worry; if he's already here, he can only nail one of us at a time. Your odds are fifty-fifty."

"The hell they are," Harvey said. "He'll shoot the man carrying the rifle first."

"Maybe *you* should carry it."

"Nice try."

Nathan toggled his transmit button on the radio. "Grangeland, radio check."

"Loud and clear," came her response. "I gagged Ernie just in case he has the notion to sound off. He's livened up a bit. Mad as a hornet."

"Good thinking. Five-minute check-ins from now on. We left the helicopter's master switch on. In the event Malmstrom calls, you'll hear it through your headset. If you need to contact Malmstrom for any reason, all you have to do is pull the red trigger on the cyclic—the control stick. Copy that?"

"Copy," she said. "Good hunting."

"Despite her gritty personality," Harvey said, "I rather like her."

"Me too. She's a trooper. Okay, we're going stealth from here on. Ten-meter separation; I'll take the lead. You've got my six."

"Copy."

"How long before our next surveillance bird's overhead?"

Harvey glanced at his soap-smeared watch. "Twelve minutes."

## ⊕ Chapter Twenty-six

Her nausea having passed and her equilibrium returned, Special Agent Grangeland was feeling a lot better. She surveyed her surroundings. Light to moderate tree cover surrounded the helicopter to the north, east, and west. From the south rim of the canyon, the helicopter was in plain sight. From the other directions it wasn't totally screened, but unless someone was purposely looking for a parked helicopter in the middle of nowhere nestled within a canyon surrounded by trees, they'd never spot it from those directions. She supposed Leonard could be looking for just such a situation. She'd overheard Nathan and Harvey talking; this spot was nearly a mile and a half from the money stash. Would Leonard Bridgestone reconnoiter out to this range? Would he start at such an extreme distance and spiral in, checking the perimeter all the while? No doubt he'd be exhausted from a twenty-two-hour drive and need to get some sleep, unless he was wired on caffeine pills and gallons of coffee.

*Shit.* Too many questions without answers. She felt vulnerable in her current position, exposed from the south. Keeping her headset on, she climbed across the rear seats and sat down in the sand on the north side of the helicopter, facing east. She had a patchy view through the trees and overhanging branches. Given all the variables, she felt the north side of the helicopter was the best place to wait. Or was it? Maybe she should be inside the trees, under deeper shadow, but then she remembered her headset. The coiled cord wouldn't reach more than five feet from the helicopter. She wasn't going anywhere. If Leonard Bridgestone spotted her, there was little she could do about it. Besides, the air force was watching the place; if anyone approached, they'd be giving her a heads-up.

*Except during the satellite blackout . . .*

She glanced at her watch, cursing herself for not knowing the blackout period. Was the blackout just starting? Or ending? What were the odds of Leonard arriving during the blackout period? She tried to calculate them. Thirty minutes of three hours was the same as one-in-six odds. Would she bet her life on one-in-six odds? Hell, no. She fought an overwhelming urge to look behind her. *Relax*, she told herself. *You're just being paranoid.* Besides, she had a vest under the Windbreaker. She'd be fine.

Two seconds later an invisible brick smashed into her torso.

Her mind tried to register the event, but she struggled with the truth.

As she lay in the sand, losing consciousness, she saw Ernie leaning under the helicopter—smiling through his gag.

The high-powered rifle shot ripped down the canyon, echoing off thousands of exposed limestone ledges. Nathan and Harvey hit the deck simultaneously.

From the prone position Nathan whipped around. "Harvey!"

"I'm okay. You?"

"Okay." Nathan pressed the transmit button, "Grangeland, you copy?"

No response.

"Grangeland, do you copy?"

Nothing.

"Harvey, form up. I think Grangeland's down."

Harvey ran in a crouch over to Nathan's position and settled in.

"That was a rifle, not a handgun."

"Agreed," Harvey said.

"I'm going back. Stay here and keep your head down."

"She's dead, Nate."

"I'm going back. Radio silence from now on. We have to assume Grangeland's radio's compromised." Nathan knew changing frequencies was useless; the devices had scanners and would automatically switch to any active channel.

"We should go together."

"Harv, the endgame is at that rock formation down the canyon. It all comes together there. Ernie will tell Leonard there're only two of us out here. They'll try to take us down and recover the money. Leonard knows that if he doesn't get his money now, he never will. He won't leave without it."

"Shit," Harvey said.

"I'll stay on the north side of the canyon and try to flush them down the south side. I doubt Leonard has a ghillie suit, but he'll be in camo fatigues. Ernie will be easier to see in his civilian clothes. Stay covered and wait for me."

"Nathan—"

"No matter what happens, I won't leave the north side of the canyon. If you get seen or pinned down, give me three quick shots with the SIG and stay put. I'll come get you."

"Nathan." Harvey shook his head. "Man, we're brothers. Closer. I just want you to know . . . Aw, shit . . ."

Nathan grasped both of Harvey's shoulders. "Keep your head in the game. We're going to win, Harv." Nathan opened and closed the bolt of his rifle in two crisp movements, chambering a round. "They don't stand a chance."

Moving from tree to tree, bush to bush, and boulder to boulder, Nathan worked his way back upstream to the west, always staying in deep shadow. In one sandy stream bed feeding the main creek, he had to drop to his belly and crawl across the semiopen ground. He hated being exposed, even though his ghillie suit made him all but invisible. The thirty-foot-wide flash-flood area of sand offered only thinly scattered buck brush for cover. Once on the opposite side, he'd have roughly a three-hundred-yard visual shot of the helicopter through the eastern tree cover. If Grangeland was down, he knew it was a good bet Ernie would be long gone. It was also a good bet Ernie would tell Leonard everything he'd seen about his captors. What kind of weapons they carried. What they were wearing. The direction they went—east, toward the money drop, along the north side of the canyon. He hoped the bastards wouldn't smash up his helicopter. It was more likely Leonard would make a mad dash, free his brother, and get back into cover as soon as possible. Nathan doubted he'd waste any time out in the open.

*Advantage, bad guys. For now . . .*

Once out of the sandy wash, he crawled the last few yards

through thick underbrush and oak fallout, being careful not to bump any of the bushes or dead branches. He also kept an eye out for ants. Crawling through a fire ant nest was never a good idea. He felt a stinging dampness in his right arm. The stitches had torn and he was bleeding again. *Damn it.*

Ignoring the renewed fire in his arm, he cleared his thoughts and put himself into Leonard's head: *I'm going to take the high ground on the opposite side of the canyon with the sun to my back. The enemy knows I'm here; he heard my shot. McBride'll double back to check on the woman and Ernie. When he approaches the helicopter, I'll nail him from a bench-rested position on the southern rim of the canyon.*

*Wrong, Leonard. Sorry to disappoint you.*

Secured in deep shadow, Nathan slowly brought the sniper rifle up, shouldered the weapon, and flipped the front and rear lens caps up. With a piercing blue eye, he peered through the scope. A few yards away, a clump of sagebrush blocked his view of the chopper. He made a slight adjustment of his position and reshouldered the weapon.

Three hundred yards distant, Grangeland was down. She lay on the north side of the helicopter with her back to him. He steadied his rifle and tried to determine whether she was breathing. He couldn't say. She looked like a lifeless heap. Wait . . . movement. A slight motion of her left arm. Her hand lifted above the sand for a moment before falling. Nathan kept watching until the movement was repeated.

*She's alive.*

And, of course, Ernie was gone. Anger began to flare, but he forced it back and slowly pivoted his rifle through an arc covering a hundred-yard radius, centered on the helicopter. Nothing. No movement at all. Approaching the helicopter was suicide, an obvious trap. No way to make a mad dash to Grangeland and tend to her. Not against a trained sniper.

Gritting his teeth at the fire in his arm and Grangeland's situation, he backed away from his current position and tucked himself behind a fallen branch offering solid cover from the south rim of the canyon. He couldn't leave Grangeland. Nor could he save her. He could almost feel Leonard's rifle scope sweeping back and forth past his location.

*Two can play that game. . . .*

Moving with caterpillar-like speed, Nathan maneuvered himself into a cross-legged position and bench-rested his cloth-wrapped rifle on top of the log. He began a slow sweeping scan of the canyon's opposite rim beyond the helicopter, zigzagging back and forth from the ridge down, concentrating on rocky spots with deep recessed shadows.

*There.* A flash of white.

Possibly Ernie's T-shirt. He swung his rifle back, focused on the spot, and held his breath, unmoving. He was looking at two huge slabs of fallen limestone three-quarters of the way up the canyon's wall that had formed a narrow triangular area of shadow.

There it was again.

"Got you," Nathan whispered.

Through his Nikon scope, Nathan watched as Ernie slowly ducked up and down with a pair of field glasses in his good hand and a handheld radio in his wounded hand. The white flash Nathan had seen was the gauze wrapping Ernie's hand. Good ol' Ernie had wisely removed his white T-shirt, but overlooked the gauze. *Oh, that's too bad.* Pure exhilaration coursed through Nathan's body like electricity. "Steady," he whispered to himself. He turned the elevation knob of the scope, counting ten clicks for a four-hundred-yard, slightly elevated shot. He gauged the wind as being nearly calm, maybe three to five miles an hour from the northwest. He'd be shooting directly into the wind, so he didn't make a windage correction.

"You're blowing it," he whispered to Ernie. "You're too regular with your movements." Every fifteen seconds Ernie would come up from his hiding place, focus on the helicopter for five seconds, and then duck back down.

Nathan placed the crosshairs where Ernie's head would appear in the next ten seconds and waited.

Nothing happened.

Ernie didn't come back up.

Well after the fifteen-second interval had passed, there was still no Ernie. What the hell was he doing? He couldn't leave the crag of rock without Nathan seeing him. Thirty seconds went by. *Have I been made? Shit. No way. No friggin' way Leonard's seen me. Not in this soldier's world.*

Forty seconds.

Fifty.

A full minute.

*Patience*, he told himself. *Breathe in deeply. Let it out slowly. In deep . . . Out slowly . . . Stay focused. Ernie's still there; he'll be back up. Patience . . .*

After ninety seconds Nathan had his answer. It was almost as if Ernie had sensed Nathan's presence, for when he reappeared the bright white gauze on his hand was gone. But it was too late.

"That's a bingo," Nathan whispered, and pulled the trigger.

The Remington 700 bucked against his right shoulder and sent a white-hot jolt of agony through his wounded arm. *Son of a bitch!* For a few seconds his vision teared up. When it cleared he didn't see Ernie, but he *did* see what was left of him on the limestone wall behind his hiding place—the unmistakable splatter of a head shot. "Promise kept," he whispered. "Marine to marine."

Feeling the sudden flood of moisture on his arm, Nathan knew the wound was really bleeding now. How long did he have before blood loss became a real concern? He couldn't worry about that right now, because the *real* struggle had just begun. Removing Ernie was moderately helpful in the battle against Leonard Bridgestone—as much psychologically as logistically—but there was no safe way past an entrenched sniper. Leonard was playing a waiting game, counting on Nathan's compassion for Grangeland or his need for the helicopter—his sole means of transport and communication—to draw him into the kill zone. *Sorry to disappoint you, Leonard, but that's not happening.*

Nathan saw another way: To reach Grangeland he'd need to create a diversion, and that meant getting back to Harvey. Two against one, they might just pull it off.

Like oozing molasses, Nathan slid himself down from the fallen branch, hunkered down behind its cover, and slung his rifle over his shoulder for the return crawl to the east. *Hang in there, Grangeland; we aren't going to abandon you.*

How much time had passed since she'd been shot? Twenty minutes? Thirty? He wasn't sure. He thought back to the image of her prone form and didn't recall seeing any blood. She'd been wearing her dark blue FBI Windbreaker to conceal her piece and her bulletproof vest. *Her vest.* Maybe the only reason she'd still be alive at all. How long did she have?

Harvey turned his head toward the sound of the shot. "Nathan," he whispered. Had Leonard just killed Nathan, or had Nathan killed one of them? He considered moving back up the canyon toward the source of the report. Nathan could be down, wounded. Slowly bleeding to death. If Harvey stayed put, would he be condemning his lifelong friend to death? He wanted to use the radio, *needed* to use the radio, but Nathan had called for silence. He weighed the repercussions. Okay, if Leonard had Grangeland's radio, so what? He couldn't use it to triangulate. The receiving transmission would be silent, coming out of Nathan's tiny ear speaker.

Decision made, he pressed the transmit button. "Five by five?"

A few seconds later he heard, "Five by five. Stay put. I'm coming to you."

Relief washed over Harvey like warm wind. Although he doubted Leonard possessed Nathan's shooting skills—only a handful of people in the world did—Leonard could've seen Nathan first, and in a long-range sniper duel, the shooter who spotted his opponent first, won.

*Stay put.* Harvey took a deep breath and exhaled. Nothing so simple had ever been more difficult.

\* \* \*

Nathan didn't blame Harvey for breaking radio silence. From a tactical perspective Harvey needed to know he was okay and still in the fight. Had Nathan been killed Harvey would have an agonizing decision to make: stay and fight and possibly die, or bug out and possibly die. Nathan doubted Leonard would let either of them just fly out of here. Harvey was a family man; he had more to consider than his own life—his wife and kids being at the top of the list. Harvey would *never* abandon the fight if he knew his partner was still alive; Nathan was certain of that.

Nathan's plan was simple. Since Leonard couldn't be in two places at once, he and Harvey would separate. He'd head toward the money cache while Harvey doubled back to the helicopter. Through a series of purposeful ploys, he planned to lure Leonard to his end of the canyon, leaving Harvey free to fly Grangeland to safety. He hoped Harv was ready for his first solo flight.

Setting that thought aside for now, Nathan crawled down the length of the fallen branch, shouldered his rifle, and scoped the canyon's southern wall. Although he had a pair of field glasses, he always used his rifle. If he saw his mark, he was instantly ready to send a bullet. If his opponent was on the move, he didn't see any evidence of it. The few sandy areas he could see were virgin, lacking discernible footprints. He steeled himself for what lay ahead—that damned thirty-foot expanse of sand and brush. If he were going to get nailed, he knew it would happen out there. It looked as vast as the Sahara Desert, but there was no avoiding it and no way around it. He had to traverse it. Simple as that.

*Here goes . . .*

Moving no faster than a foot every five seconds, he started his crawl across the sand.

He ran the math through his head to distract himself from the pain and wet sensation in his arm. *Thirty feet times five sec-*

*onds per foot. One hundred and fifty seconds. Two and half minutes. That's not so long, really; after all, it's—*

Halfway across the sand, he froze.

Had he heard something behind him? A crunch of leaves? If Leonard was back there, Nathan was a sitting duck out here in the open. He knew his ghillie suit transformed him into a shrub, but what about the tracks he left crawling out here? Moving his head slowly, he sneaked a look over his right shoulder and was surprised when he didn't see any deep tracks. He hadn't remembered brushing them flat with his legs as he moved, but he must have. He'd done it on autopilot, on pure instinct from his old training. *I'll be damned*, he thought.

There it was again.

The crunch of dried leaves.

He was certain this time.

Staring through the thinly spaced stalks of underbrush, he watched for any sign of movement. Expecting to see a pair of combat boots, Nathan felt a chill rake his spine when he saw the source of the noise.

## ⊕ Chapter Twenty-seven

A mountain lion.

A damned big one. Probably a male. Probably close to two hundred pounds. Correction, probably close to two hundred pounds of solid muscle, sharp claws, and yellow fangs.

Taking slow, deliberate steps, the animal slunk forward with its head low, its eyes searching for the scent of blood it followed. Had the rifle shots awakened it? Nathan knew mountain lions were night predators. The rifle shots should've spooked it, made it haul ass out of there, but following a fresh blood scent was a powerful instinct, especially if it was hungry.

When it reached the edge of the fallen tree branch Nathan had traversed a minute earlier, it sniffed the ground and froze. Then it looked him straight in the eyes from no more than fifteen feet away.

*Go away, damn you. Go away!*

Like something out of a slowly developing nightmare, it took a step into the sun-bleached sand, then another. And another. Directly toward him.

Moving as slowly as humanly possible, Nathan eased his hand down to his gun belt and pulled out his SIG Sauer. There was no way to unsling his rifle without significant body movement, which would certainly make the animal charge. It would be on top of him in one bound. He searched his database of survival training for encounters with mountain lions. *Never run* was at the forefront of his memory-bank readout.

The animal, now less than two body lengths away, was still coming.

Something else shot through Nathan's mind: movement. The cougar was a damning source of movement, and movement was what caught the eye.

From deep shadow on the south rim of the canyon, Leonard followed the big cat through his rifle scope and smiled. It seemed to be following an invisible scent. Quite possibly his opponent's. Seeing only its back, he watched the animal pace along a fallen branch and approach the edge of a dry streambed that fed the larger stream in the middle of the canyon. It froze for a few seconds before stepping out onto the sand.

If Nathan were going to shoot the lion, he had better do it within the next two seconds, while he still had the angle to manage the shot from the hip. If he wasn't precise with his aim, he could easily blow a hole in his own foot. *Damn it.* He didn't want to kill such a magnificent predator. In many ways they were just alike, but Nathan's own survival and Harvey's had to come first. He also knew that as soon as he pulled the trigger his cover was blown, because if his first shot wasn't fatal or severely crippling, he'd have to fire a second, and possibly a third time. The first report would alert Leonard to his general location, but the second and third reports would pinpoint him. He might as well stand up and wave a flag.

Both his options were equally unpleasant.

He could lie here and be mauled to death, literally eaten alive, or he could shoot the cat and, in turn, be shot himself. All things being equal, he preferred the second option, but it had already expired. The animal was directly behind him now; he no longer had the angle to shoot it from the hip.

He could hear the sound of its paws on the sand.

He buried his face into his shoulder and stopped breathing. If he played dead, maybe, just maybe, it would lose interest and move on. Deep down Nathan knew it was wishful thinking. A mountain lion would just as soon scavenge for food as hunt it.

The cat brought its face to within inches of Nathan's head.

Its hot breath penetrated the strips of his ghillie suit and brushed the skin on his neck.

It issued a low, growling murmur deep in its throat as it realized it had found the source of the fresh blood it had been tracking. An easy meal.

*Go away. Get the fuck out of here!*

The cat issued a second, more forceful growl and jabbed Nathan's neck with a paw. It was funny what the human mind was capable of thinking at times like this. With bizarre detachment, Nathan thanked God it had missed his wounded arm, but that thought died when he felt cool air on his skin. The cat's jab had opened a hole in his ghillie suit.

The animal pushed again. Harder.

His lungs screaming for air, Nathan continued to play dead. If things kept going like this, he wouldn't *have* to play dead.

*Go away!*

When he felt the cat's sandpaper tongue lick the back of his exposed neck, Nathan had had enough.

With as much strength as he could muster, he issued a war cry, the loudest, fiercest sound he could make. He snapped his body to the left and cracked the cat in the nose with the butt of his gun.

Leonard watched the animal traverse the sand and stop at some sort of flat shrub. It lowered its head and sniffed. Had it lost the scent? If it had been following someone, where were the tracks? Looking for human footprints, he swung his scope back to the edge of the underbrush where the cat had emerged, cranked it to maximum zoom, but saw only the cat's footprints.

At the left edge of Leonard's magnified image, he caught sudden movement. He swung the rifle back. "What the fuck?" he said aloud. The mountain lion jumped six feet into the air. When it landed, it bolted away from the shrub at a full gallop.

The shrub went vertical and began sprinting across the sand. Not a shrub—a ghillie suit, and a damned fine one at that. "Oh, you're good," Leonard said. He placed the crosshairs slightly ahead of the green mass. . . .

And pulled the trigger.

Nathan's timing had to be perfect. He needed to vary his speed as he ran. *Now!* Five feet from the safety of cover, he hit the brakes and nearly skidded to a stop. A split second later he heard the telltale *crack* of a supersonic arrival. Out in front to his right, the sand exploded from the impact. If he'd kept running at the same speed . . . Using his left hand, Nathan pointed the SIG at the ground slightly left and ahead of his path and fired five shots. Sand burst into the air. It wasn't much cover, but it would have to do. He dived into the underbrush on the opposite side of the wash and scrambled behind the thick trunk of an oak. Panting like a dog, he pressed his back against its welcome mass as a second bullet tore past his position on the left.

"Shit." Leonard had missed. Before he could reacquire, the sand in front of his target erupted, obscuring his view. He heard five quick pops, like firecrackers going off, and knew his mark had fired a handgun into the sand to provide a smokelike screen. Clever move. In combination with his motion and the irregularly shaped ghillie suit, it worked. Estimating where he thought his target would be, Leonard sent another bullet before pulling back to relocate.

Harvey heard the report of the rifle roll down the canyon in a crackling reverberation that lasted for nearly five seconds. Then he heard five quick handgun shots. A few seconds later he heard a second rifle shot. What the hell was going on?

The tiny speaker in his ear went off. "Five-by-five, Harv. Stay down; he's on the south rim. I'm coming to you."

"Copy."

As Nathan made his way upstream along the tree-covered bank toward Harvey's position, the small speaker in his ear came to life. "That was some trick with the mountain lion. How'd you manage it?"

Nathan instantly knew who it was. "The money's not worth it. Walk away."

"Fat chance." A short pause, then: "You leaving her there to die?"

Nathan saw no point in responding to that.

"The shot isn't immediately fatal," said Leonard, "but the longer she *lies* there . . . *Well*, you get the idea. I guess you have a decision to make, don't you?"

Nathan clenched his teeth and felt rage begin to boil again. Leonard Bridgestone had gut shot Grangeland on purpose, causing a cruel and prolonged death and hoping to paralyze him and Harvey in the process. That lousy piece of shit. He couldn't let Leonard know how much saving Grangeland's life meant. He had to play it cool. If he showed even the slightest concern, it would both embolden and empower his enemy. Choosing his words carefully, and grateful Grangeland no longer had her radio, he called Leonard's bluff.

"She's nothing to me but a skirt with a gun."

"Bullshit. She's a looker. I can't imagine you didn't notice that."

Nathan could feel the tension inside him building, like a piano wire about to snap. He had to turn it back on Leonard. "Why'd you sacrifice Ernie?"

"What are you talking about?"

"You know damned well what I'm talking about. You set him up where you knew I'd nail him."

Leonard didn't respond right away. "Was it that obvious?"

"He was your brother. How could you do it?"

"He gave me up; I could never trust him again."

"He gave you up under torture. But that's not the real reason, is it?"

"You tell me."

"Is your love of money so perverted that you'd feed your own brother to the wolves to keep it all yourself?"

"The way I figure it, you did him a favor. Did the *world* a favor."

"What's the matter, Lenny, you don't have the balls to clean up your own mess?"

"I used him rather than wasted him. I might have found you from the shot you took. You got lucky, McBride."

"You'll never leave here with your money. Ever. I'll make sure it gets donated to charity. How about the Purple Heart Fund? You've got two of them, don't you?"

"Cute, McBride."

"Give my regards to Ernie when you see him in hell." Nathan turned off his radio.

* * *

Fifty yards from Harvey's position, Nathan issued his signature warbling whistle. Harvey returned it, and Nathan worked his way up to his partner's hiding place.

"Damn, it's good to see your sorry ass," Harvey said as Nathan crouched down beside him.

"Sorry I'm late. I had an argument with a local."

"I heard. A mountain lion?"

"Tell you about it later."

"Is Grangeland alive?" Harvey asked.

"Yeah. At least, she was. I saw her moving. There's no way to know the extent of her wound. Leonard has her radio."

"Shit."

"We can't let her die, Harv. Getting Leonard isn't worth her life."

"Yeah, but she might die anyway. Or he might go ahead and kill her. You heard the cold-blooded fuck: He served up his own brother on a silver platter."

"Here's the plan. I'll create a distraction down here and bring Leonard to my position while you work your way back to Grangeland and fly her out of here. He can't be in two places at once. If he's on this end of the canyon, he can't be watching the chopper."

"I can't leave you out here alone. And I've never flown that thing solo."

"Harv, I have to kill him. He's still got a lot of Semtex. We can't risk him coming after us, or worse, coming after your family if he doesn't get his money. You know that. You've got dozens of takeoffs and landings under your belt. You're ready. Use the checklist for startup. Get her light on the skids before you lift off. You can definitely do it."

"It feels like I'm abandoning you. You're bleeding bad."

"You're saving Grangeland's life. I'll be okay. Leonard doesn't stand a chance against me. He has to die, Harv, for your family's sake."

"Promise me you won't follow me up that canyon and cover my ass at your own expense again."

"I promise."

"Here, take four of my SIG mags. I won't need them, and you just might."

Nathan stuffed them into his pockets. "Better give me the spool of fishing line from your backpack, and your Predator knife too."

Harvey turned around so Nathan could dig the spool out. Harvey then bent down and removed his ankle sheath and handed it to Nathan. Nathan strapped it onto his good left ankle.

"How long do you need before I call in the cavalry?" Harvey asked.

"Give me two hours from the time you turn the ignition; then call Mansfield. Worry about Grangeland, not me."

"But you might not last two hours. You're slowly bleeding out, for God's sake."

"I'll be fine. Get Grangeland to a hospital, Harv; save her life."

"Shit."

"Go on. No long good-byes."

"Nathan, I—"

"I know you do. I do too." He smiled. "Get going. You'll hear me popping off pistol shots to bring Leonard down here. Be careful traversing that sand wash."

"Nail his ass, Nathan."

"Oh, you can count on it."

# ⊕ Chapter Twenty-eight

Nathan turned his radio on and pressed the transmit button. Distraction time. "You copy, Bridgestone?"

"Yeah, I'm here."

"You mad at me for the 'give my regards in hell' comment?"

"Naw, it seemed appropriate at the time." Bridgestone stayed quiet for a moment. Then, "What's *your* story, McBride? Why do you give a shit? Why risk your life over this?"

*Keep going, Harv; get to that chopper.* "I don't know. Maybe it's the good-versus-evil thing. Maybe I'm curious to know if good truly is stronger than evil."

"Who's who?"

"Well, the last I checked, I didn't murder twenty innocent people sitting at their desks."

"Point taken."

Nathan popped off two quick rounds at nothing. "Gotta go."

"What's the matter, cat got your tongue?"

"You've got a quick wit; better hope you're as fast with that rifle."

"I am."

"You'd better be. We'll see you at your money stash." Nathan had purposely said *we'll*. He turned off the radio, popped off two more shots, and moved away downstream. So far, so good. If Leonard was on the move, he couldn't be stationary and actively looking for Harvey. At best, all Leonard could do was stop every so often and make a quick sweep of the canyon. He'd never see Harvey that way. Harvey was too good. As Nathan took slow, deliberate steps through the underbrush, he kept glancing over his shoulder for the cat. He knew the scent of his blood remained strong. Although he believed the animal to be long gone, he wasn't willing to bet his life on it.

He estimated another five hundred yards or so before he had any chance of sighting the spire at the money stash. Up ahead, he could see where the canyon made a horseshoe turn to the north and knew the spire was around that bend on the right side. If he were Leonard, he'd pick a spot within three hundred yards of the spire—probably on this side of it—set up shop, and wait for his opponent to come to him. One thing was certain: Leonard had the speed advantage, even if Nathan chose to throw caution to the wind. His calf was killing him—almost as painful as his arm, though it wasn't losing as much blood. The blood loss from his arm would soon become a concern. . . .

Yeah, Leonard had quickness on his side. In truth, he could literally run downstream along the southern rim of the canyon as long as he stayed back from the lip. Nathan wondered if Leonard would have time to retrieve the money before he even got there. Three million bucks—in cash—just sitting out here, in the middle of nowhere. It seemed bizarre and hardly believable, but Leonard's presence confirmed it. He was here to collect his cash, his lifetime's worth of savings, and bug out.

*You shouldn't have put all your eggs in one basket, Leonard, ol' boy.*

Nathan smiled, feeling a certain satisfaction at denying the murderer his money, but the smile vanished. *Keep focused*, he told himself. *Keep your head in the game.* As he dropped down to crawl through a section of low underbrush, he wondered how close Harvey was to the chopper. They'd parted company . . . what? Twenty minutes ago? He should've looked at his watch. That omission had been careless. Maybe he was more injured than he cared to admit. He knew blood loss would soon take its toll in the form of shivers, nausea, and shock. He needed to end this battle, and end it soon. The early symptoms of shock were already evident. He was having trouble thinking clearly, and he felt cold. How long until his symptoms became crippling? Half an hour? Less? He doubted he'd last the two hours he'd asked for.

Approaching the horseshoe bend in the canyon, Nathan slowed his pace even more. He had to. The going was tough through double overhead growth, and he had to take special care not to disturb any of the tall stalks as he wove his way through. The good thing was, the growth was so dense here he couldn't see the canyon's southern rim at all. Which meant, in turn, that he couldn't be seen. Step after step, Nathan moved with slow precision, always watching where he placed his boots. A snapped twig or a patch of quicksand could ruin his day. . . . He hoped he wouldn't flush any birds either. Leonard could be twenty feet away and he wouldn't be able to see Nathan, but he *would* be able to hear him.

But Leonard's presence *wasn't* what he heard right then.

What he did hear warmed his soul—the distinctive whooping drone of a helicopter's blades biting into the afternoon air. *His* helicopter, with Harvey at the controls, flying Grangeland out of there. *Attaboy, Harv. Way to go, old friend.*

"McBride, you copy?"

He made Bridgestone wait.

"McBride, you there?"

A little longer . . .

"McBride?"

"I'm here. That's Harvey, flying out of here with Grangeland. It's just you, me, and the mountain lion now."

"Good."

"Don't be so sure about your odds. There's a catch, Bridgestone. You see, time is *not* on your side. In two hours Harvey is going to call in the cavalry, and you can kiss your millions good-bye. You can't know how much this breaks my heart."

"Like you said, McBride, we've got a couple hours to settle things."

Nathan yawned audibly. "I'm a little tired and I've lost a lot of blood. Maybe I'll take a little R and R. One eye on the money, of course."

"You ex-marine or army?"

"Marine."

"Sniper?"

"Sniper."

"How many?"

"Including your brothers, fifty-nine. Guess that makes you number sixty, a nice round number. Is the money really worth your life? Is flipping burgers or stuffing envelopes beneath you? Who says you can't start over and earn money honestly?"

"Naw, not my style."

"But being dead is?"

"I'm not dead, McBride, far from it."

"Soon enough, Bridgestone, soon enough . . ." He resumed his trek downstream to the east. After another hundred yards the undergrowth thinned, and Nathan could once again see the southern rim of the canyon. He figured he needed to advance another two or three hundred yards before looking for the right spot to set up.

It took fifteen minutes to cover the last leg. He'd seen the rock spire several times through openings in the underbrush. At one point he had to divert away from the creek, nearly to the canyon's wall, to keep inside the cover of growth. Up ahead, a wide thumb of greenbelt would take him back to the sandy wash, where a large copse of mature oaks and thick brush dominated the creek's bank for several hundred yards. *Perfect*. He knew he'd find what he was looking for out there. Crawling on his belly, he inched his way forward through the labyrinth of tree trunks, slowly closing the distance to the creek's bank. Even though his arm was on fire and felt as though hundreds of red ants were chewing its flesh, he fought the urge to look at it. No upside to doing that.

Up ahead at the creek's bank, the canopy of oak branches

screened him from the canyon's rim, but gave him little cover from a lower perspective. He doubted Leonard had descended into the canyon. Would he give up the high ground? Would he change tactics to confuse his enemy? Nathan didn't think so, but he couldn't be one hundred percent sure. Advancing toward the creek, he kept studying the canyon's southern rim, looking for potential shooting positions. From what he'd seen so far, there were at least half a dozen really good candidates up there.

He wondered how long Leonard would last before desperation set in. Would he risk his life and try to recover the cash as time ran out? He might as well commit suicide, because Nathan wasn't going to let him come within fifty yards of that rock spire without nailing him.

*Advantage, good guys.*

When he closed to within thirty yards of the creek, Nathan spotted what he needed directly ahead, a huge fallen oak whose roots had been undermined by a flash flood. The exposed root-ball towered on the creek side, a chaotic tangle of weathered, wormlike tendrils, clods of earth, and river stones. The main structure of the tree, trunk and branches, fanned out toward Nathan's position at a forty-five-degree angle from the creek. Its trunk had to be almost four feet in diameter, with large branches jutting out from its central structure, the dead wood bleached white from years of sun and exposure to the elements.

As Nathan scoped the tree, a plan came to him, fully formed. *Bingo.*

Nathan crawled to the oak's prone form and shucked off his ghillie suit and backpack. The trees flanking the fallen oak gave him spotty cover at best, so he made slow, deliberate movements to avoid catching Leonard's eye. He shouldered his weapon and slowly swept the canyon's southern rim from west to east, ending at the rock spire. Nothing at all. No movement. Was Leonard dug in up there? If so, where would he be? Would he pick the most obvious position? The deepest recess offering the darkest shadow? Probably not. A trained Army Ranger wouldn't choose a predictable location; he'd pick an unlikely spot with marginal cover. But he *would* pick a location from which he could relocate after firing a shot without being seen.

*Okay,* Nathan thought, *let's assign names to the four most likely shooting positions up there.* He started with the place closest to the spire, a long bowl-shaped dip in the rim with a sandy surface flanked by low ledges of fallen limestone. He'd call that spot Ledges. The next place moving west was a medium depth of shadow crevice with a thirty-foot-long fallen slab of rock in front of it. That would be a good location because the slab of rock looked to be about three feet high, suitable for bench-resting a rifle. He called it Bench. The next good candidate was a missing piece of striated limestone shaped like a coffee cup: Coffee. The final location was a leaning chunk of limestone that formed a triangular opening with deep shadow. He'd call that spot Shadow.

Nathan didn't favor Shadow as much as the others because it didn't allow a large radius of fire. If Leonard chose Shadow, he'd have to sacrifice nearly half the canyon in order to stay concealed. It also didn't offer an easy way to relocate, because it wasn't at the very top of the canyon's rim.

He studied each location through the rifle's scope again. Ledges. Bench. Coffee. Shadow. He favored Bench because, along with its length of nearly thirty feet, it offered Leonard the easiest relocation capability. He put Ledges in second place, followed by Coffee. In fourth, Shadow.

Okay, now he had to find a position that could be seen from each of those four locations. He slithered along the fallen tree trunk and, every five feet or so, peered over the top, checking each shooting position up on the rim. Five minutes later he found a nearly ideal place near a main arterial branch. From this location he could see all four of the potential shooting positions, and as a bonus this spot could also see a large section of the southern rim stretching toward the rock spire in case Leonard wasn't holed up in one of the top four spots.

*Perfect.*

Ignoring his blood-soaked shirtsleeve, he crawled back to his ghillie suit and backpack and removed a spool of fifty-pound fishing line. Dragging the pack and ghillie suit, he made his way back to the arterial branch and began looking for a piece of wood around three feet long and two inches in diameter. He found what he was looking for attached to the fallen oak's trunk. He removed Harv's Predator knife from the ankle sheath and began cutting the piece of wood free.

When the branch was detached, he cut a six-inch section off the end of it and notched the middle of it like a log cabin. He did the same to the longer piece near one end. Using the fifty-pound fishing line, he secured the six-inch piece to the three-foot piece at the notches. When he was finished, he ended up with a crude-looking crucifix of sorts.

Using two dozen loops of line around the butt of his SIG Sauer pistol, he attached the weapon to a five-inch-thick branch jutting up from the top of the fallen tree trunk. He tied the handgun to a point on the branch where only the very top of the gun could be seen from the other side. When the gun was tight and wouldn't budge, he cut the line and tied the loose end to the trigger.

He looked over his shoulder for a place to loop the fishing line around a branch or heavy rock. *Shit.* There was nothing. How could he have overlooked such an important detail? More to the point, what was he going to do now? He cursed himself for being so sloppy and ill prepared. Damn, his arm hurt. His shirtsleeve was literally dripping wet with blood; so was the upper half of his shirt. Worse, he was beginning to lose sensation in his right thumb. Nerve damage, he feared. Not to mention that he couldn't remember the last time he'd slept.

Running on fumes, Nathan considered kicking back and waiting for the cavalry to arrive. It didn't seem like such a bad idea right about now, but that might give Leonard a chance to escape. He thought about Grangeland and the chickenshit bullet she had taken. He thought about Harvey's wife, Candace, and imagined Leonard shooting her through her kitchen window. Anger flared—crucial fuel—and he tapped it, then forced it aside. Feeling a little better, Nathan studied his options again. Where would he loop the fishing line? *Think, damn it. Think.* He'd spent nearly twenty minutes setting up in this location. He didn't think he had the time, or the energy, to set up in a different location. His body was beginning to shut down.

A deeper-rooted rage began to flood his soul for being so stupid and shortsighted. *No, not now.* Nathan closed his eyes and brought his mental image forward. His safety catch. Standing under the imaginary trees, he let the autumn-colored leaves flutter past his body. They brushed past his skin with a hypnotic sensation. He slowed his breathing and relaxed his hands. He leaned his head back against the tree trunk and sighed. Falling leaves. Falling from where? *From above!* He opened his eyes and smiled. The solution had been right in front of him all along.

## ⊕ Chapter Twenty-nine

Leonard hadn't heard any additional pistol shots for over half an hour. Maybe McBride had finally scared the cat off. From his current position on the south rim, Leonard had a clear view of the canyon below, but he hadn't seen any movement at all, feline or human. Was McBride telling the truth? Were reinforcements arriving within the next hour? Maybe it was bullshit. Maybe McBride was just trying to force his hand, to flush him out. He wasn't sure. He knew nothing about McBride's past other than what he'd just learned. One thing was certain: The guy was a damned good shot. At the compound he'd killed Sammy at a distance of six hundred yards. He didn't know how far away McBride had been when he'd nailed Ernie, but as with Sammy, it had been a single shot. *One shot, one kill*—the sniper's motto. If this guy truly had been a Marine Corps sniper, taking him out wasn't going to be easy.

Was the cash really worth it? Hell, yes, it was. He'd spent ten long years amassing it, putting up with Ernie's short temper and endless baggage. Shit, he had three million dollars in cash no more than two hundred yards away; all he had to do was go dig it up. He knew McBride would be watching the spire, but from where? He silently cursed Ernie for the tenth time for bringing McBride up here. Knowing he couldn't approach the money until he knew McBride was dead, he had few options. Maybe he should try a different approach. What could it hurt at this point? Yeah, it just might work. . . .

He pulled the radio and thumbed the transmit button. "McBride, you copy?"

Nothing, no response.

"McBride?"

"I'm a little busy right now."

"I'm willing to split the money. Fifty-fifty."

"Blood money? Not interested."

"Come on, you can't use a million and a half in cash? Tax free? Last chance. I'll split it with you. Right down the middle."

"Not interested."

"I'm sorry to hear that."

"No doubt you are."

"I'm going to enjoy killing you, McBride."

"Go ahead, give it your best shot. You've already missed twice. Why not go for the hat trick?"

"You're all talk." Leonard turned off the radio and clipped it to his belt. He made a quick scan of his desert fatigues, looking for anything out of place, anything dangling, anything shiny. Satisfied, he began a slow scan of the creek's northern bank through his rifle scope. If McBride was down there, he'd be hidden in all that green undergrowth. The problem was, there was a hell of a lot of it, and McBride's ghillie suit made him virtually invisible. If McBride was telling the truth— and Leonard had no reason to assume otherwise—time was indeed running out. If he couldn't find McBride within the next twenty minutes or so, he'd have to abandon his cash and bug out. In that event, he vowed to kill McBride *and* his partner. It might not happen two weeks from now, or two years from now, or even ten years from now, but McBride would die for denying him his money.

As Leonard swung his scope across a particularly dense area of brush, he heard two quick pops of a handgun. He focused on the general location where he'd heard the reports. "What's the matter, McBride?" he whispered. "Your furry friend come back?"

A few seconds later he saw a bush move as though it had been bumped. *There!* Two more shots from deep within the undergrowth, followed by the distinctive crackle of the shots echoing down the canyon. Handgun shots, not a rifle. He'd seen the actual muzzle flashes and had an exact location pinpointed. "You're mine, McBride."

He steadied his weapon and saw the slide of a handgun near the top of a fallen tree trunk. As if looking at a gift from heaven, Leonard watched in abject fascination as his enemy revealed himself. Slowly rising from behind the fallen trunk, the hood of a ghillie materialized like a ghost emerging from a grave. He caught the glint of a pair of field glasses inside the dark recess of the hood.

Leonard added an additional click of elevation, took in a full lungful of air, and blew half of it out. Placing the crosshairs directly between the lenses of the field glasses, Leonard smiled and pulled the trigger.

The supersonic crack announced the arrival of the slug. Nathan figured he had a fifty-fifty chance of actually seeing the muzzle flash. He'd been betting on Leonard being in the location he called Bench, but that was clearly wrong. He'd been watching the long slab of limestone nearly continuously. Nothing. No movement at all. No muzzle flash. If Leonard had been on that formation of flat rock, he would've seen the muzzle flash. He swung his rifle east toward the rock spire and looked at his second pick. Ledges.

*Got you, Leonard.*

Near the left edge of the sandy bowl, half-concealed by a sprig of sagebrush, he saw Leonard working the bolt of his rifle, chambering another round. He was well concealed; only his head and shoulders could be seen as he lay prone next to the eastern rock face of the formation. Nathan took one click off the elevation knob and steadied his rifle.

Sudden realization hit Leonard. Hit him hard. If McBride had been a Marine Corps sniper, there was no way in hell he'd be sloppy enough to reveal his position by bumping against a bush, firing handgun shots, and letting his field glasses show.

He quickly worked the bolt and chambered another round, eyes scanning left and right for the *real* Nathan McBride.

Assuming McBride had fired the handgun at arm's length, he searched both sides of the fallen trunk, but saw nothing until a very slow movement caught his eye on the left edge of his scope, farther and higher than he had imagined McBride could be.

He centered the crosshairs on the movement and his heart froze in his chest.

*Impossible!*

Well concealed near the top of an enormous root ball structure, Nathan McBride was lined up with him.

Perfectly.

The movement he'd seen was McBride's left hand, waving good-bye.

In slow motion he saw McBride's rifle wink.

Half a second after the muzzle flash burned his retina he sensed more than felt something strike his forehead.

When Nathan's rifle bucked against his shoulder, he hadn't anticipated the level of agony it would cause. His vision grayed, then quit altogether. Blind and helpless, he was hammered by sudden dizziness and nausea. He remembered this feeling well—recalled it with hideous clarity from days spent in a Nicaraguan cage: It meant he was seconds from passing out. How high was he perched in the root-ball? Five or six feet? High enough to snap his neck on impact. As gravity pulled him headfirst toward the ground, his right leg slipped and hung up in the interior root tangle. He both felt and heard his shinbones snap.

*Tib-fib. One-two. Oh, man, that's a bad deal. I'm so sorry, Harv. Sorry I let you down . . .*

Just before his head struck the earth, Nathan Daniel McBride closed his eyes, and for the second time in his life waited for the mercy of death to take him.

## ⊕ Chapter Thirty

"ETA one minute," General Mansfield said.

Flanked by two Hueys of the Fortieth Air Wing out of Malmstrom, Harvey flew Nathan's Bell 407 toward the canyon. Sitting next to him, Mansfield was coordinating the approach as the V-shaped formation of helicopters screamed over the town of Dupuyer. Harvey glanced at his watch: early by nearly twenty minutes. Nathan would just have to deal with it. No way in hell Harvey was waiting the entire two hours.

"We don't know what to expect up there," Harvey said. "We could take ground fire from Bridgestone. He could do some real damage with a sniper rifle."

"That's true, but if your partner is still alive, Bridgestone won't fire his weapon and give away his location. We don't have a lot of options at this point. I'm not willing to put men on the ground until we know what's going on."

"Agreed," Harvey said. "We'll be lucky to see anything at all. If they're engaged in a sniper fight, we won't see either of them."

"We should make a pass down the length of the canyon. Either McBride will signal us, or Bridgestone will shoot at us. I hate to say this, but if Bridgestone managed to kill McBride, he might be long gone, and it might be difficult to find your partner down there."

Harvey didn't want to think about that possibility. "Let's have your two birds fly the southern and northern rims of the canyon while we fly down the middle."

"Good plan." Mansfield passed the orders along.

As the three helicopters cleared the canyon's rim and flew directly over the original landing zone where Nathan had set the chopper down, the Hueys broke formation. The Huey on Harvey's starboard peeled off to fly the north rim of the canyon. The Huey on the port side made a similar maneuver toward the south rim. Harvey slowed the Bell and expertly followed the canyon's streambed at thirty knots. He hoped Nathan would be proud of him.

When he rounded the last horseshoe bend and had the rock spire in sight, the radio crackled to life. "Civilian Delta, Rescue One has a man down on the south rim. He looks dead."

Before Mansfield could respond, Harvey pulled the transmit trigger. "Rescue One, what is the downed man wearing?" Harvey looked up to his right, where the Huey was orbiting in a tight circle above a bowl-shaped sandy formation on the rim.

"He's wearing a desert BDU."

Harvey felt relief wash over him. "Do you see anyone else? Our man is wearing a woodland BDU under a ghillie suit."

"Negative."

"I'm going up there," Harvey said. He climbed to the rim of the canyon. Fifty yards south of Leonard's body Harvey saw a sandy patch of clear ground surrounded by waist-high brush. He taxied over, made a landing, and throttled the rpm down to seventy percent. "I'll be right back. You've got her?"

"I've got her," Mansfield confirmed.

Harvey climbed out and sprinted across the rocky terrain, weaving his way through the brush and larger rocks littering the landscape. Overhead, the loud roar of the orbiting Huey drowned out the Bell's engine noise behind him.

Leonard Bridgestone lay facedown at the edge of the canyon's rim; the upper back portion of his head was gone. From the look of things, he'd had his rifle shouldered when he'd bought the farm. Harvey stepped behind Bridgestone and lined up on his position. Bone, scalp, and brain matter had been sprayed across the sand, and from the fan-shaped pattern, Harvey could approximate where the shot had come from. He sighted down Leonard's body and made a mental note of a huge downed oak near the streambed. Twenty seconds later Harvey was strapped in and lifting off. When he descended into the canyon, there wasn't a good place to set her down besides the wet sand of the streambed. In the center of the wash nearly a foot of water still flowed.

"General, can one of your Hueys test this LZ before I set her down? They're a lot heavier than we are, and I don't have enough experience to try it."

"No problem." Mansfield called Rescue One down to their location and ordered it to check the stability of the sand near the bank of the stream.

Harvey taxied Nathan's Bell away from the LZ so the Huey could take his place. Thirty seconds later the air force Huey was hovering over the moist sand. Its pilot carefully settled onto the wet surface, gradually putting more and more weight onto its skids until it was fully down. The skids sank only a few inches into the wet sand before stopping. Its pilot radioed the results before lifting off again. "You're good to go, Civilian Delta. Shouldn't be a problem lifting off again."

Mansfield cut in: "Rescue One, set down and prepare for a medevac."

"Copy."

Although it was awkward, Harvey landed the two-and-a-half-ton Bell on the wet surface and went through the shutdown procedure. Since General Mansfield was coming with him, he didn't want to risk the helicopter vibrating itself down into the moist sand by leaving the engine idling. It took three endless minutes before the engine was cool enough to cut its fuel and shut it down.

"Nice landing," Mansfield said. "Not bad for someone without a rating. Let's go find your friend."

With General Mansfield in tow, Harvey thrashed his way through the thick brush at the creek's northern bank and approached the fallen oak. Nathan wasn't there. Panicked, Harvey looked around. Nothing. But this had to be the place. *Come on!* Then he saw something—something out of place. His Predator knife, sticking straight up with its blade driven into a large branch attached to the fallen tree trunk. Harvey fought his way through the brush over to the knife and saw a SIG Sauer handgun tied to the top of the same branch. He frowned. This was Nathan's SIG. A fishing line was attached to the trigger and looped around the butt of the knife. On the ground next to the branch lay Nathan's ghillie suit, with a crude wooden cross inside it and a broken pair of field glasses attached to the crosspiece. A second fishing line, attached to the crossbar, was cleverly looped through the V-shaped crotch of one of the fallen oak's vertical branches. Harvey now knew what Nathan had set up—a dummy decoy—and from the look of the shattered binoculars, Leonard had taken the bait.

From over Harvey's shoulder, General Mansfield looked at the setup and whispered, "I'll be damned."

The two fishing lines were running out to the southeast, following the trunk of the fallen tree. Harvey worked his way along its length, maneuvering himself over and under dead branches until he saw a prone leg and combat boot screened by a boulder. He also saw blood, lots of it.

*No. Dear God, no!*

Harvey ran the remaining distance. "Nathan!"

His lifelong friend was lying at the base of a huge root-ball, not moving. Two bloody spikes of sharp bone were protruding through the material of his BDU just below his right knee. The pant leg was soaked with blood; so were his right shirtsleeve and the upper half of his shirt.

"Aw, shit, Nathan." He crouched down and cradled Nathan's head with his hands. "You can't be dead. You can't be!"

Nathan spoke without opening his eyes. "Harv, what the hell are you doing? You're gonna give General Mansfield the wrong idea."

"*Damn,* Nate, you scared the shit outta me."

"I feel terrible."

"You look terrible."

"Thanks."

"Don't mention it."

"Grangeland okay?"

"Yeah, she's gonna make it. You were right about her. She's tough as nails."

Nathan slowly brought his left arm up and looked at his watch, then let it fall. "You're early."

"So sue me."

"Did I get Leonard?"

"Yeah, you got him."

Nathan managed a smile. "It's over then?"

"Yeah, it's over."

## Chapter Thirty-one

The following day, FBI director Ethan Lansing got his headline, as promised. The two men at the top of his most-wanted list were dead, thanks to the highly trained professionals of the Federal Bureau of Investigation. In particular, the story referred to Special Agent Mary F. Grangeland, who was recovering from a gunshot wound received in the line of duty during the engagement with the Bridgestones in a remote area of western Montana.

Every network covered the story. As a bonus, three million dollars in cash had been recovered from the scene, along with the balance of the Bridgestone brothers' Semtex. The talking heads would continue to debate the threat of homegrown terrorism until another crisis took over the spotlight, or until their viewers cried, "Enough coverage already."

Currently sharing a hospital room in Great Falls, Montana, Nathan McBride and Special Agent Grangeland had definitely seen enough coverage. Grangeland had insisted she be roomed with Nathan, even though hospital policy stated that such male-female room assignments were against hospital policy. She didn't care and wouldn't take no for an answer. Harvey had camped himself out too, a bedside presence that even the most headstrong doctor could not dislodge.

After being stabilized in the emergency room, Grangeland had undergone emergency surgery to remove a ruptured gall bladder and repair a torn liver. Even though much of its kinetic energy had been absorbed by the vest, Leonard's bullet had still passed through the Kevlar, missing her heart and lungs by less than two inches. Hooked up to half a dozen machines monitoring every aspect of her bodily functions,

Grangeland was outwardly in good spirits, but Nathan knew otherwise. The Ortega betrayal had claimed another victim, alive, but another victim—just the same.

Although Nathan's upper-biceps injury wasn't serious enough to keep him in the hospital more than one night, the compound fractures of both his tibia and fibula were. Besides, he wasn't going anywhere until Grangeland got back on her feet.

"It's funny," Nathan said to her. "I never knew your first name until now."

"You never asked."

"Hard to remember your manners when you're stuck in a half nelson," Nathan shot back, laughing.

Grangeland didn't join in. She went through moments like this fairly frequently. She'd turn pensive and quiet before getting back to her usual colorful self.

"I just thought of something horrible," she said.

"What?" asked Nathan.

"Did James Ortega know the truth going in, or did he find out under torture?"

Before answering, Nathan looked over at Harvey, who looked away and shook his head.

"For his sake, I hope he knew going in. Try to imagine what learning the truth under those circumstances would be like."

"I can't," she said. "I honestly can't."

They were silent for a few minutes.

"You know," Grangeland said, "you guys don't have to stay here and babysit me." She looked at Nathan. "The doctor gave you your walking papers yesterday."

"What? You trying to get rid of me?"

"I didn't say *that*."

"Good, 'cause I'm not going anywhere until I get those doughnuts Harvey promised me." Nathan felt a little better now. At least he had Grangeland and Harvey smiling again.

"Then will you leave?" She gave him a faux-innocent look.

"You know, Grangeland, making comments like that is what keeps our relationship healthy."

On cue, she smiled sweetly.

Nathan stayed with Grangeland for three more days, grateful for the time off his feet. After Grangeland's constant reassurances that she was okay, Nathan and Harvey left Great Falls. Because Nathan's right leg was in a fiberglass cast from knee to ankle without a rubber walker on the bottom, Harvey did all of the flying back to Sacramento. In another week Nathan's cast would be replaced with a walking version. But for now he had to avoid putting weight on the leg. On the flight south he had to admit that Harvey seemed quite comfortable in the right seat, and was amazed at what a few solo flights had done to boost Harvey's confidence. After landing at Sacramento Executive Airport they rented a Taurus, and Harvey drove to Sutter Hospital under a deepening twilight sky. Harvey dropped Nathan off at the curb at the main entrance and said he'd be back in half an hour. Nathan used his aluminum crutches to maneuver himself through the automatic doors. Once inside, he diverted over to the gift shop for a quick purchase. It didn't feel right visiting Holly empty-handed. He'd spoken to her frequently from Great Falls, but it was never the same on the phone. He wanted, needed this visit to go right.

As he hobbled his way toward Holly's room, his cell phone rang.

"Hello?"

"Nathan, it's your father."

"Hi, Dad, is everything okay?"

"Yes. I'm just leaving for a meeting with the president on this Bridgestone business. I've only got a minute, but I wanted to talk with you first."

"Yeah, sure."

"I'm hoping to close the book on it."

"Fine by me," Nathan said. "Harvey and I weren't planning to do anything, if that's what you mean."

"Not everyone would take that stand. You were nearly killed."

"I was nearly killed because of my own mistakes on the ground. Believe me, Dad, we're willing to let it go."

"Are you sure?"

"I'm sure."

"You're far more forgiving than I'd be in your shoes. But I'm glad that's your decision. I don't want to see Director Lansing or Frank Ortega dragged through the dirt over this."

"I don't either."

"I'm going to let them know your position. It's not fair to let them twist in the wind."

"Yeah, I agree. What are you going to tell the president?"

"The truth."

"What will he do?"

"Lansing's his appointee; he doesn't want a scandal any more than I do."

Nathan had reached Holly's door. He stopped and lowered his voice. "I only have one request."

"Name it."

"Will you keep your eye on someone out here? Her career?"

"Sure, who is it?"

"The special agent in charge of the Sacramento field office. Her name is Holly Simpson."

"I'm writing it down. . . . SAC Holly Simpson . . . Sacramento . . . I certainly will, to the extent I can. That's a promise."

"Thanks, Dad. I'd like to stay in touch more. Let's make the effort from now on."

"I'd like that."

"Me too. Take care, Dad."

"Take care, Nathan."

Nathan knocked softly on Holly Simpson's door.

"Come in."

Holding a dozen long-stemmed red roses, he hobbled into her hospital room. "Hello, Holly."

Her face brightened. "Hi, Nathan!"

She was sitting up in the bed. Her hospital gown had been replaced with pajama-type garments with snaps holding them in place. The stainless-steel latticework supporting her legs was still there, but the colorful balloons and flowers were gone. He bent down and kissed her. "How are you feeling, SAC?"

"Stir-crazy. I'm ready to get out of here. How are you doing?"

"Never better."

"Thank you for the flowers."

He set them down on a table and pulled up a chair. "We had a hell of a week, didn't we?"

She took his hand. "Thank you for giving the reward money to the families. That was a very generous thing you and Harvey did."

"We were glad to do it. You okay, really?"

"Well, I'll never be able to pass through an airport metal detector again without setting it off. I've got more screws and plates than the Bionic Woman."

"Beats a wheelchair."

"Amen to that."

"How's Henning doing?"

"He's going to be okay. He's being transferred up here from Fresno tomorrow, but he'll have to spend another week in a hospital bed. He's got all kinds of tubes and drains sticking out of him. He told me he looks like a Borg from a *Star Trek* episode, whatever that means."

"Are you and Lansing okay?" he asked.

"He knows I know about the Ortega/Bridgestone connection. I'm playing it cool, like it's no big deal."

"Good move. I'm sure he appreciates the 'do what's best for the team' attitude. You've got a solid future in the FBI, Holly. You made some tough decisions, bent the rules. Very few people in your position have what it takes to make those kinds of choices."

She squeezed his hand and nodded. "The FBI's giving you and Harvey private awards for what you did."

They were both silent a moment.

"Are you heading back to San Diego?" she asked.

He nodded; he didn't trust himself to say anything.

"I wish we'd met a long time ago."

"Me too."

"I can't help but wonder how different our lives would have been. You might be a father with six kids."

"Heaven help us."

"Don't sell yourself short; you'd be good at it."

"I appreciate your saying that."

"We shared something special. I know I've said this before, but I've never met anyone like you, and something tells me I never will again."

"I feel the same way about you, Holly. Listen, I'm not very good at this. I'm not even sure I know how to say it. . . . I'm not ready for this—for us—right now. I'm not at a point in my life where I can make a solid commitment to you, and you deserve that. I'm not saying we can't still see each other. In fact, if we want to, it's just—"

"Nathan, it's okay. Let's just take things a day at a time and see what happens."

He bent down and kissed her on the lips. "I'll see you soon. I promise. But until then I'm really going to miss you."

She wiped her cheek. "Me too."

"I tell you what. I'll make a special trip up here if you promise to go see *The Music Man* with me."

"Nathan McBride, it's a deal."

# ☐ **YES!**

Sign me up for the Leisure Thriller Book Club and send my FREE BOOKS! If I choose to stay in the club, I will pay only $8.50* each month, a savings of $7.48!

NAME: _____

ADDRESS: _____

TELEPHONE: _____

EMAIL: _____

☐ I want to pay by credit card.

☐ **VISA**   ☐ **MasterCard.**   ☐ **DISCOVER**

ACCOUNT #: _____

EXPIRATION DATE: _____

SIGNATURE: _____

Mail this page along with $2.00 shipping and handling to:

**Leisure Thriller Book Club**
**PO Box 6640**
**Wayne, PA 19087**

Or fax (must include credit card information) to:

**610-995-9274**

You can also sign up online at **www.dorchesterpub.com**.

*Plus $2.00 for shipping. Offer open to residents of the U.S. and Canada only. Canadian residents please call 1-800-481-9191 for pricing information.

If under 18, a parent or guardian must sign. Terms, prices and conditions subject to change. Subscription subject to acceptance. Dorchester Publishing reserves the right to reject any order or cancel any subscription.

# GET FREE BOOKS!

You can have the best fiction delivered to your door for less than what you'd pay in a bookstore or online. Sign up for one of our book clubs today, and we'll send you *FREE\* BOOKS* just for trying it out...**with no obligation to buy, ever!**

If you love fast-paced page turners, you won't want to miss any of the books in Leisure's thriller line. Filled with gripping tension and edge-of-your-seat excitement, these titles feature everything from psychological suspense to legal thrillers to police procedurals and more!

As a book club member you also receive the following special benefits:
- **30% off all orders!**
- **Exclusive access to special discounts!**
- **Convenient home delivery and 10 days to return any books you don't want to keep.**

Visit **www.dorchesterpub.com**
or call **1-800-481-9191**

There is no minimum number of books to buy, and you may cancel membership at any time.
\*Please include $2.00 for shipping and handling.